THE
OLD LION

THE

OLD

LION

A NOVEL OF

THEODORE ROOSEVELT

JEFF SHAARA

ST. MARTIN'S PRESS
NEW YORK

First published in the United States by St. Martin's Press, an imprint of St. Martin's Publishing Group

THE OLD LION. Copyright © 2023 by Jeff Shaara. All rights reserved. Printed in the United States of America. For information, address St. Martin's Publishing Group, 120 Broadway, New York, NY 10271.

www.stmartins.com

Designed by Kelly S. Too

Maps by Jeffrey L. Ward

Library of Congress Cataloging-in-Publication Data

Names: Shaara, Jeff, 1952- author.
Title: The old lion : a novel of Theodore Roosevelt / Jeff Shaara.
Description: First edition. | New York : St. Martin's Press, 2023.
Identifiers: LCCN 2022056766 | ISBN 9781250279941 (hardcover) |
    ISBN 9781250279958 (ebook)
Subjects: LCSH: Roosevelt, Theodore, 1858–1919—Fiction. | LCGFT: Biographical fiction. |
    Novels.
Classification: LCC PS3569.H18 O43 2023 | DDC 813/.54—dc23/eng/20230103
LC record available at https://lccn.loc.gov/2022056766

Our books may be purchased in bulk for promotional, educational, or business use. Please contact your local bookseller or the Macmillan Corporate and Premium Sales Department at 1-800-221-7945, extension 5442, or by email at MacmillanSpecialMarkets@macmillan.com.

First Edition: 2023

10 9 8 7 6 5 4 3 2 1

FOR MY DAUGHTER,
EMMA

CONTENTS

LIST OF MAPS

TO THE READER

Throughout the history of the United States, there have been presidents measured by their greatness or their mediocrity, their courage or their lack of courage during times of crisis, men whose decency or competence might place them a head taller or perhaps a head shorter than those who have come before them. Such lists are of course subjective, the stuff arguments are made of.

This is the story of a president who would certainly appear on any list where greatness is a priority. That list is, regrettably, a short one, and includes Washington, Jefferson, Lincoln, and others over which you and I might disagree. But few, very few, would disagree that Theodore Roosevelt ranks high among the most revered, most respected, and most admired presidents in American history.

That being said, the best way to describe this book is perhaps to describe what it is not. This is not a biography (and there are many), nor is it an academic examination of the man or his political policies (and there are many of those). Consider that the definitive biography of the man, by Edmund Morris, covers three volumes and totals more than 2,400 pages. Morris's admirable work is essential to anyone seeking the most minute details of Roosevelt's life. I did not have the means to expand this story into three volumes, nor would I wish to.

A partial roster of the historians I used for my research is listed at the end of the book.

What I have tried to do is create a story, with Roosevelt as the center point, exploring his life from his perspective, through the events as he creates them, as he marches or sometimes struggles through them. This is a novel because, often, you are in his thoughts, seeing events directly through his eyes. No writer can pretend to know what any character thinks or feels at every moment. Thus, the duty of the storyteller is to fill in the blanks. Roosevelt is not perfect, is not a superhero, and I have not portrayed him as such. One thing I have learned through my career as a storyteller is that *getting it right* means accurately, to the extent possible, recounting the events of the time. After researching and examining the accomplishments and personality of Teddy Roosevelt and those around him, this story became more personal to me than I ever expected. My own ranking of presidents has changed. My top three, in any order you wish, is Washington, Lincoln, and now Teddy Roosevelt. Perhaps, after reading this story, you will agree.

One brief personal note: Throughout the considerable amount of research involved in this project, I owe a special thanks to my wife, Stephanie. Often the grunt work goes unnoticed, but not this time. I owe her an enormous thanks because without her assistance, this book would have been far more difficult to create.

—Jeff Shaara

PROLOGUE

His decline began months before, a recurring illness made worse by news of Quentin's death. His son had been taken by the war, while in his glorious flying machine, this new tool of killing that so fascinated young men who knew nothing of their own mortality. Quentin had been shot down by his German adversary in July, a few months before the war had ended, one of so many, most of them unknown to any but their families. But Quentin's death made bold headlines. He was, after all, Teddy Roosevelt's son.

The impact on Roosevelt was mostly well hidden, some of his closest friends catching glimpses of sorrow, few ever seeing his tears in those quiet places where the grief overwhelmed him. But Roosevelt had a public face: politics and friendships and the adoring crowds. Among those who watched him closely were the men who kept to their high perches, and for them, there would be decorum, always. He was, after all, the man who established his own brand of decorum, his own manners and crusty habits, and for so long, all those *important* men, if they mattered to him at all, knew they could only go along for the ride.

Fewer still noticed that he had begun to slide, his energy ebbing, the speeches not as boisterous. If the crowds noticed, they might have seen that he was no longer the charging bull. But still they hallooed and waved and cheered him as in the old days.

Throughout the summer of Quentin's death, Roosevelt's grief was made worse by a deadly fear for his other three sons, warriors all in the

Great War that only now had sent them home. There had been wounds and the agonizing viciousness of mustard gas, and despite his sons' reassuring letters that all were safe, Roosevelt, and especially Edith, still carried the fear that some horrible piece of news was yet to come. For her, it was a mother's natural anguish. For him, it became something very different, the blow to his emotions taking hold of old injuries, an unavoidable weakness that seemed to creep over him like a blanket of punishment.

He had been so very strong, so active and robust, even in the later years as president and beyond. What the public could not see, and his friends denied, was the old leg injury, surgically repaired by frustrated doctors, the wound worsening and then healing yet again. It had occurred in 1902, in Pittsfield, Massachusetts, his carriage in a vicious collision with a trolley car, killing his beloved bodyguard, Big Bill Craig. The damage to Roosevelt's shin bone had seemed unworthy of mention, and Roosevelt's own energy, still the speeches, always the confrontations with any challenge, had masked the pain and, ultimately, the seriousness of the damage. For years, infections followed, the pain rarely leaving him be. As he traveled the world, he fought to hide the limp, never speaking of such a weakness. But that changed in the jungles of the Amazon—another wound, in the other leg, striking him down with yet another vicious infection, made worse by his chronic malarial fever. In a place where healthy legs might ensure survival, Roosevelt hobbled his way through the worst conditions he had ever endured.

But now, with the Great War finally past, with his three sons safe, the loss of his youngest boy took hold even more. The grief and the injuries caused ailments that spread throughout Roosevelt's body, odd and varied pains, more desperate labor for the doctors. There seemed to be no cure for the torment, and by late 1918 the ailments had worsened, nearly paralyzing him. Despite optimistic reports fed to the newspapers, initially that he lay in a hospital bed suffering merely from attacks of lumbago and then later that he had surgery to correct a painful toothache, what the public would not be told was just how badly his spirit had been weakened. His body was losing the same fight. The pains and weakness were becoming constant, what his mystified doctors now guessed to be severe rheumatism or gout or perhaps sciatica. The vertigo came now, confining him to his hospital bed. Finally, a string of good days, stronger, the vertigo gone, and when he insisted that he could manage, the doctors allowed Edith to take him home to Long Island, to his precious Sagamore Hill. Once home, she settled him into his own private room, what had long ago been a nursery for five of his children, bright sunlight through tall windows. The separation allowed Edith a fair night's sleep, as much sleep as a wife could find with her husband suffering so.

As Christmas came, much of the family gathered in loving support, but more symptoms set in, signs of a pulmonary embolism, persistent high fever, more attacks of vertigo, forcing him to remain in bed.

Through it all, he would not stop working, a source of frustration for those attempting to care for him. But his protests were obeyed. His letters went out, some across the Atlantic, to powerful friends and acquaintances in England and France, where the wrestling match had begun to settle the catastrophic costs of the Great War. It was no secret that Roosevelt hated President Woodrow Wilson, considered him a disaster for the nation's foreign policy, and was absolutely certain that Wilson's naked idealism and mindless ambition would accomplish nothing to heal anyone's wounds and might sow the seeds for yet another war. As Wilson sailed for Europe, expecting a triumphant reception even from the villainous Germans, talk grew that the president had a desperate fear that Teddy Roosevelt would return to the presidency in 1920. Roosevelt gave few hints about any such plan, despite the energetic push from so many in his party and from the public that he should run for the office once more. But Roosevelt knew his political life was past, that his ailments, the severity of the pains and the weakness, meant that his time was drawing to a close. For most of his life, he had predicted his own longevity, insisting to any and all, including Edith, that he would survive only until he was sixty.

He was sixty.

PART I

THE YOUNG LION

*His life was the unpacking of
an endless Christmas stocking.*

—Margaret Louisa Chandler,
FAMILY FRIEND

CHAPTER 1

"The president was received by, well, some estimates say two million Frenchmen turned out, waving flags and whatnot."

Roosevelt turned away from her, said, "My sister visits me to bolster my spirits, and this is what she brings. On Christmas Day yet. Woodrow Wilson is a hero for the ages, while I lie here as a lump of bacon fat."

"Dear Teedie, I only tell you what you will read in the papers. And you will read them, despite Christmas, or whatever affliction you have today. I have never known you to ignore any news that might annoy you."

He turned to Corinne, saw a smile. "Fine. My sister insults me. But I cannot scold you. You're one of my caretakers, after all."

He flexed his aching fingers, the pain a sudden shock. He looked at the splint around his hand. "When did this happen?"

Edith was there now, a hand on Corinne's shoulder. "Last night. The doctor said the splint would help keep your hand and wrist immobile. You complained woefully about the pain in your fingers." She paused, said softly, "You don't recall?"

"Of course I recall. I'm no *invalid*, you know."

The word hung between them, and he knew his protest had been overblown.

"No, of course you're not. We're just pampering you until you're completely *not* an invalid. What should we call you in the meantime?"

"Bull Moose will do."

His sister laughed, but Edith kept a frown.

"They're still pushing you to come back, you know. More letters this morning. *Bull Moose* indeed. They want you to run. I do wish you would tell them once and for all to leave you alone. This is not the time for such foolishness. I'm not certain that agreeing to this writer's request for an interview is a good idea at all. You need your rest."

He didn't want this, not now.

"My precious Edie, the 1912 election was my final hurrah, or perhaps my final whimpering farewell. Regardless how many love the term Bull Moose, I do not. I'm not going to run for anything, not president, not local constable." He paused, fought for a breath. "But it is flattering, yes? They still love me. I rather enjoy holding on to that. If Mr. Hagedorn wishes to write about me yet again, dig into all my wonderful accomplishments, should I complain? I think not. The public does adore me, after all."

Corinne laughed.

"I see that your gift for sarcasm hasn't been damaged." She looked up at Edith. "He's right, though. Is there harm? They want him to run because he's beloved, and Mr. Hagedorn can sell books about Teedie because people want to read them. There is no harm, Edie."

Edith lowered her head.

"Of course. It's hard to argue against any of that. We've all seen the crowds." Edith clapped her hands, bringing him to attention. "All right, that's it for politics. You want to wind yourself up, wait for Mr. Hagedorn. This young man has been begging to see you again since you've been home. But be prepared for him to press you, and hard. I'm only concerned for my husband. The doctor will be here in about an hour, and I don't want you holding back anything. Not now. Please, Teddy."

He looked at them both, saw soft fear, drew more pain from their concern than from the ridiculous agony in his hand. He flexed his fingers again, habit, flinched again from the sharp pains.

"I hurt. But it is not necessary for you both to mother-hen me like this. I am no child." He paused. "Well, usually. But right now, I just hurt. And I think I've got a fever again. You're a little blurry too. Or perhaps that's just me."

Edith bent low, a hand on his forehead. She said nothing, but he knew the look.

"Fever it is, then. My wife can hide nothing from me. I suppose you should hurry that doctor along if you can."

He rolled slightly away, stared at the brightness of the window, too bright, closed his eyes.

Corinne said, "I'll leave now, Edie. Maybe he can get some rest. Call me if you need me."

She was gone in a rustle of her dress, and Edith sat now, her hand on his arm. He wanted to turn, facing her, but there was no strength, no energy at all. He tried to open his eyes, the sun blinding him again, the weight of his fever swirling through his head.

"Thank you, Edie. I'll sleep now. My hand hurts."

HE HEARD A familiar sound outside the window.

"That singing. It's a cardinal, a male." He paused, his mind drifting, the sound of the bird filling him with the kind of joy he had always felt when hearing such a variety of songs, identifying every kind of bird, a talent that even master naturalists had found astonishing.

"God, I remember it all. My father did that, opened a marvelous door to everything about nature. Egypt, the entire family absorbing so much, but none enjoyed that trip as much as I did. If I could, I would return right now."

The images were in his mind, Egypt and the great river, so many birds, the excitement of the hunting excursions, trophies he never could have imagined. Close by, the cardinal serenaded him again, brought him home. He fought through the blurriness, tried to see Edith.

"No cardinals in Egypt, you know. Saw more birds there than anyone could ever expect, species no one here can possibly imagine. Every day, something old, something new. I perfected my taxidermy skills on that trip. Laid out my laboratory on the deck of the boat, a very tedious process, you know. Arsenic is an essential ingredient, and I had a dickens of a time trying to find someone who would sell it to me." He smiled. "Apothecary fellow thought I was intending to poison my family. I suppose there's a good bit of poisoning in those parts. The smells never bothered me, but the rest of the family has a peculiar sensitivity to the odors of nature. It's their loss." He smiled, again, tried to ignore the heat in his brain. "Father would hunt with me, and we'd ride these donkeys all through the bogs and swamps along the Nile. And later, I saw mummies, touched one, black, leathery skin. Remarkable. The pyramids too."

He forced his eyes open, tried to sit up straight. His heart was beating rapidly, an unpleasant surprise.

"I'm talking too much. Too many stories. Sorry."

She cradled a glass of lemonade, held it out toward him.

"You celebrate the best times in your life. There is no fault in that. You have told me these stories often. You should tell them to the writer, he'll want to hear all of it."

He nodded, said quietly, "They had pharaohs, you know. Nobody else can say that. Remarkable." He focused on her again. "When will that young fellow, Hagedorn, when will he be here?"

"Tomorrow, Teddy. Friday."

"If I must see him, I suppose I will."

"Be kind, Teddy. You have already agreed, and he has already done a marvelous job writing about you. His book last year was wonderful. And if I didn't believe you could trust him, I would say so." She laughed. "And besides, I've never known you to avoid the chance to speak about yourself to a willing audience."

Edith stood suddenly.

"The front door. Now who . . . ?"

She was gone quickly, a swirl of color, and he stared toward the door, puzzled, had heard no doorbell. But the thoughts were swept away by her sudden return, a paper in her hand.

"A messenger, came out from Oyster Bay, a telegram."

"Well, what's it say?"

She opened the envelope, read for a long moment, wide eyes.

"My word. It's from the French government. There's to be an official citation from Marshal Pétain. They want to award Quentin the Croix de Guerre."

He was stunned, reached for the paper.

"They must not do that. He is no different from a thousand others. He should not be singled out. We will not *celebrate* his death."

"Teddy, you must accept that he is not like so many others. He is *your* son."

"They must not do this!"

His voice had risen to a shout, concern on her face.

"Teddy, we can write them, graciously refuse, if that is your wish."

"Yes, we will do that. They will not refuse me. This sounds like Woodrow Wilson's doing, feeling generous, so he asks them to toss my family a bone. I should strangle him when he returns."

"Mrs. Roosevelt?"

The voice came from outside the room, and Edith moved that way, was gone again. He felt a wave of dread, thought, Hagedorn already? Is it Friday? He kept his focus, thought of what he would say to the young man, what sort of inane questions he might have. But she returned now, her face betraying something dreadful.

"What?"

She took a breath, trying to control her emotions.

"Another messenger, a note from Washington, the War Department. They recovered part of the seat from the wreckage of Quentin's plane." She stopped, shook her head. "It's in a crate downstairs. *They thought you'd like to have it.*"

He stared at her, deadly silence in the room. There were tears on her cheeks now, the grief rising up yet again. She sat on the edge of the bed now, and he wanted to say something, to comfort, but no words would come, too much pain of his own. He thought of the macabre *gift*, was furious now, clenched his fists, searing pain in one hand. Some clerk, he thought. A perfectly stupid gesture by someone who simply doesn't care. Your son is dead. Here's where he sat when he died. Whoever did this needs a perfect thrashing.

The fury gave way to the creeping weakness, and he glanced at his fists, useless weapons. So much is gone, he thought, and now even the memories are slipping away. I had good fists, could dish out a fair thrashing to anyone who needed it, unless the asthma came. The asthma. Thank God, no more of that. So long ago.

CHAPTER 2

The creature pursued him, caught him now, long snakelike tendons wrapping around the boy's throat. He fought, struck out with useless fists, the tendons now stronger, sharp sinews strangling him, the creature growing, a dragon, fire in its face, the burn engulfing the boy, spreading all through him.

"Aaagh!"

He awoke to wet sheets and a hollow gasping, still struggling to breathe. He fought mightily, still no air, and he panicked, a faint scream, all the sound he could manage. But it was enough, the door open, light beyond, the voice of his father, the great lion, chasing away the dragon.

"Here now, Teedie. It's all right. I've got you."

In the next bed, his younger brother, Elliott: "What is it? The asthma again?"

"Yes, Elliott. Go back to sleep. I'll take him away."

His mother was there now, a silhouette in the doorway, and his father turned to her, said, "It's all right, I'll carry him outside, a carriage ride in the cool. You should stay with Elliott, put him back to sleep." He said to the boy now, "Come. It's a cool night. It will help." The man's strong arms slid beneath the boy, raised him up, clear of the sweat-soaked bed, lifting him away from the awful places, the creatures that so often tormented him, burned holes in his lungs, sucking away his air. The attacks seemed always to come at night, horrible dreams that came with the choking strangulation, the desperate gasps for air that, until he woke, took the form of great beasts. His father had always seemed to be the savior, and the boy had begun to see the man as a lion, marvelous in his strength, the powerful good in all the bad the boy suffered through.

His father carried him outside, the cool air, scattered lamplight mostly from windows of strangers. The carriage was waiting, a sharp order from his father instantly obeyed by a servant who had seen this before. The boy was aboard now, felt a slight jostling from the horses, his father dropping heavily down on the seat beside him. The boy's gasping had eased, but the twitching and cold stabbing in his lungs came still, a choking cough, the panic again, always, that the next breath might be the last one. But his father's strength was contagious, and the boy slid one arm through his, his father's arm now wrapping around the boy, swallowing him in a powerful shield.

"We'll go up Broadway, past Herkimer's house. Keep quiet, though . . . well, of course, if you can. It's very late."

The boy pushed against his father's coat, could feel the horror in his chest beginning to fade, as it so often did when his father took control. His mother could manage, and often she had no choice, when the great man was away. The boy accepted the prescribed treatments with as much stoicism as a nine-year-old could manage, his mother following the guidance of the doctors: administrations of vomit-inducing drugs, enemas, and all manner of vile potions designed to cleanse away the symptoms of the asthma. But his father's strength was the preferred treatment.

The carriage rolled steadily north, up Broadway, past Twenty-Third Street, a soft narration from his father as to who lived in most of the homes. But the boy heard only his own breathing, the gasps and choking fading away, a soft rhythm to the breaths that meant the asthma was gone, beaten back again by the great strength of the man beside him.

The carriage stopped. The chilly air pushed past them by a silent breeze.

"There, Teedie. You feeling better? I have no notion just why a little fresh air will chase away the illness. But I know never to question what accomplishes the goal. The cooler the better, that much I have observed." He paused. "You know, Teedie, though I never suffered your particular affliction, I always remember what it was like to be a child, all the torment and terror that can come from things you don't understand. I am here for you, always, to protect, to defend if necessary, though I would rather that, one day, you learn to defend yourself. No man gains the respect of any around him if he does not stand up for himself, even if it means responding to a gross insult with a hearty use of the fist. I should like to see you tighten yourself, gain some girth."

The boy leaned forward, looked up into the man's eyes.

"Girth?"

"Well, what I mean, Teedie, is that you must apply yourself to strengthening your body. Add muscle to your arms and legs. Become stronger. It is drudgery, to be sure. But, perhaps, as you grow older, you will find ways to strengthen yourself in many ways. In a few years, you might be ready to take up boxing."

"What's that?"

"The ultimate sport. Two men, toe to toe, fists for weapons. The stronger man might win, or he might not. But the better fighter, the best boxer, that's who will nearly always come out victorious. That should be you. But not yet. You're too young, and you require a stronger body."

Roosevelt hung on the man's words, wanted more, but the message had reached him. He was a sickly boy, thin, unlikely to intimidate anyone. He slipped one hand into his nightshirt, his fingers wrapping completely around the upper arm.

"I'll try, Father. Maybe if I get muscles, the asthma won't come anymore."

His father hesitated, then said, "Perhaps. Let's find out, shall we? You may make use of the upstairs terrace. I shall secure some suitable equipment, hand weights and so forth. Perhaps we can construct some additional exercise areas outside. I shall consult Mr. John Wood, the proprietor of the gymnasium. He will certainly have some ideas on the subject and will likely oversee your efforts. You should also spend more time in the outdoors, walk, climb, anything to get your heart engaged. The outdoors should become your hobby, as it is mine."

"Yes, sir. I will begin right away."

The boy was excited now, thought of those men with the great arms, the men who worked at the markets, loading and unloading every kind of barrel and box.

"Where do I go to run about, or climb? Are there mountains nearby?"

His father laughed. "Begin small, my boy. Go to the trees right along here, near Twenty-Third Street, find some large boulders. Go over to the woodlands on Nineteenth Street. Perhaps, though, it would be best not to educate your mother about your efforts until you have mastered them. Women do tend to worry."

The boy smiled, tried to offer the knowing glance he saw on the face of his father. But the lamplight was fading, darkness over the carriage, silence now between them.

Yes, I will do this, he thought. I will find some place in the parks to run or climb. And Father will be proud.

His father pushed the carriage in a tight circle. The boy knew the routine, that they would return home, that he would return to the bed, that before the night was through, he might again struggle against the dragons.

April 1869
New York City

"I'm a failure. A pretender."

His older sister sat in one corner of the room, stifled a laugh.

"You are no one's failure. You just have a . . . naturally thin body. In time, you'll grow out of that, and gain more of a man's shape."

He turned to her, tilted his head.

"Please, Bamie, tell me just how you know so much about men's bodies." If the boy didn't understand his own impropriety, his older sister certainly did.

"Teedie, you do not ask such a thing, ever. I know biology and physiology and I am acquainted with a good many adults. You are as well. Look at them, look at your father. None of them resemble *you*, do they? They are not shaped like *you*. Very few are thin boys. So, stop complaining and continue with your exercise."

He looked again into the mirror.

"I had thought there would be some change. Perhaps a single muscle, somewhere. Instead . . . a pretender. I won't scare anybody."

HE WALKED ALONG the street, caught the smells now, the market ahead in the next block, repeated her instructions to himself.

"A chicken, no head. Be sure it's freshly killed. Yes, Mother."

He knew the instructions had come from the cook, that his mother would likely never soil her hands with the carcass of a freshly killed chicken. He loved her, doted on her as much as a boy could. She was beautiful and fragile, prone to sickness, always dressed in white. Her background was so very different from nearly all the social circles in New York. She was, in fact, a Confederate, raised in Roswell, Georgia, to a staunchly Southern family. If her discreet loyalties during the Civil War brought any significant conflict into her marriage to Theodore Sr., the children rarely saw any hint of it. What they knew of the South was what she revealed to them, as well as her soft gentility and her reliance on servants to handle the carcasses of chickens.

The market was a hive of activity, the boy slipping past crowds of men in suits, some in bloodstained butchers' aprons, others behind great tables and wagons of fruit and all manner of vegetables. The smells were digging into him now, and he hurried, saw the tall, heavy figure of his mother's desired butcher, Mr. Poindexter.

"Ah, young Master Roosevelt. A chicken, then?"

Roosevelt could never figure out how the man always knew what he wanted, even when the boy had forgotten himself.

"Yes, sir. No head, please."

"Well, of course. I have some Rhode Island reds here, just received today. New breed come down from New England. No matter. What matters most is whether your mother will be happy with it. That she will."

Poindexter went about his work with the chicken, and the boy shook his head against the smells, his eyes settling on a dark shiny carcass to one side.

"What is that, sir?"

Poindexter laughed, pointed to the next wagon.

"Hey, Barnaby. Young Master Roosevelt here's caught sight of your trophy. Give him a look then, will ya?"

Roosevelt moved that way, the man called Barnaby busy with a gaggle of noisy customers. He glanced at the boy, put a thumb past his shoulder toward the carcass.

"Go on. Take a gander. We don't get many of them near here."

Roosevelt moved that way, apprehension and growing excitement.

"What is it?"

Poindexter laughed now, said,

"It's a seal. Deader'n my Aunt Millie, and she's been gone a dozen years. Take a closer look, Master Roosevelt. Don't be bashful. Even if he could bite, he won't."

He moved close, then closer, bent low, studied the eyes, the whiskers, the skin, the mouth slightly open. He reached out a slow hand, touched the skin, cold, a thin fur coat.

"Where'd you kill him?"

Barnaby said, "The harbor, of course. You ain't likely to find one on Fourteenth Street."

"What you gonna do with it?"

"Sell it, boy. That's why I'm here. You got some coin, you can buy it for yourself."

Roosevelt suddenly felt an ache of poverty.

"No, got no money of my own."

"Well, then, look all you want. But stand aside for the customers."

Poindexter held up a paper package.

"Here's your chicken, Master Roosevelt. Be quick now. Your mother will have my hide if she thinks this bird ain't fresh as daisies."

He took the package, his eyes still on the carcass, then turned and jogged home.

———

FOR SEVERAL DAYS, the boy visited Barnaby's wagon at the market, the seal still there, no apparent takers. By the fifth day, the carcass was beginning to ripen severely, and Barnaby seemed to concede that there was a feeble market for whole seals, even if the pelt was valuable indeed. As a last effort at capitalism, he skinned the seal, stretched out the hide, a liberal coating of salt, hoping to attract some interest in the pelt alone. For the boy who had stood by admiring for so many days, Barnaby offered a reward. Young Master Roosevelt was given the skull.

It was the happiest day of his young life.

THE DOOR HAD been opened to a new world, and now, the studies followed, enormous varieties of books on the natural sciences, stories of great journeys into the unknown, from the explorations of David Livingstone to the theories of Charles Darwin and the astounding detail in the study of birds by John James Audubon. The books kept coming, furnished usually by his father, and some were too far advanced for the ten-year-old reader, but when the words were complex, the pictures usually were not. The notion of fur and feathers, all encasing the same kinds of hearts and lungs, the food chain with of course man at the top—all of it opened him up to a world of the natural sciences. In New York, the studies were limited to the exhibits in museums or, as with the seal, what might be on display in the markets. But, to his surprise, New York could be rich hunting as well, even in his own backyard.

In the weeks that followed, he began collecting what he called specimens, all manner of birds, frogs, small mammals—anything he could find around the streets close by his home. Some were captured alive, some were impossible to gather except as corpses. Eventually, his assembly gained a name, the Roosevelt Natural History Museum. If no one outside his home had any notion that such a place existed, those inside certainly did. The first hint had been the odor.

In time, the studies grew more complex, books giving way to taxidermy and biology with a penknife. To his dismay, no one in his family seemed to grasp his passion for the subject, and though he rarely heard the conversations, he knew that his parents and older sister were becoming concerned that his need for the outdoors was becoming far more unusual than the usual activities of an adolescent boy. As he grew into adolescence, his zeal increased, and even his father supported Roosevelt's lust for the outdoors, though no one else in the family had expected the pursuit to include so much carnage.

April 1872
New York City

"My God in heaven! Teedie! Where in the world are you?"

He suspected the source of his older sister's shrill anger, tread slowly toward the kitchen, peered in carefully.

"Hello, Bamie."

"Hello? I just found an entire colony of frozen mice wrapped in paper on our block of ice. Since mice do not open doors, I am certain they were put there by this family's great naturalist. Is that true?"

She was four years his senior, but seemed to tower over him with all the formidable presence of their mother. He puffed out his chest as much as he dared, said, "Well, Bamie, if you do not chill them, they will soon become quite wretched. It is much more difficult to dissect and study the workings of their organs if they are beyond spoiled."

She stared at him, seemed suddenly to accept the logic of his statement. Her anger snapped back into place.

"How about this, Teedie. Dissect, or whatever peculiar thing you do to these creatures before they become . . . spoiled. Do your studies, make your notes, or whatever else you do, and then, when you're done, dispose of these creatures in the outdoors. Not where we chill our milk."

"But Bamie, there are too many for me to study. Even now, I have a colony of moles in a box under my bed, and there are two very fine specimens of snapping turtles secured to the legs of the laundry cabinet."

"Yes, I know. The housekeeper is threatening to resign if you do not keep your vermin out of her way."

He felt insulted, shook his head at the ignorance of so many who did not appreciate nature's ways.

"What about my birds?"

Bamie seemed to draw back a half step. "What birds?"

"They're dead of course. Father insisted I not allow them to flit about the house. I keep them on the terrace, lined up in order of size or color, if not both. I truly wish I had access to a larger display case, to expand my museum. I could maintain a permanent display."

Bamie put her hands on her hips, her head tilted slightly.

"Good Lord, why?"

He shook his head, annoyed by her ignorance.

"Really, Bamie. The longer I work at this, the more knowledge I will gain. I am barely thirteen. There is an entire world I have not yet experienced. The books are wonderful, but I want to go out there myself, see for myself what so many others are writing about. I am considering a career in taxidermy. Mr. Bell has been teaching me his technique, and he says I have what it takes."

"What does it take? A strong stomach, no doubt."

Her look softened, and he saw the crippling twist in her back now, the lifelong agony that kept her so often inside the house. She pretended not to notice his gaze.

"You have already been to Europe, Teedie. By pure accident, you happened to be where Pope Pius was passing through, and you actually met him, dared to accept a handshake. We expected you to draw some kind of serious wrath from the Catholic Church. Instead, the pope smiled at you. Did you not find something there to hold your interest? *Anything* else beyond taxidermy? Good Lord, drying out dead animals. To what purpose?"

He was amazed at the question.

"To *learn,* Bamie. Some people explore outside, some explore these tiny worlds inside. I am prepared to do both. And, I'm sorry, but I didn't learn anything from the pope."

She seemed defeated, let out a breath.

"Just try not to smell up the house. And store your rodents where they do not so completely offend. Again, was there nothing else in Europe you found entertaining?"

It had been the year before, a journey that stayed with him as much for his suffering, constant bouts of asthma, as for the school lessons that dogged him along the way, including an unpleasant stay in a family's home in Dresden. Though his father had done as much as possible to open up the experiences of a European journey to his family, for the boy it seemed more like tedium. Bamie seemed to read him, had mixed feelings herself about the European trip, a trip that did little to comfort the curvature in her spine.

"Never mind, Teedie. I have no doubt that you will visit every place you wish to see and bring home every manner of creature, dead or alive, that suits you. God help us."

July 1872
Oyster Bay, New York

"Eyes closed, my boy."

He waited with the kind of anticipation usually reserved for Christmas presents. He felt the glorious weight in his hands now, knew the feel, didn't wait for the command to open his eyes.

"Father! Is this . . . ?"

"It is yours now, Teedie. You've learned how to handle the gun, and it's time you had a piece of your own. Be careful, and be wise. Go about your hunting for birds or whatever else you find so appealing, but there will be no shooting near houses, no matter what creature might be close by."

"No, certainly not, Father. Oh my, but she is beautiful."

He ignored the laughter from his sisters behind him, the reaction to his labeling the weapon in the feminine. His mind focused only on the gun now, and he studied the detail, a double-barrel shotgun, twelve gauge, French made.

"The maker, sir, I forget the name."

"Lefaucheux. You'll remember soon enough. It's engraved there, on the barrel. Beware of one minor inconvenience, Teedie. You'll have a bruised shoulder now and then. That piece kicks like a mule."

"THERE TEEDIE! To the right!"

He swung the shotgun in that direction, the sky empty, the voice of his brother.

"Teedie! You let him go. Why? He was fine."

Roosevelt scanned the skies, pretended not to hear his brother's critique.

"There, another! Shoot him!"

He swung around, searched frantically, nothing, his brother's taunting now becoming infuriating. But Elliott calmed now, as though something more was happening.

"I don't understand, Teedie."

"Never mind. Here, you take the next one. You seem to conjure these ducks out of thin air. Let's go over to the small pond, there's usually something in there. Don't damage my gun."

Elliott crept ahead, and Roosevelt saw a flash of motion, little else, a sudden blast from the shotgun. The bird fell close to Roosevelt's feet, Elliott now cheering himself, running close, grabbing the fallen duck by the neck.

"How about that, Teedie! We'll make supper from this one."

Roosevelt managed a smile, said in a low voice, "I didn't see him. Good shooting, though. Maybe I'll get the next one."

"I hope so, Teedie. It doesn't seem like you can see any of them too well."

"HERE. TRY THESE on."

"Spectacles?"

He took them from his father's hand.

"Why would I need spectacles?"

He slid them onto his nose, hooked them behind his ears. The room seemed to explode in colorful detail—his father's beard, the lace in his mother's white dress, Bamie behind her, smiling. His father said,

"Those examinations from the doctor made it pretty obvious you had some sort of vision problem. He says you are severely nearsighted. This was his prescribed cure. What do you think?"

He stared around the room, the light through the window, distant trees moving with the breeze, a vase of flowers in the next room, small petals of red and blue.

"I see things. I see everything. This is incredible, Father."

His father laughed, a pat on the boy's shoulder. "There is a good-sized flock of seagulls gathering close to the shore. Let's take your shotgun outside and see if you can find them. That should be a fine test."

They moved outside, his little brother, Elliott, trailing behind. Roosevelt carried the shotgun, moved with quick, excited steps, glanced down to the grass and gravel, small stones he had never seen before. He looked up, a jay flying past, graceful motion, then another, a robin. My God, he thought. I have missed so much. I have missed all of it.

They crept up a low rise, the water beyond, and he could hear the call of the gulls, several rising up, then disappearing down behind the hill. Beside him, his father said,

"Go on, Teedie. Take one. Let's try out those spectacles." He left the two of them behind, crept up the hill, saw the birds spread out on the water. He readied the gun, then lunged forward. The gulls responded, a half dozen now airborne, and he focused on one, stared straight out along the twin barrels, pulled the trigger.

The gull dropped in a heap, and he stared at it, then the shotgun, turned now, held the gun aloft, a beaming smile.

"Thank you, Father. This changes everything!"

CHAPTER 3

September 1872
New York City

He struggled to pull on his pants, the button too tight. He sucked in his breath, and his stomach, tried again. The button held, and he dared to exhale, thought, What has happened? The pants legs are too short, and the waist too small.

He hadn't worn these particular clothes in a long while, had thought they would work well in the gymnasium. They have shrunk, certainly. Or . . . the thought warmed him, a burst of happiness. *I have grown.* He swung his arms, noticed now that his shirt was tighter, and he flexed one arm, the knot of muscle above his elbow. Finally! Finally! It is working. *Father was right.*

He moved to the mirror, studied every part of him, more hints of muscle in his forearms, and he flexed his biceps, impressed himself. Why have I not noticed? Does this mean I'm becoming an actual man? That is a question for Father.

He jogged downstairs, saw one of the maids recoiling, as though he was a madman.

"Lucille, where is Father?"

She pointed toward the study, and he moved that way, saw him seated with an enormous book spread across his lap.

"Excuse me, Father. I have news."

His father looked up, studied him, said,

"Your pants are too small. Must we go shopping?"

Roosevelt rocked on his heels, proud of the observation.

"Yes, sir, my pants are too small. Likely because I have become larger."

His father studied him again, nodded.

"So you have. Perhaps you will grow larger still. You still have much to learn about boxing and climbing."

Roosevelt hesitated, waited for more, another useful gem of advice. But there was only silence, and finally, Roosevelt said,

"Thank you, sir. I will certainly try. Might I be excused?"

His father returned to his book, waved him away.

He withdrew again to his room, sat on his bed, fought against an empty hole in his gut. His father's words came to him now, the admonition he gave to all of his children. *I hesitate to say something favorable, because a sugar diet is not good for you.* He stood again, moved to the open window, saw his hand weights on the floor. Then I shall continue, he thought. And one day, he will notice.

HE KNEW THEY were watching him, Corinne and Elliot on the far end of the *piazza* as he struggled on the parallel bars, the weights, every other means of physical torture he had been given. The lesson earlier that morning had come at Wood's Gymnasium, Mr. Wood himself leading the lessons, while Roosevelt's mother stood to one side. If not coaching, she was at least overseeing the regimen, making sure that the fee they were paying Mr. Wood was well spent. If anyone else in the gymnasium thought the presence of Mittie Roosevelt was inappropriate, it was Wood himself who would silence any teasing. Roosevelt tried not to imagine that Wood's concerns had much to do with a beautiful and wealthy socialite like Mrs. Roosevelt adding considerable decorum to the surroundings.

Now, he was outside on the porch, what his father referred to as the *piazza*. There, the family had helped construct a gymnasium of their own, while some of the equipment was of course constructed by Mr. Wood. Roosevelt had no excuses now not to apply himself. If he could not attend the gymnasium, he could certainly make do with a difficult exercise routine on his own porch.

Part of his show now was for his siblings, the obvious pride in showing off to his younger sister and brother just how strong he might be. As part of the show, Roosevelt discreetly grabbed much lighter weights, swinging and tossing them as though they were mere toys, what would impress his younger siblings as a show of great strength. With the absence of anyone else's fists to punch him in the nose, the workouts were a leisurely struggle, his own pace, but still driven by what he knew he must do. Roosevelt's greatest concern was a return of the asthma. The attacks still came, perhaps not as often as when he was younger, but even now, they were completely unpredictable and could put him into a panic, a desperate struggle to breathe. He had to believe that putting himself into outstanding physical condition would help keep the affliction away. So far, he had little evidence that it actually worked. But there was always tomorrow, and the day after that.

HE FACED THE older boy, Mr. Wood between them. The instructions came, rules of engagement, ensuring no one was injured by some unsportsmanlike punch or head butt. Roosevelt eyed his opponent, thick shoulders, shorter arms, a solid middle. And a protruding jaw. He stared at the point of the young man's chin. There, he thought. Put it right there. And keep him from doing the same thing to you.

His hands came up, padded gloves protecting his chin, one hand dropping slightly, cocked into position for the left hook, the best punch he had. Behind him, he heard Wood.

"All right. Mr. Conroy. Mr. Roosevelt. Go to it!"

Conroy swung wildly, the amateur's curse, trying to end the fight with the first punch. Roosevelt watched the boy's hand drop, a deadly stupid reflex, following his punch by leaving himself completely open. But Roosevelt didn't take advantage, not yet. He jabbed twice, then moved slowly to his left, inviting the boy to throw the right hand. It came now, another wildly errant punch, and Roosevelt didn't wait, threw his own left, landed flush on the boy's chin, the boy's head jerking to one side, his knees giving way. He staggered to one knee now, and Roosevelt's vision wouldn't let him see the boy's glassy eyes, but Wood did, stepping in quickly.

"Enough. Mr. Roosevelt is the winner. Mr. Conroy, sit down until you gain your senses." Wood took Roosevelt by both shoulders. "Fine job, lad. That's four in a row for you. You ever consider turning professional, then? You'd have a good chance at it."

Roosevelt glanced toward his mother, saw a smile, knew that becoming a professional boxer was a fantasy he would never pursue. He had seen them, the professional fighters visiting the gymnasium once in a while, with their broken noses and grotesque cauliflower ears, men who were beat up in both body and mind.

"No thank you, Mr. Wood. It's just to keep me in top condition. Today was good, for certain." He lowered his voice. "Is he really that tough, Billy Conroy?"

Wood smiled, patted him on the side of the head. "Remember this, my boy. Everybody's tough until a fist finds his jaw. Just you worry about you. You won this one. Take that home with you." Wood glanced over toward Mittie, a short nodding bow. "Mrs. Roosevelt, he done real good today. Pays attention like he's supposed to. You should be proud. This one was short and sweet." He turned toward Conroy now, still sitting on a small stool. "Come on, boy, let's get you up. Maybe you'll do what I told you and keep your hands up."

Roosevelt glanced around the gymnasium, a handful of others, practicing, exercising, some watching him, nods of approval. His mother came toward him now, and he couldn't help a smile, said,

"I can't wait to tell Father about this one. All of this work is really doing me well. It's not just muscle, you know, it's paying attention, brains too. That's how I won today, I thought it through."

"I know. I saw it. He let his right hand fall."

Roosevelt was impressed, didn't really expect her to understand it at all. She helped him remove his gloves, and quickly, they walked outside, carriages moving past, a man on horseback, who made no secret with his gaze at Mittie.

"Did you see that man, Mother? He fully winked at you."

"I didn't notice, Teedie. Sometimes it's best to keep your eyes only on your own deportment. I was impressed with you today. You still need some polishing of the apple, but in time, you'll have a reputation in that gymnasium. It reminds me very much of my brother. My entire family, really. All the Bulloch men were handy in fisticuffs. They came to my rescue more than once when I was small. That ugly fellow on that horse would have stood no chance at all." She laughed, a soft, lilting song.

"Is that the brother who went to sea?"

She looked at him, as if to scold, but it didn't come. "Have I told you those stories? I do not believe so. It was important . . . for a while that I not speak of my family. It would not look good in those circles where your father holds such importance. During the war, they fought for the Confederacy. Not with the musket so much, but in other ways. My half brother James actually constructed the CSS *Alabama*, one of the finest warships of its time. Brother Irvine served aboard that ship. We were so proud, and it was a painful thing to keep so many secrets."

"Did Father know these things?"

She smiled, lowered her head.

"Of course he knew. But he loves me, and our family. You four children, you are more important to us than anything that happened during that awful war." She paused. "It is likely I may never travel to my Southern home again. It is very different now since the Yankees . . ." She stopped herself, took a long breath. "Since the war ended. Much is gone, much has changed. My home is here, with my husband, and with you. That is what matters."

He wanted to say something comforting, felt as though she was unhappy saying the words.

"I'm sorry, Mother."

"Don't be sorry for me. After all, I have *you*." She put a hand over his, studied his knuckles. "Just see that next time, *you're* not the one who gets a fist on the chin."

CHAPTER 4

"So, Teedie, you're leaving soon."

"Yes, sir. Mother has arranged a carriage to carry me to the rail station. In New York, I will board a train at four o'clock, to Boston."

His father smiled.

There was silence now, and Roosevelt suddenly felt awkward, could see the same awkwardness on his father's face. After a long moment, his father said, "You've done well to be accepted to Harvard. The tutor we brought here was most excellent, and his student doubly so. Mathematics is difficult at any level. With this entrance score, you show me that you could have mastered any entrance exam, to any college you wished. But Harvard is where you should be. Every successful man goes to Harvard." He paused. "Well, perhaps there are a few who go elsewhere. But you . . . *you* will become successful."

Another awkward silence, and Roosevelt fought for words.

"I hope to make considerable use of the library. I will use every spare moment to enrich my brain with books."

His father laughed now.

"Oh, I do not doubt that. You'll do what you always do, attack every obstacle in front of you with terrifying and enviable passion. You will read books, you will study your courses, you will enjoy the socializing, and you will do all of it possibly at the same time." He paused again. "I will write you, and I expect you to write me. I want to know how you progress, and I want to know if you require help, academic or financial. You won't require the academic."

"I only hope, Father, that I might live up to your expectations. I will never be your equal, but I will perform as your son *should* perform."

Another silent moment. His father crossed his arms, shook his head.

"I do wish you would not speak that way. You are my oldest son, but more, you are the one I am most proud of. That is no secret in this family, that my expectations of you are the highest. You have already made me proud in more ways than I can count, and that will continue. Elliott is pretty, and he will do well with such. The girls need no help from me. They are both brilliant and beautiful. You . . . you are not beautiful. That's a compliment, Teedie. You will work hard for whatever you achieve. No one, not me, not your mother, and not Harvard, will hand you anything for free. It is my pride, Teedie, that I have been able to offer the world around us a good bit of philanthropy. The Children's Aid Society, the Natural History Museum—these are, I suppose, my trophies, those things for which I'm known. But you . . . you are the greatest trophy of all. You are the son who is most like me, and you will succeed, like me. You have been the one who lifts me up, and not the other way around. You have never been a bother, a nuisance, you have never done anything to suggest we should use the whip." He smiled. "We never had to hand you over to a constable. Some of the boys I have known . . . well, never you mind. So, now? Harvard? You will continue to give me great pride."

Roosevelt felt tears, struggled to push them back, made a short bow.

"Thank you, Father. I shall do all I can to . . . to . . ." He ran out of words, and his father smiled again.

"Just go off to Harvard and try to have the best time you can."

December 1876
Cambridge, Massachusetts

His first weeks at Harvard were a ride down the rapids of a river he never knew existed. For most of the other freshmen, the goal was fun, and Roosevelt enjoyed his share. But beyond that, there was the more serious social life, clubs to join, fellowships to form, all of those connections that would supposedly serve these young men in whatever careers they chose. Many would follow their fathers, join banking or manufacturing firms. Harvard groomed the young men for the finest positions, the top tier of business and commerce. For Roosevelt, it was as though a blueprint had been laid before him, and so for the first two years, he followed the trends, joined everything open to him, forming mostly superficial friendships. That followed one piece of advice from his mother, that making good acquaintance with those with the right names could prove profitable, whether or not they were likable. But his father knew that advice was unnecessary. And so it was.

For Roosevelt, the academic curriculum confused as much as enlightened him. It was not that the courses were so difficult but that the goal behind each seemed a mystery. He knew some of what drove him, what he wanted to do with his life, and it didn't seem to have much to do with the classroom, the corporate or banking life, or even philanthropy, one of his father's great strengths. As time passed, he began to pay more attention to another area of fascination, one that inspired very little respect among the school's elite young men. It wasn't something he could aspire to in the classroom—there was no particular course he could take that would open doorways. For a long while, he wasn't sure why this should be a goal anyone should aspire to, thinking that perhaps his classmates were right when they suggested that only the low, the overly ambitious, the level of thieves would even suggest it as a profession. If Roosevelt didn't know just what to make of all of that, or just how he might apply it to his love of nature, he was beginning to be inspired nonetheless. It was politics.

No matter the gymnasium or the improvements in his physique, Roosevelt was at best a mediocre athlete. Though he played sports when the thought struck him, his primary interest was books. The social life was there as well, but he was not a heavy drinker, never smoked, and so, by default, excluded himself from some of the more boisterous crowds. But if the parties weren't entirely to his liking, the library was. His reputation grew as the young man with the literary mind who could speak on nearly any subject, although most often he would expound on those things that seemed most precious to him in the natural world around him. And when he did speak of his personal adventures, what seemed normal to him was often outrageous to others. This was a fellow, after all, who, as an eleven-year-old, had shaken hands with the pope, not long after fondling the hand of a three-thousand-year-old mummy. It had never occurred to him that any of it was truly unusual.

June 1877
Franklin County, Adirondack Mountains, New York

"Over here, Harry. I hear a peculiar one."

"Of course you do. You always hear them first."

"That's not true. But listen."

The shrill whistle came, far distant. Roosevelt was excited now, something new for the afternoon's exploration.

"Write that down. It's a gold-crowned wren."

Minot wrote on the pad, said, "That's a good number for today. This list is lengthening nicely. How many more do we require?"

"I don't know. We require all of those birds who are in these mountains. How many do *you* require?"

Minot smiled, nodded. "As many as you, that's for certain."

Roosevelt was enjoying himself immensely, far beyond the discovery and cataloging of birds and their calls. Harry Minot was the one young man he could truly call a friend, and it had little to do with social status or athletics. Minot had a love of ornithology barely surpassed by Roosevelt's own, and so they had begun to explore together, hiking through the various mountains within a couple of days' ride from Cambridge. Today it was the Adirondacks, and the following week they had plans to move out farther, possibly to the White Mountains in New Hampshire. The goal was simple: catalog bird descriptions and sounds to make a comprehensive list of the birds that inhabited this part of the world. Roosevelt had no idea when their mission might be complete, or if they would discover new species of birds that no one had ever seen before. It mattered not. He and Minot were having an enormous amount of fun.

He stopped, cupped his ear. "Wait, do you hear that?"

Minot did the same, shook his head in frustration.

"Too many at the same time. Wait, I hear it. A hermit thrush."

"Excellent, Harry. Write it down. I'm very sure you're right. That's a hermit thrush. I tell you, my friend, we're very fortunate. If it were September, the songbirds would be mostly mute. Summer is always the best time to hear the songs. And so . . ."

"You're giving me a lesson now? You don't have to tell me that this is the best time of year to be out here with you and this pad of paper."

Roosevelt stared off, said, "No insult meant, Harry. We've both done our share of this work. I assume it's all right with you if we share equal credit for it. We might sell a million copies."

Minot laughed.

"If my name's on the cover, there's a half dozen people in my family who'll buy it."

Roosevelt tried to imagine that, a book with his name prominently displayed. And Harry's of course. He had been sorely disappointed that among his classmates at Harvard, almost no one seemed to pay much attention to any part of the world around them that didn't involve alcohol. Except Harry.

Roosevelt glanced toward the setting sun, felt the first chill of the day. He stopped the relentless motion, pointed toward another songbird, and Minot said, "Swainson's thrush."

Roosevelt nodded. "We have that one already. I thought maybe it was . . . well, no matter. I was wrong." He began a silent lecture. Pay attention, he thought. If it's not the right bird, just look at all there is around you. There is nothing more beautiful than what you will find out here.

"We publish this book, Harry, we'll be famous. The world needs books like this, studies of things few people ever see. Even when people happen to be in the right place, they have no idea what they're seeing or hearing. We're telling them. You picked out a couple tough ones today. That chickadee you found is unusual in June."

"Thanks. It's getting kinda late, Ted."

Roosevelt felt his first jab of disappointment. "I'd love to stay out well after dark. A whole new world opens up. Have you been out west?"

"No farther than Pennsylvania. My family vacationed in the Pocono Mountains a couple years ago."

Roosevelt shook his head. "You must go, Harry. You absolutely must. I will go myself when my studies are completed. I'm not sure how, or with whom. But I'll go. The *West,* Harry. Indian territory, the great Rocky Mountains. Full of beasts like nothing we will ever see here. I hear that a sunset out there lasts an hour or more, lights up the entire sky with great oranges and reds and purples."

"Where'd you hear that?"

Roosevelt thought a moment, was stumped.

"Read it somewhere. So many good books on the subject, and I hope to read them all. Maybe write a few as well. The point is, Harry, that what we're doing right now is the first step. Nature is everywhere, and most people look right past it. I want to change that. I want everyone else to be as excited about the world on this mountain, on every mountain, as you and I are."

"I admit, Ted, *you've* done that for me. Ornithology is the most fascinating thing I've ever done, or ever tried to do. I'm searching for birds, for crying out loud, and what I didn't already know I learned from you. You've taught me how to tell the difference between a nuthatch and a brown creeper." He held up the pad of paper. "Now, we're writing a book. Thank you for that, Ted."

"It's *our* book, Harry."

"Well, thank you anyway. But we should get back. It's a good walk and I hear there's bears out here."

"Plenty of 'em. All black bears. Not as interesting. One day I'd love to come up on a brown bear, the kind they have out west."

"Who would eat who?"

Roosevelt laughed.

"Whom. It's *who would eat whom.*"

"Exactly what I said, Professor Roosevelt. Look, it's getting dark. Since you always know where the trail is, you can lead the way."

In mid-1877, Samuel E. Casino, of Salem, Massachusetts, published a reference book titled *Catalogue of Summer Birds,* by Theodore Roosevelt Jr. and H. D. Minot. It was well received, though it did not sell a million copies.

CHAPTER 5

February 1878
Cambridge, Massachusetts

Christmas in New York had been a marvelous family affair, the weather providing the delicious scenery of snow in the parks, carriages led by horses adorned with bells and wreaths. He had come down from Cambridge on the train, passing through farmlands and small towns that could have inspired the great painters. But once home, there was an odd current of discomfort, denied by all but made plain by occasional outbursts of pain expressed by his father. The pains seemed to subside, so much so that Roosevelt had felt comfortable taking his leave, returning to Cambridge on January 2. His studies were paramount, midyear examinations requiring every moment of his attention, even at the expense of his long walks through the hills he adored.

The letters flowed back and forth, all of his siblings keeping him informed of his father's condition, most of them cheerily optimistic. But there was an ominous hint here and there of something worse, his older sister Bamie mentioning the single word: peritonitis. To Roosevelt, that word seemed only to be a catchall phrase for any number of abdominal ailments, most of those minor afflictions having as much to do with indigestion as with anything truly medical. He took the reports from his family in stride, tried not to dwell on any hint of the negative, which was all that he could do. He was far away and had issues of his own that pulled him deeply into his studies.

He sat with Minot, each of them burrowed deeply into massive tomes of the natural sciences, subjects far more friendly to both young men than the mathematics texts staring down at them from the shelf above.

After a long silence, Roosevelt glanced upward, said, "We're delaying the inevitable, Harry. Professor Long is right now preparing his algebra exam with the two of us in mind. As much as I despise the mathematics classes, we might as well put aside our strength and work on our weakness. If we don't, Professor Long certainly will."

Minot looked up from his book, shook his head.

"You're a pessimist, Ted. Do well in your strong subjects, and let the weak ones take care of themselves."

Roosevelt was surprised.

"And that's how you expect to get through Harvard?" Minot seemed to hesitate, a small red flag rising in Roosevelt's mind. "What, Harry?"

"This might be the end for me, Ted. Harvard is great for some people, like you, I guess. But by this summer, I might go in another direction, even pursuing a career in ornithology."

"My God. You're serious." Roosevelt thought a moment, ran names through his head. "Harry, you're the only friend I have here. Real friend."

"Nonsense. You're popular, certainly more than I am."

"Popular because people laugh at me. They think I'm strange and loud and I'm fun to have at parties. But . . . you're my friend."

Minot pointed to the book across his small desk. "Look, let's get back to the studies. Summer's a long way away, and anything could happen."

Roosevelt turned again to the text. "Yeah, I suppose so."

There was a sharp rap at the door, a low voice, familiar.

"Mr. Roosevelt?"

"It's not locked."

The door opened slowly, a wide-eyed freshman.

"Sir, there's a telegram for you, addressed to Theodore Roosevelt Jr."

Roosevelt looked at Minot, then again to the boy. "What's your name, freshman?"

"Dalrymple, sir. Here's the telegram."

"Thank you, Mr. Dalrymple. Next time, be a little quicker about it."

"Yes, sir. Thank you, sir."

The door closed, and Minot said, "Well, what is it? Telegrams aren't usually good news."

Roosevelt held it up toward the lamp. "Hmm. Can't tell. Maybe I should open it."

"Quit playing, Ted. What's it say?"

He ripped open the paper, unfolded the telegram, read the first few words, felt himself sink into the small chair. "My God. No, it can't be." He paused, stumbled over the words again. "This is some kind of hideous dream."

"What has happened, Ted?"

"My father . . . has died. The greatest man I ever knew, or ever will know. How did this happen?"

"You said he was ill."

"Peritonitis, they said. Nothing to be concerned about, they said. But he was better, they said. Everything was fine. *They said.*"

He stood now, a burst of motion, but there was no place to go in the small room.

"My God. Mother, my sisters. This is awful. I must get to New York."

"There's the overnight from Boston. That'll be the fastest."

"Then that's where I'm going." He stopped, looked at Minot, felt a wave of panic. "I don't know what to do, Harry. He was the answer to all the questions."

Minot stood, put a hand on Roosevelt's shoulder.

"Your family needs you, for certain. Your mother will need you. You're the head of the family now."

He fought back tears, to still the fierce beating of his heart, his hands shaking.

"No. That's Bamie. I need *her*. We'll all need her, especially Mother. She'll know what to do."

"I'm so sorry, Ted. I'll see to the professors here, let them know about this. There's nothing else for you to do but go home."

The crowds had gathered around the Roosevelt home for several days prior to Theodore Roosevelt Sr.'s death, word passing quickly of the seriousness of his sickness among those circles who were so well connected to him. But word had continued to spread, and soon children came from the Children's Aid Society and from the Newsboy Lodging House, keeping watch with dirty faces, street urchins who only had a place to sleep and food to eat because of the work of the man who had lain in agony, painfully dying in the house on Fifty-Seventh Street. Others came as well, secretaries and supervisors, staff from the Natural History Museum, from other offices around the city, all of whom owed their subsistence to this man who was now too sick to know them. From his own company, Roosevelt & Son, the workers and foremen had come, joining the throng that spread out to Fifth Avenue and well up Fifty-Seventh Street.

They were brought there primarily because of the stories in the newspapers, reporting that one of New York's most renowned and beloved philanthropists was on his deathbed. The family had kept the reporters away, and so the reporters assumed the worst, and said so in their columns. For several days well into January, it had seemed to the family and close friends that the worst was past, but the pains returned, again and again, the family enduring Theodore's suffering cries, an agony in his abdomen no one could seem to cure.

On February 9, the agony ended.

"You MUST TELL me everything."

Elliott looked down.

"I already have, Teedie. Once we knew . . . it would happen soon, he seemed to calm. He had been hurting so badly. The doctor used the chloroform to allow him to rest, but by yesterday he was already gone. That's when we sent you the telegram." Elliott paused. "He spoke of you, Teedie. He said he was proud, that he knew you would do great things. I suppose he was proud of us all. He loved us all. But he especially loved you."

He didn't need that, not now.

"We will speak much more of this later. This is a time for quiet, for mourning. I will sit with Mother now. I must try to be of some comfort to all the women. And they must try to comfort you and me."

"They are very distraught."

"Elliott, we are all distraught."

"This is so very hard. Teedie, he was only forty-six. How does this happen? He was so healthy, so strong. I felt as though he was . . . *mighty*."

"Does that matter now? He was the most wise and loving father that ever lived. I owe everything to him. Somehow, we must learn to survive without him."

CHAPTER 6

June 1878
Cambridge, Massachusetts

My Dear Bamie,

I have offered myself the luxury of thought, for taking time away from my studies, from the other activities which can distract me. The one great distraction, of course, is Father. I have breakdowns occasionally, which shames me not at all. Even my friends understand that grief is perhaps healthy. Yet I will never be worthy of him. I must try, for he would have had it no other way. I shall try to lead a life as he would have wished. I actually feel that he is here with me, that his discipline aids me in my studies. I allow myself to accept that the longer I am at Harvard, the more successes have come my way. I have a growing number of acquaintances, have quite the social life, and with the conclusion of my junior year, my standing in the class has improved. I am now number nineteen out of two hundred thirty, a standing that even Father would approve. And, I must announce with some fanfare, beseeching your approval, that I intend to remove my whiskers. If I am to embark on being a man, I must look the part. And yet, I beseech you again, that you do what you can to guide me. You are in many ways more like our father than anyone in the family. I do not label Mother as weak, but she is not you and you are not her. I am there for her, and you, though I believe she needs me more. I wonder every day how I could have been more

of a good son to Father, knowing that I failed him in his worst
hour, able to offer him no solace, no cure when he was so very ill.
Yet, dear sister, I will not fail Mother, nor any of you.

Your Loving Brother,
Teedie

September 7, 1878
Aroostook County, Maine

It was the ideal end to his summer vacation, the promise of a glorious wilderness journey. He still carried his father's spirit wherever he went, but the grim heartache had mellowed just enough so that, now, new experiences could be shared even if he felt his father was somehow there, watching him. He tried his best, often in vain, not to ponder that. Too often the result would be a tear-filled breakdown.

For a long while now, throughout most of his stay at Harvard, his asthma seemed to look the other way, and when the attacks did come, they were brief and mild. Roosevelt had no idea why Harvard had offered him such relief, and there was no one he could ask. He preferred it that way.

He truly missed hunting—there were few places near Cambridge where a man could sling a rifle over his shoulder for small animals or the occasional deer. But Maine was very different, extremely appealing to one who treasured the rough nature of the wilderness as well as the plentiful varieties of game.

The journey northward was far longer than he had expected, the rail lines stopping well short of his destination. For the final thirty-five miles, he rode by buckboard, sweating horses and log-strewn pathways through thickets of trees that blocked out the sun. He had companions, a pair of his cousins and one doctor he barely knew, none of whom seemed as passionate for the journey as he was. It was a price he had to endure for making this trip in the first place. No one in his family was willing to approve his making this potentially dangerous trip all by himself. If his companions insisted on taking part, they could try to keep up. It was Roosevelt's usual level of loud confidence, that no rural county in Maine, or anywhere else, would prevent him from enjoying the most dee-lightful adventure.

HE WOULDN'T ADMIT how sore his rump was, saw the small huts with a silent wheeze of relief. The wheeze came again, and he crossed his arms in front of his chest, too familiar with what was coming. He crawled down from the buckboard, the others watching him, concern on all faces, the doctor seeming to know this might happen.

"Here, Mr. Roosevelt, take this. It's reliable, should help clear you up."

Roosevelt swallowed a vile liquid, the potion almost drowning him as he fought to breathe. He dropped to his knees, fought the congestion, felt the first relief, one cool breath breaking through. He sat, his back against the wagon wheel, his breaths coming more steadily now, slow, rhythmic. He coughed, a wet, phlegmy mass expelled, his breathing easier still.

"Thank you, Doctor. I am better. It has been so long. I didn't expect . . ."

"You didn't *expect* this? What do you expect? You brought a cussed doctor along with you. What kind of woodsman are you, anyway?"

Roosevelt followed the voice to an enormous man now standing tall above him, a thick beard half covering a ragged face.

"Can you stand up? Don't want a pale youngster like you hurting himself."

Roosevelt pushed away the helping hands, rose to his feet. He held out his own hand, said, "I am Theodore Roosevelt. You would be . . . ?"

"Bill Sewall. Your *host*. If you've come here to hunt, I'm the man to show you where. I'm not sure what any of you've come here for. We don't sit around and drink tea."

The doctor stepped forward, an air of rebelliousness.

"I assure you, Mr. Sewall, Mr. Roosevelt is a man of grit. You'll not tire him out."

"That so? Well, we'll see. Tomorrow we'll do twenty-five miles. You start squalling about how sore your feet are, you can stay where I leave you. You keep up with me, and I'll show you some fine country, better country than any of you city boys have ever seen."

Roosevelt discreetly checked his breathing, said, "Mr. Sewall, I cannot speak for my companions, but I can tell you that I am willing to walk any number of miles you feel are necessary to accomplish the purpose of this journey."

Sewall laughed, big and toothy through his beard.

"And just what is that purpose, then?"

"Sir, I've come to hunt."

FOR A FULL week, Roosevelt hiked alongside Bill Sewall for as many miles as necessary to carry out the great hunt, whether the goal was deer, moose, or bear. To Sewall's enormous surprise, the young man he had first described as "mighty pindlin" soon moved alongside Sewall step for step. The rest of the party quickly fell back, and kept miles to the rear.

With the hunt drawing to a close, Roosevelt returned to Harvard for the start of his senior, and final, year. He left behind Bill Sewall, who could only say of Roosevelt that there was nothing in the young man that Sewall didn't like. Though, *Mr. Roosevelt was not remarkably cautious about expressing his opinion.*

CHAPTER 7

October 1879
Cambridge, Massachusetts

The evening had been one of so many: what had once been dreaded now blossoming into an enthusiastic social life. Much of that had come at the hand of Harvard men who seemed willing to offer up their sisters or cousins to available and capable suitors. To Roosevelt's surprise, he was among those considered appropriate. A greater surprise was that as the social engagements grew in number, he actually enjoyed the company of most everyone who took part.

Most of the events took him to fine estates; others, to the more modest homes of the families of his friends. His favorite haunt had become the home of his classmate Dick Saltonstall, one of the finer homes situated on Chestnut Hill, a short distance from Cambridge. Through Saltonstall, and several other young men, Roosevelt was presented with the hands of various young ladies, dancing and dinners, snowy sleigh rides and walks along wooded paths. If they found him to be a little too boisterous, a little too loud and ingratiating, there were several of those ladies who hoped he would come around again. More often, he had obliged them.

"MY WORD, DICK. You've done it. You've opened the door to my heart."

Saltonstall shook his head.

"I'm not certain I care for that description. I have enough challenges opening my own heart than to crawl into yours."

"Oh, stop that. Can't you see I am smitten? This is serious, Dick. I have met so many perfect young angels, and I have you and so many others to thank for that. But last evening, the most perfect of all. I should like to see her again, and soon. Do you think you can arrange it? Your family is so close to hers—your homes practically touch, after all."

Saltonstall looked at him, puzzled.

"You've been seeing these same ladies for a number of occasions. I had no idea you were focusing in on any one of them. I certainly had no idea any of these ladies stuck the arrow so deeply. You were doing so well with the lot of them, my own family included. You're never at a loss for a dance partner. Why settle for just one, when they tend to flock around you like so many birds? And I am at a loss to know just which one you're talking about. Miss Lane? Miss Bacon?"

Roosevelt was annoyed.

"You're toying with me. How could anyone not see when and where my attentions have turned? She is the prize above all others, the angel who soars far beyond the rest. I am smitten, Dick. I am in love."

"Um . . . with who?"

Roosevelt shook his head.

"You are indeed dense. Who else could it be? There are nice girls, and then there are goddesses. I have found my goddess. I am in love with Miss Alice Lee."

December 1879
Chestnut Hill, Massachusetts

He was in torment, his stomach twisting with an ache that spread through every part of him. It wasn't the asthma. It was Alice Lee.

He had arranged a photograph be taken, a tintype in a well-known local studio, a portrait of the two of them standing alone, a memento that he would keep close to him, or close to his line of sight if she wasn't there, which was too often. To his enormous disappointment, Alice had agreed to the photography session only if Dick Saltonstall's sister, Rose, joined in. Thus did Roosevelt sit dejectedly between two young ladies, every part of him wanting to lean much closer to the one on his right. He had to accept the obvious, that it was Alice's virtue that prevented her from joining him alone in the photographer's lair.

The rest of the courtship was proving as awkward. In the best of times, Roosevelt seemed overly enthusiastic about most everything, but when doubts crept in, as they did now, he compensated by adding a hearty dose of exuberance. The results could be embarrassing to others, if not to him. And to his horror, it seemed to push Alice ever so slightly away.

THE MUSIC WAS awful, some sort of minuet with a violin player who seemed to be engaged in some other occupation altogether. Roosevelt hesitated, saw Alice waiting for him, her hand extended his way. To his enormous relief, she was actually smiling.

He stepped forward, took her hand, led her onto the makeshift dance floor that the Saltonstall family converted on this one Saturday into a festive gathering place for the area's eligibles. It was one more opportunity for Roosevelt to impress on Alice just how much he loved her without actually saying it. Dancing and refreshments, a small orchestra—all designed, or so he thought, to inspire as much longing in her for him as he felt for her. And yet, for so long now, as those moments would raise the tide inside him, she would seem to drift back out to sea. It was maddening.

He began to step, flowing in time to the hideous music, a glance to one side, his friend Dick watching approvingly, sitting alongside most of the Lee family, who did not approve at all. Roosevelt did his best to convey charm, a short bow to her stone-faced parents, then a more pronounced one toward Alice. She seemed to gaze away, deflecting another soft advance from him, and he began to compensate yet again, this time with his feet.

Do it now, he thought. Take charge of her attention, and the rest of them as well. Be serious, but be light. Smile. Not too much. All right, dance.

His feet took on a life of their own, the music obliterated by the sheer beauty of her, and the feelings inside him that gave every ounce of energy to his anxious pursuit. He glanced again to one side, saw a small herd of young men, all of them staring at her with evil designs in their faces. He felt a chill, wanted to throttle the lot of them, knew from his friend that a number of these young men had been calling on Alice. The thought that any one of them felt the same ache for her as he did made him sick.

All right, don't think. *Dance.* He moved with heavy steps, as if to emphasize his power, the strength he would use to keep the others away. And if she insisted, he would show her the strength behind his resolve, his love and devotion. He moved with thunderous steps now, held a grip on her fragile hand, saw a glimmer of agony on her face, let go, horrified. He tried to back away, saw that his heel had snagged her dress. He raised the errant foot, stumbled, felt a burn in his face, others staring at him as he tried to salvage the dance steps. He continued to move, pretending to ignore his clumsiness, made a single hop, one hand high, the music gone from his mind. He felt desperate, his mind racing through a fog, urgently seeking for some way to avoid any more embarrassment. He clamped a wide grin on his face, shouted out, "My, but this is dee-lightful!"

The words were very loud and came out of him from some odd place, but he held the great toothy grin, as if all was well. The young men stood watching him with arms crossed, and he glanced at his friend Saltonstall, saw a look of embarrassed misery. Alice's father seemed ready to locate a dueling pistol. Then miraculously, silence in the enormous room, and he realized the music had stopped. For a long moment, he wasn't sure what to do. He looked at her now, realized he had failed to pay proper attention, that somewhere in the midst of his disaster, he had released her gloved hand. He tried to keep the grin, but it failed him, and he glanced at his own hand, thought, What do I do now?

She answered the question herself, extended her hand once more.

"My dear Teddy, would you accompany me in a glass of Mother's punch? It isn't proper, you know, for me to go myself. After your magnificent performance, I require some refreshment."

He heard the sarcasm, waited for her to pull away, felt a heavy ache in his chest, but she remained, and he said, "Dee-lighted, Miss Lee. I could use some punch myself. Perhaps the kind that comes with knuckles attached."

His joke carried more volume than he intended.

He turned, saw a pair of her alleged suitors seeming to tag along, keeping some distance, as though with the slightest lapse in his attentions to her, they would pounce.

"I say, Miss Lee, let us move away. I shall have one of the servants bring us the punch. I feel as though we are the center of attention at these proceedings."

She laughed, like soft music.

"Oh, dear Teddy. I would gladly go wherever you lead. And, perhaps after so much time together, you should start calling me Alice."

Her words engulfed him like a tidal wave, and he stared into her eyes, let her beauty fall over him.

"Does this mean . . . dear Alice, that you will reconsider my proposal?"

She led him now, out past the refreshments, a slightly more private corner of the great hall.

"Teddy, I am only seventeen, far too young for marriage."

He glanced back across the room, saw the expected glare from her father, realized he didn't hear a *no*.

"An early engagement, then. Marriage can come much later, if you prefer. I am just . . . afraid someone will step into my place. You are so very special, and you mean so very much to me."

"Teddy, we can speak of this later. I am being rude to our hosts."

She moved away, all pearls and lavender, ivory skin and soft lace. He knew her eighteenth birthday was coming soon, the great *coming out* would follow, the elaborate ritual that seemed so important to the parents of eligible young women. He saw the young men again, so many pairs of lustful eyes, watching her swaying walk, none of them with any respect for his aching passion. What must I do to win her? She teases and then she withdraws, then back again. Alice. She insists I call her Alice. Finally. So, what must I do now?

He felt the first choking wheeze of a new assault of asthma.

ON FEBRUARY 14, 1880, Roosevelt was reluctantly granted permission by George Cabot Lee, Alice's father, to make public their official engagement. The Lees agreed to Roosevelt's request that there be an autumn wedding, eight months later. Finally, Alice the coquette, the tease, seemed to accept that this boisterous and exuberant young man was to be her husband, that the infuriating games that had so tortured him were over. For him, it was the happiest time in his life.

What followed was momentous as well. In June 1880 Roosevelt graduated magna cum laude from Harvard, although his senior thesis nearly cost him the respect he had earned, both from the faculty and his classmates. It was titled "The Practicability of Giving Men and Women Equal Rights." Despite the fashion of the day, and the mores of most of those around him, Roosevelt came down convincingly on the side of the positive.

Advocating for a woman's right to vote, to hold office, and to have a vast number of other male privileges did not endear him to even some of his social acquaintances. But from those who mattered, especially the women in his own family, the responses were mostly supportive, and he did not hesitate to speak out on the subject, whether he was asked to or not.

WITH PLANS FOR an October wedding blossoming around him, Roosevelt wisely accepted the opportunity to embark on a very different kind of excursion, a hunting trip with his brother Elliott. They would seek game throughout several stops in the Midwest, but there was little to cheer about, the experience more of a mud-soaked chore than any real adventure. Unfortunately, Elliott, though a capable hunter himself, seemed mostly miserable, unsatisfied with the shoots that Roosevelt had always enjoyed. Worse, as their trip drew to a close, Roosevelt observed what his mother had described as Elliott's bad habits, a dismaying tendency to drink to excess.

By the time Roosevelt boarded the train to New York, he was as happy as Elliott seemed to be to bring the entire experience to its conclusion. For Roosevelt, the trip had opened up another sense of longing, the Midwest offering him only a hint of what the hunter's life could be farther west, the *real* West. But that would be an adventure for another time.

Upon leaving the train in New York, he stepped into the firestorm of his mother's and Alice's planning for the wedding. Wisely, Roosevelt knew to stay mostly out of the way. His role would come soon enough.

October 19, 1880
New York City

The parlor was dark but for a pair of candles to one side. Mittie sat across, the light reflecting on her weary face.

"Where have you been? It's past eleven."

Roosevelt placed his hat on the rack, loosened his vest.

"You know, Mother, I was with the gaggle of single ladies, Miss Edith Carow, Miss Fanny Smith. They seem quite determined to fatten me up before the wedding. If they had lavished this much attention on me when I was available, I'd be as fat as a turnip now."

He watched her as her arm moved across a small marble table, delicate and fragile. She took a painful breath, said, "Those women are going to miss your company, but it doesn't always have to be so. They are all very fond of you. I'm certain they want you to be happy, and Alice is quite the friend to all of them. You should not lose the friendships of the women in your life just for being married. With proper etiquette, of course."

He smiled toward her.

"Of course, Mother."

"Alice is so very lovely. The loveliest young woman I have seen in many years. Her mother and I have grown close, you know. That's a very good thing. Their family is welcome here any time, and she has extended the same invitation when we travel to Massachusetts."

He stared at her for a long moment, then said, "What of Elliott?"

She shook her head.

"He is quite busy preparing for his journey to India. I'm not even sure where he is right now, just that he will not be available for your wedding. It is all so . . . discouraging."

It had been a surprise to Roosevelt, even more so than to the rest of the family. Elliott, who so disdained the hunt in the Midwest, was now planning an excursion of his own, considerably more exotic than his time in Iowa.

"He must do what he must do, Mother. He is searching for something, and I am not able to assist him."

Mittie shook her head, and after a quiet moment, said, "Who shall you ask to be your best man?"

Roosevelt knew this was coming.

"No one. I shall stand alone. I shall not rely on some last-minute substitute, just for decorum's sake."

To his surprise, she smiled.

"Excellent, Teedie. Your decorum is no issue. However, I am concerned with the amount of money you have been spending. We are sharing quite a bit of expense with Alice's family as it is."

"I surprised myself, Mother. I have been spending money like it is water, but I assure you, it will not continue. Once I am married, we shall become the most frugal of couples."

She smiled at him again.

"Your father said that, many years ago. I was not to lavish great sums on our household, and in return he would pay close attention to our expenses. It didn't work. We both exploded our conservative budgets. I suspect you will too. If not you, then perhaps your charming new wife."

"We'll see, certainly. I must make ready now for the next stop on this railway to matrimony. I'm off to a friend's cottage near Salem in the morning. He has promised all the solitude I require, considering that in a week, I shall no longer be solitary."

He was surprised to see concern on her face.

"Do I know this friend?"

"No, Mother, I don't see how you could. A classmate from Harvard. His family has a wonderful estate, and I have been promised absolute privacy to do what I require to get all the tastes of the single life washed away from my brain."

She cocked her head to one side.

"Why do you require privacy? Washed away how? Be honest with me, Teedie. Is there debauchery afoot? You are your own man, and you may do as you please. But these things rarely remain secret. It is no way to begin a marriage."

He was confused.

"I can only tell you what he told me. They are providing a fine axe. I am to spend as much time as I would like chopping down trees."

ONE WEEK LATER, on October 27, 1880, Theodore Roosevelt Jr. married Miss Alice Lee in the Unitarian Church in Brookline, Massachusetts. It was his twenty-second birthday. To no one's surprise, when the ceremony required him to respond to the vows, his voice rose high above the volume of any other. There was no confusing his meaning. He was marrying the love of his life.

CHAPTER 8

November 13, 1880
New York City

It had been a whirlwind, a brief informal honeymoon at Oyster Bay, dinners with friends and various family members, some he knew well, some whose kinship was to Alice. As a break in the continuous festivities tossed upon them from so many well-wishers, Roosevelt and his new bride had returned to New York, at the request of his mother, Mittie determined to embroil them in yet another social whirl. The culprits this time were Corinne and Bamie as well, everyone in the family drawn to Alice and having as much affection for her as their brother did.

"BY GEORGE, IT was a true feeling of power, wonderful, absolutely."

The four women sat around the table, seeming to hang on his words, with only one, Bamie, holding a hint of a scowl. Roosevelt didn't miss that, knew where it originated. But he plodded onward.

"Voting. There is no greater sense of loyalty to the country, no greater sense of responsibility to our Constitution. I tell you, I walked out of that polling place . . . no, I strutted out of there with a pride I had never felt. To be of voting age finally. By George."

Bamie could keep silent no longer.

"How very nice for you, Brother."

He expected this, was prepared for it.

"Bamie . . . all of you. The day is not that far removed when we may all assemble around our parlor table and argue about who inspired us to vote his way. I will tell you that this election, my first, I voted for Mr. Garfield for president. I would dearly enjoy listening to the four of you label me a scoundrel or a fool, with very good reasons why you chose a competitor. Alas, it is not to be. Not yet."

Alice said, "Why is that? Why are we denied?"

Roosevelt felt a storm brewing.

"Because, my love, they are afraid of you. Men are manipulated by talk of power and finance. Men are easily corrupted. Women are not. I believe it is that simple. If you all gained suffrage, we might elect the very best candidate for the job every time out. Then . . . the reformers would have nothing to do."

He hoped the bit of humor would calm the waters, and it seemed to have worked. After a moment digesting his words, Mittie said, "Are you serious about the law? A career as a lawyer?"

Roosevelt welcomed his mother's change of topic.

"I like the law. There is an enormous amount of reading, on every topic. To pursue research on some arcane point, to dig into ancient lawbooks, writings on every type of legal precedent . . . I find that enormously appealing." He paused, took a deep breath, his words coming out in a flood. "The greatest hero we have in this country is Abraham Lincoln, a country lawyer. Granted, I would become a city lawyer, but I would aspire nonetheless to a life that earns the respect of a Lincoln. Consider the opportunity he so ably grasped. He was the one man capable of steering this nation through its greatest tragedy. The Southern states were determined to destroy the one great free republic on the face of the earth, to engage in a war that would drive their own states into ruin, all to perpetuate slavery. It took a great man to bring us out of that pit of misery. Thank God for Lincoln." He looked self-consciously at his mother, expected at least a hint of protest from the woman whose family was so devoutly Confederate. To his relief, Corinne held up her hand.

"Well, Teedie, if I should ever be handed the right to vote, I shall cast mine for Abraham Lincoln."

He knew he had gone overboard.

"I wish we all had that opportunity. We must settle for what is, and perhaps what will be. But I admit, I'm drawn to the notion of a life in politics. To perform a service that benefits the entire people . . ."

The word seemed to surprise his mother.

"Politics? Your father did great good for an enormous number of people with charity work, advancing the culture in less dreadful ways. He considered the professional politician to be a man with no other opportunities in his life except to defraud and scandalize the people who could be persuaded to give him their vote. They are scoundrels, all of them. Are you seriously considering politics as a profession? Surely the law would offer you more reputable opportunities. I fear, my son, you will draw the wrath of those professional politicians who will see you only as a disruption."

"*I hope so!*" The words came out with more volume than needed, all four of the women leaning back under his barrage. He tried to back down, but his passion overtook him yet again, the words flowing like an unstoppable river. "If there is a governing class in this society, and others not considered worthy of that class, then having someone like me cross that line should be welcome. If that life is not for me, then I should quit. But I would not quit until I had made the effort and found out whether I really was too weak to hold my own in the rough-and-tumble."

He sat back, saw all four staring at him, smiles now spreading across the room. Bamie spoke first.

"I do not believe, Teedie, you will have any difficulty measuring up to any decision you make, no matter how *rough-and-tumble*."

Corinne said, "Tell me, then. What office would you strive for? Governor first, then on to Washington?"

He knew he had invited the jesting—let his sisters have their say.

"I would begin at the beginning. State assembly."

Bamie laughed.

"The beginning? The beginning is the block captain for the local ward boss. Shake a few hands and pet a dog or two. Assemblymen go to Albany and find ways to steal from the poor."

He crossed his arms, glanced at Alice.

"Which is why I would prefer to go to Albany. Someone needs to stop that nonsense."

By spring, Roosevelt had begun to seek an assemblyman post in earnest, hobnobbing with those who had the connections that led straight to the state capitol in Albany. In the meantime, the social tornado that surrounded the newlyweds and their families only seemed to grow: great parties in honor of the bride and groom, the Lee and Roosevelt families reciprocating with parties of their own. If there was a pause in the attention paid to the newlyweds, there was renewed clamor toward his sister Corinne, now *coming out* as a beautiful debutante. Through it all, it was Alice who held the most attention, so that even the natural reluctance of her mother-in-law had melted away. Mittie and Alice had become very close, so much so that Bamie and Corinne both welcomed her as a sister, not merely a sister-in-law.

To Roosevelt's dismay, party politics in New York was a more difficult wall to breach than he had imagined. Despite his outgoing glad-handing and obvious passion for living up to the expectation of Republican Party elders, the powers that controlled the road to Albany were not yet convinced he was the man for the job. Though sulking might have been his natural reaction, he had very little time to wallow in self-pity. The time had come for a proper honeymoon.

On May 12, 1881, the couple boarded the steamship *Celtic*, for the ten-day journey that would take them to the British Isles. After several days at sea, Roosevelt began to feel homesick for what he was missing in New York. But soon his greater concern was for the awful attacks of seasickness that were affecting his wife. Finally, with the crossing complete, Alice emerged from the cocoon of misery, and the couple embarked on the experience each had hoped for through England and northern Europe. The excursion carried them through Switzerland, where, true to form, the intensely excited Roosevelt saw a challenge he couldn't resist. He succeeded in climbing the Matterhorn. With yet another extraordinary physical accomplishment behind him, the Roosevelts made their way back through Belgium and the Netherlands, finally returning to England.

The boxes and crates were loaded first, their personal treasures from so many weeks of shopping. Alice's personal baggage came after that, followed by his own. He stood back, watched the process, thought to himself, this ship seems seaworthy enough for this much baggage, *as long as no one else has any.* He laughed at his own joke, backed away, let the longshoremen do their work. He loved the ships, all the details, the smell, the ropes and cables, smokestacks and anchor chains. And, of course, the men whose hands made it all work.

He heard her voice, unmistakable.

"My darling! There you are! Something dreadful has happened."

He saw her now, as she scampered across the dock, men stepping aside, low comments he ignored.

"What?"

She held out a section of newspaper, out of breath. No more words were necessary.

"My God. President Garfield is dead. I thought he would recover." He paused. "Now, it's murder. He was murdered by an assassin. Like Lincoln." He looked around, as though someone would have more information. "We knew when he was shot back in July that it could have been serious. But some of the papers here made it sound like some kind of foolish accident, that he would be fine. He was not fine at all. We should have paid more attention instead of indulging ourselves with shopping and sightseeing."

She took his arm now.

"We did nothing wrong. We could not have done anything. You know that."

He let out a long breath, focused on the paper.

"This says he died five days ago."

She seemed to read him, said, "We are going home today. It will not be long, and you can talk to your friends, find out what this will mean."

He looked at her, her beauty sweeping away so much of the horror of the moment.

"This has been the happiest time of my life, all these weeks with you. But I must know what is happening in New York, whether I can do anything, make any contribution. The government must be in turmoil. Chester Arthur is now president, a man my father knew well. I don't know what it all means for the country, for Albany. I am so very far away."

"Then, my husband, let's board the ship."

ON OCTOBER 28, 1881, the name Theodore Roosevelt was placed in nomination by the Republican Party assembly convention. He was chosen on the first ballot over a long-established candidate who had been expected to walk into the nomination. The surprise from most of the party elders was complete. But with the death of President Garfield, the public seemed to have awakened from the shock of such a loss with a determination to sweep away the corrupt and shady politicians who had become so well implanted in their governments. This young fellow, Roosevelt—he was only twenty-three—seemed to bring the breath of fresh air, if not a hurricane, into what had been the dusty backroom procedures that had determined policy for years. It would now be up to the young man himself to prove that he was able to withstand the business-as-usual temptations that were certain to come his way.

November 9, 1881
New York City

"It is complete! I am done. Well, perhaps not completely done. It must be edited certainly, by someone at Putnam's whose eyes are not tainted by my personal bias."

Alice took the manuscript from him, felt the heft.

"My word, Teddy, this is quite a work. I wasn't sure you would ever finish it, with so many distractions."

"The ship home from England. That was the key. Nothing else to do for ten days but write. That was the incentive I needed to complete this, to establish a rhythm that would not be interrupted. I must put this into the hands of my publisher immediately. No one has completed such a work before, and I am nervous that, suddenly, every author in the land would pen the same work."

"*The Naval War of 1812.* No, my husband, I do not believe anyone shall beat you to publication. In less than three years, you have done a lifetime of research on this. I offer my congratulations."

"Offer me a kiss. That shall suffice for every congratulation I might receive anywhere else."

He heard footsteps on the stairway below, and now Corinne's voice.

"Teedie? Forgive me. A gentleman from the newspaper is here. *The Times.* He wishes to speak to you."

Alice stood aside, smiling.

"You see? They already know about your great work."

He didn't share her mirth, looked out through a window, thick darkness, the clock nearby showing nine o'clock.

"Why would a newspaperman want to talk to me? And why so late?"

"It's November ninth. Isn't this Election Day for the assembly?"

It struck him like a bolt of lightning.

"Well, of course. I voted first thing this morning. I had quite forgotten. Tidying up this manuscript absorbed all my thoughts." He called out to Corinne, "Coming right now. Tell him to wait in the parlor."

He dropped down the steps two at a time, his usual gait, the entire house seeming to shake. The man was small, a tight beard, wearing an ill-fitting suit.

"Yes, sir. What may I do for you?"

The man responded with a smile, said, "Harvey Glatton, sir. *New York Times.* I'm only seeking your reaction, perhaps a quote. I came by at the request of my editor to see if you had anything to say to the good citizens of New York, perhaps some comment we can use. Quite a momentous day for you, is it not?"

Roosevelt felt open-eyed honesty in the man, tried to detect some corrupt motive under the surface.

"Uh, yes, certainly, sir. It is a momentous day. I have completed a great work. Well, great to my eye. Others will have to judge."

Glatton seemed confused, said, "You mean, the election?"

Roosevelt stopped cold, said, "You are here for my reaction to the voting. I have not received any kind of tally." He paused, swallowed. "Is that why you're here?"

Glatton smiled now, rocked on his heels, the look of a man who brings great secrets.

"You have not been informed, then. First, however, allow me to read to you what you already know. It is your own handbill, dated November one. 'Having been nominated as a candidate for member of Assembly for this District, I would esteem it as a compliment if you honor me with your vote and personal influence on Election Day.'"

Roosevelt had his own share of confusion now, felt an edge of caution.

"I am familiar with that. I wrote it. Those circulars were handed out throughout the city, wherever possible. I see nothing improper in that, certainly nothing illegal."

Glatton laughed.

"Sir, not only were these legal and proper, they were extremely successful. It is my job to wade through the morass of campaign literature, pages upon pages of flowery promises, men claiming to bring the right hand of God to their elected office. No, sir, you put it simply and plainly, and I congratulate you. It worked. You have defeated the Democrat, Mr. Strew, by a sizable margin. Sir, if you allow, I should like to shake your hand. I firmly believe I am in the presence of a rising star."

Roosevelt shook the man's hand.

"Reaction. You want my reaction. 'Thank you, voters. I will do the job. There will be no shame.'"

Glatton jotted the words on a pad of paper, slid the pen back into his coat pocket. "Very good, sir." He backed away now, placed his hat on his head. "I will take leave, Mr. Roosevelt. Enjoy Albany, sir. Pray you're not devoured by those people."

Glatton was shown the door by one of the servants, and Roosevelt felt an odd euphoria, realized there were ears above him, Alice and Corinne on the staircase. Alice moved down now, a wide smile.

"Congratulations, my Teddy. You have succeeded at what you worked so hard to achieve."

He seemed distracted, tried to focus on her face, her words, glanced at Corinne, another smile, heard now their mother coming up from the cellar. Corinne said, "Mother, this is a glorious day for Teedie. Tell her, Teedie, tell her!"

He looked at Mittie's frail beauty, felt the contagious joy that seemed to pass through all of them. He felt it himself now, nodded with his usual energy, both hands clenched, raised his arms above his head in triumph.

"It is a bully day! By George, I finished my book!"

CHAPTER 9

Spring 1883
Albany, New York

"Mr. Speaker! Mr. Speaker! I will be heard! Mr. Speaker!"

The great hall had echoed with the same cry for a year now, the gathered assembly accustomed to the piercing bellow from its youngest member. At the head of the room, the speaker of the assembly had long understood that Roosevelt would not give up until he was heard. It was best just to give in.

"The Republican gentleman from New York City may speak."

Roosevelt straightened himself, had been leaning far out over his desk. He tugged at his coat, took a long breath, his energy and frustration level at full boil.

"It is to the credit of every man in this august body to pass those bills which benefit all New Yorkers. Sadly, such is rarely the case. I do not understand why such learned men as these cannot see past their own corrupt influence."

May 5, 1883
New York City

He scribbled furiously in his diary.

I fear I may become an outcast in the very position to which I have been elected. They seem unable to face themselves in the mirror, to see what kind of body they have become. There are some twenty-five Irish

63

Democrats in this house, a stupid, sodden, vicious lot, most of them being equally deficient in brains and virtue. Those holding their power by the grace of the Tammany machine are totally unable to speak with even an approximation of good grammar; not even one of them can string three intelligible sentences together to save his neck. For that gentleman named McManus, he is a huge, fleshy unutterably coarse and low brute, who was formerly a prizefighter, at present keeps a low drinking and dancing saloon, and is more than suspected of having begun his life as a pickpocket.

He saw Alice standing in the doorway, put down his pen.

"You know, they can't even elect a speaker worth respecting. The man who is to lead us is yet to be selected from among a dozen good candidates for the position. But it is the will of the parties that we be deadlocked, time and again, or worse, that we choose a speaker who is little more than a puppet of those few who control nearly every vote we undertake. And if the votes are not preordained by corrupt influence, it is as though these men thrive on inactivity, small children when told to eat their supper, instead sit cross-armed with a chin pooched out. Yes, stubborn children. Most of them, anyway."

She seemed concerned, said, "Are you feeling all right, Teddy? You are flushed, more than usual. I am concerned for you. I do not completely understand why you subject yourself to this kind of punishment at the hands of so many men you do not respect."

"They make the law. I find myself in a grotesque situation, but what comes out of that great building in Albany changes our piece of the world. If I could control those bills, determine what has value to the people, well, of course, I would be happy, and no one else would join me. So, my job, my responsibility is to prevent some thieving lowlife in the aisles across from me from controlling those bills for himself. It is a god-awful system, but, strangely enough, it seems mostly to work. But I admit. I am unduly frustrated. And a good many of those people are frustrated having to listen to me. Of that I am certain."

"How much longer will you put yourself through this, Teddy?"

He was surprised at the question, turned fully to her, one hand out. She moved close, sat on his knee.

"I must do this, at least for now. I have few other opportunities awaiting me. And, slowly, I find that some men there respect what I say. I am amazed by that, but it means I must, at least for now, continue to serve those who elected me."

She leaned closer to him, the soft air of her perfume drifting over him. He put a hand around her waist.

"My, but you are pleasant . . . no, make that *magnificent* to touch."

She laughed softly.

"You have proven that on so many occasions, my husband. This is perhaps the best time to reveal to you what I have only just determined. It seems I am expecting."

"Expecting what?"

She laughed again, sat up straight, then stood now, looking at him.

"Teddy, I am going to have a child."

He stood as well, stared at her, his mouth slightly open. After a long moment, he managed the words, "By George. A child. I am to be a father."

Her smile was contagious.

"Yes, Teddy."

"When?"

"Well, according to the midwife, we may expect the birth to come after the end of the year."

"This year? Well, of course, this year. So, next year."

She laughed now.

"Yes, Teddy, February."

"My word. I had not considered this. Are you all right?"

"I am fine, Teddy. The doctor will be examining me often, to be sure all is well. Your mother has offered her hand, as has Bamie. My mother is positively beside herself, so she will be a great help as well."

"It seems everyone knows about this but the father."

"Well, you spend your weekdays in Albany. This has to wait for a weekend for me to tell you. After all, I wasn't going to send this in a letter."

He reached out to her shoulders now.

"No, of course not. It seems you are in good hands for now. Good woman hands. I would likely become an enthusiastic nuisance."

She laughed again.

"Aren't you already? That's what they seem to think in Albany. The newspapers do mention something about that once in a while."

"Never mind the newspapers. Since the assembly will adjourn this week, I have their next headline: Assemblyman Theodore Roosevelt Junior is set to become a father. And he is dee-lighted."

May 28, 1883
New York City

Though many in Roosevelt's Republican Party did consider him a nuisance, the respect they felt for him continued to grow, so much so that with the end of the legislative session, a party was scheduled in his honor at a well-known bar and eatery in the city.

"Yes, I do support free trade, though I suspect there are some in this city who vote for me regularly who would tear up their ballots if they heard me say such things."

The laughter was uproarious, no one seeming to take him seriously, and he let that fall any way they wanted it. The alcohol was flowing freely, the mood much more celebratory than political, which suited him just fine.

"I have learned that when a party is in full enjoyment, it is best to keep one's politics to himself. No need to spoil the fun."

A hand slapped his back, more following, the loosening in the mood of some of his critics made easier by the spirits he avoided. The men seemed to settle down now, food appearing, their focus more on their bellies than on him, which, again, suited him just fine.

"Mr. Roosevelt, would you sit with me?"

He followed the voice, a middle-aged man, unfamiliar. He hesitated, and the man seemed to sense that, said, "I understand you are a hunter."

"Yes I am, sir. Quite, as time and circumstances allow. Too infrequently these days."

"Sir, if you will join me, then?"

Roosevelt followed the man's lead, a small table to one side, both men sitting heavily.

"I don't believe I know you, sir."

"Commander Henry Gorringe, United States Navy, at your service, sir. You may be familiar with my work, if not my name. I commanded the effort required to bring Cleopatra's Needle out of Egypt and relocate it in Central Park. Quite an undertaking, I assure you."

Roosevelt knew of the project, the enormous stone obelisk transported so carefully across the Atlantic. He saw the pride in Gorringe's face.

"Yes, I know your achievement, if not your name. Most impressive."

"I would offer that same compliment to you. Your book, *The Naval War of 1812* . . . magnificent."

It was the finest compliment Roosevelt could receive, coming from a man who no doubt had a vast knowledge of ships himself.

"My word, thank you. Um, you mentioned hunting? My brother has recently returned from India, quite the hunter himself. His trophies are amazing, many of which I had never seen before. It rekindled the dormant fire I had to get once more into the field." He knew he was bombarding Gorringe with more than he needed to know. "Why did you bring up the subject, if I may ask?"

"I have heard it said that you have expressed some interest in going west. I am in the process of creating a hunting ranch in the Dakota Territory. Such an enterprise depends on paying customers, and I believe with your public influence, having a good word from you could help me considerably."

Roosevelt felt an itch of warning, but Gorringe continued.

"Are you interested in hunting buffalo?"

The words settled on his brain as if brought by angels.

"My word, sir, I would be most dee-lighted to embark on such a hunt. I was not aware there were buffalo left to shoot."

"There are, if you know where to look. If you're interested, I would ask you to accompany me on my next trip to the Badlands, likely in the fall. You wouldn't have to confine yourself to a buffalo hunt, of course. We have ample supplies of deer, elk, antelope, sheep, and bear, plus a good many small game and birds. Would you be interested?"

Roosevelt sat back, a wide toothy smile.

"Sir, you just tell me when."

"WHEN?"

"Most likely the fall, September. The rail lines run very close to where he has his ranch, so the journey is fairly swift."

He expected more resistance from her, glanced now at his mother, who said, "Alice is in capable hands, Teedie. Clearly, you are going on this adventure, no matter what the women in your family say, so go. Enjoy yourself. Shoot things. In that, you have much in common with your brother."

He knew that Elliott seemed to be avoiding him, wasn't certain as to why.

"I am pleased to be compared to my younger brother. He has accomplished much, and I know that his trip to India was a resounding success."

He expected more of a positive response, looked again at his mother, who said, "He is not well, Teedie. He claims that he is merely tired, but he lost considerable weight on his trip, and that continues. And . . . oh dear."

Alice said, "Say it, Mittie. Teddy, your brother drinks excessively. You are gone so often to Albany that you don't see it. But rarely is he here without the smell of alcohol on his breath. He is infatuated with this new bride of his, but she has had no better success trying to clean him up. I'm sorry, Mittie, but it's all true. Elliott has developed some very bad habits."

Roosevelt was angry, but not at them. His brother was obviously causing the rest of the family considerable pain.

"I shall straighten him out. A good talking to, or perhaps a good lashing."

Mittie struggled to stand, a concern all its own.

"You will do no such thing. He is a grown man, and he will solve his own problems. I do not see any of this as our affair. As Alice said, it is bad habits. He can break those as easily as that. I will hear no more of this. Teedie, plan your adventure, with our blessing. Do you agree, Alice?"

"Quite so. You have done so very well in the assembly. It is time for a pause, to rejuvenate yourself. Go, and do not be concerned about any of us, least of all me. I have the best women I could hope for to take care of me. Besides, you will return months before I am due to give birth."

He moved closer to her, started to reach for her belly, knew it wasn't done in front of his mother.

"It is only a few weeks. And I will take time beforehand to oversee the new house. It will be for you, Alice, and for all of us. We shall have a great piazza, where we can sit in rocking chairs and look at the sunset, a library, great fireplaces, my gun room of course, and every convenience we can include. We shall raise our child there, my love. And there will be much love in every foot of our home. I admit, it causes me considerable excitement to think of all this. Our new home, our child, my trip out west."

He paused, caught his breath. "No, not now."

It came as so often before, the hard, hot squeeze inside him, the tightening in his throat. He sat, one hand on his chest, fought to breathe, saw the concern on their faces, Mittie calling out to a servant, the instructions they had heard before, the tonics and elixirs that only Mittie believed would work. He tried to raise his hand, but there was no strength, all the energy fighting his lungs, begging to breathe. The asthma had come back.

FOR MOST OF that summer, he and Alice luxuriated at a spa in Rich-field Springs, in the Catskill Mountains. For his pregnant wife, the spa offered every kind of indulgence, a variety of pampering that Alice accepted with grateful abandon. For him, it was about health more than simple well-being. A doctor had been summoned, instructing Roosevelt to imbibe a concoction that Roosevelt described as "soaking sulfur matches in dishwater, and drinking it from an old kerosene can." By the end of their stay, the tonic seemed to have worked, the asthma gone once again, the greatest concern being Roosevelt's boredom. For Alice, the daily meals, great platters of food, seemed to be a tonic of its own. Roosevelt was very pleased to see that his wife had come to resemble a "pink boa constrictor."

By the end of the summer, Alice was in full strength, preparing for the second half of her pregnancy, which opened the way for Roosevelt to make his journey west. With less than a week before he would board the train, Commander Gorringe notified Roosevelt that he was forced to withdraw from the trip. If Roosevelt hoped for a new adventure, he would be on his own.

CHAPTER 10

September 7, 1883
Little Missouri, Dakota Territory

The journey had taken two days, the sleeping accommodations on the final leg virtually nonexistent. During the day, he had stared with dismay at the flat lands the tracks had crossed, the dismal nothingness of the Dakota Territory. After dark, the view might as well have been the same, Roosevelt staring into nothing, feeling only the shaking of the train.

The conductor roused him, unnecessary, the train slowing with squealing brakes. The train lurched to a halt, and he stared out, expected to see lights, a platform perhaps. But there was nothing but the darkness, and he eased himself off the train, felt for whatever lay below him, his foot finding only hard dirt.

"Got it, yes."

He took one step away from the train, the conductor tossing him his duffel bag. Roosevelt felt the weight of his gun case, and, with the duffel, more baggage than he knew he would need. The conductor produced a small lantern now, waved it toward the engine, where the engineer waited for the signal. Abruptly, the train jerked again into motion, the conductor calling to him, "Good luck, Mr. Roosevelt. Be safe now. You'll likely find a place to sleep across the way there, that way."

The lantern barely illuminated the ground close by, sagebrush and a small water tank, unlit buildings barely visible.

"Much obliged, sir."

He tried to lift his duffel to his shoulders, no lighter now than when he had boarded the first train in New York. By damned, he thought, use your brains. If you pack it, you have to carry it. Unlikely to find a porter out here. He moved as best he could, dragging the duffel, one hand hoisting the gun case. He stepped through ragged sagebrush, focused on what seemed to be the largest building, no lights, no sign that anyone lived in this place at all.

He reached a door, dropped the duffel, set the gun case down gently on hard dirt, knocked softly. He waited, no response, repeated the knock, much louder now. There was movement inside, the door jerked open, dull lantern light and a short stump of a man.

"What in blazes do you want? It's three damn o'clock in the damn morning. Jesus B. Christ, you done woke me out of a good damn sleep, damn you. What do you want anyway?"

It wasn't the reception Roosevelt had expected. He could smell the whiskey, as though the entire building was soaked in the stuff.

"My apologies, sir. I am looking for a bed for the night. I was told to seek out the largest building, and that appears to be you. If I've made an error, I'm dreadfully sorry."

The man turned away with a slight stumble.

"You're in the right place. Lucky too. I got one bed left. This here is the Pyramid Place Hotel. Fanciest hotel in these parts. Pay up front, one dollar."

They climbed a flight of stairs, and the man stopped, looked at him in the lantern light.

"You wear glasses. You might as best be prepared for some trouble over that. Around here, it means you got defective moral character. And you can be sure you've already got a name hung on you, no matter what your real name is. *Four-eyes*. Beware of a fist or two. There'll be some around here wanting to test just what you can see. You carry a pistol? No, don't see one. That's another thing. Folks around here like to sometimes shoot at each other. Sometimes they miss. It's good for sport when folks drink a good quart of Forty Mile red-eye. Watch that stuff, or it'll make a gunfighter out of you too. Damn near kills me every time I drink it. It's kinda tasty, though."

"Shut the hell up, Hobart! We're sleepin' here! For the fifty cents you charge, I expect peace and quiet."

Roosevelt stared into the darkness, could hear stirring, thought, Fifty cents. Don't ask. A dollar just means I'm from out of town. And there's likely no one sleeping now. He tried not to have second thoughts. He had heard tales of men bedding down right out in the sagebrush, an idea that was beginning to have some merit.

The man they called Hobart launched a line of spit to one side, didn't change his volume.

"There's the last bed I got, over there against the wall. Don't step on nobody, you might get a knife in your softies."

ROOSEVELT AWOKE TO a kick in the side of his cot.

"What the hell we got here? Easterner, I bet. Hey, Hank, lookee here. We got us a eastern punkin lily."

Roosevelt was fully awake now, glanced at the pistol hanging off the man's side. He slipped his glasses on, the unbreakable habit, could see the man's face clearly, a stubble of gray beard, a face creased by decades of bad weather.

"Yes, I'm from the East." Two voices began a debate in his head. *Don't let this man shove you back,* fighting with *keep your mouth shut.* The latter argument could never win, and he said, "I've come here to hunt, if that suits you all right. I have no argument with you."

The man stood straight, looking him over, a handful of the others eyeing Roosevelt with curiosity, none seeming particularly hostile. Roosevelt slipped off the cot, stood, at least now on equal terms with the man closest to him. Another man stepped closer, a smile across red-cracked lips.

"What you aiming to hunt, then? You'll be needing a guide and such. Don't do for a man to go traipsing across the Badlands on his own. I get five dollars per day, and another two for using my horse."

There was a whistle, and Roosevelt understood liars, knew what was happening. So, apparently, did the rest of them.

"I'm to see a man named Vine. He's expecting me, and will be making my arrangements."

The lying man seemed disappointed, had clearly missed out on a lucrative opportunity.

"You done met him. He's the one robbed you last night for the price of a bed. He did, too, didn't he? Charged you a dollar."

"Oh, shut up now."

Roosevelt looked toward the voice, saw the man he had met last night. He walked close with a slight stagger, and Roosevelt could smell the whiskey again, wasn't sure if the room had a permanent odor.

"Nah, Easterner, you don't want me. I don't do guiding much anymore. My son, Frank. He'll see to you, get you set up with the right man. Frank's been expecting you. Heard from your buddy Gorringe, that navy fellow. Gorringe said not to cheat you too awful bad. But you can't have your extra fifty cents back. Call it newcomer tax."

Roosevelt saw all eyes on him now, some men standing, others still lying in the cots. One man sat up in his cot, said, "So, four-eyes, what you aiming to shoot?"

Roosevelt's enthusiasm for the hunt now took over from his caution.

"Buffalo, I hope."

"Haw!"

The laughter was scattered, the message clear.

"There ain't been a buffalo brought down around here in a month of Sundays."

Vine seemed to ruffle.

"If there's a buffalo to be found, my boy Frank knows who can find him. Now, four-eyes, you come with me. I'll find my boy, and you can be on your way."

Roosevelt waited, scanned the room, tested just how nasty this bunch might be, saw mostly curiosity.

"Excuse me. Gentlemen, I know I'm fresh from the East, but I would appreciate at least some of you calling me by my name. It's not four-eyes. It's Theodore Roosevelt."

HE STEPPED OUTSIDE, the air cool and clean, his eye caught by the distant buttes beyond the railroad tracks, far across the wide spread of table-flat land. Behind the hotel was a shallow river, snaking through a wider sandy gorge, and, across, a tall steep bluff lined below with a scattering of ragged cottonwood trees. His new escort, Frank Vine, was as short and round as his father, red-faced, with a far better attitude toward life and Roosevelt than his father had shown.

After a long moment, Vine said, "What do you think?"

"It's beautiful."

Vine laughed.

"You'll change your mind after a piece. Your horse throws you or breaks a leg well out in the Badlands, well, there's a reason this place is called the Badlands. A few days out here, and you might wish you were back in New York."

"I doubt that, sir."

Vine laughed again.

"Stop that, Mr. Roosevelt. Anybody hears you call me *sir*, and I'll have to stick up for myself over there in Jess Hogue's place. A piece of advice: Stay out of there unless you're dog-thirsty. And if you've got any money on you, and plan to keep it, hide it real good. If you're a gambler, you *will* lose it. Not one of the regulars there plays a straight game. It's all in the cards, you might say."

Roosevelt stared out across the river, a cluster of smaller buildings, distinctly separate from Little Missouri.

"What's that place?"

"Hmph. That's Medora. There's a cock-eared Frenchman built it, owns it outright. You'll learn about him soon enough. We need to get you supplied up, and you need to meet Joe Ferris. He's the best man to haul you across this land out here and not get you lost or dead. There he is, by the buckboard."

Roosevelt was getting used to tiptoeing around these people, and approached Ferris slowly. He was a man Roosevelt's age, with a great horseshoe of a moustache, the ends hanging down below his chin. The man's eyes seemed to give him away, softer and curious, none of the hard glare that led to such rough-talking bravado, a condition that seemed to infect most of the men Roosevelt had met. As he got closer, Ferris said, "You ain't never been on a buffalo hunt before."

There was no challenge to the statement, just plain fact.

"No, sir, I haven't."

"Gorringe wired Frank and me that we should take you seriously. So, I will. Can you see anything without those damn spectacles?"

"Sorry, no."

Ferris grumbled.

"I hope, for your sake, we don't come across any gangs of especially bad men. There's a few out there, and they take one look at you, and try to see who can shoot them things off'n your face. And they can't shoot worth a damn."

Roosevelt managed a weak smile. "I'll take care of myself, Mr. Ferris."

"Unlikely. All right, Frank and I have talked about it. We're to head up Little Cannonball Creek, fifty miles or so upriver. First, we'll stop at my brother Sylvane's place. We can spend the night, then start out fresh in the morning. It gets mighty hot out here in midday. Best to do as much travel as we can in the cool. What we don't have here in the buckboard, Sylvane and his partner will set us up. He probably won't hunt with us. That's my job. That's the way I like it."

Roosevelt tried to find enthusiasm in Ferris's words, the man's expression unchanging, Ferris now eyeing Roosevelt's clothes.

"Is there some problem, Mr. Ferris? I was told you and Frank would handle my needs. I assure you that just because I wear spectacles and my clothes are clean does not mean I do not have considerable experience with a rifle. *This* rifle. I have hunted in Egypt, in the state of Maine, and a good many places in between. I am no New York City dude, if that's what you believe."

Ferris ignored his words, eyed Roosevelt's rifle.

"That's too small for buffalo. We get to my brother's place, I'll set you up right. You want a buffalo, Mr. Roosevelt, by God, we'll do our best to find you one. But you'll do it how we say, when we say, and you'll follow my instructions or I'll leave you behind. Got no patience for dudes who think they know it all. This can be a nasty place to hunt, or it can be glorious. You'll likely see both parts of that. But that don't make you an expert."

Roosevelt looked at his Winchester, had no idea just how much larger his rifle should be. But he felt the nagging truth, that it was best not to argue.

———

THEY REACHED CANNONBALL Creek and slept in a house belonging to an old Scotsman, Gregor Lang, a man with muttonchops that made Roosevelt envious and with another characteristic that set him up far closer to Roosevelt's heart: he wore spectacles.

The next morning, the hunt began in earnest, a driving rainstorm that did nothing to slow Roosevelt's passion. His enthusiasm was contagious, even Ferris admitting that if this New Yorker wanted to suffer the weather, the least Ferris could do was oblige him.

By dusk, no buffalo had been seen, the hunters pushing their tired horses through the muck of the Dakota gumbo, much of that sticking to the men themselves. Back at Lang's, after a meal of beans and dried venison, Ferris had wrapped himself in a heavy buffalo hide and gone to sleep. For Roosevelt, there would be no sleep. The single day in the saddle had rekindled the fire that brought him west. Instead of rest, Roosevelt found a man willing to forego sleep for the sake of a good conversation. It was Gregor Lang.

"CATTLE?"

"Of course, cattle! Nothing else to do in these parts. The Badlands don't grow cucumbers, you know."

Roosevelt smiled, saw in Lang's face the same light he carried in his own, the sharp blue eyes, the man spitting out his words faster than his mouth seemed able.

"How many cattle?"

"I've about fifteen hundred head. Sylvane and Mr. Merrifield have done well managing for me, and some of the other ranchmen around here." Lang drank from a bent tin cup, what Roosevelt could smell to be iron-gut coffee. "You know what you got here, Mr. Roosevelt? America. I come here two years ago looking for some hope, and here I be. You got a country here that lights up with hope for the rest of the whole world. There's no place on earth where a poor bugger like me can show up in a place like this, and in no time a'tall, I'm a bloody cattleman!"

Roosevelt's head was swimming, the coffee unnecessary.

"Do you think it's profitable? Is it worthwhile?"

Lang's eyes squinted.

"What isn't worthwhile, Mr. Roosevelt? If you have a good damn time, and maybe put some money in your pocket doing it . . . well, that sounds pretty worthwhile to me. I ain't sayin' you're gonna get rich running cattle. But look where you're sitting right now. No big city is gonna give you what you'll find here. You wanna hunt, you hunt. You wanna sleep the sleep of angels, you do like Mr. Ferris there. You wanna drink yourself to death, well, there's a place in Little Missouri to do that too. This place . . . it done made me a free man. I'm free to face each day and do whatever the hell I want. Can you say that about your New York?"

Roosevelt absorbed the man's words, thought for a long moment, staring into a log fire, another pleasant experience.

"Mr. Lang, since I've been out here, my head has been positively spinning. I am thinking seriously about going into the cattle business. Would you advise me to pursue that?"

"I'd rather not give you advice of a kind like that. I told you why I like it, why it's for me. I'm prepared to follow it to the end. I have full faith in those four-legged beasts out there and the men I hire to run them. As a business proposition, for me it's the best there is. That's all I'll say."

A WEEK'S HUNTING had produced a trail or two, scattered tracks of buffalo whose ability to hide far outweighed Roosevelt's ability to find them. Even when spotted, the scattered few seemed to vanish in the sights of Roosevelt's rifle, exhausted horses trailing the animals into holes where none but the hunters emerged. The going was hard, far out away from the Lang homestead, nights spent on muddy ground where every shape lurking nearby could be seen for sagebrush in the morning.

The morning broke through heavy gray clouds, Roosevelt shivering, tugging at his wet blanket.

"You awake, Mr. Roosevelt?"

It didn't escape him that Ferris never returned to the epithet "four-eyes."

"Yes. What is the hour?"

"Five. Time to move."

"Yes, very well. Up we go. What do we have to eat? Same as last night?"

Ferris stood slowly, seemed to work the kinks out of his back.

"One hard biscuit apiece. I swear, I'm gonna make Lang eat one of these things right in front of me. He swears by 'em. I'll swear at him. Everybody knows you have to use grease to make biscuits, and his boy told me that Lang insisted that all you need was *elbow* grease. I'll elbow him."

Roosevelt took the biscuit, gnawed, absorbing the wetness out of his mouth. He worked it for a while, a few crumbs breaking off, said,

"I rather like Mr. Lang. But when it comes to his cooking, I'm with you."

They rode all day, faint trails crossed, few other signs of buffalo except for small black dots a mile or more away that vanished as quickly as the men could attempt an approach. Once more, they slept in the open, Roosevelt wishing against rain, a wish that was mostly ignored. After a second day, their tracking of the latest buffalo had taken them too far away from Cannonball Creek to return in a single day. It was another night on the ground, another night of drizzling rain, soaking Roosevelt's blanket, waking him in the morning with half his body in a muddy puddle. They started now back from where they came, the necessity to resupply and perhaps take a full day to dry out clothes and blankets. As they made their way toward Lang's homestead, Roosevelt couldn't fight the ongoing enthusiasm, energy coming from some deep place inside him, the words of Frank Vine about the glorious scenery, the joy of Gregor Lang to be free. Along the way, he kept an eye on Joe Ferris, aware that out here alone, Roosevelt would likely be dead by now, the scenery he so admired so much like the rest in every direction, the beauty hiding more dangers than Roosevelt could guess. Ferris at least seemed to know the way home. But along the way the watering holes were poor, sloppy with gumbo, the mud filtered with your fingers, barely drinkable one swallow at a time, the horses suffering through the same misery. After ten hours in the saddle, the ground grew more uneven, arroyos and small buttes, and with shadows lengthening, Roosevelt stopped his horse, copying the move from Ferris.

"There. Right there."

Roosevelt could see past Ferris, the light dim, but the targets plain. Three buffalo stood in a shallow depression, unwary of their pursuers. Ferris whispered, "Four hundred yards. Have to get closer. This is it, Mr. Roosevelt. Let's work our way on foot, then down to our knees along that edge of sagebrush. It'll disguise our silhouettes. Let's go. Now."

Roosevelt dismounted, slid his rifle from the long holster, made a slow trot along the ridgeline. He measured his steps in slow, easy rhythm, the animals seemingly unaware. Ferris went to his knees, Roosevelt the same, following close behind Ferris. And now it began to rain.

The rain splattered the ground around them, fat, cold drops covering both men with light gray mud. They kept on, Roosevelt's pant legs soaked in the cold, mud inside his boots. He looked to his rifle, wet but not filthy, gripped it hard. The wind shifted now, the rain blowing into their faces, and Roosevelt lowered his head, his hat pushed into his face. Ferris stopped, a soft whisper.

"This is it. Take your time. They haven't seen us."

Roosevelt couldn't help the cold chill, the quivering shake in his hands and arms. He slid out prone, aiming just over a hump, through wet, blowing sagebrush. The animals seemed still unaware, and he brought the sight down on the largest one, tried to keep steady, let out a slow breath, and pulled the trigger.

They ran as one, disappeared into a low draw, and were gone.

He hung his head, rain blowing down his shirt, chilling his neck. He looked back at Ferris, saw him doing the same.

"Sorry, Joe. I missed."

"Yeah. You missed. Let's go."

They trudged slowly through the mud, the rain in their backs now, the horses waiting, nosing the small puddles forming close around them. Ferris climbed up on his horse, wasn't looking at him, and Roosevelt wanted to say something, an apology, something stronger.

"I don't understand it, Joe. I'll look back on this one, I promise you. I just missed."

"You missed. Saddle up, Mr. Roosevelt. It seems like bad luck's following us like a dog follows a drunk."

With such luck as seemed to plague his client, Joe Ferris seemed ready to surrender, but Roosevelt would hear none of it. It was Ferris, the man who doubted the resolve and the skills of the four-eyed eastern tenderfoot, who finally had to admit that his client was a surprise, that Roosevelt's enthusiasm for the hunt and for the land they crossed produced a cheerfulness that Ferris found difficult to mimic.

As they rode through the chill of a driving storm on their way back to Lang's, Roosevelt remarked, "By Godfrey, but this is fun!"

FERRIS WAS ASLEEP again, and Roosevelt felt the warmth of Lang's fire, wiggling the toes of his bare feet.

"Mr. Lang, I have definitely decided to go into the cattle business. I require someone to run the cattle for me, and to take management of my cattle under some arrangement to be worked out. Will you take charge?"

Lang seemed surprised, the first time Roosevelt had seen him arch his considerable brow.

"Me? Thank you, but I am tied up with other obligations, to other herds."

Roosevelt felt like he had been kicked, had never considered Lang wouldn't do the job.

"Well, then, is there someone else you would recommend?"

"Yep. Joe's brother, Sylvane Ferris, and Bill Merrifield."

"COULD YOU BOYS handle the cattle for me?"

Sylvane had come prepared with the right answers.

"Certainly, sir. If you are in a position to afford such a herd."

Roosevelt knew this was coming.

"How much will that cost?"

"I anticipate forty thousand dollars, with one-third to start."

"And if I manage that, you'll take care of them?"

Merrifield had more trouble than Sylvane containing his enthusiasm.

"Well, I guess so, Mr. Roosevelt!"

Sylvane smiled now, for the first time.

"I'll go along with Bill, sir. You put together the right kind of contract, and we'll do it."

"Perfect. That's just perfect."

Roosevelt pulled out a checkbook, scribbled, handed the check to Sylvane.

"This is fourteen thousand dollars. The rest will come when you require it. And we sign our contracts."

Sylvane showed the check to Merrifield.

"Well, then, sir, our next step is to head over to Minnesota and buy us some cattle."

Merrifield said, "Um, sir, do you want some kind of receipt?"

Roosevelt slid the checkbook into his pocket.

"Oh, it's not necessary. If I didn't trust you men, I wouldn't go into business with you."

WITH THE WINDOW closing on Roosevelt's hunt, Joe Ferris forced himself to exercise the patience to match Roosevelt's unbounded energy and enthusiasm. As if to reward the sheer willpower Roosevelt had put into the hunt, the buffalo finally cooperated. Two days after agreeing with Sylvane Ferris and Bill Merrifield to run his cattle business, Roosevelt faced another heart-pounding opportunity at a trio of buffalo. This time, to Joe Ferris's relief, Roosevelt didn't miss.

As Roosevelt made ready to return to Little Missouri and the train that would carry him back east, Gregor Lang made his own observation about Roosevelt: "He is the most extraordinary man I have ever met. I shall be surprised if the world does not hear from him one of these days."

———

THE JOURNEY HOME had seemed an eternity, his mind ignoring the scenery he passed, focused instead on memories of the place he had just left. Already, he knew there would be changes, his dreams sharpening, but his feelings were different from any he had felt before. He knew that, above all else, he would return soon to the Badlands.

CHAPTER 11

November 17, 1883
New York City

"You've changed, Teedie."

He barely heard the words, studied his mother's face.

"Are you feeling well, Mother?"

"The same. I feel weak, then stronger. It passes, day to day. I am more concerned with you."

He couldn't shake the feeling that she wasn't being completely honest with him.

"If you say so. If you're up to it, I have a few things I wish to discuss." He paused. "I would be greatly pleased to tell you of my Dakota adventures again and again. Such is the impression made upon me, and such is the level of enthusiasm I have for returning there, for the life of a ranchman. I'm in the cattle business, Mother. I own cattle!"

She managed a smile.

"So you've said." She seemed to think deeply, a frown on her face.

"What is it?"

"Teedie, what of the law? You spoke so highly of that as a profession. Has that changed now?"

He saw Alice coming down the stairs, knew he would have to do this, that the moment would come when he could hide nothing from them. He smiled at Alice, moved to assist her on the last few steps, her round belly swaying with her slow, plodding steps.

"No, Teddy, I'm fine. I want to hear your answer about the law.

You told me once I would be a lawyer's wife. So, you've decided otherwise?"

"I had thought . . ." He stopped, sorted out his words, something unusual for him. "I had once believed that becoming a lawyer meant you would have a place in our world where you could help people, all sorts of people—the disadvantaged, those who had no other means to fend for themselves. Since I have been in the assembly, I have seen firsthand what lawyers do, whom they represent, how they ply their trade." He paused again, a self-conscious glance at Mittie. "I had thought the law was a respectable way to earn a good living. What I have seen in Albany is that people of our means use the law . . . use lawyers to place themselves at a greater advantage over all others. If I thought I could be of benefit to those people downtown, those people for whom Father was such a savior, then, well, the law would be an excellent field of pursuit. But studying law has become boring. That's the word. Boring. It's all about using the law to gain an advantage over your opponent. It's not so different from boxing. Include a lawyer by your side so you may more effectively pummel your opponent. The better the lawyer, the greater the victory." He stopped again, looked at Alice. "I don't know what will become of my venture into the cattle business. But those people, the people I met and dealt with and hunted with—those are people with a spirit and an independence unlike anything I've seen in Albany or, frankly, in New York City. I like those people, even the ones who don't wish to be liked. I like the people who don't care much for me. I will never truly be one of them, but I do hope to try."

He was wound up now, felt the stories coming again, boiling up inside him, the buffalo hunt, Joe Ferris, the Scotsman, Lang, so many more. But his mother's stare stopped him, her face pale, the firmness she tried to show far weaker than usual.

Alice moved to her side.

"Teddy, she isn't well. Let's take her upstairs."

"She was fine yesterday."

"She weakens easily." Alice smiled at him. "You can do that to her, you know. It takes all our energy sometimes to keep up with yours."

Mittie stood, pushed Alice's hand away gently.

"You need not speak of me as though I'm deaf. I will go up to my room on my own. I believe I'll take a nap."

WITH THE COMING of the new year, the New York General Assembly went through the customary process of choosing a new speaker. After his first two years stirring the considerable pot in his own party, Roosevelt had been selected by the Republicans to be the minority leader. But in the local elections just passed, they had won a majority of seats, and thus, should Roosevelt maintain his leadership, he would become the Speaker of the House. He assumed the post was his, that by his good work underwriting and debating so many useful and constructive bills, he had earned the respect of his peers, so much so that no one would even oppose him for speaker. He was wrong. He had underestimated the great political machine, and at the eleventh hour of New Year's Eve 1883, that machine came to life. The backroom manipulations moved into the open, and to Roosevelt's chagrin, and bitter disappointment, he was shoved aside for a relatively minor and ineffectual local politician named Titus Sheard, handpicked from a Democratic county purely for the influence his new position might give him so the Republicans could gain control of Sheard's home county in the next election. Even those members of the assembly who were staunchly supporting Roosevelt could not resist the wild under-the-table promises from machine bosses should they place their vote for this man Sheard. With various straw votes showing that Roosevelt was certain to be defeated, he grudgingly accepted the inevitable and threw his own vote to Sheard, a hollow show of party unity.

February 13, 1884
Albany, New York

The session had yet to begin, and he sat in his newly designated seat, on the back row. He had resented that fiercely, but he had been approached more than once by Titus Sheard, who seemed guiltily to recognize that his appointment had nothing to do with his qualifications, which were virtually nonexistent. Roosevelt had been granted the right to choose the men for various committees, an unheard-of gesture from a speaker, but entirely appropriate for a speaker who had essentially no idea what he was doing.

Roosevelt sat alone in the far reaches of the assembly's seats, shuffled through his diary, slid it beneath another book, read her letter again. He glanced up, no one of importance in the hall yet, so he returned to her letter, read slowly.

My dear Teddy,

I am so very grateful for your mother, and your sisters. Now that Corinne is married, and with child of her own, I suspected she would be scarce at 57th Street. But she has a generous heart far beyond my own meager cares. She would manage for all of us, and Bamie would do the same. I so admire their strength and beauty. I do so wish you were here. I am doing well, though I appear about to burst. I am told that I am larger than is usual, but the doctor says there should be no worrying. I am, as he put it, healthy as a horse. I am not certain I should accept that with a smiling face, but he is a kind man. I would rather think of myself as your beautiful pink boa constrictor. At least I know those words to be original to my loving husband himself. The baby has been kicking up furiously, so I guess him to be a boy much like his father. If it is to be a girl, she is certain to force her way through life with her father's energy.

With Deepest Love from
Both of Your Family,
Alice

I do so wish you were here. The words stung him. I have been so terribly busy, he thought, and there is so much yet to do. It has been productive, and my back-row seat at least allows me to see every conniving conversation, every hand reaching for another. He felt distracted by her letter again, slipped it down with his diary. We shall beat these people back, he thought. I made a promise to the entire state that I would do all in my power, and perhaps beyond my power, to break down the machines, Republican *and* Democrat. The people have virtually no voice in this assembly, and here we issue all those laws and bills that dictate how people live and work. It cannot be this way. By Godfrey, I will be heard if I have to bring a bass drum in here and wail away with a tree limb.

"Excuse me, Mr. Roosevelt. There is a telegram for you. From New York City, sir."

The young man held out the paper, and Roosevelt stared at it, felt a sudden rush of fear, one very dark memory, his father's death. Beside him was John Doud, a young assemblyman from far upstate.

"What's it say? I get those, it means I owe somebody money."

Roosevelt ignored him, ignored the smiles, others curious, moving up close to his seat. He took a deep breath, reached for the paper, broke the seal, read for a short moment.

"By George! By George! I am a father! My dear Alice has given birth to a daughter, just last night! By George, but this is bully!"

The hands came out now, boisterous calls of congratulations, nothing of party loyalties or political allegiance. Word spread through the hall, and now applause broke out, smiling faces and huzzahs from some of the men Roosevelt despised. He waved to them, a beaming, toothy smile of his own, shook more hands, one man close by, "Your wife doing okay?"

Roosevelt obeyed the question, looked at the rest of the telegram, annoyed that the man would toss cold water on the moment.

"She is . . . *fairly well*. Well, the doctor said it was her first, always the most difficult. No matter. I shall take the express down to the city."

"Sir, there is one in about two hours."

"Excellent, yes. Excuse me, if you will. Thank you all. By George!"

"Mr. Roosevelt! Mr. Roosevelt! I'm glad I caught you. Another telegram came for you, sir. At the capitol they said you had gone to catch the train."

Roosevelt glanced upward, above the platform to the enormous clock, another twenty minutes before the train departed.

"Yes, so you found me. What's it say?"

"Oh, I don't know, sir. It's private."

"Yes, yes, fine. Hand it to me. Well-wishers, no doubt."

He read, felt his hands shake, the sounds around him growing softer.

Come as quickly as you can. Mother is dying. Alice is not well. There is a curse on this house. Elliott

HE WILLED THE train down the rail line into the city, cursed the slow crawl of the fastest train of its day. As the train finally pulled to a stop in Grand Central Station, he stepped down quickly into dense fog, a ghostly haze that covered every light with a wet gray shroud.

The walk was quick but lonely, no one else visible on the street, the clocks in scattered church towers tolling eleven. He stumbled through the wet streets, potholes and ruts hidden by soft mud. From a block away, he could see the house, and finally he rounded the corner off Fifth Avenue onto Fifty-Seventh Street. He looked up, was surprised to see very little light, flickers of lamps mostly on the third floor. He pushed through the heavy door, annoyed now no one was present, thought, Where could they have gone? I come all the way here . . .

"Teedie!"

He saw Corinne on the stairs, saw tears.

"Come quick, Teedie. Alice is not well, and Mother is worse. Go to your wife. Your baby is beautiful. Go see."

He felt overwhelmed, but he had to see Alice, bolted past Corinne, pushed up to the third floor. He was surprised to see the room empty of anyone else, only Alice in the bed, soft blankets, soft lamplight. To one side, a cradle, *his* cradle, and, within, a small, silent bundle. He went to the bed, knelt, took her hand.

"Oh, my dear wife, my dear, beautiful wife. How are you doing? How is the baby?"

She nodded slowly, faint words, "The baby is well. She is beautiful. Will you still name her Alice?"

It was an odd question, and he nodded furiously. "Yes, by George, she is Alice. There shall be two of you. More for me!"

He tried to keep his voice low enough to match the stillness of the house, but the enthusiasm for the moment rose up, unstoppable, and he put hands on both her shoulders, wanted to pull her up to him, had second thoughts, knew it was a bad idea. He released her gently, pulled his hands away, smiling now, tears from both of them, and now a sound, behind him, Elliott.

"Teedie, you should come downstairs. Right now. If you wish to say goodbye to Mother, you must come."

He looked again to Alice, saw her nod slowly, more tears. He rose, followed Elliott downstairs. The smells changed abruptly, pungent and grotesque, and he followed Elliott into Mittie's room, saw the others around the bed, the doctor there, a man Roosevelt didn't know.

The doctor said, "I am sorry for you all. The typhoid is winning this fight. There is nothing more I can do."

Roosevelt pushed forward, saw her face, more beautiful now than he had ever seen. She seemed to stare past him, and he waited for recognition, begged she would know him, saw now a blink, focus coming into her eyes, her hand rising slowly toward him. Her voice came softly now, but her head began to turn away, no strength, her voice with the single word, "Teedie."

He bent low, kissed her cheek, felt an awful chill, none of the soft warmth. He stood again, hands on him, Bamie and Corinne. He watched as Elliott bent low, words of his own, gentle kisses, now the women, farewells of their own. Roosevelt realized the doctor was still there, standing quietly in the doorway. He had questions. Why? How is this happening? His mind leapt with angry frustration, a moment so much like his father's death. There was nothing the son could do. Corinne stayed close to her, a soft goodbye, words he couldn't hear, prayers, and many tears.

And then Mittie was gone.

3:00 AM

"Mr. Roosevelt, please come with me. You may certainly ask for the others if you like."

He stared at the doctor, shook his head, didn't know what to say or what the doctor meant. He followed the man up the stairs, back to Alice's room, but the doctor stopped short, whispered to him,

"Mr. Roosevelt, your wife has Bright's disease. Her kidneys are certain to fail. There is no cure, I'm afraid. Your baby has survived and is strong. But the only thing I can do for your wife is suggest you comfort her."

"What? But my mother . . . what happened?"

"She had a severe case of typhoid fever. She is at peace now. I am more concerned for your wife. Right now, you should be as well."

"Yes, certainly."

The doctor looked at his watch.

"It is close to three now. I will return late in the morning, to see how your wife is doing. Try to sleep if you can. There is nothing more I can do for her right now. You must take care of yourself to be strong for her."

The doctor moved away, eased down the darkened stairs toward the soft, whimpering sobs in the bedroom below.

Roosevelt moved back into Alice's bedroom, dropped again to his knees, took her hand. He could feel her sleeping, soft breaths. *Does she know? She must, certainly. The doctor has to have been honest with her. She would have it no other way. She sleeps, though; that is good. It is best, at least for now. When she regains her strength, we'll talk about Mother. Oh God . . . Mother.* He rested his head on the side of the bed, the hour catching up with him, exhaustion and sadness, one part of him believing this was all a cruel nightmare, another voice in his head, his brother's: *a curse on this house.* No, there is sadness. It is life, it is a passing. But it is no curse. I will never believe that. It will be better tomorrow. Tomorrow.

1:00 PM

He woke to a soft nudge, realized he was sleeping beside her, had not removed any of his clothes or shoes. He rolled slightly, saw Bamie.

"Teedie, come eat something. Mary Anna has made biscuits, your favorite."

He was suddenly angry.

"I can't leave her! She might need something!"

He knew the look on Bamie's face, stern and unyielding, the big sister who knew so much more of everything.

"Teedie, you have to eat. She'll be fine. I'll stay here with her. Corinne sat with you all morning, and you never stirred. Alice is fine now. You have to eat. Go on down. I'm here."

He wanted to argue, but had used all his strength. He rolled over, off the edge of the bed, had a sickening thought.

"Mother."

Bamie seemed to fight for composure.

"She died, Teedie. You were there. She had been weak for a long time; we just never knew it would turn to such a sickness. We always just thought she was fragile." She paused. "She loved you most of all, Teedie. Don't ever forget that."

"That doesn't help, Bamie. Just like Father, being the favorite doesn't mean I can help them, protect them." He had a burst of thought. "The baby! Where . . ."

Bamie smiled. "Corinne has her. Alice is too weak to nurse, so when the time comes, Corinne can help."

The words stuck in his mind. When the time comes. What time?

"I don't want to leave her side, Bamie. Alice is the dearest thing in my life."

Bamie managed another smile.

"You have two Alices now. You have to be strong for both of them."

He forced himself to stand, fought through dizziness, and Bamie took his arm. He put his head on her shoulder, said, "You were always the strong one."

He slipped away from her, moved unsteadily downstairs, stepped slowly past his mother's room without stopping. He glanced through a window, saw daylight and rain, had no idea what time it was. He pulled out his watch, was surprised to see one o'clock *in the afternoon.*

He obeyed Bamie's orders, sought out the dining table, the housekeeper responding immediately. He saw tears on her face too.

"Mary Anne, it's all right. This is a terribly sad day for all of us."

"Mr. Roosevelt, I've been working for Miss Mittie since before you were born. I was there when she birthed you and all the others. My heart hurts, sir. It hurts for you, and for me. And most of all, for Miss Mittie."

He took her hand.

"Don't hurt for her, Mary Anne. She has no pain now. Maybe she's with Father." He didn't really believe that, had never accepted the teachings of the church. But now was not the time for raw truth.

"Oh, I'll get you some breakfast, sir. I made biscuits and there's some fine apple butter."

"Teedie! Come up, please."

It was Bamie's voice, far above, and he jumped up, jogged up the stairs. He reached the top floor, out of breath, and Bamie said, "Go in. She's asking for you. She's panicked a little that you aren't here. Go."

He moved past his sister, sat on the side of the bed, wrapped Alice's hands with his own, calmed himself.

"Hey, my beautiful wife. I'm right here. I went to get breakfast, that's all." He smiled, tried to find a smile in her. "It's Bamie's fault. She's always telling me what to do. She does that even more than you do."

She didn't respond, then rolled toward him with half-shut eyes.

"Hold me, Teddy. Just lie here and hold me."

He pushed away tears, a cold twist inside him, fear rising up, raw helplessness. He slid slowly onto the bed, saw Bamie at the door, moving away. He waited for Alice to roll into him, but she didn't move, and he put one arm across her shoulder, gently turned her to him. His face was close to hers now, and he leaned forward, kissed her softly, but there was no response. He felt his heart beginning to pound, the sickening fear inside him, and he put one hand against her face, soft and beautiful, saw her eyes open, quiet words, "Oh, Teddy."

He felt her grow limp, held her tighter, squeezing her into him, but there was nothing there, no movement, no more words.

"Alice?" Then louder, with the voice that shook the house. *"Alice?"*

There was no response.

PART II

THE BADLANDS

*The worst of all fears is
the fear of living.*

—THEODORE ROOSEVELT

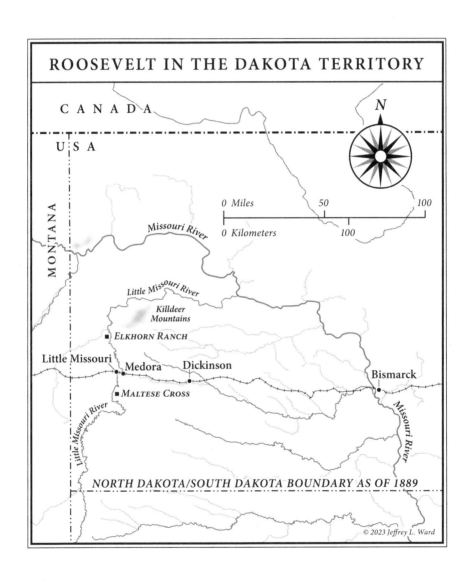

ROOSEVELT IN THE DAKOTA TERRITORY

C A N A D A

N

U S A

MONTANA

Missouri River

0 Miles 50 100

0 Kilometers 100

Little Missouri River

Killdeer
Mountains

■ ELKHORN RANCH

Little Missouri

Medora

Dickinson

Bismarck

Little Missouri River

■ MALTESE CROSS

Missouri River

NORTH DAKOTA/SOUTH DAKOTA BOUNDARY AS OF 1889

© 2023 Jeffrey L. Ward

CHAPTER 12

December 28, 1918
Sagamore Hill, New York

"How is he, Edith? I got here as quickly as I could. The trains were dreadfully slow, and you know how little patience I have for that sort of thing."

He heard Alice's voice, kept his eyes closed, the voice too familiar, the same melody as her mother. Edith responded with a soft whisper,

"Alice, you must not carry on. He is in a fragile state. The doctors don't know what else they can do. We're fighting the fever—ice water and alcohol compresses. It has helped some. But he seems to need a great deal of sleep."

He was fully awake now, still with closed eyes, fought the sudden flood of memories, the beautiful baby from the beautiful mother. He had insisted then that she be named Alice, as he had promised, and so now she was, the living image of those days, so grown up with a life and cares of her own. He knew how spoiled she was and that she had a personality as strong as his, both questionable gifts from father to daughter.

It had been painful at first, and he could not be both father and mother to an infant, and so Bamie had stepped in, as she always seemed to, capable hands, a loving heart, and young Alice was raised with a mother after all. The child seemed to thrive, though Roosevelt wasn't much help. It was inevitable that when he looked upon the child, he saw her mother, and he would never want to see her mother, ever. That pain was all-consuming, a devastating emotional blow that the child only brought back to him. He knew he was a failure as her father, was thankful for Bamie and Corinne, who would know what a young girl required of childhood, the correct behavior. He was terrified of that, had learned the awful truth that nothing is forever, that when you love with all your being, it matters not to God or to anyone else how important or how fragile that could be. It could be swept away like so much dust with a broom. His mind focused on that one page in his diary, written the day after the horror of their deaths, that one entry, dark and scribbled: *the light has gone out of my life.* I wasn't wrong then, he thought. It is just . . . a different light now.

And then there was Edith. From his very childhood, she was one of several young women who had surrounded the awkward young Teddy, gracious all, and when they were older, they were gracious even to Alice Lee, who had stood out among them and then, finally, stood alone as his wife. For all the years he knew Edith Carow, she had been nearly as special, but Roosevelt had seen her more as a charming friend. With Alice suddenly swept away, the charm began to grow, closeness becoming love, and two years after that one terrible day, Edith Carow had become the second Mrs. Roosevelt.

As had Bamie, Edith had taken to the young Alice, had made it very clear that there was no jealousy and no conflict that could not be overcome. To a child who could have recoiled at anyone new, Alice had accepted Edith as she had her Aunt Bamie, and so Roosevelt had the family he had sought after all. If he had believed that the child's mother was the only wife he could love, Edith had eased those thoughts aside. She filled the void, anchored herself into that awful, lonely place. She never complained that he seemed to overcompensate for his first wife's absence, that he would never speak of her, never refer to her by name. For years, it had put a wedge between father and daughter, a wound he carried as much as the young Alice. But now, the adult Alice was very much her own woman, as headstrong as her father, and finally, after more than thirty years, the two could face each other without the tragedy of her mother's death to come between them. Or so she seemed to believe. He knew better. He had great difficulty looking her in the eyes, and to him Alice was only her mother's name. He called her Baby Lee.

He tested his breathing, felt stronger, rolled slowly toward them, saw them staring down at him, no smiles, so much of the worry he was tired of seeing.

Edith leaned low, said, "You're awake. Finally. You do cause us a fright, Teddy."

He clamped his jaw tight, knew better than to protest.

"Call me Teedie. Makes me feel young."

Edith didn't need prompting, but Alice, always the rebel, said, "Teddy, Ted, Teedie, Theodore, Mr. Roosevelt, Colonel, Mr. President. Perhaps you should designate one, so we know our proper place."

There was the edge in her voice, always, and Edith put a hand on her arm.

"Please, Alice. This is not the time for a squabble. Come, let's go outside. Kermit says he has some books you might like to have."

Roosevelt was alone now, heard the voice again, *her* voice. Why now? he thought. I have not thought of her in so very long, so what is it? the fever? Is this what my illness is about, bringing back those memories, the horrors, so much death—my father, my mother, my wife? It stung him, his brain not latching on to her name, even now. How many more deaths am I to fester over? those men in Cuba? out west? murdered presidents? my dear Quentin? Oh Lord, if this is what fever does, I truly wish to be healed.

Edith had returned, said, "I am so sorry for Alice. She is hurting, and frightened for you, and she doesn't know how to show it. She is too much like her father, so, of all of us, she must be the strong one."

"She is the oldest child. She has to be."

"That's ridiculous. But I won't stir you up with an argument. How do you feel?"

"Weak. Tired. Hungry. Much better, actually."

"Being hungry is good. Mr. Hagedorn is supposed to be here later this afternoon, unless you say no. Please say no. You're too weak for a lengthy interview. Just lie here quietly, no moving around. I'll have some lunch prepared. Clara has some chocolate pudding that might suit you."

"I'll be fine. I'll just answer questions, give him something to write on his little pieces of paper. Maybe offer him some lunch. Venison."

"What?" She laughed now, then stopped, knew he was drifting off, somewhere else, somewhere *back there*. "Yes, my love, maybe venison. Sleep now."

CHAPTER 13

June 10, 1884
The Badlands, Dakota Territory

They sat in a semicircle, Roosevelt on one end, Gregor Lang and his teenage son on the other. Between them, Sylvane Ferris and Bill Merrifield sat, joined now by a younger man, George Myers, the newest ranch hand Roosevelt had employed.

"By Godfrey, this is some fine stew."

Lang nodded his appreciation, said, "Sylvane brought him in. White tail. Took him down at near three hundred yards. I just cook 'em, leave the shootin' to these younger fellows with the sharper eyes. This ain't a bad dish. The secret is flour. Tempers the rough taste of some of these bigger bucks. Onions help too. I used my last one just for this here special occasion. On behalf of all of us here, welcome back, Mr. Roosevelt."

Roosevelt glanced around, unfamiliar surroundings.

"Why'd you move from your homestead? This is fine and all. I'm just curious."

Merrifield laughed, a smile from Ferris, and Roosevelt knew he was about to embark on a journey that required a stretch of the truth.

"Dang cattle outfit out of Texas, set up their operation not a half mile downstream of my place. Too close for me. One of us had to move. They had about thirty gunslingers and such in their employ, so I decided the moving would best be done by me."

Ferris laughed out loud.

"Tell 'em the real reason."

Lang crossed his arms, a show of silent stubbornness. Ferris looked at Roosevelt, said, "Out here, sir, there's all kinds of varmints. Some big, some little. One, in particular, of the little variety, decided to move into Gregor's home. Made himself a nest of sorts right under his bed. We tried sweet-talking the varmint into leaving, but nothing would work. Gregor here, he's more aggressive. Decided to use the direct method. Got his pitchfork and launched his attack directly."

Lang scowled even more, said, "Well, by dickens, nobody told me how bad a skunk can stink. He didn't take kindly to my pitchfork. Made it a whole heap of unpleasant for me to sleep in my own bed. So, now that you've heard a story that's longer than it need be, you have the answer to your question, sir."

Roosevelt fought the urge to laugh at Lang's predicament, buried his gaze into the bowl of stew.

"This is dee-lightful. Best venison I've had."

He couldn't avoid their stares, looked up, scanned their faces, no smiles now.

"I do something wrong?"

Lang said, "We're mighty cut off from things back east, usually. But the telegraph brings us news of a sort. It's hit-and-miss, but the important stuff makes it here pretty quick. Forgive me, sir, but all of us, we're wondering just how you're doing. None of our business, none of us. Just concerned. No man oughta go through what you been through. I ain't gonna say no more."

Roosevelt knew his personal tragedy had been news, was surprised that word had made it this far west.

"I'd rather not talk about my family, if that's all right. I would share anything with any of you, more than any other folks I know. There's not a gossiping snake among you, and I've learned that in my profession as a state assemblyman, snakes are a regular concern." He paused. "I admit, I've had a very bad time, and some days are worse than others. But some things are best kept inside."

Lang nodded, and Roosevelt could feel their concern, knew he could open up to them, if he chose to.

Ferris said, "Any time you change your mind, you can spill anything out to us. You know that. But I got another question. I know you come here after leaving Chicago, that Republican convention. How'd that Blaine fellow get the nomination? We kinda thought they might choose you. You'd get every vote out here, that's for sure."

Roosevelt appreciated the kindness in Ferris's words.

"Not me, Sylvane. I'm too young, for one thing. The U.S. Constitution says you have to be thirty-five. I'm ten years away. No, this whole Blaine thing is what politicians like to refer to as a *careful and intense negotiation to choose the finest man for the job*, the one most likely to get elected in the general election."

Lang asked, "What do you call it?"

Roosevelt paused again, chose his words, grateful he could speak freely.

"That entire convention was a disaster. Machine politics at its worst. Blaine's a loyal Republican, loyal to the people who pull all the strings, so they're loyal to him. It's always about putting up a man for high office who will remember how he got there, so he'll pass along the favors when the time comes. For the typical delegate, somebody not attached to any powerful interest, a candidate like James Blaine is propped up before them, and they make their decision based on no more than, well, he doesn't seem like such a bad fellow, I suppose he'll do. And, I admit, Blaine's a decent fellow, kind to your mother and small children, that sort."

Lang said, "Who'd you get up for? Which one of them made sense to you?"

Roosevelt lowered his head, then looked up at Lang.

"George Edmunds, senator from Vermont. For some reason, a few of us thought he had a chance of winning the nomination, and maybe even the presidency. I'm still convinced he'd be a lot more effective leader than Blaine. But the convention had already been decided, long before we got there, long before anybody had a real chance to be heard. It's like when you wade out into the edge of the ocean and try to stay upright against a big wave. Not likely. The wave broke over us." He saw the faces, a smile or two, realized it was unlikely any of these men had ever stood in the ocean. "So, now, Mr. Blaine will most certainly lose the election. He's got some bats flitting around in his closet, some financial shenanigans that the Democrats are certain to use against him.

And, likely, the Democrats will nominate the governor of New York, Grover Cleveland. I've had some dealings with him, and he seems to be a straightforward sort of man, gets things done. That's what the people want. But when Mr. Cleveland wins, my political career will have concluded."

"Nonsense, Mr. Roosevelt. You're young. It's all in front of you."

Roosevelt swallowed another spoonful of the venison stew.

"The train from Chicago deposited me in Saint Paul. Before I boarded the train for here, I saw a newspaper, handed to me by some young reporter, big smiles and bigger ambition. He knew I was on the train, so he made all kinds of insinuations *why,* as though I had run off from the convention, that I might have run off from the whole Republican Party, rather than support Blaine. Idiot. But that newspaper . . . some are already talking about how the group of us abandoned the party, turned traitor, since we didn't support Blaine. Bolting a party is the worst treason in politics. In Chicago, and to this young snake in Saint Paul, I tried to explain . . . even though *explaining* is a deadly sin . . . that I was coming west to do precisely what I'm doing right now. I have a cattle herd to look after, and I have some other concerns here that require my attention. They didn't believe me in Chicago, and I'm quite sure that young squirt in Saint Paul was hoping for a dirtier story, as though I was running away and hiding my sulking head. Those were *his* words. By Godfrey, I didn't let that nonsense stop me from ignoring him, and boarding that train. That might be a mistake. Reporters don't like being ignored."

Ferris seemed puzzled, said, "Well, sir, we are most pleased to have you back, but I'm wondering: What other concerns do you have out here? Three hundred head of cattle are here, with more on the way. We've established your Maltese Cross brand, and the boys and I are building your homestead as you instructed. Maltese Cross is a fine name for your ranch as well. We've got four miles fronting the river, with no one to interfere."

"I am dee-lighted for all, Mr. Ferris. But I had to be here myself for a very different proposition which involves you and Mr. Merrifield. I wish to purchase a thousand more head of cattle." He saw the surprise on Ferris's face. "I'm committed to this thing, Mr. Ferris. I'm committed to whatever it takes to be a legitimate ranchman. I'm not a cowboy, and I'm not out here to drink myself to death, any more than you are. I see this as a business, and I'm rather enthusiastic about it."

Lang said, "And what else? You said you had concerns."

"Well, yes. I want a custom-made buckskin suit. And I want to shoot an antelope."

THE CATTLE HAD been purchased, Ferris and Merrifield again traveling into Minnesota to gather up the herd Roosevelt had grown so excited for. They were beginning to know him better, understood that this easterner had no less love for the West than anyone who lived there full-time. And they had also learned that if Roosevelt had an inkling, a yearning, it might soon grow into an infatuation. Such was his passion for acquiring more cattle. As Lang noted, if Mr. Roosevelt wanted something, it was best to stay out his way when he went to get it. And if he instructed Ferris or Merrifield to secure supplies, whether timber and leather or the cattle on the hoof, there would be no second thoughts. Roosevelt didn't change his mind.

The buckskin suit had been a simple matter. The seamstress's name was Maddox, the woman's ramshackle homestead a short day's ride from the Maltese Cross. To his surprise, there was very little about the woman that could be called feminine.

"WHAT IN BLAZES do you want, four-eyes?"

Roosevelt eyed the rifle in the woman's hands, pointed dangerously at his chest.

"Hello, madam. My name is Roosevelt. I understand you are handy with leather and a needle. I was hoping . . ."

"You want some dandy duded-up fancy stupid buckskin suit. I done heard about you, Mr. Roosevelt. You got a first name, or are you too good to let us know that?"

"It's Theodore, madam. Madam, if you please, could you lower that rifle? It does make my horse nervous."

Beside him, Lang's teenage son, Lincoln, Roosevelt's temporary guide, said, "Mrs. Maddox, Mr. Roosevelt here is a fine man, respected by everyone out this way. He's no big-city fool, come to parade around like a clown."

She spit a thick brown stream onto the ground beside Roosevelt's horse.

"I heard about all of that too. So, you ain't decided to come out here and take advantage of all us ignorant dirt-poor cattle rustlers, eh?"

She lowered the rifle, and Roosevelt let out an inaudible breath, was beginning to understand the woman's hostility. He saw movement to one side, a man's head briefly peering out from the side of her home. Roosevelt saw an opening, a chance to be more sociable.

"Is that your husband, madam? I'd be happy to make his acquaintance."

The rifle came up again, and he heard a low groan from young Lang, soft words, "No no no."

"That's my hand, Crow Joe. He don't talk to strangers, and he barely talks to me. My husband's done gone. He made the mistake of getting blind drunk and comin' after me with a couple of fists. I leveled him out with a frying pan, and the rest of his drunken gang hauled him off. Ain't seen him since. Might have killed him, hard to say. But he ain't been back, and if he does, I'll kill him again. Now, what the hell do you want? Oh yes, a fancy hide suit. Well, come on, get down off that nag and come inside. I'll take some measures, and you can pay me. Half now, half when the suit fits you."

He obeyed, the rifle still hanging in a rough aim near his midsection.

"WHAT A MARVELOUS character! A regular Calamity Jane."

Lincoln laughed.

"No, sir. They say she can outshoot Miss Jane, and about every man around here. I wouldn't test her on that one, sir. She's liable to take off your ear just to prove a point."

"I'll take your word for it, Mr. Lang."

Lang had stopped his horse, Roosevelt doing the same, curious. He glanced around, then followed the young boy's stare, and now a whisper.

"Sir, out past those scrub trees. Antelope."

Roosevelt tried not to move in his saddle, a nearly impossible task, the sudden rush of excitement focused now on his rifle. He slid it clear of the scabbard, still didn't see the antelope, but the boy had a fixed stare, and Roosevelt followed that way, aching to see. The two animals moved now, spooking, and Roosevelt raised the rifle, a quick instinctive aim, fired. The first antelope dropped, and Roosevelt threw his arms in the air, whooping, shaking his fists, Lang now yelling, "Shoot the other one!"

Roosevelt could see the second antelope, a panicked gallop in no particular direction, no more than a few dozen yards away.

"Shoot him, sir!"

Roosevelt looked down, his rifle in the dirt beneath him. The calm was forced on him by a feeling of utter foolishness. There was nothing else he could do.

"It appears, Master Lang, I cannot." He laughed now. "Seems I dropped my gun."

They both watched as the uninjured antelope scampered away.

"Um, well, sir, we should dress this one, get him back to home. My pa makes a good mess of steaks out of these varmints. He calls 'em goats. But he'll be happy. And, if I may, sir, so will you."

"I already am, Master Lang. I already am."

THE LATE-AFTERNOON SKY was crystal-blue and cloudless, the horse gliding beneath him as though the prairie was the smoothest sand. In fact, it was grass and rugged sagebrush. But the horse seemed not to notice, or, more to Roosevelt's liking, was overly respectful of its rider.

From the beginning, Roosevelt had been deathly afraid of a bucking horse, not just because of the potential for injury but because the behavior suggested that this great beast simply didn't like you and would very likely ignore anything you wished it to do. Roosevelt had been duly impressed with Ferris's skill, calming or even breaking a wild horse with the smooth touch of his hand. It had become a joke between Ferris and him that when a horse was broken by Ferris, what seemed to Roosevelt to be almost mystical, the horse would be handed over to him with Ferris's assurance that this one, sir, is plumb gentle. For reasons Roosevelt could only guess, that only meant the horse would attack the new rider with at least one more episode of violence, designed to rid itself of this New York dude before settling down once more to the soothing hand of Sylvane Ferris.

He called this horse Manitou, for no more complicated reason than it was the first name that came to him. For two days now, man and horse had eased along the base of the larger buttes, climbing the grassy slopes of the gentler hills. Often Roosevelt would dismount, crawling gingerly through the thorny bullberry bushes, one more effort to sneak up on whatever creature might lurk beyond the crest of the butte. So far, those creatures had been mostly jackrabbits and magpies, who seemed to laugh at the intrepid hunter as they scampered or flew away. There had been one deer, a large blacktail, amusing only in that Roosevelt had forgotten to load his rifle. For a brief while, it had brought home the reminder that on this one solitary excursion into the Badlands, he was truly alone. Any big game he might bring down would be his to dress and haul the miles back to his homestead.

He had built the small fire from anything around him that would burn, more brush than timber. He watched the roaring blaze, soon to die away, gathered more of the same brushy fuel, felt a strange desperation that once the fire died out, he would begin to feel the anxiousness that came from being truly alone.

Ferris and the others, Merrifield and Myers, had gone to Minnesota, one more excursion to complete the purchase of Roosevelt's growing herd. Ferris, in particular, had shown considerable reluctance to Roosevelt's making this trip by himself, had coached him in the art of saddling his horse, packing his provisions, and undertaking any other survival necessity Roosevelt might need. It annoyed him that his men still thought of him as something of a four-eyed dude, even if none would ever utter the words. His fear of the bucking horses had been one hint of that, and he had done all he could to take hold of that particular fear and squeeze it away. The rest had been easier—Roosevelt the good student taking heed of everything Ferris had taught him about riding alone in country that could kill a man as easily as the man might kill a deer.

He sat now, one last pile of brush on the fire, a signal to any large predators that he was there, with a rifle and a shotgun, and would take no quarter. Or, at least, that he would make every effort not to be eaten.

He unrolled his blanket, tried to relax, the fire nearly gone, smoky ashes drifting just above him. When they cleared, he was staring into stars, a great blanket of speckled light, something far more grand than anything he had seen through the lantern light of New York. He had admired the night skies in Maine, but there was a difference he couldn't quite figure. In Maine there were trees. Here, there was nothing to block your view all the way to the horizon, in every direction. He marveled at the brighter stars, thought, I should know more about astronomy, identify what I'm looking at. There are books, certainly, and perhaps one day I can write my own.

He saw a streak, what his father had called a shooting star. Then another, and he smiled, wondered if anyone, anywhere in the world, had seen the same thing. Or was it only me? Was it meant for me, perhaps? Some would call it a spark from the hand of God. Maybe. He could not really embrace that.

It had been when he was very young, a Sunday visit to a church in Madison Square, near their home in New York. It was the preacher's sermon, quoting a Bible verse, "For the zeal of thine house hath eaten me up." He smiled now, but there was no humor about that verse then, the small boy convinced that in every great, cavernous church there must lurk a creature certain to devour him from some hidden place. The creature of course must have been a *zeal*.

More than a child's silliness, there had been something in other sermons that had struck him the wrong way, the notion that bad things awaited all people unless they conformed to the lessons as presented not just by the Bible, or by God, but by the preacher, just because he said so. He would never admit to being an agnostic, and certainly not to being an atheist. But accepting the lessons as handed down by a man in a robe seemed unacceptable. His brief encounter with the pope in Rome hadn't changed the view. To the eleven-year-old, the pope was just one more preacher, albeit with far fancier clothes—perhaps a chief preacher who held sway in a great many churches. As he got older, he discovered that he had been correct about that, more or less. But still, they were all just *men*. If God had a lesson, or a message, there shouldn't be a go-between. So now he watched the stars, watched the fascinating streaks of light pass through the utter silence, and wondered if there was more here than shooting stars.

He closed his eyes for a brief moment, a sickening sensation that he was seeing more than he wanted to. He had tried so very hard not to recall that awful day, could picture his mother always, dressed in frilly white, her choice and his father's, that seemed to suit the strong-willed yet soft-spoken Southern belle. But her image faded quickly, replaced by the most painful of all, the loveliest, most beautiful woman he had ever seen, ever would see. And he had to stop it, stop seeing her, hearing her name. Why did we name the child Alice?

He tried to lose himself again in the stars. Don't look down upon me, don't send me signs, don't show me your face among the lights. Please. I will love you forever. But please allow me to forget that one terrible day.

He heard a distinct sound, sat up, a burst of heartbeats, knew he was in a place where the only such sounds were from a creature as large as he was. He reached for his shotgun, more effective than the rifle at close range, rose to his feet. The darkness was absolute, the only light from the stars, and he crept forward, heard another crack of the brush, closer now. He froze, the shotgun at his waist aimed ahead, had no idea what to do next. Speak? *Hello?* No, if it's Indians, they'll be on me. Mountain lion? *Hello?* That might scare him off. He couldn't hide his breathing now, his chest bursting cold.

Now he heard a loud *snort*. The ground in front of him seemed to erupt with motion, and he fumbled to fire the shotgun, hoofbeats now galloping away. He stood with the gun pointing ahead, heavy breaths, his heart trying to slow.

A deer, certainly.

Well, he thought, his heart's beating too. Maybe I'll find him tomorrow.

He moved back to his makeshift bed, the air growing chillier, and he pulled his blanket over him, closed his eyes for a long moment, then opened them, looked again at the stars.

CHAPTER 14

June 26, 1884
Little Missouri, Dakota Territory

For reasons of which I am not yet certain, and I hesitate to tempt the fates by saying this at all, but it appears that my asthma has ceased. I must of course credit the clear air of this place, and the kind of hearty living one must endure to survive. I have not only survived, but am prospering, strengthening myself in body and spirit. And, without asthma.

Your Loving Brother, Teedie

He had been writing to Bamie more often than to anyone else in his family, which, to him, seemed perfectly reasonable. She was, after all, the matriarch now, and Roosevelt never ignored the pull of guilt he had that she was serving as mother to baby Alice.

The telegraph building was closed, the haphazardness characteristic of a town where few seemed to live by a schedule. But not all the townspeople were unreliable. Near the telegraph building was the office of the town's fledgling newspaper, operated by a pleasant and seemingly civilized man named Arthur Packard. Packard happily accepted Roosevelt's letter, and the two men enjoyed a brief but convivial chat before Roosevelt hastened back to his horse. It had never escaped him that Packard was one of the few who seemed to recognize that there was nothing wrong with Roosevelt's wearing spectacles. But in a town where hostile strangers might happen by for no reason other than to pick a fight, Roosevelt, when by himself, assumed it was best if he moved with purpose.

He crossed the shallow river, more shallow now given the lack of rain, and moved through Medora, which could, at best, be called the little brother to Little Missouri. The town was owned and planned out by a flamboyant Frenchman Roosevelt had not yet met. But the man's odd reputation was everywhere, inspiring both laughter and greed.

"Ah, finally! The man with the four eyes!"

Roosevelt turned in the saddle, saw a small group of men, one very different from the rest. He wore a vastly oversize sombrero and carried a pair of revolvers at his waist and a massive knife in his belt, his upper body wrapped in a pair of cartridge belts. The four men came closer to Roosevelt now, and he could see the man's handlebar moustache, perfectly waxed tips—a fiercely handsome man with dark, piercing eyes.

"Welcome to my side of the river, Mr. Roosevelt, the town of Medora. I understand you have come to take over the cattle business, yes? A challenge, since I will beat you to it. I am Antoine de Vallombrosa, Marquis de Morès. You may call me Marquis. It is how I am known through this territory. You are certainly known as Mr. Roosevelt."

The marquis had money, a great deal of it, and was spreading it around the Badlands like tumbleweeds. If he liked you, or perhaps feared you, you might find his money in your pocket. If he didn't like you, you were just another obstacle in his way.

Roosevelt absorbed the man's arrogant syrup, eyed the others alongside him. Roosevelt knew one, Jake Maunders. For reasons Roosevelt didn't understand, Maunders simply hated him. And Jake Maunders was a man whose hate could be dangerous.

He looked again at Morès, was impressed at the man's near-perfect English, a rarity in a place where good grammar marked you for an eastern dude and thus a target for relentless ridicule. But what Roosevelt knew of the marquis told him that the man cared very little for what anyone else thought of him, his dress, or his manners.

"It's a pleasure to finally meet you, Marquis. I assure you, I have no interest in expanding my cattle business beyond the land I have now. I have come here to manage my own herd of cattle, to hunt, and to enjoy the territory. I seek no challenge beyond that."

"Well, then, we should become the closest of friends. It is my goal to process every head of beef from this part of the country, to build an enormous slaughterhouse right here, bring in refrigerated railcars to transport the beef and lamb and pork to Chicago and New York, and every city in between. This place, my Medora, which I named in honor of my wife, we shall soon see another Omaha, right here on this river. I have come with many millions of dollars and have a guarantee for millions more. It is only a matter of time before I create my stage line through here, add to the rail stops, and bring even more civilization to this place than is here now. As we both know, Mr. Roosevelt, one can never have too much civilization."

Roosevelt scanned the other three men, saw the glare from Maunders he had seen before.

"If you will excuse me, Marquis, I must return to the Maltese Cross. It was my pleasure meeting you. Enjoy this warm weather."

He turned, nudged the horse firmly, put distance between himself and the heavily armed men still watching him, thought, Civilization, indeed.

"I met the marquis finally. Oily sort of chap."

Lang seemed to come awake.

"He's worse than oily. He's a liar, a dreamer, a scoundrel, and he surrounds himself with some of the worst varmints in the territory. I'd steer clear of him, if I were you."

Roosevelt was curious.

"He seemed friendly, gracious, a glad hand, once he knows you're not his rival. I didn't feel that he thought of me as an enemy. I take some relief from that, since he clearly has some people working for him who enjoy carrying guns."

"Well, sir, while you're shaking his hand, you can believe that those gunslingers might try to stick you in the back. I'm offering you some good advice, Mr. Roosevelt. He's got men working for him that not only carry their weight in guns, but they don't seem to hesitate shooting a man in cold blood. I'll never tell you what to do, sir, but I'm just offering you friendly advice."

Roosevelt heard an edge in Lang's voice he hadn't heard before.

"Your advice is noted, sir."

He heard hoofbeats, and Lang stood, clamped a pipe in his teeth, moved to the door.

"It's the Ferris brothers, both of 'em. In a hootin' hell of a hurry, looks like."

Roosevelt started to stand, the Ferris brothers already at the door, moving in quickly, sitting with sharp nods to the other men.

"What is it, gentlemen?"

Sylvane seemed to interrupt his thoughts, looked at Roosevelt.

"By Jesus, Mr. Roosevelt, I do wish you wouldn't call us gentlemen. It just don't look good hereabouts."

"Sorry. Just habit."

Joe spoke up now, all seriousness.

"Jack Baxter lost eighty head of horses last night. That's the fourth ranch stripped of stock this month. The horse thieves are getting bolder, don't seem to care if we know who or what they're doing. There's a pretty good notion exactly who's behind them, and just how they're running the horses into Canada. You're lucky, Mr. Roosevelt, since you're not herding horses. These rustlers don't seem to care about cattle. They're too slow to move, and too hard to sell on account of their brands. But from what we've heard, the horses are being sold to Indians north of the border."

Roosevelt felt the usual stir of excitement, spoke quickly.

"What happens now? A posse goes after them? Marshals come in from the bigger cities? Forgive me. Never had to deal with horse thieves before."

Sylvane couldn't help a laugh.

"This ain't storybook stuff, sir. Out here, there ain't no law you can depend on, and hiring a gunfighter is a sure way to get that man killed. It's kinda secret, and I'm not sure of the facts, but we heard . . . there's a gang of vigilantes being put together by Granville Stuart, head of the cattleman's association in Miles City. He's being extra careful, and extra . . . discreet. Too many people around the territory have friends among the thieves, and if Stuart's plan gets out, there'll be a good deal of blood."

Roosevelt felt a rising heat in the back of his neck.

"Can't have this. We just can't. This part of the country is on its way to civilization, to being a place for families and businessmen, men like Mr. Packard, who aren't raising cattle at all. You make it too dangerous for those folks, and this place might as well dry up. You men have done admirable work making a living, prospering from land that some might see as nothing more than sagebrush and rattlesnakes. By George, I want to find out more of this, learn how this Mr. Stuart is organizing. If I can help him, then I will."

The Ferris brothers eyed each other, and Roosevelt could see alarm.

Sylvane said, "Sir, that's not what we had in mind. We brung you this news, 'cause it's news. That's all. But my guess is that Stuart's people are gonna get their pound of flesh from the thieves, and that might go both ways. With me and Bill set to gather up your herd over east, you won't have nobody hardly backing you up. Pardon me for saying, Mr. Roosevelt, but you're not likely to back down anybody around here who has bad intent toward you. I'd steer clear of Stuart and his people. There could be something of a war if this goes badly."

"That's two pieces of advice I've received today. With respects to all of you, I'm not certain I can follow either one of them. For all your concerns about me, Mr. Ferris, I am confident I can take care of myself."

"I WAS JUST wondering, Marquis, with your considerable interests hereabouts, if you've heard of some bad people doing bad things. Thievery and such. I find it hard to believe that such things can still thrive among a community like this."

Morès was eyeing him, smiled now.

"You are a master of flattery, Mr. Roosevelt. You know better than to come right out and ask an indelicate question. So you will let me answer it without a question at all. Nicely done, sir." He sipped from a small glass of sherry, then held it out toward Roosevelt. "None for you? Surely."

Roosevelt shook his head, again.

"No, thank you."

Morès seemed to take his time, spoke slowly, and Roosevelt could see the man might have doubts of his own, about just whom he could trust.

"In your travels hunting and so forth, have you happened to meet a man named Stuart?"

Roosevelt smiled, appreciated the chess game.

"Granville Stuart. Cattleman's association. No, I have not met him, but I understand him to be a man with a strong sense of decency."

"One would hope so. One problem for Mr. Stuart is that should the men he is seeking learn of his enterprise, the enterprise will collapse. Worse, men could find themselves in a bloody trap. Certain men react angrily when their flow of money is interrupted. I know I would."

He could feel Morès itching to say more, and Roosevelt was never one to say less.

"If Mr. Stuart intends on doing good, as I have been told, I should like to join him. Wouldn't you?"

Morès sipped the sherry, another deliberate pause, seemed as though he was measuring Roosevelt.

"You are a popular man in New York. You have fought against those who seek to strangle your political party. You have had tragedy in your life."

Roosevelt was annoyed now.

"You read newspapers."

"I read *you,* sir. There is a man you do not know, Jameson, an Englishman, very good with a gun, so he says. He and I will be making a trip westward. The train shall take us to Glendive, in Montana."

Roosevelt knew now he could find out anything the marquis knew.

"Why?"

"I am one of a dozen men who knows what Mr. Stuart is planning. He is choosing men very carefully, men who are expert with the rifle, and silent of the mouth. Secrecy is vital, essential, or we are all wasting our time. The outlaws must be surprised, or nothing good will come. Do you understand, Mr. Roosevelt?"

He was truly excited now, flexed his fingers with nervous energy, one foot bouncing on the carpeted floor.

"I understand. When do we leave for Glendive?"

Roosevelt found it hard to like Stuart, because, clearly, Stuart had no use for him. And Stuart seemed to feel the same about Morès and Jameson.

"The answer is no. First, I don't know what you're talking about. Second, you're not the kind of men I need." He leaned forward in his chair, stared hard at Morès, a glance toward Roosevelt. "Honest men, I have no doubt. But you're not gunmen. None of you has killed a man, and I assure you"—he glanced at Roosevelt again—"it's not like killing a deer."

Morès looked at Roosevelt with desperate gloom. Roosevelt said, "Sir, I have a hearty dislike of lawbreakers. There is nothing to stop these very bad men from plying a very bad trade. I should like to assist you. I might not be a gunslinger, but I can shoot, and I am not afraid. I assure you, sir, I would be an asset. We all would."

Stuart shook his head.

"You're wrong. You would be a liability. You, sir, are quite well known. Someone puts a bullet in you, and it will make the papers all the way to Boston. Can't have that. Hell, the marquis here, somebody plugs him, and they'll know about it in Paris. No, sir. Leave this to me and the men I'm choosing. We'll do the job. All I ask is that when you leave here, you keep your mouths closed tight."

In the weeks that followed, Granville Stuart and his handpicked vigilantes wreaked havoc with the bands of horse thieves, surprising and, in some cases, killing men who had believed themselves untouchable. Within months, the plague of horse thievery had come to an end.

Roosevelt, along with the Marquis de Morès and young Mr. Jameson, would only know the details of Stuart's raids as the word spread throughout the territory. For now, they had no choice but to board the train in Glendive and return quietly to Little Missouri.

CHAPTER 15

He planned to return to New York in a few days, though he had very mixed feelings, feeling the need, on the one hand, to explore more of this fascinating land and its people and, on the other, to surround himself with the kind of love that comes only from family. Part of the reason for the trip back east was to see his young daughter, to eliminate the unforgivable crime of having her grow older with no image of her father. There were other reasons for returning than family. Aside from his lukewarm commitment to campaign for James Blaine for president, he was still a member of the New York State Assembly, and there would be expectations attached to that. As a prominent member of the Republican Party, he was expected to support every candidate in that party, whether he actually liked them or not. Roosevelt was learning hard truths about politics: that very often, no matter what decision you make, it's the wrong one.

There was another reason for the return trip. From his earlier hunting excursions to Maine, he had formed a long-distance friendship with his guides there, Bill Sewall and Bill's nephew Wilmot Dow. Roosevelt's cattle operation had expanded beyond his crew's ability to efficiently manage the herd, and hiring reliable and honest men around Little Missouri could be a problem. Roosevelt knew that Sewall and Dow were as rugged as anyone he had met in the Dakotas, regardless of whether they were inclined to brandish a pistol. But both men were honest and could be depended on to do the job Roosevelt required.

Sewall, in particular, had been hesitant, but his own spirit of adventure for the unknown had finally prevailed, Dow going along. The greatest objection was put up by their two wives, and Roosevelt was forced to guarantee that both men could return one year into their three-year contract. As an added incentive, he paid each man, or rather each woman, the sum of three thousand dollars. It had the desired effect. Roosevelt would meet with the men in New York, and in early August he would escort both men out to a homestead they were expected to build themselves.

WITH ONLY A few days before he was to leave the Maltese Cross behind, Roosevelt had made a move, relocating downriver a few miles, to a homestead farther removed from annoying visitors. His first home had been situated on the main trail along the river, which ran so close to his front door that he was frequently invited into conversation with passing drifters. Roosevelt's perfect idea of isolation was to sit down with a good book, but the frequent visitor too often became an infuriating interruption. The new piece of land was available for squatters' rights, and would offer him both solitude and enormous beauty. He had accepted the move with a hearty smile.

He was taking one last solitary ride, heading northward first, then to the west, well away from the river, and for a long while he relied on the horse to take him where Manitou thought he ought to go. For the most part, game was scarce, the rifle secured in its scabbard. He reached down, touched it, a habit of a man not yet fully comfortable alone in these surroundings. There was a row of buttes to one side, sagebrush and patches of grass, and he was surprised to see a small cluster of cattle bunched against the steep wall of a small canyon. Well, he thought, someone's got claim to this place, that's for sure. Maybe I better check the brand, then find someone around here who might know.

He pushed the horse that way, saw a pair of riders now, and he waved his hat, attracted their attention. They moved close, more curious than hostile, halted their horses a few yards distant, and both men started to chuckle.

Roosevelt glanced downward, absorbed what they were absorbing, the fringes on his buckskin suit, the rest of his attire complete with silver belt buckle and alligator boots. His pistol attracted attention as well, engraved silver and gold inlay, with a bright-white ivory handle.

One of the men seemed to gather himself.

"Wait a minute. I know you. You're that dude fella they talk about over at Little Missouri. I got kin over that way. Yep, the spectacles made it for certain."

The other fellow still smiled broadly.

"Where'd you get them clothes? New York, I bet."

Roosevelt had ridden with full pride in his attire until now.

"No, I had everything made around Little Missouri, and I ordered the boots from Saint Paul. I was mighty pleased with the whole ensemble, if I do say so."

The men glanced at each other.

"If you say so, friend. You might want to steer clear of Mingusville, though. There's a handful of drunken-fool sheepherders over there now, claiming to own the place as they see fit. Bad for business."

The other fellow pointed at Roosevelt's glasses, said, "Might be bad for four-eyed dudes too."

Roosevelt was hoping to find some sort of settlement where he could refill his canteen, which was woefully dry.

"Where is this Mingusville?"

One man pointed back over his shoulder.

"Right past these buttes. Ain't much. You might get to meet Gus and Minnie, if them drunks ain't shot 'em to pieces."

"They founded the town. They run the hotel there too. It's gettin' late in the day, if you're planning on holing up for the night, all it takes is a dollar for Minnie and ten dollars' worth of courage."

Roosevelt's brain wrapped around the names. Min-Gus-ville. "Thank you, I understand." He pointed toward the canyon now. "There's a small herd of cattle bunched up over that way. I assume you might know their owner."

The first man nodded.

"Most likely Gus. He owns most everything around here. We work for him. You need a job to help pay for all that glitter, he might hire you."

The second man reached out in a playful slap to his friend's shoulder.

"Fool. Any man dresses like that's gotta have enough money to hire his own crew of gunfighters to protect him. I bet there's fellas with rifles watching us right now."

Roosevelt was relaxing now, raised his hat high with a toothy smile.

"That's my signal to those boys that you're friendly. I'll not comment further on that. Perhaps I'll see you boys in Mingusville."

HE RODE SLOWLY, cautious, the town not more than a small cluster of buildings, a picturesque scene with a wide creek behind. He was surprised to see a train station, the other main building beside what passed for a hotel and saloon.

He dismounted at the saloon, walked his horse to a shed nearby, tied Manitou up beside a row of others. There was a back door to the saloon, and he eased that way, suddenly heard two gunshots crack past him from the bar. His heart jumped, *leave, now,* his first instinct to avoid any place where gunfights break out. He put one hand on his pistol, useless gesture, no one exiting, hearty laughter now coming from inside.

He glanced out toward the horses, daylight fading, no water and no choice now but to find dinner and a place to sleep. He eased through the door, saw lantern light and cigar smoke, a dozen men seated at rickety tables, some leaning against a bar. But it wasn't congenial, the men all staring at one man in particular, a staggering drunk moving along the bar, pistols in each hand. Roosevelt tried to absorb what he could, saw the clock on the wall with two bullet holes, saw men keeping their hands purposely away from their gun belts, saw that the drunk's pistols were both cocked.

And now the man saw him.

"Four-eyes!"

Laughter followed, forced and anxious, and Roosevelt tried to join in, his eyes on the muzzles of the man's pistols. The man staggered slightly, said, "Four-eyes is gonna treat. He's payin'."

Roosevelt laughed with the others, moved to a darker corner, sat, trying his best to disappear. But the man had his target in sight now, kept advancing.

"I said four-eyes is gonna treat." The man leaned closer to Roosevelt now, the stink of whiskey washing over him. "Bartender, set up drinks for the whole crowd. The four-eye dude here is paying."

Roosevelt kept his eyes on the man's pistols, waving close to his face. His heart was racing, the sickening thought that he might die *right here*. His mind swirled, no chance to draw his own pistol, no one else at the bar willing to pull the man away. He was growing angry now, knew he couldn't back down to this man, that he would inspire more laughter and disrespect than he already did. He glanced down, the drunk hovering right over him, Roosevelt's mind working feverishly, the man's feet too close together. That, friend, is a mistake. He stood now.

"Well, if I have to, I have to." He looked past the man, eyes on the bartender, who seemed to think Roosevelt was serious. The drunk glanced away as well, already glowing with his personal victory over the dude in the buckskin suit.

Roosevelt stood straight, leaned slightly forward, focused on the man's chin, launched a sharp right hand against the man's jaw, then a quick left, then another right. The pistols fired, wildly, the man dropping in a heap, his head striking the bar. Roosevelt was shaking now, still watched the man's guns, wisps of smoke from the barrels. He felt frozen in place, a sudden thought that the man might still react. He prepared to pounce on the man with his knees, rip the guns away, voices at the bar, moving closer.

"You done kilt him."

"Naw. He's breathin'."

"He ain't nothin' but a bully, nohow. You done the right thing, friend."

"He comes in here, shoots the place up, and nobody's got the guts to stand up to him. A man gets that drunk, there's no use talking to him."

The last man was older, not dressed like a trail hand. Roosevelt said, "You would be . . ."

"Gus. I appreciate you handlin' this like you did. Now, you boys, get this heap of stupidity out of my bar, and keep him out." He looked at Roosevelt now.

"How are your hands?"

Roosevelt hadn't felt the pain until now.

"All right. Thank you."

"How 'bout some dinner? Wife makes some good lamb stew. And drinks are on me."

"Just the stew, and a pitcher of water."

"Whatever you say. If you're looking for a place to stay, costs you a dollar, and you sleep upstairs. I wouldn't worry about those fellows coming back after you, looking to start something. You made your point. Hellfire, you made it for all of us, clean across the butte country."

Roosevelt was puzzled, flexed his aching fingers.

"What do you mean, sir?"

Gus laughed.

"What's your name?"

"Theodore Roosevelt, sir. From over near Little Missouri."

Gus put his hands on his hips.

"Well, ain't that something. Heard of you. Didn't believe all that nonsense about what a dandy dude you were, that is, 'til I seen your outfit. But you done it now, Mr. Roosevelt. You done made yourself an honest reputation. All those sheepherders piled out of here with this story on their lips. Within a week, the story'll grow 'til you don't recognize it, but don't worry about that. After all, you done defanged a rattlesnake with your bare hands. They might still call you four-eyes. But now, it'll be with respect."

CHAPTER 16

July 12, 1884
New York City

He was more than nervous, felt his entire insides curling over, his breathing in short chops, inspiring fears of the dreaded asthma. He walked to the window, looked out onto Fifth Avenue, a beehive of activity, carriages pulled through muddy ruts by filthy horses. A good deal of rain, he thought, his brain trying to take his mind elsewhere, away from this moment. But he heard voices, knew them well, clenched his fists, the nervousness complete. He took a deep breath, turned toward the door, saw Bamie first, tried to avoid her stare, could not, nodded with a hint of a smile, and now, behind her, Corinne came in, holding the bundle. It was larger than he recalled, larger than he expected now. Bamie stood to one side, a hint of scolding in her expression, silent instructions. *Do this right.*

Corinne focused more on the baby, moved closer to him, a tearful smile.

"Teedie, Alice welcomes you. Say hello to your daughter."

He looked down into the blanket, saw pink, her face, her tiny dress, small sounds, chirps, coos, nothing like he had ever heard before. For a quick moment, he wanted to turn away, the pink too much like her mother, her color of choice for most every occasion. But he knew Bamie was watching him, would just as likely launch a bolt of lightning at him if he failed this moment.

Corinne said, "Take her, Teedie. Hold her."

He hesitated, a glance at Bamie.

124

"I'm not sure I know how."

Bamie said, "She has no teeth yet, Teedie. She won't bite you."

Corinne laughed softly, said, "She might spit up her latest feeding. She's unpredictable about that. But it seems to me that she's smiling at you."

He stood frozen, said, "Well, that's a positive thing." He looked at Bamie again. "It is, right?"

Bamie shook her head.

"Take your daughter in your arms. If you don't do this now, you will despise yourself later on. I promise you."

Her words sank heavily into him, and he looked now at Corinne, saw the same soft smile. She held the baby out toward him, and Roosevelt extended his arms, felt the softness of the pink blanket, more small sounds from the baby, heavier now than what he had expected.

"She is six months old, I suppose."

"Almost, Teedie."

He hadn't quite taken her from Corinne's hands, looked at his sister.

"And I suppose she's being cared for, fed and such."

"I'm taking care of her, Teedie. I'm nursing my own child and he's but a few months older. Call me her wet nurse."

Roosevelt felt embarrassed, had never had this kind of conversation.

"I'm sorry. That was too inappropriate."

Corinne laughed.

"Teedie, she's your daughter. You're supposed to know how she's doing, and *what* she's doing."

Bamie moved closer now, said, "You're supposed to do more than that. You're her father."

The words made their point, and he put his hands fully beneath the blanket, lifted the baby away from Corinne, pulled the bundle against his chest.

"Is this right?"

Corinne said, "Of course it's right. She's looking at you. She knows. She knows you're her father. She already loves you, Teedie."

He forced himself to look at the baby's face, the tiny hands and arms, was fascinated by her fingers. He could see Alice in her, the baby's eyes, tried to look away, but the baby's smile held him. He fought it, closed his eyes for a brief moment, knew he had to do this, not just because of his sisters' scolding, but because it was important. And if he was hurting from the image of his wife, that didn't matter, not nearly as much as the soft bundle he held right now. He looked again at the small hands, one tiny arm now extending, the fingers reaching up toward his face.

He began to cry.

July 18, 1884
Nahant, Massachusetts

Henry Cabot Lodge was older by nearly a decade, enjoyed a solid reputation among Massachusetts Republicans as a man of both intelligence and breeding, covered perhaps with a blanket of Harvard arrogance. But, to Roosevelt, he was a friend. The two men seemed to share similar attitudes about most of the politicians in the respective assemblies they were forced to work alongside, and, even more important to Roosevelt, Lodge had been among the small minority who had fought against the nomination of James Blaine for the presidential ticket. Now, Lodge was absorbing some of the same criticism Roosevelt had, some of the more progressive and independent Republicans branding both men traitors to their party.

"What would your father have done?"

It was an odd question, but Roosevelt knew that Lodge understood the power that Theodore Senior still held over his son.

"He would have, above all else, maintained a clear conscience."

Lodge sipped from a china cup.

"Well?"

Roosevelt smiled.

"Yes, my conscience is clear. But the newspapers insist I provide them a comment nearly every day, and I will now tell them that I shall support Blaine, no matter what the *people* might wish me to do."

Lodge sat back, stroked the short beard on his chin.

"That stance is risky for both of us."

Roosevelt ignored the coffee in his own cup, felt his energy rising.

"If I leave the Republican Party over this Blaine fiasco, I am finished in politics. If I come out in support of him, at least they will say that I tossed my hat into the wrong circle, along with a great many others. Cabot, we both know we are likely to be the beaten party. I, for one, can live with that. Can you?"

Lodge smiled now.

"Of course. I just wanted to know your reasoning."

"Well, here's more of my *reasoning*. I am not accepting nomination for the assembly this fall. I can offer no benefit to a body that will be universally hostile to me, no matter what happens in the election. Cabot, you and I are, by inheritance and by education, Republicans. It is that affiliation that has allowed me to accomplish much good in public life, much as my father did. I will tell the papers that I am supporting Blaine, but it is my firm decision now that I will not be available to actively campaign for the election."

Lodge seemed curious now.

"Why do you think you will be ineffective in the assembly?"

"If I support Blaine, I am a traitor to the progressives. If I support Blaine and do not actively campaign for him, Blaine's people will know I'm just being patronizing, for my own good. They're probably right. But no matter what I do, it will please no one. Not the papers, not the party, not Mr. Blaine, and possibly not even you, my friend. In a few days, I am returning to my ranch in the Dakota Territory. There is one great truth I have discovered riding my horse through that extraordinary place: Nowhere else can I describe myself as truly free. No matter how much displeasure I might inspire in Albany or elsewhere, I assure you, out west, the pleasure is *mine*."

"And if Blaine wins? He will feel that you abandoned him. There will be no place for you in his government. Thus, your great rising star will extinguish."

Roosevelt pondered the question.

"I'm a politician because I have thought I could do good for those people who cannot help themselves, not because of a lust for power. That is the role my father handed me. I take that seriously." He paused. "Do you believe Blaine will win?"

Lodge sipped again from the china cup.

"I prefer to leave prognostications to others. To you, perhaps."

Roosevelt shook his head. "Blaine will not win. Our next president will be Grover Cleveland. And I do believe that, even for a Democrat, he actually likes me."

Lodge laughed.

"Oh, that will extinguish that star soon enough. I can hear the epithets clearly. Traitor. Scoundrel. Backstabber."

Roosevelt shrugged.

"If politics is to be my lifeblood, I must do it on my own terms, and I will find a way to survive. If it is not in my future, well, I have my cattle. And a clear conscience."

CHAPTER 17

August 10, 1884
Little Missouri, Dakota Territory

He felt as though he could breathe again, felt even more excited about sharing this magnificent life with two men from Maine. But Bill Sewall and his nephew were not horsemen, few opportunities existing for a long prairie ride in the backwoods of Maine. And so, to Roosevelt's annoyance and entertainment, it took time to train both men in the art of rounding up cattle from the backs of beasts totally alien to them.

Roosevelt was adjusting himself in his own saddle, the curse of weeks in the East. Ferris pretended not to notice, and after a short and painful moment, Roosevelt said, "How's the herd?"

Ferris was looking past him now, watching Sewall straighten out the stiffness in his legs.

"Herd's good. We're fully at sixteen hundred head, including what Bill and I just brung over from Iowa. We've got a deal made with a broker there for four hundred more, if you give the word, sir."

"Excellent, Mr. Ferris. I'll think about that."

"Um, Mr. Roosevelt, I know you've got money behind you and all. I'm just a little concerned that you're taking an awful risk out here. Bad things can happen, and I don't mean human. The weather turns, a rough winter, and you could lose half your herd just like that. Disease . . . hell, there's all kinds of plagues can affect a herd."

"There is risk in everything we do, Mr. Ferris. I accept that. I have confidence in those who work for me to do their best to see us through the difficult times."

Sewall walked over now, still unhooking the kinks in his legs. Ferris seemed to scan him from top to bottom, said, "You done hefted your share of Maine timbers, right?"

Sewall tried to accept the compliments with a smile.

"You could say that. I could likely pick up one of these ponies easier than I can ride one."

Ferris laughed, and Roosevelt was relieved that there had been no east-west conflicts, at least not yet. Sewall and Dow seemed to accept readily that they were the children out here, with a great deal to learn.

Sewall said, "It does seem strange to me, though, how cattle can survive in this place. Looks kinda rough to me. Don't get me wrong, it's got a beauty to it, for sure. Just not much of cattle country."

Ferris seemed to bristle, but a glance toward Roosevelt calmed him down.

Roosevelt said, "Bill, if these fellows say they can run cattle here, they'll do it. They know more than I do, and I assure you, I know more than you."

Sewall stretched his back, still working on days of soreness.

"Fair enough to me, sir."

Merrifield came close now, a glance at Sewall, who stood a head taller.

"Um, Mr. Roosevelt, we might have a different kind of problem."

"The marquis?"

"Yes, sir."

"I heard when I was in town. He's laying claim to my new ranch downriver. I need to go see him and straighten this out."

Ferris said, "He's laid claim to anyplace in this whole territory that anybody else finds suitable. You like it, suddenly, he owns it. I wouldn't give it much thought, Mr. Roosevelt. He's a big bag of air looking for someplace to blow."

Roosevelt thought of Maunders and the other gunmen who seemed to flit around Morès like bees.

"All the same, fellows, I'd rather have peace with the marquis and a clear understanding."

"We'll grab a bunch of the boys, go over there with you."

Roosevelt shook his head.

"No. The marquis either respects power or he respects equals. We don't have the kind of gun-wielding renegades that he does. So, we don't need to get into some contest over who can shoot each other. He's already invited me to come by and visit his château, or whatever he's calling that grand house, and I've heard that his wife is even more highbrowed than he is. If I go alone, I'll show him I have my hat in my hand, or else I expect him to respect me. Either way, I'll be welcome. I can put on a few airs when I have to." He laughed. "I did go to Harvard, you know."

"Have you ever fought a duel, Mr. Roosevelt?"

He was beginning to understand that when Morès asked a question, it had two meanings, friendliness and danger. So far, Roosevelt kept steering the responses toward the former.

"No, sir. Haven't really sought out the opportunity."

Morès seemed to puff up more than he had already been. "I have, you know. Twice. Successfully, I might add, though I suppose that would be obvious. I have killed two men. Unpleasant affair, but sometimes it has to be done. You certainly know about honor, sir, being so versed in politics."

Roosevelt saw an opportunity for levity.

"Sorry, I'm unfamiliar with the term. Never saw much *honor* from politicians."

He had the desired effect.

"Ah! Yes, very well. The same is true in France as well as New York. Some professions are naturally attracted to the worst classes of people."

Roosevelt realized he had just been insulted, let it go.

Morès sipped his sherry.

"You must have noticed how Medora has grown over the summer months. The word is out, to be sure. I am creating a great marketplace here, for livestock, for the meat industry back east. The word is spreading through all the big cities, that Badlands beef is something you must have. I'm building a stage line myself, and Mr. Packard, the newspaperman, he is putting word out on the telegraph that is already drawing Easterners this way."

"Yes. Quite impressive."

"I know. You should come to work for me, sir. Your herd is growing nicely and would be the bait, so to speak, for others to bring their livestock to my slaughterhouses. With your name in front and mine above, it will be an irresistible attraction."

Roosevelt was surprised and felt like laughing, held it in tightly.

"How many slaughterhouses do you have, sir?"

"Oh, just the one. But a dozen or more will be built before much longer."

Roosevelt still didn't respond to Morès's offer to become his boss, was relieved that Morès didn't pursue it.

There was a fluttering of bright lace, the unmistakable aura of French perfume, and Roosevelt stood, watched as Morès's wife swept into the room.

She held out a hand toward Roosevelt, said, "I am so very charmed to meet you, sir. You have quite a reputation."

Morès faked a smile.

"This is a land, dear wife, where *everyone* has *some* kind of reputation."

Roosevelt bowed slightly, kissed her gloved hand, felt washed in memories of such greetings years before, the formality of so many balls and cotillions.

"It is my pleasure as well, madame."

"Please, let us sit. Our chef is preparing a marvelous dinner." She laughed. "Not a buffalo in sight, I'm afraid."

Roosevelt sat as she did, eyed her face, beautiful, an aristocrat's bearing, everything one should expect in a woman of such breeding. And he knew she came from serious money, perhaps more than Morès did. He waited for a long second, curious if there would be recognition, or at least a confession from her that they might have met before. He smiled at the thought, that Medora von Hoffmann had on occasion been a social acquaintance to his sister Bamie. But that was the past, and now the present was a world her husband was desperately trying to change to fit his own ambitions.

Morès said, "Now that the formal pleasantries are out of the way, and before dinner is served, I must clear up one particular matter. I suspect that is why you are here, sir."

"Perhaps."

Morès sat back, as though taking the stage.

"You have chosen a piece of property downriver for your homestead. I'm afraid that is a problem for you. I own that range. In fact, I own most of the range downriver, and quite a bit upriver as well. I have allowed your Maltese Cross to remain where it sits, mainly because I respect you, and frankly I rather like you."

"I am flattered, sir. However, I'm afraid you are mistaken, certainly an honest mistake. We have done some research into land grants and so forth throughout this area, including my new homestead, and we have determined that ownership of that property is now mine. It would be severely unfortunate should anyone attempt to relocate my herd and my home without my permission. Thus, I'm certain it will not happen."

The scowl on Morès's face made Roosevelt want to laugh, but he wisely kept his composure. Madame Morès seemed to know when to fill an uncomfortable void, picked up a small bell, gave it a tinkling ring.

"Josephine, if Henri is ready, you may serve the dinner." She leaned toward Roosevelt now. "Henri Bouchard is our chef, arrived last month from Paris."

The activity was brisk, six servants emerging from a side room, surrounding the table, wine and covered dishes, revealing elegant blue china, the smell of roasted bird, what Roosevelt assumed to be squab, imported of course. He was impressed, but he eyed the marquis once more. No smile there. No matter what this dinner might be, he seems to be eating crow.

CHAPTER 18

As Roosevelt had predicted, the November general election saw Grover Cleveland elected president of the United States. The only surprise, to Roosevelt especially, was that the margin of victory was slight, as though even the disenfranchised Republicans had made some attempt to rally around their candidate, Blaine.

Though Roosevelt remained at his homestead near Medora and Little Missouri, he couldn't escape the sticky hands of politics. For months, hard rumors had abounded that the Dakota Territory was to become a state, or possibly as many as four states. With the election of Cleveland, those rumors gained steam, many assuming that the Democrats would be energized to add states to their arsenal of voters. For more than a decade, as the romance of the West became fashionable, enhanced by the discovery of gold in the Black Hills in the southern part of the territory, the population of the area had grown to such a level that Washington could no longer ignore what had been, to many, a wasteland.

Roosevelt had heard the rumors and paid little heed. If the land around him was suddenly an official part of the United States, it would make very little difference to his cattle operation, which had become his first priority. But one change confronted him right away: His name was being bandied about as the new state's first representative to the United

States Congress. The opportunity seemed appealing, especially to a man who had so many political enemies in the East. But careful thought gave way to plans of a different kind. Instead of making his presence known at local stump meetings, and without committing himself to a political position at all, he put together plans of another kind. Once again, he was going hunting.

"By GODFREY, I'm as tired as any man ought to be. The horses feel the same way, quite certain of that. It was most successful, I'll say that. Mr. Merrifield is a fine guide. That buckboard is overflowing with game, furs, and heads. I've not seen anything quite like it. I must say, though, to return to my homestead is a dee-light. This is fine stew, as always, and the biscuits . . . well, they're excellent. Like sponges, soaking up the gravy. Outstanding."

Merrifield sat low against the log wall near the hearth, nodded slowly, a slight smile. Roosevelt pointed toward him, said again to the others, "He did a fine job. Truly fine. We brought down just about every game creature that populates that range. And a few that just wandered by out of curiosity. The grizzly was the best challenge—something I predicted. Well, then there was the blacktail deer. Took him down at better than four hundred paces. My best shot ever."

Merrifield dabbed at a plate of beans perched on his knees, glanced up at Roosevelt.

"You missed that mountain lion. A few deer too." His smile grew now. "You got to learn to follow orders, Mr. Roosevelt. Well, not orders, exactly. Maybe *directions,* I mean. I tell you to hold up, to stop moving, you need to heed the words." He looked at Ferris and the two men from Maine. "He tends to get excited."

Roosevelt laughed.

"Quite right, Mr. Merrifield. But I tell you, all of you. Being out there, in a place where no man has been, or at least where no man wants to be, well, that's bully."

Roosevelt felt the boiling heat sweeping through the room. The smell of the food was intoxicating, and he dipped another ladle of stew into his bowl, added a scoop of beans. Sewall began to speak, then seemed to hesitate, and finally said, "You planning on spending the whole winter with us, sir?"

"Well, Bill, you boys have done most of the work building my new cabin, and there isn't much else for me to do. I need to rest the horses after that long hunt, maybe rest Mr. Merrifield too. I heard that Gregor Lang has completed his new place as well."

Ferris laughed.

"His wife did all that. She's brought him some back-east culture. It shows in his place. They got curtains, for crying out loud."

Roosevelt had heard that Lang's wife was due to arrive, was wondering just what kind of woman would be married to the cantankerous Scotsman.

"I'd like to go meet her. I must say, I'm curious."

Sewall said, "So, go meet her. There's plenty else you can do around here, if you decide to stay a bit longer. I'm just wondering why you'd do that. You got a whole life back east. Somebody back there is missing having you around."

Roosevelt let out a breath, hadn't expected to mention anything of this to his men. But he knew that Sewall would likely understand. Of the two Maine men, he was the quiet one, his enormous physical size belying just how thoughtful he could be. Dow was the jokester, had a keen wit that fit right in with Ferris and Merrifield.

Roosevelt looked at Sewall, saw the dark eyes staring back at him. Sewall expected an answer, whether Roosevelt wanted to give him one or not.

"I've not decided when I'm leaving. I should like to experience at least some of the winter out here, to understand just what my own livestock must endure, my horses, and of course all of you."

Sewall said, "I've been told by these boys that it ain't likely nothing as gentle as Maine. Not sure about that. I've pulled ten-pound icicles off trees. Not too many trees around here could handle that."

Dow laughed, and Roosevelt could tell it was a rare joke from Sewall. Roosevelt didn't laugh, his mind taking him elsewhere. After a silent moment, broken only by the sounds of the men eating, Roosevelt said, "I'm not sure what's waiting for me back east. Not sure at all. My career is likely ended. No one would support me for any elected office, not if they believe I could end up betraying them. I feel more at home out here than ever before. I'm a ranchman, until I figure out that maybe I can't do that either. I'm feeling like I don't really belong in either place."

Sewall stood, his huge form towering over Roosevelt.

"You can stop that kind of talk right now. You ought not let yourself get all wrapped up in how miserable things are, in how miserable *you* are. For one thing, you've got a child, and that's enough for most men to want to live forever."

Roosevelt tried not to look at Sewall's bearded face.

"Her aunt can take care of her a good deal better than I can. The baby wouldn't ever know much about me anyway. She's better off growing up with my sister."

"What if your sister gets married? Things change, you know."

Roosevelt didn't respond, thought, I hadn't considered that. Surely, she wouldn't . . . but of course she could. A good man might see in Bamie what the rest of us do, and even though she's crippled . . . well, that doesn't change what a good soul she is.

He felt like an idiot now, waited for Sewall to sit down again, watched as the big man dipped himself another bowl of antelope stew, a handful of hard biscuits. There was silence, no one prepared to speak unless Roosevelt opened the door. He stared at the floor between his feet, said, "I have a great deal to be thankful for."

Sewall sat with his food, clearly wasn't finished speaking. "You feel like you're standing in some swamp, is that it? You've had a tough time this year. But time heals. You ain't gonna stay here and drive cattle the rest of your life. There's too much you'll want to do elsewhere, and too many who will expect you to do it. If you can't think of anything else to do, go back east and start some kind of reform movement for something. You've said yourself, there's all kind of things need reforming, not just politics. Well, maybe politics too. That's what you do, ain't it? You're a reformer. So, go home and reform something. You always want to make things better than worse. You can do a whole lot more for the world back there than what you'll do here. So, go do it. And when you get home, kiss your daughter on the cheek. That's all she'll need to know."

THE WINTER WAS more intensely cold than anything he could have imagined, ice on the river, deep snowdrifts along the edges of the buttes. The journey from his old homestead of Maltese Cross, where Sylvane Ferris and Merrifield called home, was a good ride to Roosevelt's new cabin, now called Elkhorn, named after a locked pair of elk antlers he had discovered on his first ride through the country. There, Sewall and Dow made their beds, still completing the last bit of work to make the cabin as weatherproof as possible. What Roosevelt learned of the daily chores was that the tasks themselves were not so different from what he might go through at Oyster Bay. But the amount of labor was far greater, and the severity of the conditions far more difficult. Even though he wore extra fur clothing and boots and pants designed to protect him on horseback, the wind seemed to mock such defenses, slicing knifelike through any buckskin or fur. Fortunately, there was a vein of lignite coal along a bluff on his property, a godsend for keeping the fires burning in his hearth. But the cattle had no such luxury, and he was alarmed at how many seemed certain not to survive, the weaker, thinner animals they would find only when the snow melted in spring.

Roosevelt planned his trip east to be home in time for Christmas, but his men would continue their work, doing what they could to keep the cattle fed and doctoring some of the weaker animals as best they could by bringing them into shelter. The questions were asked, just when he might return. But the men knew what he knew. Roosevelt would return to the Badlands when the notion struck him. In the meantime, his cattle operation would continue without him.

January 14, 1885
New York City

"All right, Mr. Roosevelt, hold still now. Just a moment more."

He tried to obey the photographer's instructions, was challenged by a nearby mirror just slightly out of his line of sight.

"I do say, Mr. Bain, I'm feeling rather uncomfortable. As good as I look, and no doubt, this is impressive to any Easterner, the buckskin is allowing a good bit of sweat to gather. Even my feet are sweating. How much longer, sir?"

"Just a moment, please, Mr. Roosevelt."

He caught a glimpse of color at the doorway, a soft giggle, then another, and now a woman's voice.

"Oh, good gracious. This is why you wanted all of this material? You weren't happy in the West, you had to pretend it was in my parlor as well?"

He glanced at Bamie, disobeying the photographer's instructions yet again. Her laughter was contagious, and he smiled, realized the second voice belonged to Edith Carow. He nodded a brief smile, then forced himself to ignore them, staring ahead with all the fierceness he could muster.

"This shotgun is getting heavier, Mr. Bain."

Bamie laughed again.

"Oh yes, Mr. Bain, do take his photograph in all haste. Make certain you capture the essence of his manly viciousness, the knife, the boots, and of course the rugged buckskin suit. Tell me, Teedie, did you also slay the dragon that you're standing on, or is that fake grass merely a rag of carpet?"

He kept his stare straight ahead, both women stifling laughter. He kept his fearsome stare forward, obeying the photographer, hoping all of this would end.

"It's for authenticity, Bamie. It's supposed to look like grass, the plants scattered around like the genuine outdoors. The tapestry behind me doesn't really look like the Badlands, but it will have to do."

They were still laughing, and Bamie said, "Now, be sure to clean up this mess when you're finished. You too, Mr. Bain."

"There, got it, Mr. Roosevelt. All finished. You may, um, lower your weapon. I shall have the photograph for you in a few days, and as many copies as you would like. Just let me know."

The man began breaking down his equipment, and Roosevelt looked at his sister, hands on her hips, more of the smile. He focused more on Edith now, caught himself staring at her face, a spark of loveliness he hadn't really noticed before. Edith returned the gaze, said with a smile, "Really, Teddy. What's this for? Can't you have someone out west make this photograph for you? At least it would appear proper. Or do you not actually wear such an outfit out there, for fear of laughter louder than what you will hear in New York?"

He was stung by her teasing, went finally to the mirror, saw himself through their eyes for the first time.

"I rather like the outfit, though I admit, here in New York, it would draw more derision than admiration. If one of my men could take the photograph out there, it would be far better. Unfortunately, none of them know how to operate a camera."

"How ARE YOU, Teddy? I do not wish to pry."

He watched Edith discreetly, a teacup in her hand, the two of them alone in Bamie's parlor.

"I am acceptable, most of the time."

"In case you were curious, your sister invited me here, possibly to care for you. They are concerned for you. I've been told that you are not yourself." Edith laughed. "After today, seeing you in your western costume, I would argue that."

He tried to feel hurt at her jibe, but he knew she was right.

"It's not really a costume out there."

"Does everyone dress like that, then?"

He laughed now.

"No, not especially. This is more of a hunting outfit. I have spent some time rounding up cattle with my men, very much the student to a number of good teachers. I might be their boss, and they show me deference, but I know very well that I am the greenhorn. Often, it's best to just let them do what they do and stay out of their way. I do admit, I have become a far better horseman than on the foxhunts on Long Island. The challenges and dangers are far greater, and the horses far more savage. It takes a strong hand to break them to where they can be ridden in a useful way. I don't have the knack for that. I try to *gentle* them. Doesn't work as well, from what I've seen." He paused. "I fear I am sounding like a braggart."

Edith smiled again.

"I don't mind a bit, Teddy. All of us have wondered just what you're doing out there. I suppose I have wondered more than most."

He realized she was flirting with him, suddenly felt much younger, as they once were, two close friends sharing childish silliness. But there was nothing childish now, her eyes lighting up every time he spoke. She suddenly looked down, a slight scowl, breaking the spell.

"I fear I am acting inappropriately. I am not a schoolgirl."

He felt something he had not experienced, had not allowed himself to experience in a very long time.

"Neither of us is being inappropriate, dear Edith. These few moments are as happy as any I have experienced since . . ."

He stopped, and she said, "No. It is not necessary for you to relive any part of the past. I suppose that's why I'm here. Perhaps, just perhaps, we are part of the future."

April 4, 1885
Dakota Territory

He was impressed with the work that Sewall and Dow had done, the new house called Elkhorn now complete, outbuildings going up for storage and shelter for the weaker livestock. The house itself stood on stout logs, was single-story, and had a covered porch facing the river. At Roosevelt's specifications, his bedroom adjoined a large central room where he could comfortably read his various new volumes. At night, the larger room would convert to the living area for the men. After what had been a painful lesson to Sewall and Dow, the fireplace in the large room was larger still, an enormous hearth, with andirons Dow had fashioned from errant railroad tracks. If the heat seemed excessive to Roosevelt, the two men from Maine were taking no chances on suffering through another winter shivering under blankets.

He rode out through the muddy ground, dancing the horse carefully through the worst of the soft pools that seemed to be designed to suck the unsuspecting cowboy completely out of sight.

Roosevelt had not yet enjoyed a cold spring here, the late-melting snow making misery of the land that usually was a delight to explore. The misery extended both to the men and the cattle, the constant need to rescue the wayward cows from an infinite number of bottomless bog holes that would otherwise drown them.

He pulled on Manitou's reins, brought him gently to a halt, scanned the horizon, the cottonwood trees along the river showing their first speckles of green. He smiled, listened carefully, sorted through the sounds of so many birds, creatures waking with the warmth as well as the trees that housed them. There were the grouse as well, scattered out through the muddy brush, and on any other day Roosevelt would be the hunter, gathering up what he could for his larder. Now, he was merely Roosevelt the birder, counting to himself the familiar songs, delighted as each new bird presented itself.

He moved closer to the river, avoided more muddy traps, the roar of the high water drowning out any other sound. Medora lay just downstream, but that was not his destination. Across the river, Joe Ferris was waiting for him, Ferris's general store now a source for much of what Roosevelt needed to buy. It was a friendly agreement, no one in the area concerned about Roosevelt's credit. And if Roosevelt or his crew couldn't find time to pick up the merchandise, Joe would happily deliver it to the Maltese Cross.

He reached the usual crossing, a footpath alongside the railroad tracks, did not expect to see what he saw now. The river had swollen to a level that he had only heard about and hadn't quite believed. But the sound and the raw fury was convincing enough. Others were there, most just staring at the torrent burying the footpath, some of the men angry at their helplessness, as though raising one's voice might slow the water. He looked downstream, nothing to see, but like the others he knew the marquis had constructed a dam for the purpose of backing up the winter freeze for the ice he could then harvest. The dam was invisible now, but Roosevelt had crossed it before, knew the location. He nudged the horse that way, saw others watching him, one man following.

"What you aimin' to do? You can't cross the dam, not like this."

Roosevelt looked at the man, knew him, Fisher, one of Morès's men.

"Show me where the dam starts. I'll make it across."

Roosevelt could barely hear the man through the tumbling roar of the river.

"You're crazy, sir. It'll take you and your horse right on downriver. And it's a mile or more to the next crossing."

"I have faith in my horse, sir. Where's the end point?"

"Right here, sir. But it's gotta be under four feet of water."

"Manitou's a good swimmer. We're going across."

He pushed the horse, who obeyed without hesitation, stepping slowly, deliberately onto whatever firm surface was below the surging water. He urged the horse on, still no hesitation, the cold now rolling up Roosevelt's boots, his legs, splashing high around him. The horse stumbled, then caught himself, Roosevelt gripping the reins, the first twist of fear now, and he called out to the horse, "Come on, boy. A few more steps. You can do it. Come on!"

His eyes were locked on the water, and he heard loud voices, glanced up, saw Joe Ferris, others, arms in the air, some waving *no*, all of them calling out to him. He focused again on the horse, felt the steps unsteady, the horse slipping to one side, then back up, slipping again.

"Come on!"

He was fully submerged now, a sharp, cold blast, but the horse found its feet, righted himself, Roosevelt coming up high, clear of the water. He went down again, thick ice crushing into both of them, Roosevelt shoving blocks of ice away from the horse. But the river was shallow here, the horse finding the edge, easing up the far side, clear of the dam, the danger past. Roosevelt heard the cheers, saw Joe Ferris, scratching his bare head, slapping his leg with his hat.

"You are a madman, Mr. Roosevelt. I give credit to your horse. You're just the fool who rode him."

"Mr. Ferris, might I trouble you for a pair of dry socks?"

Ferris leaned low, both hands on his knees, relief and laughter.

143

"I won't even charge you. I gotta say, sir, that was among one of the more reckless things I've seen."

Roosevelt led the horse forward, felt the water sifting down through his soaked clothes, a hard shiver from the cold.

"It might have been reckless, Joe. But it was a lot of fun."

Ferris stared at him now, a silent moment, then said, "One thing I don't understand, sir. How in God's name did you keep your spectacles on?"

CHAPTER 19

April 24, 1885
Dakota Territory

"We're up to thirty-five hundred head, Mr. Roosevelt. That's a pretty stout number for cattlemen in these parts. You certain of the risk?"

Roosevelt rocked slowly on the horse, stared out across the massive spread of livestock.

"Sylvane, there are ranches not that far from here, the south mostly, where they're marketing ten times that number. I've no such ambition. So far, we've made a fair profit, and I'd like to see that continue. You and Bill have done fine work. But tell me honestly. Have my two friends from Maine worked out to your satisfaction?"

Ferris laughed.

"At first, I doubted them both pretty hard. They were pure tenderfeet around the horses. But they came around. I've never seen harder workers, and your Mr. Dow has come to fit right in around the campfires."

Roosevelt was curious.

"What about Mr. Sewall?"

"Well, I wouldn't want to get in a wrestling match with him. He pulls stakes out of the ground with his bare hands. But he's mighty quiet, seems to think more than he talks, which, I suppose, is a good thing."

"It's an excellent thing. He's not a Westerner; he's a lumberman. They both are. I'm not sure how much longer the two of them will keep with us. They're making money on their part of the bargain, so that will help. And I know that both of them have talked about bringing their women out. Dow told me he's going to take a trip back east, finally marrying his fiancée."

Ferris tilted his hat back on his forehead.

"Two more women for the Badlands? Well, I hope that don't drain the work out of either one of them fellows. The women will need caring for. Nobody comes out here and just fits in without some adjusting."

Roosevelt laughed, stared out again at the cattle, the vast chorus of lowing animals. "I wouldn't worry too much about those women. Mr. Sewall's wife, in particular, was raised the same way he was, hard hands and a strong back. And, according to him, she can shoot better than any man out here. I'd believe him."

June 2, 1885

He bent low, his face engulfed by the steam from the stewpot. He inhaled again, then stood, his spectacles coated with the fog.

"By George, Mrs. Sewall, this is some fine stew."

She didn't stop her labor, said, "You haven't tasted it yet, Mr. Roosevelt. But thank you."

There were more smells as well, and he stepped closer to the oven, wanted desperately to look inside.

"Not yet. The bread needs another five minutes. When that's finished, I'll put the cake in."

"Cake?"

She looked at him now.

"You men work hard enough. I'm happy to offer you a little dessert once in a while."

"What kind of cake?"

"Buttermilk and wild plum." He stiffened, and she read him again. "I know, Mr. Roosevelt, you have no taste for buttermilk. Don't worry. You can't taste it in the cake. It just adds moistness, makes it rise more. It's just better to eat. Not sure what kind of cakes these men have tried to make you."

Roosevelt laughed now. "Not once. Never had cake out here. Not even the marquis's chef does cake very often. How'd you learn to do this, madam?"

She shook her head. "In Maine, sir, every respectable woman who hopes to find a husband learns her way around a kitchen. Mr. Roosevelt, I was wondering. With the river out there running cold for a while yet, I assume you could hang some milk jugs in the water. I had to buy this quart of buttermilk from Mr. Ferris, in town. Could you . . . um . . . have someone gather up some fresh milk from your herd?"

He stared at her with an open mouth.

"I can't say we've ever had use for milk."

She faced him now, hands on her hips.

"You're telling me that you have thousands of cattle and don't keep one cow close by for milk?"

He shook his head, felt as though she had opened up an entirely new way of thinking.

"No, Mrs. Sewall, we haven't. But, by Godfrey, we will. I'll have the boys choose a good one, and we'll milk her."

She laughed now.

"Do you know how?"

A noise interrupted them, boot steps on the piazza, and now Sewall and Dow both came in, clouds of mud and dust.

Dow said, "We got a good dinner tonight. I can tell by the steam rising. And we'll do well tomorrow too. Bill took down a deer, got it outside, so we'll have venison for a few days."

Roosevelt said, "That's excellent. Have either one of you ever milked a cow?"

Dow laughed, but Sewall said, "I watched my pap do it. Why?"

Roosevelt didn't answer, saw the light coming on inside each of them.

Dow said, "We got about three hundred milch cows out there, at least. I suppose one of 'em could provide for us. Come on, Bill, let's go find one."

They thundered out, and Roosevelt said, "There you go, madam. You ask, and we'll provide."

She moved to the corner of the large room, retrieved a broom.

147

"Well, then, if I ask you to sweep out their mess, is that *providing*?"

Roosevelt made a short bow, took the broom, began to sweep the dirt the men had tracked onto the plank floor. She watched him for a minute.

"You use that thing like you're from the city. Tell you what, Mr. Roosevelt. I'll do the sweeping, if you make sure those boys take off their boots when they come in the house."

HE LED THE three horses on a long rope, Manitou following the grassy trail. He could see Elkhorn now, Sewall with a hoe in his hand, churning up the rugged ground close beside the house, what had become a potato patch. Sewall saw him now, stepped out that way.

"What you got here, sir? Those look like Indian horses."

Roosevelt stretched his back. "They are. They were stolen from an old Indian down south a ways. I told James that I'd get them back to their owners. The Indians are supposed to be sending someone up here to collect them, maybe the old man himself."

Sewall stared at him. "I don't know that fellow James all that well. How many men in this place would go to all the trouble to get these animals back to some Indians. I'm just wondering."

"James didn't seem to like handing 'em over. But he knew I saw the whole thing unfold, and he didn't like having a witness. What appeared to be the thieves rode off just as I happened by. Whether they expected to be paid by James, I can't say. But it was pretty obvious that James knew he had someone else's horses. I just tried being sociable, asked him where his new mounts came from, since they seemed to be broken and all. He was pretty edgy about it, finally just handed 'em to me, and if that didn't surprise me enough, he then told me about the old Indian. Funny how he knew all about it." He thought a moment. "Since Mr. Stuart cleaned the horse thieves out of most of this territory, I think that anybody so inclined thinks twice before selling off someone else's mount. Horse thieves are a vanishing breed around here, and I guess James didn't want to be the next one to vanish. I think sometimes a man steals something and thinks no one will know, and then his conscience, or his common sense, tells him maybe he's not that smart, and he's about to buy a world of trouble."

"James. Guess he's one of those fellows none of us need to get friendly with."

"Maybe. No matter. We'll hold the horses right here until someone shows up to claim them."

THE INDIAN WAS old, no expression, and Roosevelt stood back, let Sewall hand off the reins. The man looked at Roosevelt, knew clearly who was in command of the homestead, still no expression. The horses were in hand now, and he turned, led them away.

Sewall stepped closer to Roosevelt, said, "Well, that's gratitude. No thank you, no anything. Is that how they act out here? I was wondering if maybe some of what I've been told about those folks is true."

Roosevelt shook his head. "Maybe he doesn't know how to say thank you. But he could have nodded his head, anything. I feel like I've been taken." He paused. "Never really sat down with any of those people. Took it for granted that what most everyone says out here is true, that nine of out ten Indians aren't worth shooting. And the tenth one is questionable. Not sure if that's the right way to look at those people, but it's all I've been taught. How about you?"

Sewall shrugged. "Never gave it much thought. Used to see some of the Penobscot people when I was younger, but I haven't seen any of them for years. Guess they went into Canada or Vermont, or maybe just stayed on reservations. Never really had reason to pay attention. The boys down at the Maltese Cross have just said that you keep a close watch when you're out in the prairie, especially if you're alone. Maybe they're just like us, trying to make something out of this god-forsaken land."

Roosevelt watched the old Indian disappear past a line of buttes.

"They've got it tougher than we do, that's all I know. They're not farmers, don't operate ranches. They hunt until the game runs out, then hunt somewhere else. That doesn't open any doors to prosperity. Doubt any of them are educated, except what they can do to fend for themselves and their families. If they speak English, it's probably from the schools at the army posts. Hard to know how they think about any of this."

"You think they're dangerous, sir?"

"I haven't heard about any real problems. Horse thieving is maybe the worst of it, and . . . well, I guess that can go either way."

Sewall turned, moved toward the house.

"Come on, sir. My wife's plowed up some real fine venison steaks, and she makes a terrific brown gravy." He smiled. "She says the milk helps a lot. Forget about that Indian. It looks like they ain't worth worrying about."

THEY HAD STILL not perfected the art of cow milking, Dow holding the cow ungraciously by the neck, while Sewall struggled with the udder. Roosevelt fought the urge to laugh, stayed back, no room yet for a third pair of hands. The cow kicked mightily, Sewall wrapping an arm around the cow's back legs, curse words flying. Roosevelt saw an opening where help might be needed, but he stopped, his attention caught by a horseman on the horizon. It was an Indian.

"Hold off there. We have a visitor."

They backed away from the cow, all three motionless, curious, a hint of caution they were used to. The old man approached slowly, and Roosevelt recognized the horse from a few days before.

Beside him, Sewall said, "It's the Indian fellow, sure enough."

"You're right. Let's see what he wants."

Roosevelt waited for the old man to draw closer, saw a long thin bundle in the man's hand. The old man stopped, reached out, and Roosevelt stepped forward, obliged by taking the bundle. The old man pulled the horse away, turned, and just as quickly as he came, he rode off.

Roosevelt looked at the bundle, tied with a crude strip of buckskin. He knelt down, unrolled it on the hard ground, the other two men coming close. The bundle was a hide, tanned and supple, a painting spread across one side.

Dow said, "What is it? Looks like a bunch of Indians, and men in blue."

Roosevelt stood, stared down at the extraordinary piece of work.

"That's exactly what it is. It's the battle of the Little Big Horn."

"Is that some kind of nasty message?"

He looked at Sewall. "I'm not sure. But certainly this is a symbol of a great victory for them. Not much has gone their way since. But I'll tell you both"—he bent closer, examined the colors, the details—"this is a piece of art. And that's *thank you* enough for me."

CHAPTER 20

June 10, 1885
Dakota Territory

Earlier that spring, Roosevelt had been a welcome part of the great roundup, an annual affair where the cattle from every ranch in the area were gathered up from wherever they had endured the winter months and sorted by their brands. This year, as many as sixty men had taken part from a dozen ranches, bringing in cattle from hundreds of square miles of range. There were casualties, always, those cattle who wandered so far afield that they might never be found, others too weak to withstand the winter, their remains discovered in ravines or on the open plain.

Throughout the roundup, Roosevelt had been the greenhorn, but there was no embarrassment and no shame in that. Even if he could match up to many of them with his skill on horseback, he simply wasn't as seasoned as the other men, including his own. Yet to those men, he was always the *boss,* but he would never be satisfied merely to be a spectator. He had learned to pitch in at every opportunity, rescuing errant cows from bog holes, keeping them clear of the river, which was still carrying enough water to drown the weaker animals. Other cattle, some solitary, some in small groups, tended to wander farther from the main herd, the men working their horses to head them off, driving them forcefully back to the herd.

As exhausting as the roundup could be, Roosevelt welcomed the latest task as much more reasonable: to drive the thousand head he had most recently purchased, the cattle unloaded from railcars to the stockyard at Medora. Now, Roosevelt's latest herd would be pushed northward, toward Elkhorn, to join Roosevelt's existing herd in the ranges around his homestead.

This day had been like the one before, and the one before that, though this drive was on a far smaller scale than that of early spring. This time, there were no other ranchmen involved, Roosevelt working only with his own men, Dow, Ferris, Merrifield, Sewall, and Myers.

At night, the men slept the sleep of angels, but it was brief, cut short at three in the morning, the men roused up quickly to more bacon, more deadly coffee, then back in the saddle to do it all again. Roosevelt rose with the rest of them, baffling anyone near him with his astounding show of energy, mounting the horse with the kind of enthusiasm the Dakota men had lost years before. But his was contagious, his men drawing energy from him, the whoops and hollers punctuating the steady roar of so many cattle on the hoof.

It had been yet another eighteen-hour day, the men starting early, their breakfast a slopped-together mix of bacon and cornbread. Now, the dinner wasn't much more appealing, beans and more dry cornbread, coffee that seemed wrung through sagebrush. But as happened every evening on the roundup, by the time the men could climb down from their horses, it was nearly full dark, and any kind of meal would seem like the finest steak in Chicago.

He moved toward the fire, aching in every joint, would never admit it, sat on one wheel of the buckboard, a mistake, punishing the same muscles awakened by a long day on the horse. He saw Merrifield, pouring a thick ooze from the coffeepot, said, "Hey, Bill. Good day's work, certainly, wouldn't you say?"

Merrifield smiled, shook his head. "Yes, sir. Good day. Barring any trouble, we should get them put up around Elkhorn by tomorrow night."

"Where are we now? I don't exactly recognize the place. I know that most often we drive these fellows right up the riverbed."

Merrifield shook his head. "Not this time, sir. There've been just enough flash storms that the river's too dangerous. We could lose a mess of the weaker cows. Best stay inland."

"Of course. I understand."

"Excuse me for saying so, sir, but you're the trail boss of this outfit right now. It's proper for you to make the decisions about such things."

Roosevelt was annoyed with himself now. "I know. My apologies, Bill. I'll do better. I suppose we should bed down. What time should we rise?"

Merrifield dropped his head, laughed. "That's your decision, sir. But if I had my way, I'd say we rouse up at three, just like every day so far."

Roosevelt finished off the last of the beans. "Yes, of course. I shall sound an alarm at three."

Sewall was there now, said, "Um, sir, I wouldn't sound no alarm around the herd. We're riding patrol around them right now, Ferris and Myers, and they mentioned that the herd is mighty jumpy. It must be the weather."

Roosevelt felt a stab of fear. "What weather?"

"Well, sir, there are storms out to the west. There, you can see the flashes on the horizon. Anything gets closer, it could cause a . . . *stampede*." He had whispered the word.

Merrifield looked at Sewall, said, "You don't need to whisper it. The cows know what a stampede is. Point is, Mr. Roosevelt, to prevent one, we need to keep moving, not leave them critters to their own thoughts. Ride around 'em, singing, soft words, keep 'em calm."

Roosevelt waited for the joke, could see that Merrifield was serious. "What do we sing?"

"Nonsense, anything comes to mind. Cattle don't know much about music. It's just the sounds. Take their minds off the weather, any sharp noises, all like that."

Roosevelt looked again toward the west, the unmistakable line of thunderstorms clearly visible. He knew enough of the weather here to know just how rapidly squall lines can move.

"All of us, gentlemen. Get everybody in the saddle. There's no time for sleeping. If that line of storms gets much closer, we'll start hearing the thunder."

Both men rose, coffee poured away, horses mounted, hushed orders, no one complaining. Roosevelt was impressed, thought, they've done this before. Guess it's better to prevent a stampede than to have to stop one. He climbed up on his mount, not the comfortable Manitou, but a horse much more accustomed to driving cattle. He rode slowly, deliberately through the dark, guided the horse through ragged ground, the horse returning the favor. He felt the night air, soft, dry, nothing like the night before, snow flurries that dropped the temperatures to freezing, one more oddity of the Badlands.

He had been through a stampede once before, several dozen experienced cowhands fighting through the night to calm and gather the herd. Then, it had been lightning, a memory he never could escape, a single crash of thunder that ignited the thousands of cattle as one force. Now, it could be anything, the storms still distant, the changes in temperature, the thirst of the animals, necessarily kept far from the danger of the river. He felt his gut churn, heard hoofbeats out in all directions, the men doing what they could, and this time they were not sixty, but six.

And then the cattle rose up and began to move, one great dormant force suddenly coming to life, all shuffling in a single direction, the lead animals picking up speed, the great mass behind them following. Roosevelt jabbed the horse with his spurs unnecessarily, the horse knowing its own job: to keep up with the movement of the herd, to pull out in front, as close as necessary. Roosevelt gripped the reins, held tight, the darkness terrifying, no hope of testing the uneven ground, small gullies and rocks, testing his faith in the horse's talent for self-preservation. He passed by small trees now, couldn't see them until they were nearly past, each one deadly to both the horse and its rider.

The sounds from the other men were wiped out now, the hoofbeats and lowing of the panicking cows the only sound he could hear. He pushed the horse harder, gripped with his legs, steadying himself, coaxing the horse to do the right thing. His eyes adjusted slightly, a sea of cattle moving as one wave, down and then up, the undulating ground, a sharp cry, a cow stumbling into a ravine, more following it down. The horse carried him down the soft sides of the depression, and Roosevelt called out in a sharp voice, could see the shuffling movement of the cattle, and he moved the horse closer, used his whip, driving the cattle up and out of the ravine, sending them back to the rest of the herd. He spurred the horse up to level ground now, saw a man, hat waving, driving cattle back to where they had to be. The others had ridden hard to the front of the stampede, trying to slow the herd by coaxing and calming the lead animals. Roosevelt ached to see more clearly, focused on mass shapes, guided the horse that way, slowing another small part of the herd. The horse suddenly gave way beneath him, stumbling, Roosevelt going down to one side, impact on the rocky ground, hard on his shoulder, rolling over in thick wet dirt. He struggled to stand, felt panic that he was left behind. But he saw the horse now, upright, seeming to wait for him, head bobbing, impatient. Roosevelt flexed the pain in his shoulder, climbed up, the horse jerking slightly, Roosevelt's only thoughts, I'm alive, and he wants to go.

The loudest sounds now were the horse's hoofbeats and his own breathing, and he nudged another cluster of cows back along a gully, pushing them into the herd. He saw the other cattle now, the main body, circling, slowing, and he slowed his own horse, struggled to hear, the lowing of the herd now blending together into a single call, cows in front of him settling down, spent. And now he heard a new sound, looked that way, Merrifield. He was singing.

Roosevelt sat in the saddle, exhausted, breathing heavily, aches in every joint, his clothes soaked through. He leaned low, patted the horse's neck, kind words, then thought, I've forgotten your name. But thank you, sir, for the job you did. And for not killing me.

As JUNE PASSED, the already-hot summer gave birth to strange predictions that flowed through the saloons and around the campfires. The old hands began to talk of desolation, saying that the early heat offered dangerous signs of drought, that the grass across the prairie, so essential for feeding the range cattle, might be so dry that the herds would grow thin and weak. Even worse, Roosevelt began to hear talk in Medora that the danger might extend to the homesteads. Dry grass could mean fire, and once a prairie fire started, only rain could stop it.

He listened to the dark tales, the dire predictions, would not accept that this kind of tragedy could be as severe as the old voices said. Besides his curiosity about how anyone predicted these things, he readily accepted that there was absolutely nothing he could do about it. Of more importance to him, a wire had come from a building contractor, a man named Wood, who had been supervising construction of Roosevelt's new house at Oyster Bay. It was to be a homestead of a very different kind from the one he enjoyed in the Dakotas, a grand house that would have satisfied Alice, who no doubt would have embraced every part of it. For a while, Roosevelt had thought of stopping it altogether, settling elsewhere, one more step in erasing that tragedy from his mind. But his own conscience prevailed, his love for the property, for the scenic overlook toward Long Island Sound, the home that would be his, built for his taste, his hunting trophies, the new life he was desperate to begin.

In late June, with the contractor Wood's telegram in hand, Roosevelt boarded the train once more and returned to New York.

CHAPTER 21

June 29, 1885
Oyster Bay, New York

He stood on an adjoining hill, hands on his hips, stared out with more pride than he had felt for anything he had done.

"By Godfrey, it's beautiful. Mr. Wood, you are to be commended."

The contractor stood slightly behind him, allowing Roosevelt the full view of the estate.

"Thank you, sir. It was a pleasure putting her up. I think you'll be satisfied with her. We done give her all what you wanted, changed them things you wanted changed. You ought to go inside her, sir. We did some good work in there."

It didn't escape him that the man who did the work called the house by the feminine. I suppose I would too, he thought. You learn to love that which you care for so intimately, even if it's a house.

He turned, could see the older estate beyond the next hilltop, the house called Tranquility, where he had spent so much time so many years ago, a home that held many memories. The house was occupied by others now, tenants, who most likely had little appreciation for all that the place had meant to a family of four children, who spent many hours in the salt water, and many more nestled by their fireplace with the parents who cared deeply for them. But there were memories here as well, long walks along the water, boat rides during which he had shown Alice the various nooks and harbors along the shoreline. Those happy times had been driven away by the painful memories, digging at him even now. He had originally called this place Leeholm, a play on Alice's name, a home he had begun to build for her, for their life together. He fought with himself to ignore all of that, forced himself to see the wonderful view from the crown of the hilltop, where the house perched high above the water, a grassy plain spread out from the wide veranda, where Alice would have made her perch, reading, napping, or just sharing with him the sheer beauty of the estate. At least, he thought, it's finally finished, fully completed. He used his critical eye now, the house bereft of landscaping, the new colors yet to fade into harmony. In time, he thought. Bamie will help with the bushes and flowers and such. She has a talent for it. I certainly do not. He thought of the contractor standing behind him, his encouragement to see the interior. But he hesitated to move closer. It would take time to push through those memories of her, the soft colors in the bedrooms— those things he would say to no one, not even his sisters.

And behind him, coming up closer, a woman's voice.

"It is beautiful, Teddy."

He welcomed her kindness, knew she had stayed back, allowing him a few moments of solitude, but he felt her move closer now, caught a hint of her perfume, her arm now sliding in beside his. The contractor moved away, as if on cue, allowing Roosevelt the private moment, his thoughts no longer solitary.

"Thank you, Edith. I have been thinking a great deal about this. I do not believe it is appropriate to retain the old name I have chosen for the estate. Much has changed in my life, just as much has changed right here. There is an Indian word, meaning 'chief.' I should like to use that. I should like to call this place Sagamore."

His time in New York had been spent mostly with Edith, but there was another change for him as well. As a child, the old estate at Oyster Bay had been the scene of laughing children, outrageous play, wrestling with his brother, bird hunting, tending rowboats with his sisters and so many others, including a very young Edith Carow. It was the one place where Roosevelt enjoyed the muscle-building routines his father had so insisted upon, rowing the small boats all up and down the rugged coastlines, delighting those passengers he might have brought along. But now there was a childish giggle of a different kind, a different voice. For the first time, he began to accept his own fatherhood, to accept that young Alice was not merely the namesake of her mother but his daughter as well. To the delight of his sister Bamie, Roosevelt began to play with the toddler, the two of them scurrying through the rooms of the house to peals of laughter that even his more-staid servants found entertaining.

He sat heavily in his office chair, exhausted, the little girl wrapped around one of his ankles. He straightened the leg, picking her off the floor, more laughter, his foot bouncing slightly, as much as her weight would allow. Bamie was there now, said, "Well, I see I have another child to care for. Little Alice and Teedie. A handful, to say the least."

"I FEAR SHE has worn me completely out. It's your turn," Roosevelt said to Bamie.

"Oh, no, sorry. Your sister-in-law Anna has *deposited* . . . no, that's crude. She has *requested* that I care for their infant, Eleanor, for a couple of days. Anna is seeing to some problem with our brother."

"What kind of problem? What has Elliott done now?"

Bamie shook her head. "She chose not to say, and I chose not to inquire."

Roosevelt shook his head. "Is the infant old enough to play with this little creature stuck to my leg?"

Bamie laughed, looked at Alice, still clinging tightly. "No, of course not. Eleanor's less than a year old. For all of Alice's energy, or yours, playtime might be dangerous for an infant."

"Well, then, she's yours to care for. I'll tend to this one right here, if she'll allow me time to take a breath." He bounced Alice a few more times, then said, "Edith hasn't arrived, has she?"

Bamie put her hands on her hips. "Don't you think someone here would inform you?"

There was more, Roosevelt knowing his sister too well. "What is it? You disapprove of Miss Carow?"

"No. I rather like her, always have, and I think she would fit this family very well. She has been, after all, practically a part of this family since we were all children. Especially you. You're a child still. So, just how seriously are you courting her? Have you something more substantial in mind?"

He had not yet revealed his growing feelings for Edith to either of his sisters, suspected there would be disapproval. He could see now that he was right.

"We are close. We enjoy each other's company. I cannot say more."

"All right, then I will. Should you become engaged to her, it will cause something of a scandal. It is less than two years since Alice's death, and for you to reattach yourself to another woman so quickly will be seen as an impropriety. Teedie, it just isn't appropriate. It could cost you considerable public stature."

He peeled the toddler from his leg, held her up in his lap.

"Bamie, I appreciate your concerns. But right now I have no public stature. If I choose to attach myself to Edith, it will happen on our terms and no one else's. If I choose to announce our engagement, it will be because we are serious about becoming man and wife. We are in no rush, I assure you."

Bamie seemed relieved. "Good. I just hope you consider what this might do to Edith's reputation, if not your own. You are widowed less than two years. It just isn't done."

He was annoyed now. "Not done by whom? Why?"

Bamie shook her head, smiled at him. "If the entire world could be shifted on its axis to please you, I have no doubt you could find a way to make it happen. But if you and Edith become engaged so quickly after . . . well, *after* what has happened, it will make her seem to be an opportunist, with no respect for . . . your place in society."

He was even more annoyed now, knew that Bamie was right, that polite society had infuriating rules about this sort of thing.

"My dear sweet sister, I am far less concerned with the rules of propriety than I am about how I feel about her. She and I have been friends since we were children. No one can dispute that, and it certainly doesn't make her an opportunist. It is my intention, eventually, to ask her to marry me, to offer her an engagement, with no fear of *opportunism*."

Bamie seemed resigned, nodded slowly. He stood, held the toddler in his arms, the child's energy fading as well as his own. He moved toward the window facing the water, his eyes cast outward, saw distant sails, small boats caught by the soft breeze on Long Island Sound. She would have so loved this place, he thought. But it is time to move past.

He turned to his sister again, said, "I will leave for my ranch the end of August. I will return later this fall, and if she will have me, I will continue my courtship of Edith. Bamie, if our relationship becomes serious, the *opportunist* will be me. I would seek the opportunity to enjoy my life moving forward. I will not suffer the past." He paused, didn't enjoy issuing ultimatums or making these kinds of pronouncements to his own family. He studied her face, saw the love he had always seen, mixed with a hint of disappointment. "My sister, I cannot predict what will occur beyond that. But what we do is our affair. It must be this way or not at all. There is no more to discuss."

There was a soft knock, and Roosevelt saw the housekeeper, who said, "Pardon me, sir. Miss Carow has arrived."

Bamie raised her hands toward him, seemed to surrender the point.

"Go to your love, Teedie. Here, I'll take Alice. She can meet her little cousin. I'll occupy her until you regain enough strength to handle her. Though I suspect you might require strength aplenty for Miss Carow."

IN LATE AUGUST, Roosevelt returned again to the Dakotas. To his dismay, the dire predictions from so many of the crusty old ranchmen seemed to be coming true. The prairie had singed under rainless skies, fires had broken out to the west, far out into what was known to be Indian territory, driving the Indians to safer land even farther away, though their livestock could rarely be moved in time.

Roosevelt had been reassured that, despite the drought, his herd was strong, most of the cattle healthy enough to endure until winter, assuming the winter brought relief in the form of moderate snowfalls. Once again, Roosevelt recognized the helplessness of his being there, that nothing he could bring, no instruction he could give, would change the conditions that his men, and now their wives, had to cope with. As if there weren't enough to concern him, the boys from Maine smilingly announced to him that their women were pregnant. By spring, the population at Elkhorn would increase by two.

After several more weeks in the Dakotas, Roosevelt returned home again to spend the winter season with the family, including of course toddler Alice. As he and Edith continued their subtle relationship, he knew that, in time, the public, or whoever else cared to make his life their business, would come to know about their mutual feelings, and would hold opinions about whether those feelings were appropriate. Despite his ongoing political ambitions and what the cost might be for any sort of personal scandal, Roosevelt was becoming completely over-whelmed by Edith Carow. He pursued Edith with the same vigor and passion it had taken him to reach through to Alice, the same vigor and passion that seemed to drive everything he did.

CHAPTER 22

March 23, 1886
Dakota Territory

He had written a handful of pages, slid the papers up onto a shelf in one corner of his bedroom. By George, he thought, another good day.

The writing had been episodic: some days, no words came; others, a steady flood. He knew he was no great scribe, found writing to be tedious and difficult. And yet the more he took time to hunker down, the words somehow flowed out in a river that filled pages on end, piecing together the next wave of chapters for his new book. Besides the book on the naval ships of 1812, which had become surprisingly successful, he had continued to write on any subject that seemed to please him. All he required was paper.

He stepped outside to the veranda, felt the chill of early spring, could hear the roar of the river. He paced now, moved around one side of the house, saw the pregnant women working a small garden, tilling the soil with more energy than he thought wise. They were scheduled to give birth in midsummer, a frankness from both Dow and Sewall that Roosevelt found refreshing. In New York, it was unusual, at best, for any woman to discuss her own pregnancy, but, here, these two women had accepted their condition with smiles and cupped hands on their bellies as they continued the work of preparing whatever the men required of them. What will that be like? he thought. Crying infants. I never know what that means, whether they're just hungry or in some kind of agony. No matter. If the men are happy, and the women continue making a delightful home here, I am not one to complain.

He saw the figures coming past the rough hills to the east, beyond the river, called out to the women, "They're back. Seems they're empty-handed. That's strange."

Sewall and Dow rode closer, a quick wave toward Roosevelt, a more energetic wave toward their wives. They dismounted, tied the horses up to the pony rope, the usual place, slid a hefty flat-bottomed boat toward the water's edge. Both men climbed aboard, paddled the short distance, the only effective way anyone could deal with the flow of the river until the water went down later in the spring. They tied up the boat on the near side now, moved toward Roosevelt with purpose.

Dow seemed eager to tell the story, said, "Dang cougars, a pair of 'em, pretty certain. We had four deer, strung up nice to keep coyotes and other varmints off 'em until we were wrapped up to go. Hunted a bit this morning, then went to haul 'em down, and they had been stripped near clean, bones busted up. Cost us the whole hunt."

Roosevelt said, "This is a problem. If those cougars are staying around this country, they'll ruin every hunt. Deer won't stay put, that's for sure."

Sewall said, "You're right on that, sir. We've got to track 'em, take care of the situation. There's some snow in the hills, which will help us follow 'em."

Roosevelt was intrigued by the idea, looked at Sewall. "You ever done that kind of hunt before?"

"Back in Maine, more than once. Damn cats came down from the hills in wintertime, would play havoc with the farms, livestock, even house pets. We can't let those things run free around here. Might even cause a stampede."

Roosevelt said, "Maybe I should talk to some of the other ranchers, let them know. Should also talk to Mr. Ferris and Mr. Merrifield. Maybe they'll help us out, send a couple of fellows up this way from the Maltese Cross."

Sewall said, "Nah. Don't need any help, sir. Just need to get out there on the trail as quick as we can. Give me a fresh canteen of water, and I'm ready to ride right now."

The women had come close, heard Sewall's request, and filled canteens and passed them out to all three. Roosevelt hurried inside, retrieved his rifle, then a quick trot toward the boat as the other two checked their rifles and followed him. They slid the boat quickly into the current, paddled furiously, and, once across, Roosevelt climbed out, moved toward Manitou. The horse responded to the obvious urgency of its rider, something it was certainly used to. He moved the horse toward the others.

Sewall said, "Just one thing, sir. You see one of those cats, take your time, get a good shot. It ain't likely a good idea to wound one of those things."

THE HUNT HAD been fruitless, darkness settling over the hills before any real tracking could be accomplished. The best plan now was to wait until morning, start with a fresh day's light. Even better, as the night settled over Roosevelt's ranch, a light coating of snow settled in as well, an inch or more, which no big cat could avoid.

HE ATE HIS breakfast with the usual vigor, and Dow did the same, silent, his mind set on the day's hunt.

Roosevelt said to no one in particular, "They call them mountain lions too, you know. I suppose it depends on where you're from. Same beast, same problems." He focused on the women now. "Ladies, these biscuits are as perfect as any can be. I've learned if you slide a piece of the venison inside and add a touch of grease . . . well, it's better than anything they're serving on Fifth Avenue, I'll tell you that." He stuffed his mouth, struggled for a long moment to swallow, then said, "Any more biscuits?"

Mrs. Sewall shook her head, smiled, then said, "I was saving these last two for my husband. But I'm certain he wouldn't mind."

Roosevelt laughed, a spray of crumbs on the plate in his hands.

"I'm certain he would, madam. No, I'll never steal another man's breakfast. He'll be back soon, pretty certain. Once we secure a couple more hands to assist us and load up the boat, we'll head downstream. We can cover a great deal more ground that way. Those cougars won't get away from us today, right, Wil?"

Dow glanced up from his plate.

"Right, sir. We'll get 'em."

The boot steps came across the piazza, Sewall at the door now, a quick glance at his wife's bountiful feast.

"Might I have some of that, missy? Haven't had so much as a cup of coffee."

He was obliged by both women, coffee and biscuits, thin slices of venison steak. Roosevelt studied him, waited for the word of approval, ran out of patience.

"We set? Ready to go? Boat all loaded up? Mr. Tompkins going with us, then? We could use the extra pair of eyes, I'm assuming. I can hardly wait to put one of those beasts in my sights. A cougar hide is a fine trophy, for certain."

Sewall sat across the rectangular table, jammed a biscuit in his mouth, shook his head.

Roosevelt was confused.

"What is it? By George, are we hunting or not?"

Sewall swallowed, cleared his palate, pulled a small piece of rope from his pocket.

"We're not going anywhere on that river. Somebody stole the boat."

Roosevelt stood, bumping the table. "Stole the boat? By George, let's find the thieves. They could not have gotten far." His anger was growing now. "What good is a boat anyway? It's not worth selling, and once the river falls, it sits on the shore for ten months. *Who in blazes would steal a boat?*"

He was shouting now, and Sewall held up a hand, pointed to Roosevelt's chair. It was a request that Roosevelt had seen before. He sat down.

Sewall said, "There's only one other scow on the river anywhere near here, and it's a pile of useless leaking timbers. Those who own her need a better boat. Find them, find your boat."

Roosevelt absorbed Sewall's advice, said, "Boat thieves. That has to be the most idiotic enterprise I've ever heard in this territory. I'm not aware of any body of water around here where a boat is required. We're not in Boston, by Godfrey. When do we start? We should take the horses and follow the river that way. We'll surely come across them."

"I wouldn't get all upset about it, sir. It's just a boat. Can't be worth more than ten or twenty dollars."

"Hardly the point, Mr. Sewall. These are thieves. If they were stealing horses, Mr. Stuart and his vigilantes would be stringing them up. I feel inclined to do the same. I have no tolerance for lawbreakers. And I understand the minds of men, gentlemen. You let a man steal from you, it just invites more of the same. I'll not have it." He paused, nodded. "Yes . . . it just occurred to me that there are three hard characters with a homestead downriver, bad reputations all, led by a fellow named Finnegan. If it's not him, then I'll apologize to him. But first . . . by George, gentlemen, let's go find Mr. Finnegan."

"Sir, I would suggest, rather than wear out the horses in the mud and snow along the river, that we build us another boat. Wil and I can do it in three days. If it's Finnegan, he won't be leaving the country in our old scow anytime soon. We'll catch him quick enough."

March 30, 1886

With Sewall steering with a long pole and Dow in the front with a pole of his own, Roosevelt had very little to do but read the books he had brought along. For three more days, the current carried them downriver, Sewall and Dow cursing the brutally cold winds, which seemed always in their faces, while Roosevelt hunkered down in the center of the boat under blankets and a heavy coat. With no other responsibility until something changed the routine, he passed the time by reading Tolstoy.

The winds weren't all that was brutal for the three men. Though the skies had cleared, the temperatures had offered no respite, at night dropping to zero or below. As their food supplies ran low, the three men relied on game, but that too was scarce, until the prairie provided the enormous gift of a pair of deer.

"HOW'S THE BOOK?"

Roosevelt looked up, Dow standing over him, ice on the man's hair.

"Book's fine. I'll write a review one day. It has problems. I can't really say it's a good book, though Tolstoy writes a lot better than I do."

He saw Dow pull his shoulders up, a futile barrier against the wind.

"That's nice, Mr. Roosevelt. I best get back up front. The wind's calmed a bit right now. Nice change. But lots of ice."

"There!"

Dow looked toward the voice, Sewall in the stern of the boat. Roosevelt turned toward him, saw the long pole motionless, one hand rising slowly to a point. Sewall said, "There it is, sir. There's your boat."

Roosevelt scrambled up, saw what Sewall saw, his boat tied up against the right bank of the river. He had a sudden burst of indecision. What do we do now? Sewall seemed to read him, said in a hard whisper, "Wil, take your shotgun. Sir, your rifle. I'll tie up the boat, be right behind you."

Roosevelt checked his rifle, jumped from the boat, crept low to a line of brush, Dow quickly following. Beside him, crouched low, Dow seemed to pulse, the shotgun at his waist, taking aim at a target not yet there. Roosevelt stared through the brush, aching to see anyone at all, felt a jolt inside, ice in his chest. On the ground a few yards in front of him were the heels of a pair of boots. He raised the rifle, stood slowly. Roosevelt stepped through the brush, eyes glancing all through the area, an obvious camp, a spent fire and a scattering of rolled blankets, the carcass of a deer nearly stripped bare, hanging from a scraggly tree.

He saw more of the man now, old, sitting against a small tree. His head was low, the man obviously asleep, or dead drunk, an empty bottle of some horrifying potion beside him. The words skipped through Roosevelt's brain, the only liquor he knew anything about here. Forty Mile red-eye. He took one more step toward the man, Sewall now joining Dow, spreading out to both sides. He looked at Sewall, saw a sharp nod, and Roosevelt stepped forward again, a sharp kick on the man's bootheel.

"Put your hands up!"

The old man sprang awake, hands high above his head.

"Don' shoot me. I got nothin' to give ya."

Roosevelt kept the rifle aimed at the man's chest, tried to ease the shaking in his hands, the ice in his chest as severe as the air around him. Dow lunged forward, sweeping the man's gun away, retrieving the man's pistol and a pair of large bowie knives.

Roosevelt still scanned the area, a fading campfire, no horses, short grass perfect for a camp, surrounded against the prairie by thick sagebrush.

"Where's your friends? Finnegan, right?"

"Finnegan's out huntin'. Him and the half-breed, Bernstead, they be out huntin'. Ain't got no meat."

Roosevelt heard the sharp edge of a German accent, said, "What's your name?"

"Wharfenberger. I tend the fire. Oh, it done gone out. I better get it built up again."

Sewall eased closer, still probed the sage with a sharp eye.

"He's a half-wit. His only job is to keep the fire going. Done a lousy job so far. That right, old fellow? You're supposed to keep the fire hot so your friends will see the smoke."

The old man seemed eager to please now, nodded his head.

"Ya. That's what I do."

Roosevelt glanced aloft, the skies starting to darken, said, "Well, friend, do it right now. Your friends need to come home before dark."

The old man crawled to the fire, a pile of small timbers to one side. He stoked the fire with his own breath, Roosevelt glancing at the empty bottle, wondering if that was a good idea. But smoke rose quickly, the wind more calm, a black column drifting up over toward the river, easily visible out in the prairie.

Sewall said, "No offense, Mr. Roosevelt, but we got the sharper eyes in case we need a good aim. You shoot at a man, it ain't like stalking a deer. Wil and I will spread out to both sides of you, and you keep look-out in the center. I'm betting we'll hear those varmints before we see 'em. They got no reason to keep quiet."

Roosevelt kept his eyes on the old man.

"What about him?"

Sewall moved close to the old man, poked the barrel of his shotgun under the man's chin. "You'll be quiet now, won't you?"

Dow seemed to flinch, came forward.

"Uh, Bill, careful with that double-barrel. The right-hand barrel's mighty touchy. It goes off on its own sometimes."

Sewall kept the barrel under the old man's chin.

"Yeah, I recall that. Well, I'll try to be careful. You too, right, old fellow?"

"Yes, sir. I'm quiet, for certain."

Sewall backed away, turned toward Roosevelt, a hint of a smile. Roosevelt followed him out to the edge of the sagebrush, a glimpse back at the old man, who stayed low beside the fire, nowhere else to go. Sewall moved close to Roosevelt, said in a low voice, "They draw close enough for shotguns, you stand up, call out 'hands up.' Wil and I will have the shotguns on them. They try to run, or shoot, we'll have 'em in a pretty bad fix."

Roosevelt felt a rush of excitement, mixed with a blanket of dread, thought, We're planning on killing men who might try to kill us. I guess it has to be. I'd rather they just give up.

The time passed slowly, the agony of straining to hear any sound, the crack of the sagebrush usually some sort of bird. He kept his gaze to the sky, darker still, wondered if they would travel in the dark. That would be insane, he thought. You'll die trying to find your way in the cold black night.

He heard them now, his heart jumping in his chest. There was low talk, meaningless chatter, no alarm in the voices. The sagebrush cracked more loudly, a pair of men pushing their way toward their campfire. He could see them clearly now, moving in a tight line straight toward him. He stared at their rifles, both men carrying them in a relaxed hold. He recognized Finnegan by description, a redhead, scraggly red beard, a pair of pistols at his belt. Aim at him, he thought.

He glanced toward Sewall, saw the shotgun at his shoulder, and the men were close now, thirty yards, less . . .

He jumped up, the rifle poised.

"Hands up!"

The other man obeyed immediately, his rifle tumbling to the brush at his feet. But Finnegan seemed to wait, glanced at the other two men, as though measuring, appraising his chances. Roosevelt felt the fear, that he might kill this man, pushed forward through the brush, his rifle trained on the man's heart.

"Put up your hands, thief!"

Finnegan smiled, shook his head, tossed his rifle out in front of him.

"What you want with us? We ain't done nothing. You robbin' us?"

The other two stepped forward out of the brush, shotguns pointed. Sewall said, "You build that boat, then? Or maybe steal it upriver?"

Finnegan smiled now, hands on his hips, the silent message. *I'm caught.*

Roosevelt said, "We're not here to shoot you. If you try to get away, we will. Let's go, to your camp."

The dark settled low, Roosevelt and his men struggling to stoke the campfire, keeping it flaming throughout the night. Roosevelt knew it was inhumane to bind up the men, either hands or feet, that being immobile on a freezing night could cause frostbite, or in the worst case, might kill them. The idea came to Roosevelt himself, that no man would run very far through this kind of territory if his feet were bare. To the amusement of Dow and Sewall, and the relative disgust of Finnegan and his men, Roosevelt ordered them to surrender their boots. They could keep warm enough, though each would have to rely on the warmth of the other two. Roosevelt provided them with a single buffalo blanket.

April 2, 1886

"What are you thinking, sir?"

Sewall's words came without a whisper, some of that for the benefit of the thieves, who seemed keenly interested in the answer to the question. Roosevelt cradled his rifle in his arms, said, "We're taking them to jail."

"It'd be a whole lot simpler to just hang 'em out here. Shooting 'em would be easier still."

Roosevelt lowered his voice now.

"That talk isn't necessary, Bill. I'll not tolerate lawlessness from us, any more than I'd tolerate it from these three. The nearest jail is at Dickinson, likely about due south of here, on the railroad line. We'll load up as much of their provisions as they've got and take a boat ride until we find a ranch, maybe some horses we can borrow."

Sewall shook his head.

"Ice, sir. Plenty of it. It could take us days to get anywhere. Not sure how much food we'll have, and from what I can see, there ain't game to speak of in this part of the territory."

"We'll do the best we can. Give them their boots."

Dow moved close to Roosevelt, his shotgun aimed at the three men, sitting now close to the dying fire, spoke in a whisper.

"They ain't likely to run off. More likely to kill us if they get the chance."

There was nothing encouraging about Dow's observation, a thought Roosevelt had been carrying himself.

"Let's just stay awake."

THE ICE WAS even worse than Sewall had predicted, massive floes that stopped the movement of the boat completely. They worked as best they could, poling the ice to one side or the other, tedious, back-straining work. But the boat was making progress, if only a few feet at a time, until the ice became a solid wall, blocking the river entirely. There would be nothing to do until the current would loosen the floes, the boat able to move once more, only to be halted again a mile downriver.

April 6, 1886

There was no need for secrets, the situation as dangerous for all six as it was for Roosevelt.

He watched Sewall push through the icy bank, now at the river's edge, and Roosevelt called out, "Anything?"

Sewall seemed disgusted, stepped onto the boat.

"Not so much as a prairie chicken. Coulda shot a magpie. That was as close to big game as I saw. No sign, no tracks. If there were ever deer in these parts, they're long gone."

Finnigan spoke now, the menace in his voice replaced by obvious fear.

"If'n we can't eat, what you gonna do with us?"

Roosevelt understood the man's concern. They had barely a day's rations for three men, which meant that six were a severe handicap. Roosevelt tried to ignore the man, said to Sewall, "We can't shoot them, and we can't feed them. It seems we'll have to let them go."

Sewall pounced on his words. "No, sir. Not after what we been through catching up to 'em. We still have some rations. The flour will last another day or two. We'll keep finding a way, maybe locate a ranch hereabouts, and still might find some game. We turn 'em loose out here, they're just as likely to die anyway."

Roosevelt thought a moment, as much for theatrics as for pondering Sewall's words. "All right, we'll hold on to them." He looked at the ice jam in front of the boat, then said to Dow, "Listen, Wil, Bill needs a rest. We'll leave him here, guarding them, and you and I will head out the other side of the river, see if we can find any kind of settlement, or maybe a deer or two."

Dow nodded. "Yes, sir."

Sewall said, "I'll use the rickety shotgun. Still not sure of that one barrel. Anybody gets jumpy, no telling what might happen."

He sat now, the shotgun across his legs, aimed directly at Finnegan.

THEY HAD WALKED for several miles, Dow leading the way, mostly flat ground, unbroken swaths of sagebrush, low buttes to both sides. Dow stopped abruptly, one hand up, the signal Roosevelt had learned to obey. He saw Dow raise the shotgun, aiming at a dense cluster of sage, a sharp blast from the gun. From the sage, a prairie chicken burst out to one side, Dow firing again, the chicken rolling over, a trail of bloody feathers.

"You got him!"

"I got two. Other one's in the brush. At least we'll have a little meat."

The birds were gutted, quickly deposited into their coats.

Roosevelt felt energized, more hopeful now, both men picking up the pace, aiming for a line of the buttes to the south. He stopped, pointed. Dow said, "Yep. About time."

It was smoke.

"YOU'RE ON THE C Diamond Ranch, boys. Don't get many trespassers up this way. Mostly cowboys chasing lost cows out of Dickinson."

Other men were gathering, younger, the first man clearly the boss. Roosevelt removed his hat, said, "Sir, we are in a dire strait. My name is Theodore Roosevelt, the Elkhorn Ranch north of Medora. We've captured a trio of thieves over on the Little Missouri, but our boat is being held fast by the ice. We're low on rations, and fear we must let our quarry go free unless we can deliver them to Dickinson without all of us starving to death."

"You're the greenhorn wants to be a big-time cattleman. Heard talk about you. The only four-eyes in the territory that dares to parade himself through a saloon or a cattle camp. Not sure if that makes you brave or stupid."

"I'm not sure myself, sir."

The old man laughed.

"I can loan you a horse, but I expect him returned. Those hills to the south, the Killdeer Mountains. Follow the trail and you'll come to our main ranch there. Ask for Henry Jessup. He'll fix you up, and most likely hire himself out to you. Word is, Mr. Roosevelt, that you come from money back east. He'll want a piece of that. You steal my horse, I will too, and I'm good at tracking folks down. I'm not sure but what the thieves you're talking about ain't standing right in front of me, four-eyes or not. But I'm a trusting fellow, to a point. You get down to the ranch, you give Jessup the horse for safekeeping. I won't charge you nothing for the loan."

Roosevelt asked himself, How do these people find out so much about me? He thought of Mingusville, the fight with the drunk. That Gus fellow was right. Word gets out.

Dow stepped forward, said, "Sir, I don't mean to sound ungrateful, but my boss here ain't no broncobuster. It would be best if you could offer him something of a gentle ride."

The old man laughed, the cowboys behind him joining in.

"Mr. Four-eyes, if you want a horse, you'll do with the one I give you. He's broke, mostly. Since you found your way into this country, you best know how to ride what somebody gives you."

Roosevelt tried not to be annoyed with Dow, said, "You're correct, sir. I am grateful in the extreme."

The old man motioned to his men, and a horse was led out from a small corral. Roosevelt turned to Dow, said, "Thank you for concerning yourself, Wil, but I'll be fine. You go back to the boat, help Bill push his way through the ice, and if it stays stuck, just wait for me to come back. If this all works out, we'll all end up in Dickinson. If I can hire a rancher with a wagon, maybe he'll provision us so we won't starve."

"A WAGON, YOU say? Yessir, got a whole barnful. You going far?"

"Dickinson, sir. But, first, I need to provision my men over on the river. We're hung up in some bad ice."

Jessup pushed his hat up on his forehead.

"Of course you are. This time of year, that river's one big ice floe. What in blazes you doing in a boat?"

"Two boats, actually. We were in pursuit of boat thieves, and we caught them."

"In another boat?"

Roosevelt was feeling tired and frustrated.

"Sir, we have three bad men at gunpoint over on the river. I will pay whatever you wish to provision a good wagon, travel there, and take those men under our guard to the jail at Dickinson."

Jessup nodded, seemed to talk to himself.

"Twenty dollars. But I drive the wagon. This is something I gotta see."

He found Sewall and Dow almost exactly where he had left their camp, the ice in great, thick sheets, tentlike mountains of white that had stopped all progress of the two boats. Jessup halted the wagon, gave out a chuckle. Roosevelt dismounted the wagon, relieved to see that both of his men were still in command of the camp. He looked to the thieves, sullen still, clustered together near a small campfire. He saw something new now, the third thief, the one they simply called half-breed looking at Jessup, a sign of recognition from both men. Roosevelt said to Jessup, "You know these men?"

Jessup shook his head.

"Nope. Strangers. I gotta ask, Mr. Roosevelt, why on God's earth are you hauling them around? Out here, a good hanging is all it takes, and you go on your way. There's no law for near fifty miles."

"That's Dickinson, and that's where I'm taking these men. I'll have no more talk of hanging or shooting. If there's no official law out here, we're making some the best we can."

He saw a smile on the half-breed's face, another strong look at Jessup. Roosevelt felt an uneasy stir, saw Sewall watching the same interaction.

Jessup said, "All right. You're paying me. What we doing next?"

Roosevelt moved closer to Sewall, motioned for Dow to keep a close eye on the prisoners. Sewall said, "I don't trust that driver. He's too familiar with those fellows."

Roosevelt let out a breath. "Bill, we can't stay here, and we can't pretend this ice is just going to break up." He paused. "We've got two boats to manage. I'm leaving you and Wil here. Handle the boats the best you can. The goal is to get them over to Mandan. That's the next good crossing. We can sell them there, or, well, it doesn't matter. What matters to me is getting these fellows to jail. I'll take the wagon, load them up inside, and go overland to Dickinson."

Sewall responded with an urgent whisper. "Sir, you heard that rancher. It's near fifty miles. It'll be three against one . . . well, maybe four. I don't trust that Jessup fellow."

Roosevelt fingered his rifle, felt the ammunition in his belt.

"Neither do I. There's just one way to do this. I'll have my rifle in case anybody runs off or tries to leave me behind."

"What do you mean?"

"Bill, take the boats. I'll manage the thieves on my own, and Jessup too."

He moved away, Sewall still puzzled.

"Mr. Jessup, we'll unload the provisions for my men. Then, we'll load up the prisoners in your wagon."

Jessup said, "You'll be sitting up front with me, then?"

Roosevelt shook his head.

"You'll drive the wagon at a slow pace. I'm an excellent shot, sir. And I'll be walking behind you."

April 10, 1886

He couldn't remember when he had last slept. The going was slow, thankfully, the thawing clay beneath his feet sucking and clawing at his boots, the muck also slowing the horses and wagon in front of him. But the effort was enormous for all, the old rancher occasionally resting his horses, as though he knew Roosevelt would require the same.

The day was finally ending, a hard chill that gnawed at the sweat in his clothes. For the first time, his mind swirled around the thought of nighttime, just what he would do with three men who might make every attempt to escape, or simply kill him. No matter the obedience of the rancher, keeping the wagon to a pace slow enough for Roosevelt to step, he still didn't trust him, had no idea if the old man would hold a gun on the thieves while Roosevelt slept or join in and cut Roosevelt's throat.

He could feel his breathing, the cold eating into his lungs, his head pulsing with a headache he could not cure. His feet moved with as much rhythm as he could manage in the slop, and he spent long stretches looking down at the wreckage of his boots, his mind dancing around the notion of a new suit, new boots, all manner of fantasy of his early days in the West.

"*Shack up ahead.*"

His brain snapped awake, and he tried to focus, could see now a small structure a few hundred yards in front of the wagon. He hurried himself up closer to the wagon, said to the rancher, "What is it? Anybody there?"

"Nope. Drover's cabin, for the roundup. Forgot it was here. We can hole up there for the night, start out again in the morning. If that's all right with you, deputy."

The old man laughed at his own joke, and Roosevelt's mind was slow, the word sinking in like the goo beneath his feet. *Deputy.*

"I guess, maybe so. Let's everybody get in that cabin. Will you make some coffee?"

The old man shook his head.

"Got none. Besides, you're wanting to keep an eye on me too, and I'd have to light a fire outside. Let me offer you one word of warning, and I don't mind if these boys hear me. There's three of them and one of you, and you're gonna find out if you can keep your eyes open all night long. 'Cause at least one of them will. Me? I'm going to sleep. Good luck to you, Mr. Roosevelt."

The cabin smelled of sagebrush and dust, no different from the air outside. Nobody's been here in a while, he thought. The three thieves were put into a corner, close together, and Roosevelt sat in the opposite corner, his rifle propped on his knees. The rancher had a bundle, various rations from his wagon, mostly dried beef and hard biscuits.

"Best I got, Mr. Roosevelt." He handed the rations to the other three, looked at Roosevelt again. "Don't stuff yourself too good. You'll want to take a nap worse'n hell, for sure." The old man laughed, what sounded like an evil cackle.

Roosevelt said nothing, gnawed on one piece of beef, the old man's words echoing into his brain. All right, that's enough. There'll be time to eat in Dickinson.

"Hey there, four-eyes. Why you going to all the trouble to haul us all the way to Dickinson?"

It was the first time Finnegan had spoken since morning, and Roosevelt saw the brown stubble that passed for the man's teeth, the sickening smile that told Roosevelt all he should know about the man's intentions.

"So you'll be tried as thieves."

"You might shoulda done that when you had your friends with you. You coulda been judge and jury, and then the man with the rope. Now that's it's three to one, you gotta figure that the closer we get to Dickinson, the more we're likely to rip your heart out. I'm just wondering how long you can stay awake. Good night, four-eyes."

Finnegan and the others wrapped themselves in blankets, the rancher doing the same. Roosevelt felt his eyes droop, pulled them awake, adjusted the rifle, flexed his fingers around the stock, swung his head from side to side. He watched the men, heard their breathing, soft rhythm, the rancher now starting to snore. Roosevelt took a long deep breath, then another, his mind carrying him to soft places, drifting into a half slumber, but he jerked awake again, shouting at himself, No! You fall asleep, and you're dead. You'll be shot with your own rifle. I won't end up that way. He rocked his head in a circle again, stretching his neck, stared at the dark shapes across from him, heard a low voice,

"'Night, four-eyes."

THE MEN STIRRED, boots on the rough wood floor, Roosevelt snapping to full awake. He realized now that he could see, the men in their blankets clearly visible, the rancher, no snoring now, moving as well. Roosevelt stood, knew it would wake him further, working the stiffness from his joints, the soreness in his backside from sitting all night long.

"Well, now. I give it to you, Mr. Roosevelt, you done survived." The cackle came again, the rancher rolling up his blanket, moving to the three prisoners, kicking boot bottoms, rousing them awake.

Roosevelt said nothing, moved to the ramshackle door, felt the cold blowing through, a harsh wind from the north. He saw Finnegan, the awful smile.

"Well, good morning, four-eyes. You done what I thought you'd never do. You stayed awake. I was watching you too. All night long. Now, you gotta walk again, while we ride. This'll be fun to see if you can keep up. Them horses are in a whole heap better shape than you."

Roosevelt aimed the rifle from his waist.

"Outside, now. Mount up."

They obeyed without speaking, all of them battered by the cold wind as they staggered out of the shack. Roosevelt watched the three prisoners into the wagon, the rancher now close to him.

"Keep sharp, Mr. Roosevelt. The closer we get to that jail of yours, the more likely they are to try something nasty. I can't say I'm too comfortable riding up in front of them, in case they decide it's my throat that needs cutting."

Roosevelt was skeptical.

"These men aren't strangers to you."

The rancher smiled.

"No, one of 'em ain't. That half-breed, the one who don't say much. He used to work for me. Stole a horse, stole half the food out of the larder, took off. Been wondering if I'd ever see him again. You're doing me a favor, Mr. Roosevelt. He makes it to Dickinson, and I'll file my own complaints against him. He'll hang. If . . ." He slapped Roosevelt on the back. "If he don't hang me first."

Roosevelt was still skeptical, but he knew he had no choice but to trust this man at least to push the horses in the right direction.

"When should we reach Dickinson?"

The man gazed around, nodded, talking to himself.

"We done passed by the Knife River. I'd say we'll be there before dark. You know, ain't no need of you walking. We can tie these fellows up, and you can sit up front with me."

Roosevelt felt an odd itch, an alarm coming from the old man's smile.

"I'll walk. It worked yesterday, I'll do it again today."

"If you say so. I'm mountin' up. Let's go."

It WAS NEARLY dark, his feet screaming with every step, raw blisters, the rifle in his hands heavier with each passing hour. He had perched the rifle on his shoulders, no relief, his shoulders cramping along with the calves in both legs. He moved with automatic steps, the wagon rocking in front of him with a sleep-inducing rhythm. He was kept awake by the faces watching him, Finnegan, the others, the filthy smiles, waiting for him to falter, to stumble. It was the faces that gave him the energy, the sheer ugliness of the prisoners, of all they represented. He stared out past the wagon, stepped outside of the wagon's ruts, a mistake, the soggy clay grabbing him, sucking the strength from his legs. His heart jumped, panic, Finnegan watching, emerging from the wagon, Roosevelt raising the rifle, driving him back. And now, the voice of the rancher.

"There you be, Mr. Roosevelt. I only missed it straight on by a quarter mile. Them buildings. Dickinson."

He staggered again, struggled not to fall, the pain ripping through his feet, the face of Finnegan . . . and now a horse, another, coming close, stopping, words with the rancher, and now close to him.

"We don't see many people come out of the prairie from the north. Why are you walking, mister?"

Roosevelt glanced up, said, "It's a long story."

Roosevelt looked again at Finnegan, saw anger and desperation, a man prepared to do anything to survive. Roosevelt aimed the rifle that way, and the man on the horse said, "Whoa there, mister. There'll be no shooting in this town. I'm Deputy Sheriff McTavish. Lower that rifle, sir."

Roosevelt looked up at the deputy, did as he was told, pointed a hand to the wagon.

"Three prisoners for you, sir. Thieves. I'm happy to file any papers you might require. I would keep a good watch on them, though. They're not the nicest chaps."

And then, for the first time in two days, through the film of mud and clay, hard, chapped lips, and dreary, sleepless eyes, he smiled.

WITH HIS PRISONERS safely installed in the Dickinson jail, Roosevelt had yet to sleep. But luck was still with him. The only doctor in more than a hundred fifty miles, Dr. Victor Stickney, happened to maintain his office in Dickinson. For an hour or more, an astonished Dr. Stickney heard Roosevelt's story while he patched and mended Roosevelt's bloody and blistered feet. Roosevelt was already fully energized and, despite not having slept in forty-eight hours, he convinced Dr. Stickney and others who saw him that he would be fully capable of performing the entire adventure all over again.

Word spread quickly of what Roosevelt had done, one more legend piling on the man who seemed simply to love all of life, who poured himself into every enterprise. In Medora, a cattleman, hearing the story in the local saloon, was heard to say, "He's the only real damn fool in the county." But most agreed with another assessment: "He's a fearless bugger."

CHAPTER 23

August 24, 1886
Dakota Territory

"I have some news, sir."

Sewall seemed unusually anxious, and Roosevelt looked up from his book.

"What sort of news?"

"I was at Joe Ferris's store, and Mr. Packard, the newspaperman, was there, said to pass along to you that the thieves got their due. Finnegan and Bernstead each pulled twenty-five months in the Bismarck Penitentiary. The Dutchman, the half-wit, was acquitted. That's what you wanted to hear, right, sir?"

Roosevelt nodded, rubbed a hand on his chin.

"That's what I wanted. That German fellow was mighty slow, just doing what he was told. He was probably scared of Finnegan like everybody else around here. I can't fault him. But twenty-five months . . . that's justice, I suppose."

"If it had been horses they stole, they'd have been hanged. I guess a couple years at hard labor is punishment enough for a leaky old boat."

Roosevelt sat back in the chair, tried to avoid a scorching sun in his face.

"It's not the boat, Bill. It's the act. Thievery. They're trying to bring the modern world, civilization, out here. You can't have people acting like the only law is frontier justice. Sooner or later, there has to be a real sheriff in Medora, or a U.S. marshal. There is no place for people like Finnegan, not when families are settling the area, children are being born."

Sewall laughed.

"And the cattlemen are griping loud and long that any kind of civilization that comes here means fences and taxes. That rubs some the wrong way."

"I've got no patience for that, Bill. If people want a civilized government, whether it's a sheriff or courts, or any other organized systems, it costs money. The cattlemen have more of it than anyone else out here, except maybe for the marquis. But I'm pretty sure that if some tax law is passed, he'll end up paying his fair share too."

Sewall sat down beside him now, a hot breeze drifting across the veranda.

"Wil and I had wondered if you were gonna stay out here all summer. I'm glad you're here to see what all is happening."

"What do you mean?"

"In Ferris's store, the talk was mostly about the drought. I ain't never seen a season this dry in Maine, but I wasn't sure if it was normal out here. The fellows in the store said no, that this kind of dry is dangerous, and not just for fire. You walk out on the open prairie and it crunches under your feet like broken glass. Not sure how a cow is supposed to eat that and survive. The old-timers say it bodes evil for the winter."

"Have faith, Bill. We've done pretty well so far, and we've all made a profit."

"Well, yes, sir, I know. It's just worrisome, hearing all the talk."

Roosevelt smiled.

"Talk is just talk. We'll see what happens when Wil gets back from Chicago. If cattle prices stay strong, we'll do very well for the year, drought or no drought."

"Yes, sir. If you say so."

Sewall looked down, and Roosevelt knew there was more.

"Say what you have to, Bill."

"Well, sir, Mr. Packard also said he was gonna print something that came off *The New York Times,* copied in the paper in Bismarck. He said people out here ought to know, so they can give you a hearty salute."

"What are you talking about? *The New York Times*?"

"Yes, sir. Word is that you and your new lady have been officially engaged now for a while. Just curious if you'd bring her out here."

Sewall's words opened a wound. Edith had agreed to marry him back in November, and for the couple, that was as official as the relationship needed to be. But they had kept it quiet, for all the reasons Bamie had drilled into him: Roosevelt might face a mountain of disapproval, even from his family. So, no one had been told at all, no official notice posted anywhere. Until now.

He stood, paced angrily on the veranda.

"This is terrible. How did the papers find out? Who told them? This is awful."

Sewall stayed in the chair, seemed sheepish now, said, "Sorry if I did something wrong, sir. Folks here say they're happy for you."

Roosevelt continued to pace, slammed a fist into his open hand.

"I have to repair this, and immediately."

"What's wrong, sir? Does this mean you're not getting married?"

Roosevelt stopped his manic movements, looked at Sewall.

"Yes, we're getting married. But no one knows. No one. No one in my family, not my sisters, cousins, no one." He made a sarcastic laugh. "Well, they do now. Watch for the next mail run, Bill, see what arrives. Bamie, for one, will stick a knife in me with her words. She's good at that. I have to write them, Corinne and Bamie both. There's no time to waste."

He moved inside, gathered up his satchel, prepared for a hard ride into Medora. He was back out on the veranda now, said to Sewall, "There is no more privacy, Bill. I don't mean you. You have every right to know what's going to affect your own future. But I doubt Edith would fit in here at all. Not that she's some kind of society dilettante. I assure you, she's not. But I don't think she'd much enjoy the prairie life." He laughed. "No, I'm quite certain she wouldn't."

"Well, sir, you know we'd welcome her. Three wives are better than two." Sewall caught himself. "Sorry, sir. I know you're not married yet. It's not my business when that will happen."

Roosevelt surrendered to the inevitable, thought, If I can't trust him to silence, there is no one in the Dakotas I can trust.

"Edith left for England back in April, to spend some travel time with her family. She plans to be there for the rest of the year."

"Sorry, sir. That's hard, being away that long from somebody you care about."

"No, I have plenty to keep me occupied out here. But, yes. I do miss her. Every day. Her travel was agreed upon by both of us. She's staying over there, waiting for me to join her later this fall. That's where we'll be married. It was the best way we could figure to keep it a secret. Did Packard say if the article made mention of marriage? Or just the engagement?"

"I believe just the engagement."

"That's good. I'm not sure how anyone could know about us going to England, unless they're mind readers."

Sewall stood, held out a hand.

"It might be early, sir, but congratulations to you. I swear to you, no one around here will say a single word. And even if they knew about it, nobody would think bad of you *or* your wife."

Roosevelt took the hand.

"Thank you. All this effort at secrecy might sound ridiculous. But in New York people think differently than they do here. My brother probably doesn't care. But my sisters . . . all I know is that if my family wants nothing to do with me when I go back east, I might as well figure out a way to teach Edith about cattle."

HE WENT HUNTING, two weeks in the steep mountains of western Montana territory, pursuing grizzly and any other big game he could find. To his amazing good fortune, he succeeded in bringing down a white goat, one of the most elusive game animals on the continent. But the ranch called him back—Roosevelt was touched just enough by the concerns of Sewall, as well as others, including Gregor Lang, all of whom were preaching doom, signs of a hard winter to come.

There were signs that Roosevelt never would have known, the fact that geese were flying south far earlier than usual, that beavers were working doubly hard to take down trees for their dams. The Indians seemed to know much more about these kinds of signs, many of them leaving the area, anticipating a severe shortage of game. To Roosevelt, it was amusing talk, though one part of him knew not to laugh, knew that when there was consensus on anything, pay attention.

In mid-September, he left Montana and returned to Elkhorn in time to meet Wil Dow, who had delivered a trainload of this year's cattle to the stockyards in Chicago.

"I'M SORRY, SIR. Here are the papers. The best I could find was twenty-five per head."

Sewell whistled. "That's ten less than it costs us to raise 'em and haul 'em. What happened?"

Roosevelt listened to both men with his arms crossed, leaned back in the chair, stared at the barely flowing river, the numbers running through his head. Dow stood to one side, said, "They say that western cattle just aren't as desirable as eastern. They say that folks are particular and that unless the cattle are fatted up for several months in the stockyards back east, they just don't taste good."

Roosevelt thought of Morès, his grandiose plans to take over the cattle industry with western cattle.

"I wonder how the marquis is taking this."

Dow said, "I ran into some of his people there. They were going through the same thing. None of them even wanted to come back here to face him. It's not good, sir, not at all."

Sewall paced a few steps, back and forth across the veranda. "Sir, I'm not concerned with the marquis, or anyone else out here. We have a contract with you that calls for us to share the profits, while you bear the losses. This is hitting you hard, sir, and we're off scot-free. I was doubtful we'd ever see a profit at all, that all we'd make here was wages. You proved me wrong. But that's changed now. What we have here is a one-sided trade. We have our wives and babies to think of, and you're paying the bill."

Dow said, "I agree with Bill, sir. Watching you lose money ain't much fun. From everything I heard in Chicago, it feels like the boom out here is past."

Sewall sat now, leaned closer to Roosevelt. "Sir, I don't think we have any choice. We have to terminate our contract with you. Wil and I just don't want to watch you lose money like this. This drought is scaring people, and if the cattle are poorer still, next year's herds could sell for cheaper yet."

Roosevelt thought a moment, rapped the palms of his hands on the arms of the chair. "I can take losses like this. And I don't know what this drought means for next year. I will certainly discuss this with Mr. Ferris and Mr. Merrifield. They're part of this too."

Sewall said, "Sir, they're part of this *place* too. I've talked to both of them, and neither one thinks he'll ever leave here, no matter the price of cattle. You can count on them to help you, no matter what you want to do. Wil and I . . . it's a whole different circumstance."

Roosevelt thought a moment, absorbed the gravity of what he was facing. "I respect you both and consider you to be my friends. But watching friends gamble is not a fulfilling enterprise. I can take the risk. You cannot."

Sewall said, "Sir, right now, the risk is *all* yours. Neither of us wants to help you to lose money."

Roosevelt nodded.

"I will figure out where we stand and settle up with you, if that's what you want. You may change your mind at any time, and our contract will continue. But if you wish to leave, quit this business, then you had best go back to Maine, with no ill feelings from me."

Sewall said, "I never want to fool away anybody else's money."

Dow moved closer, put his hand on Sewall's shoulder. "Me neither, sir. It ain't right."

"How soon would you go?"

The women emerged from the house now, obviously aware what was taking place.

Roosevelt forced a smile.

"How are those Badlands babies doing?"

Both women forced smiles of their own, said in unison, "Very well, sir."

Sewall looked at his wife, said, "Three weeks, perhaps?"

She nodded. "We'll be ready."

Roosevelt gave her a genuine smile. "Those babies of yours . . .

189

they're frontier babies. You might have your hands full when you get back east."

Mrs. Sewall laughed, said, "Sir, we've had our hands full of *you,* and have done just fine."

HE RODE WITH Sewall, a quiet time, the horse drifting around and past the herds.

"You're coming east too, sir?"

Roosevelt waited before answering, watched a bony calf struggle to keep up with its mother.

"Yes, same train, most likely."

"I knew this was coming, sir. So did you. I predicted it two years ago, when you were so down about your life and all. You were full of questions, all that you wanted to do, and you thought you'd found it here because you had lost it back east. I didn't believe you then, and I feel even stronger about it now. Most everything in your life is back east. You're going to get married. You'll travel, and not to places where sagebrush stabs your feet and outlaws steal your boat."

Roosevelt stopped the horse, watched the cattle, felt the rhythm of the lowing, the cattle as tired of the heat as he was.

"I miss her, Bill. Powerfully. I won't argue with what you say because I can't. I'm wondering if maybe I should think again about going into law."

"You'd make a good lawyer, for certain." Sewall paused. "But maybe you ought to think again about politics. You're a good man, sir. Good men should go into politics."

Roosevelt didn't respond, thought, There's surely plenty of bad ones. After a quiet moment, he said, "There are friends in New York who want me to do exactly that. I do have to think about it. Most of the time, I'd rather be writing my books and articles. It's difficult work, but it's good work."

He followed Sewall's gaze upward, staring at the endless sky, the sun drawing low, bright orange and dark blue, shimmering heat rising from the prairie, no rain in more than four months. He gazed over the herd again, saw their bones, their weakness, felt a desperate helplessness.

After a long silence, Sewall said, "You can write your books any-time. But we need good men to lead us into good places. If you decide to do that, well, sir, I'll be grateful. And I think you'll end up being president."

HE DIDN'T TAKE Sewall seriously, knew only that both men from Maine, along with the Dakotans, Merrifield and Ferris, had become true friends.

The ride now was alone, another trek out past the herds, the rugged butte country, what had once seemed so utterly beautiful now transformed by the drought into something dismal. The sage crackled beneath Manitou's hooves, dust spreading out where once had been smooth, hard clay. The smaller creeks, the trickles that fed into the Little Missouri River, were dead dry, no sign of water anywhere out from the river itself, which seemed to hold on to the title in the most desperate way, an amazing contrast to the early spring. Then, Roosevelt's boat had been essential merely to cross from one side to another. Now, a man could step across, barely wetting his pant legs.

He rode with the heat pressing him down, put a hand on the horse's neck, thought, Kind old friend. You can't be enjoying this, and so we'll make it short. I just wanted to come out one more time. I'll be leaving you, leaving all the rest of this in a few days, and I don't know when I'll return. So many people hoping for so much from me back home. Talk of running me for mayor of New York. Ridiculous. And yet . . .

With Sewall and Dow preparing to leave for Maine, Roosevelt had expanded the contract he had with Sylvane Ferris and Bill Merrifield so that the Maltese Cross assumed control of Roosevelt's herds at Elk-horn. It had been a smooth negotiation, both men understanding that the Maine men were never likely to remain in the Dakotas permanently. Roosevelt had been blunt with the men, no guarantee if he would return at all this year, and no idea if 1887 would be any different. Like so many, they had been pessimistic both about the drought and about what it might mean for the herds this winter: that with brittle, short grass where that lush green had been, a good many of the weaker cows would simply not survive. He didn't want to hear that, would trust them to do what was best, save what could be saved. After all, just because the beavers were busier than usual didn't mean anything unusual to him.

He let Manitou lead him down through a shallow arroyo, a black deer startled, a fast gallop up and out, a hopping scamper across the open ground. He reached for his rifle, let it go, the deer too far, too fast. Roosevelt watched it, measured the shot he could have taken, but this wasn't a hunt. One more deer for next year, he thought. Sylvane will get him. Best shot I've ever seen. And they'll need the meat.

The horse carried him back up to the flat ground, thick sagebrush in a flat depression, a shallow valley, a wet-weather creek dusty dry. This was so beautiful, he thought. What has happened? This place hasn't changed so much. It has to be me. Big dreams about being a cattle rancher, but if we have another year like this one, I cannot afford that. Certainly not with a new wife, with a new home to manage. She says she's good with money, can manage our finances. I hope so, because, plainly, I cannot. I gambled. And I am losing. I have to believe it will be better next year, but no one here believes that.

He turned the horse away from the afternoon sun, followed the hoofprints back the way he came. Yes, this was once the most beautiful place I had ever seen. My new home, perhaps for all time. Now, it's time for me to go back east. No matter what dreams I thought I had, I truly miss Edith . . . and Sagamore Hill. That's where I belong.

THE WINTER OF 1886–87 fulfilled the grim expectations of even the most pessimistic of the old-timers, the drought giving way to the most brutal cold, with blizzards dropping feet of snow. Throughout the Badlands, the herds of weakened cattle were wiped out, most of the ranchers losing half to three-quarters of their stock. The weakness of the cattle extended into the following year, calves not surviving to add to the herds.

The game animals weren't immune, the spring thaw revealing hundreds of deer carcasses, mostly in the deepest draws, where these same animals had once found safe refuge.

With the snowmelt came the flooding, the Little Missouri River spreading far outside its banks, sweeping away groves of trees and nearby homesteads, along with a good many of the people who had hunkered down in those homes, believing they could survive the worst winter in anyone's memory.

Though the boomtown of Medora lost most of its residents, Sylvane Ferris and Bill Merrifield continued to operate Roosevelt's Elkhorn and Maltese Cross ranches. In the fall of 1887, Roosevelt made one last visit, his final duty as a cattleman, to oversee the last remaining part of his herd. Roosevelt cut his losses, settling with the two men as generously as possible, overseeing his final sale. Again, prices had dropped so low at the stockyards of Chicago that Roosevelt lost money on every animal he sold. It was the final straw. His dreams of living as a ranchman were extinguished. He was, after all, an Easterner.

PART III

THE COLONEL

War takes all the
"littleness" out of men.

—Theodore Roosevelt

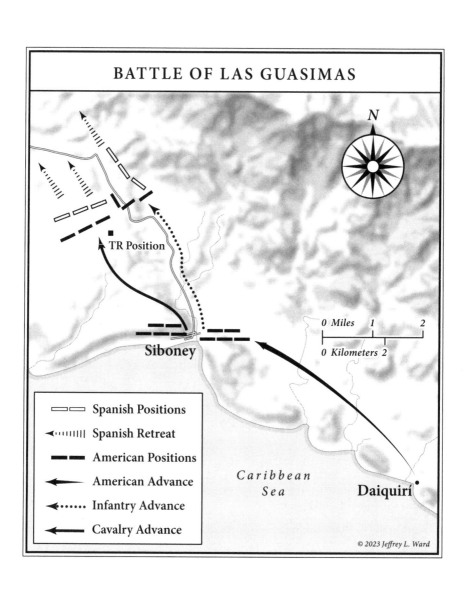

BATTLE OF LAS GUASIMAS

N

TR Position

0 Miles 1 2

0 Kilometers 2

Siboney

Caribbean
Sea

Daiquirí

Spanish Positions
Spanish Retreat
American Positions
American Advance
Infantry Advance
Cavalry Advance

© 2023 Jeffrey L. Ward

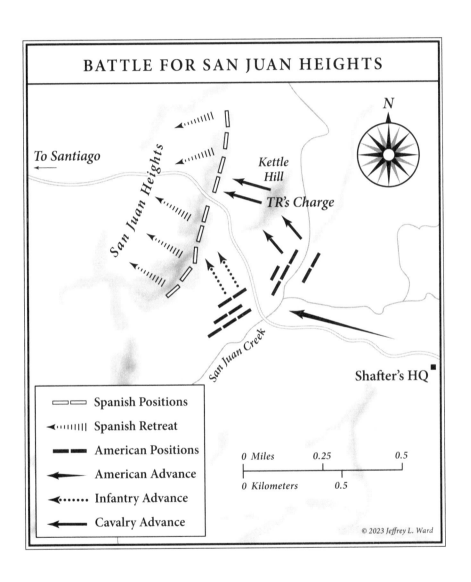

BATTLE FOR SAN JUAN HEIGHTS

N

To Santiago

San Juan Heights

Kettle
Hill

TR's Charge

San Juan Creek

Shafter's HQ

Spanish Positions

Spanish Retreat

American Positions

American Advance

Infantry Advance

Cavalry Advance

0 Miles   0.25   0.5

0 Kilometers   0.5

© 2023 Jeffrey L. Ward

CHAPTER 24

December 29, 1918
Sagamore Hill, New York

"Was it fun being a cowboy?"

Roosevelt looked at Hagedorn with ill-disguised annoyance.

"Let me tell you something. Those cowboys you blithely dismiss are the hardest-working people I've ever known. They live by a code that city people can't possibly comprehend. Meanness, cowardice, and dishonesty are not tolerated. One's word is absolute. A cowboy looks at death, courts death, every day he's working, and I never heard a single complaint or saw anyone shirk his duties. I played at it, I tried, I had my cowboy outfit and toted my six-gun like one of them. But I could never measure up to those men, no matter what I thought I could do."

The response wore him out, Hagedorn seeming to know he had stepped on a very sore toe.

"I meant no offense, sir. It's just that people in New York see cowboys in magazines and motion pictures, and it's so adventurous."

Roosevelt took a long, painful breath.

"I know. You're right. Those good men are portrayed like cartoons, or by some actor like Tom Mix, all fists and six-guns and shooting Indians, something for an eight-year-old to pretend about. It's embarrassing."

"Did you see men killed, gunfights and so forth?"

"Listen. When a room is full of people all wearing guns, it's a great equalizer. Unless someone is dead drunk, no one's likely to go on the shoot just to prove himself. This ridiculousness about well-organized gunfights between masked gangs . . . well, I never saw it, and I suspect neither did anyone else."

"If you don't mind, sir, could you talk about hunting? People in New York are curious about that, what all you've done. Do you still go out west?"

He wondered if Hagedorn had any idea just how sick Roosevelt felt.

"The last time I hunted in the Dakotas or Montana was 1903. It's not like it was then. Most of the game is a great deal harder to find; the ranges are fenced in. It's hard for me to think about having fun now on the backs and efforts of those good men. If there's deer to be killed, let them do it. They need to eat more than I do."

"I can come back to that a little later, if it's all right. Can we talk about your political life, well before you were president?"

"There is no political *life* even when you become president. It's more of a very slow death, that every day someone tries to take something away from you, bring you down just a bit, steal your effectiveness. Anyone who stays in politics, in elected office, after decades? All they lose is their own effectiveness. One lesson I had to learn, and quickly, is that I am not all-important. None of those people are. They can inspire fear by their status or intimidate by their skill at manipulation. But what they're missing is respect. Most of those people don't know what respect is anymore. They're just trying to stay in power. And make no mistake. Power isn't respect. It's just power."

Hagedorn wrote furiously, Roosevelt trying to regain the strength he had felt a half hour ago. He saw Edith at the door now, the rays of sunlight falling across her dress, a soft moment.

Hagedorn looked up from his pad, shook his head.

"It just amazes me, sir, that you ran for mayor of New York."

One hand on a cane, Roosevelt leaned toward the young man's chair.

"What's so amazing about it, Mr. Hagedorn? I once ran for president and *won*, or didn't you know that?" He paused, Hagedorn writing again. "I've never gotten over that New York thing, you know. I didn't expect to win, mind you, but I didn't expect to finish third in a three-man race. A horse does that badly and they shoot him."

Hagedorn smiled at the joke.

"Of course, sorry. There's just so much to write about you. I'm not sure there's enough paper."

"Don't flatter me, son. I know my successes and my failings, and believe me there are plenty of both. If you're going to keep writing about me, you need to keep that in mind. Running for mayor of New York isn't anything to crow about. Winning is. Losing is best just forgotten. Which I had mostly done until you brought it up."

Edith had remained quiet, but Roosevelt caught a flicker of movement, knew that words were coming.

"Now, don't be mean, Teddy. *You* mentioned the New York race, not him." She spoke to Hagedorn now. "He's very touchy on that subject. He much prefers talking about the battles he's won."

Hagedorn laughed. "Oh, yes, ma'am. I know that for certain."

She leaned close to the young man. "Time for lunch, Mr. Hagedorn. My husband will take his right here. We have prepared a table for you downstairs. Is that all right?"

"Oh, by all means, ma'am. Thank you. I'll go now."

"After lunch, you may have my husband for one hour more. That should be sufficient for today."

"Yes, ma'am. I understand. Thank you again."

The servant waited at the door, escorted the young man away.

"Clara, bring Mr. Roosevelt's tray in here. He's ready."

"Yes, ma'am."

Edith looked at him now, a scolding frown.

"You abuse him, Teddy."

"Why the hell not? It's good sport. He can take it. It's part of the job."

He looked past her, sorted through a flutter of thoughts.

"Still, you know you were quite pleased with his first book. Rudeness is not necessary."

Roosevelt grumbled, said, "He agitates me."

"And you agreed to it."

Roosevelt leaned back on a pillow, pushed the cane away with a clatter.

"Never should have done that. Writers are all the same. No matter how pretty a picture you try to paint, they find the ugly. *Increases their readership,* so I've heard." He fought to breathe, let out a long breath, inhaled again.

"Are you all right?"

"Hmm? Yes, just winded. That's what they say about me, isn't it? Long-winded. Well, these days I'm more short-winded. Makes for better speeches."

She lifted his feet, removed his shoes, what had been a good show of decorum for Hagedorn. He wiggled his toes, felt the annoying deadness, tingling now, like so many bees inside his socks. She pulled the blanket up to his waist, and he saw the servant there with the tray.

"What's that smell? Dead fish?"

"It's roast beef, Teddy. You wanted a sandwich, remember?"

"If you insist."

She shook her head, said, "Would you like something to drink?"

He thought a moment, fought against his mind, drifting away from her.

"I'd like to be back in Venice with you, do our honeymoon all over again. God, but you were beautiful, and I was so stupidly young, and we were in love and everything we did or saw or ate was romantic."

She said nothing. He focused on her, saw crossed arms, her head shaking.

"And now?"

He sorted out his words, realized he had just insulted her and their marriage.

"Oh, for Godfrey's sake, I didn't mean anything. It . . . just . . . it was so very different, our first time together as a couple. So many beautiful places."

She was smiling now.

"I know what you meant. I recall that your knowledge of the languages was so poor you kept ordering us the strangest food or, sometimes, no food at all."

He laughed now, a coughing wheeze.

"But Venice . . ." He laughed again. "You insisted we take one of those gondolas. It was February, for Godfrey's sake. I expected ice in the lagoons. At least that fellow with the pole had the brains to wear a coat."

"The blanket he gave us . . . fine velvet. I remember the smell, soft perfume."

"You have an insane memory, my dear. Though I do recall, we snuggled nicely underneath it."

She laughed. "Of course, that would be your finest memory of Venice. Perhaps all of Italy."

Roosevelt didn't answer for a long moment. "Yes, I think so. We were so young, and every touch of you was magical. Is that silly? We must have been like giggling schoolchildren."

"You still are."

"Oh, very nice. Insult me in my pain." He thought again. "Venice was perfectly lovely. Truly appealed to me, as if I had been born five hundred years too late. And I was with *you,* and we were young and ridiculous and every piece of a good life was all before us."

He looked away from her, his eye catching a small painting on the wall, a distraction, said slowly, "And now it is behind us."

She shook her head.

"No. It is all right here, right inside us, right in this room, this home, our children, and their children."

"Grandchildren? Oh, dear Lord, I had forgotten."

He looked back at her, past her, glanced around the room.

"That writer . . . Hagedorn. He's gone?"

He knew the look, her worry, her face not hiding the alarm.

"He's eating lunch downstairs. I have allowed him to return for one hour only."

He tried to focus, to remember the young man's face.

"Did I tell him about sneaking off on that ship to London so we could get married? Bamie came with me, pretended to be my wife, fictitious names, so no one would know who I was. As if losing the mayor's race made me famous. The church . . . what was it called?"

"Saint George's Church. And no, you haven't revealed that part of our personal life."

"Yes, well, good. I know how you treasure our privacy." He thought for a long moment. "December third. I bet you thought I wouldn't remember our anniversary date."

"It's December second, Teddy."

"ALL RIGHT, MR. Hagedorn. What else is eating at you? And why'd you decide to invade my privacy, anyway? You're mighty young."

"I'm thirty-six, sir. Not that young."

"Answer the question."

"I very much enjoyed writing my first book about you, and I know there is so much more to tell. I also know there are a number of qualified biographers itching to tell your story. I thought I had better hop to it. My editor agreed, and they offered me an advance to begin the work. I don't mind telling you that, sir."

"It's all right. Nobody writes because they want to be a humanitarian. It's a living. Good for you."

"Sir, if I may . . . I have read how much you admire Abraham Lincoln. But who would you say you *least* admire in American history?"

Roosevelt laughed.

"Most everyone. But a few stand out. If I had to choose a single person, I would begin with Jefferson Davis. I happened to mention to an audience somewhere that I considered Davis to be comparable to Benedict Arnold. Someone happily, or unhappily, conveyed my comparison to Davis himself, who then wrote me an astonishing letter. It was ill-tempered and undignified, to say the least, claiming that I am ignorant of American history and that my outrage against his deeds and character are unproved." He paused, smiled. "I had a good laugh over that. I would thoroughly enjoy it if Davis was still among us to discuss these points publicly. Since he's not, let's move on. What's your next question?"

"Can we discuss your first wife?"

"No."

He could see disappointment on the younger man's face, wouldn't help him, wouldn't say anything more, thought, Why must they know?

Hagedorn gathered himself, consulted his pad.

"I understand, sir, that you foxhunt around this area. That must afford you a good substitute for the Dakotas."

"It doesn't. Leave it at that."

"What about the Indians, sir?"

"What Indians?"

"The ones you must have met or fought in the Dakotas. Or did you get along with them?"

Roosevelt shook his head.

"You watch too many western movies. When I first went west, I was like everyone else in the East. The Indians are mindless savages, best swept away so we can have free rein. Well, I learned something out west, and it applies to the Negro right here in New York. I have had my share of prejudice, assuming the worst about a race just because they had a name: Indian, Negro, Hindu, Chinese. I have judged entire races as inferior or unable to compete with the white man. I admit there are times when I slip back into those feelings, no matter how hard I try to escape that. The point is, Mr. Hagedorn, there is one thing I have learned in my life: race doesn't mean a thing when compared to achievement, skill, competence, ability. Give me a Negro any day who can outthink or outspeak a white man. Give me an Indian engineer who can build a bridge better than any white engineer, and on and on. You get my drift, right? A man has value because of what he can accomplish and the power of his brain, not the color of his skin. And I know full well, this kind of talk just gets me more enemies. Bring them on."

"Do you feel the same way about women?"

"Absolutely. Most men are imbeciles when it comes to women. The notion that you can keep an entire gender down, subservient, is patently ridiculous. If I tried that with any of the women in this family . . . moot point. It could never happen. The fact that there are men firmly entrenched against a woman's right to vote astounds me. Suffrage is an inevitability, starting with Abigail Adams, Elizabeth Cady Stanton, and all the rest. They created a wave that grew slowly, then more rapidly, until it was unstoppable. I admire the suffragettes as much as I admire all the women in my family. Mark my words. They'll have the vote in another year or two. They've earned it."

"Thank you, sir. I didn't know you felt so strongly about these particular things."

"You'd better feel strongly about these things, son, or the world will leave you behind. Some of the old politicians I've suffered through, they think they can turn back the clock, reverse the flow of history. I can't, and I know better than to try. Nobody ever has."

"Yes, sir. To change topics, sir, can you tell me about the Boone and Crockett Club?"

Roosevelt thought a moment, long breaths, gathered strength.

"There are three kinds of hunters: those who kill to eat, those who kill for a trophy, and those who kill just to kill. There was a time when I was the latter. Never gave much thought to ruining a hunting area for someone else or wasting game just to do it. That was a mistake. Over time, I became more the second type, seeking trophies. I have enough of those. In the Dakotas, there were times when we killed to survive. So, I believe I can speak with some authority on the value of hunting and what it means to be a conservationist. I have come to understand that wild game is a precious thing. That isn't a contradiction, though some think it is. If you manage game correctly, set laws in place to limit numbers killed, protect habitat, it is my belief that you will preserve the very game you're trying to hunt and provide the means for future generations to enjoy the same activity, with the same good fortune I have had." He stopped. "This is difficult to explain, Mr. Hagedorn. But it's why I formed the Boone and Crockett Club. We assembled some pretty influential members, men who could apply pressure to Congress. We pushed through the Lacey Act of 1894, which protected Yellowstone Park for all time. We've done so much, so much. Protecting everything from seals and whales in Alaska to the great sequoia groves in California, and so much more." He paused, exhausted. "I'll get off my soapbox now. This is a pitfall of interviewing me, Mr. Hagedorn. I talk a great deal about things I care about."

Hagedorn scribbled again, and Roosevelt was impressed with the man's stamina for writing.

"You know, I used to write like that. A thousand words a minute . . . well, not quite. But when I was in my thirties, like you, I wrote like a madman, all manner of books and articles. Some are actually worth reading. Some . . . well . . ."

"I've heard you were a great friend to President Harrison."

"Where did you hear that?"

Hagedorn seemed embarrassed now. "Not sure, sir."

"What I did was campaign for Benjamin Harrison, and so I helped put him in the Executive Mansion. In return, he appointed me civil service commissioner. It's a thankless, miserable job that pays almost nothing. I loved it. Made people mad by preaching civil service reform. You ever want to kill the mood of a party? Bring up civil service reform. But you know what? I stirred up the old men, the entrenched and the comfortable. They hated me, in every state in the nation, and even more so the men I worked with, the other commissioners. And in return, I energized the notion of fairness, that workers of all stripes should be regarded with respect and a decent living. Do you know that before I drove a cattle prod into that agency, men could be denied a job because of their political beliefs? We changed a system that had rewarded favoritism at every level, a system in which the incompetent and useless would get the job best filled by the able and the skilled. And one more thing. I actually liked Benjamin Harrison. It seems that made me the exception in Washington. No matter. He liked me too. That made *him* an exception. Terrible thing to be a president with a moral backbone. You pay an awful price in bad publicity and haranguing speeches. And in his case, it got him tossed out of office after a single term, and it brought back in Grover Cleveland. God help the USA."

Hagedorn stared at his pad, and Roosevelt knew he was hesitating.

"What is it? A good biographer has to ask all the questions, no matter how idiotic. Go ahead."

"Sir, might I be allowed to ask you about your brother, Elliott?"

Roosevelt had expected this, but he searched for words, a rarity.

"He died about twenty-five years ago. He was too young. Abused himself terribly, and his mind paid the price for that. His body followed. There was nothing anyone could have done to change his ways. That's all I have to say." He watched the young man scribbling again, then said, "There is another loss you should know about, whether or not you write it down. About the same time that Elliott died, we lost Wilmot Dow. He and his uncle, Bill Sewall, helped to change my life in the Dakotas, and they're not even Westerners; they're from Maine. The finest men I've ever known. Write that down, Mr. Hagedorn."

"Yes, sir. Thank you."

"I got along all right with President Cleveland. I assume you were going to ask me that. The world always seems so interested in how presidents get along. Mortal enemies, best friends, playful antagonists? Cleveland supported most of my efforts, and allowed me to make my own enemies. I always appreciated that. Without enemies, you know, politics is no fun at all."

"Have you always fancied yourself a police officer?"

Roosevelt sat back, stared.

"What an odd question. You mean did I enjoy being police commissioner of New York? By jove, I did. Just like the reform movements in Washington, reforming the New York police department was a challenge, and utterly fulfilling. And a good many of those people hated me in the process."

Hagedorn laughed now, a surprise.

"I sense there is a recurring theme in your life, sir."

Roosevelt was recalling why he liked the man.

"You want to lead the dance, you have to step on some toes. I rather enjoy that. But New York in 1895 was different. Those people, those police officers, all the way to the top . . . well almost to the top . . . they had been doing a difficult and dangerous job since the city was founded. It's one thing to attack a complacent bureaucrat and swat him in the backside with a broom. Dealing with corruption when men carry guns, men who tend to put up a united front against you, well, that requires tact, skill, diplomacy. And an occasional show of force. There were powerful people fighting against me. I succeeded in firing a few of them. That helped. Got their attention, anyway. The newspapers too. I found myself reforming again, whether those people wanted to be reformed or not." He paused, smiled. "I closed the saloons, you know. It was a hotbed of corruption for the bad officers. So, I just shut them down. I thought the German New Yorkers would hang me, since I took away their beer. I was quite possibly the most unpopular man in New York. No, I was *definitely* the most unpopular man in New York. And yet my name was rising everywhere else. Very strange."

"But you campaigned for President McKinley. Were you still police commissioner?"

"I took some good advice, something I don't often do. General Charles Collis, good man, fought in the Civil War, Medal of Honor. He was public works commissioner at the time, had his share of problems too. Told me to leave New York while I still could, with my head up. So, I did. When William McKinley began his campaign, I threw in with him. You have to find opportunity where it might lay, and I had other dreams. I also had children to feed and a home to take care of. For all the magnificence of my literary accomplishments, the fact is, Mr. Hagedorn, my books don't sell all that well."

"Sir, how did you go from police commissioner of New York to vice president?"

Roosevelt was surprised.

"You're missing a chapter in your research, Mr. Hagedorn. Recall McKinley's campaign. The opposition, if you can call him that, was William Jennings Bryan. I have never experienced a more thunderous, obtuse, malevolent big mouth than Bryan. In 1896 he launched into the Democratic campaign, spouting some of the most ridiculous claims about all he would do to save the world. McKinley and his intimates were terrified that Bryan could so bowl over the mindless voters, and there are plenty of those in every state, that he could take the presidency. He insisted, for God's sake, that we return to the halcyon days when agriculture ruled the world, as though the Industrial Revolution was an unhappy accident. The man makes a career out of becoming hysterical and pushing his audience to do the same. At first, I didn't believe Bryan would win, but, nonetheless, I offered to take to the stump and do a speech-making jaunt for the McKinley campaign. It seems to have worked. To my enormous relief, McKinley won by a sizable margin. But where one would expect an immediate show of gratitude, I found myself groveling for the job I truly wanted. It took until April 1897 for the president to finally grant me the plum I was after. I became assistant secretary of the navy."

"And is that when you started the war with Spain?"

CHAPTER 25

He couldn't keep his eyes from the rich blue sea, a marvelous reminder of so many journeys across the North Atlantic, the cruises to Europe. He watched the horizon, searching for other ships, but there was nothing to see. Until now, Roosevelt had merely been a passenger, and quite likely an inconvenience to those whose responsibility it was to manage a great ship. Now, as the *Iowa* moved away from the Virginia coast, he carried real authority, was by all definitions the senior naval official on board. Even the commander of the great battleship, a stern, well-seasoned seaman, Captain James Sampson, deferred to Roosevelt with what seemed to be genuine politeness, characteristic of a naval officer who had spent a long career expressing obedience and deference to his superiors. Roosevelt returned the respect, saw Sampson's age and experience as an asset to the department Roosevelt was struggling to move forward.

He stared out over the railing, the bridge of the ship just behind him, could feel the presence of a young officer standing a step back, allowing Roosevelt free rein. The horizon was flat, the seas calm, the coastline of Virginia now out of sight, no need to search for any kind of land. But there was a speck in the distance now, and Roosevelt turned to the young man.

"What is that, far distant, there?"

"Oh, sir, that's our target buoy. We'll be engaging in practice shortly.

This ship is so new, much of the crew has yet to experience battle conditions or general quarters. That's really the purpose of this cruise."

He felt the excitement he was looking for, stared out at the target. He kept the words to himself: By Godfrey, I'd love to fire one of these big guns. I'd never hit anything, of course. But it would certainly make a lot of noise.

After a quiet moment, the young officer said, "Do you think we're in for it, sir? I mean, a real war?"

"I hope so, Lieutenant. It's something I've given a great deal of thought. This entire world is very much a world of empires. Right now, the British are most dominant in many parts of our world. But every colonial nation—Spain, Holland, Germany, Japan—they're all in possession of a great deal of territory beyond their own boundaries, and they hunger for more. In all our history, the United States has been most content to occupy our own continent, guided by the Monroe Doctrine. But that doctrine also calls for us to beware of expansion by other powers into our own part of the world, primarily Central America, or even the Caribbean. There is great concern in Washington that, besides blatant colonialism, what the Spanish are doing in Cuba is nothing short of vicious brutality against the Cuban people, people who have a right to their own destiny." He stopped, realized he was making a speech best designed for some gathering in Washington. "Sorry, Lieutenant. I tend to exhibit a bit more enthusiasm for my *causes* than suits my audience."

"Oh, that's all right, sir. I understand. Word around here is that we might go to war against Spain. From what you say, there might be good reason."

Roosevelt laughed, his eyes still on the distant target.

"If only the powers in Washington had your clarity of insight, it would be a better world. Never mind. Is there a schedule for when we shall aim for that target?"

"Fourteen hundred, sir. Right after lunch is concluded. You are welcome to go below. The captain has provided a menu for you in his quarters."

"War by time clock. A luxury for your captain, assigning orders and duties by his watch. Enjoy that, Lieutenant. Once a war begins, nothing will be done *after lunch*."

Roosevelt sat back silently, allowed Lodge to smoke his cigar.

Lodge said, "They're afraid of you, you know."

"By Godfrey, who?"

Lodge laughed.

"Most everyone, of course. But especially your own superiors— Secretary Long, and perhaps even the president. For an assistant, you have the amazing tendency to issue instructions to your own superior. It feels like you're telling Secretary Long what to do rather than the other way around."

"Secretary Long is past his time, Henry. He'd rather go on a nice, quiet vacation than manage the Navy Department. I won't just sit quietly in my office and pretend I care about whether or not he'll approve of everything I might do, every thought I might have."

"What kind of thoughts?"

"The navy is in excellent condition, though we need more of everything. The morale of the sailors, the fighting preparedness of our ships is as good as it can be. But that's not enough. We need more ships, more men, more ammunition, more powder, and more of . . . well, whatever a navy requires."

"I don't hear much about that in Congress."

"No, of course not. There you have lawyers and bankers and rich businessmen who insist on peace at any price. Well, that *price* is weakness. It goes back to the Civil War, the notion of horror, that war can only be a scourge, costly, and disastrous. That wave of public opinion affects Congress, which influences the War Department into believing that we can do nothing that might be seen as aggressive. Strength could be seen by our allies as *offensive*. So, we shy away from improvements to our military, offensively and defensively. George Washington once said, 'to be prepared for war is the most effectual means to promote peace.' He was right, of course. And right now, we are not prepared for anything. That could have deadly consequences in this world. There are a great many others who view what we possess as ripe for plucking. Weakness invites aggression. I truly believe that, and I truly believe we are dangerously weak. We need a show of strength, some pushback against aggression, a demonstration that we're capable of defending ourselves, and any other territory who looks to us for protection. Peace at any price is a direct contradiction of that. Cuba is a perfect example. Those people are struggling against the iron hand of Spain, who are using Cuba as nothing more than a source of raw materials. Worse, I am certain they have designs on other islands in the Caribbean, especially those controlled from far away by weaker powers—the Dutch, certainly. You know your history, Cabot. The Spanish once controlled most of Central and South America, and I'm betting that it smarts in Madrid that most of those nations now have their independence. The question is, how far are the Spanish willing to go? I don't know, do you? Does the president? But there are a great many governments in this hemisphere who look to us for security, who see us as allies. We cannot ignore that. We cannot embrace our weakness, especially with the Spanish ninety miles from Key West." He paused. "Cabot, what we need is a war."

He stared out toward the Executive Mansion, imagined President McKinley staring back at him. Hardly, he thought. He's more likely entertaining the bland and weak-kneed opinions of a handful of the most powerful congressmen, all of them counseling him not to listen to the firebrands in this government who are pushing for a confrontation with Spain. Poppycock. And we argue and debate and pretend we are immune from the world's problems, while our president has no more backbone than a chocolate éclair.

There was a quiet knock on his office door, the voice of an aide.

"Mr. Secretary, Colonel Wood is here."

Roosevelt spun his chair around, stood. Wood entered now, tall, firm of posture, every bit the appearance that fit Roosevelt's notion of what a senior officer should look like.

"Do come in, sir. Is it time, then?"

Wood cracked a slight smile, the most pronounced show of emotion he was likely to offer.

"By all means, Mr. Secretary. It's time."

"Then, by George, Rock Creek Park awaits."

They seemed to race from the building, Wood usually in the lead, a quick jog to the park, then their typical race through the obstacle course Roosevelt had fashioned for himself since his first days in Washington. He had created a fearful reputation by leading his various guests, including congressmen, other officials, even foreign dignitaries, up and over the hills and rocks, climbing, running, sliding down, often leading men who wore clothing ill suited for what was, by all measures, a track meet. But the only man who could regularly defeat Roosevelt in the challenge was Leonard Wood.

Wood was two years' Roosevelt's junior, another Harvard man, who had become a respected army physician. To Roosevelt's enormous admiration, Wood had been awarded the Medal of Honor for his part during the Plains Indian wars, primarily for the capture of the Indian chief Geronimo. His reputation expanding, Wood had then been named the official physician to President Cleveland and, now, McKinley.

The other partner for Roosevelt in these vigorous jaunts was Commodore George Dewey. Dewey's only disadvantage in handling Roosevelt's competitiveness was age, the man twenty years' Roosevelt's senior, who much preferred attacking Rock Creek Park on horseback, and if Roosevelt preferred to attack the great boulders, Dewey preferred to walk around them. But these days, Dewey was far away, commanding a flotilla of warships patrolling the waters along the Asian coast.

As different as Wood and Dewey were in age and demeanor, both men quickly gained an ally in Assistant Secretary of the Navy Roosevelt, who believed, as they did, in a strong military, one capable of exerting pressure worldwide when necessary. In late 1897, the most urgent cause that all three men pressed for, whether to Congress or other officials in the executive branch, was war against the government of Spain. Roosevelt knew, as did the others, that if a war was to happen, neither Congress nor President McKinley would be eager to start it. The spark would almost certainly have to come from the Spanish.

CHAPTER 26

It began with simple discomfort in her abdomen, then a fever, what might have been a nasty by-product of something she ate. But days passed, and Edith seemed to sink into the fever, hovering always over one hundred degrees, usually higher, the doctors administering all they knew how to administer, but still the pains continued.

Roosevelt began to feel a familiar panic, tried to keep that away in the quiet times when he sat beside her in the temporary home he had secured for them in Washington. He could feel the fever even through her hands, felt the utter helplessness of a husband who has no control, who might be watching his wife, *another wife,* drift away.

The birth of his son Quentin in November had been without incident, a relief not only to Roosevelt but also to every other member of his family, all of whom had too many thoughts of what had happened to Alice. But Edith's fever was very different, a relentless and unshakable fever lasting now for nearly three weeks. Roosevelt began to agree with the doctors, who suggested it was typhoid, but there was no relief to that diagnosis, just a sharp memory of that awful day, the disease that had killed his mother. He stayed with her as often as he could, but the Navy Department pulled him away, unavoidable, Edith often left in the hands of the doctors. Those men were doing all that was possible. Through it all, there was Bamie, caring now for the teenage Alice, a challenge all its own. The younger children needed more attention than Roosevelt could provide, and so Bamie was once again fulfilling the role of mother. The younger children could not understand much of what was happening, beyond the obvious, that their mother was gravely ill and that no one seemed to have a cure. As well, they were too young to understand the difficulty Roosevelt was enduring trying to maintain the household in Washington while pouring himself into the challenges that he had taken on in his official position as the navy's assistant secretary and in his unofficial position as master of everything else.

At Roosevelt's own suggestion, the frustrated doctors finally gave way to a gynecologist, who changed every diagnosis, determining that Edith had an infected nonmalignant growth in her lower abdomen. Roosevelt stood holding her hand as the surgery was completed, a show of confidence in the doctor that barely hid his terror that something still could go terribly wrong. But the surgery was successful, and Edith's fever dissipated quickly. Within days, helped no doubt by Roosevelt's and his sister Bamie's attentions, Edith was making a full and energetic recovery. Though he still carried a fear that there would be some relapse the doctors couldn't predict, his only remedy was to return to his own working world, to focus on the government's business.

THE RESTAURANT WAS completely full, the voices appropriately hushed, the quiet conversations of the *important*. Roosevelt continued eating, realized he was making a fair amount of noise with his lamb chops. He weighed the consequences, shrugged to himself, picked another one up with greasy fingers, began to gnaw the meaty remnants from the bone. He glanced up from his solitary feast, saw faces watching him, some with the usual cast of disapproval. He responded with his customary nod, hoisting a denuded bone skyward.

"Try the lamb. Dee-lightful."

He drew the usual chuckles, shaking of heads, knew that many of those men had the clout, if not the authority, to cause him trouble at the Navy Department. No matter, he thought. I do love these lamb chops.

The meal complete, he sat for a long moment, embraced the fullness of his belly, one hand smoothing over the increasing roundness beneath his belt. Edith does not approve of my gluttony, he thought. Best enjoy this sort of repast out of her sight. Hard to disguise the effects, though. He couldn't avoid a burst of worry, had tried to escape the horror of what might yet happen to Edith. Is this how it is for everyone else? If you have a loved one, can you not avoid the fear that something awful will happen? I cannot tell anyone of the stabbing terror that I feel every time she sneezes, coughs. It was one very good reason why he attacked his work so completely, and if it was not the Navy Department, it was his writing. He needed the distraction.

He knew that he was scowling now, but the faces around the restaurant were mostly trying to ignore him, some speaking in low voices with Roosevelt as their subject. He rose with a clatter, the napkin still attached to his front, the faces turning toward him again, and he made a short bow to his detractors, a wide, toothy smile.

"Gentlemen, enjoy your daily dissatisfactions and your dismal desperations. I'm dee-lighted to return to work."

He moved out onto the street with his usual quick steps, looked at the odd mix of vehicles, from the usual horse-drawn carriages to the smoke-belching noisemakers that had begun to eliminate the horse from its usefulness. Odd world, he thought. Is this what change is, gradual, a blend of old and new, until one prevails completely? And *old* rarely wins. Yes, very strange, very interesting.

He reached his building, bounded up the steps two at a time, ignored more stares, moved inside, felt the cold isolation of the Navy Department. He climbed again, two at a time, slowed as he passed the second floor, the weight along his waistline betraying him. He was breathing heavily, didn't care, moved to his office, burst into his private space, dropped hard into his chair. Now, he thought, what might we accomplish this afternoon?

The knock on the door fit the question, and he saw Secretary Long peer in.

"A moment, Theodore?"

"Certainly, sir."

"I prepared a note for you, in the event you were still absent."

"Lunch, sir."

"Oh, of course. Nonetheless, I am removing myself from the office for the rest of the day. Perhaps tomorrow as well. Things have been profoundly hectic the past few weeks, and I prefer to simply take a break. Of course, in my absence, you are in charge of the department. Thus, my note. Read it at your leisure. Good day, then, Mr. Roosevelt."

Long was gone now, and Roosevelt fingered the note, opened it, saw Long's difficult handwriting:

> *Do not take any such step affecting the policy of the*
> *Administration without consulting with the president or me. I*
> *am not away from town and my intention is only to have you*
> *look after the routine of the office . . . I am anxious to have no*
> *unnecessary occasion for a sensation in the papers.*

He stood, began to pace the office, stared out briefly toward the white Executive Mansion. He felt a sudden breath of satisfaction, thought, No one can deny that, for whatever time Long has allowed me, I am the chief of the Navy Department. It's time to go to work.

The papers began to fly, Roosevelt ordering the shipment and movement of all manner of naval supplies, including of course ammunition and fuel, to bases for deployment to ships in ports all over the country. For months, purchases of various smaller warships had been languishing in Secretary Long's files. Roosevelt ordered the purchases to be completed. To a reluctant Congress, he requested in the strongest terms that legislation be passed authorizing increased enlistment quotas for naval volunteers, as well as the promotion of the most capable men into positions of command.

As the day passed and the next one followed, Roosevelt's memos and orders flowed through Washington, and now more than just faces in a restaurant began to pay attention to this loud voice from navy. For some, their condescending smiles had become growls. For others, he was seen to have blasted the stale air out of the Navy Department. But, quickly, the talk and the arguments had less to do with Roosevelt than what it was he had ordered and proposed. It was the best he could hope for.

"WHAT ON EARTH are you doing?"

Roosevelt looked up from a sheaf of papers, put down his pen, said, "May I help you, Senator Lodge?"

"I hope I don't have to help *you*. Word is passing pretty quickly that you're pushing paper out of this building at lightning speed. I'm concerned about you, my friend. Have you gone crazy, or have you just had too many cups of coffee?"

"Either one is correct. I have an opportunity here, Cabot. Things operate at less than a snail's pace in this place, as in most of Washington. No one can fault me for lighting a few fires."

Lodge shook his head, wasn't smiling.

"I don't know exactly what all you're ordering and decreeing and specifying. But if you push too hard against too many brick walls in this town, one of those walls might fall on you."

Roosevelt ignored the warning, said, "Look here. I'd like you to read this one."

Commodore Dewey,
Order the squadron . . . to Hong Kong. Keep full of coal. In the event of a declaration of war with Spain, your duty will be to see that the Spanish squadron does not leave the Asiatic coast, and then, offensive operations in Philippines Islands . . . until further orders.
Roosevelt

Lodge looked up at him.

"You're ordering him to prepare for war."

"Cabot, no one should have to be ordered to prepare for war. It's a dangerous world, and there is one great danger right off our southern coast. The Spanish have been imprisoning the Cuban people in concentration camps, and yet no one around here seems alarmed by that. Whom else might they imprison, especially if they have no fear that we will intervene? Do the Cuban people not have the right of independence?"

Lodge stood, moved toward the door.

"You're doing good work here, Theodore. But you're not in

command of much of anything. You may very well find yourself tossed out of this place."

It was a warning Roosevelt took seriously.

"I'm doing my job. Someone has to look after things when no one else will. If that's likely to see me unemployed . . . I can't help that. I have to warn these people, and do what I can to prepare for a war that is certain to come."

Lodge looked down, and Roosevelt could see sadness on his friend's face.

"No one wants a war, Theodore."

"I didn't say I wanted one. I said we *need* one."

HE HAD NEVER seen Long's face so red.

"You know what you are, Mr. Roosevelt? You're a bull in a china shop. Have you been possessed by the devil himself? I have discussed your actions with the president. He agrees that what you've done, all that paper you've sent out of here, it has been most discourteous to *me,* your superior. You have communicated to the entire navy and most of Congress that only *you* are capable of ordering these actions, since, apparently, I will not." Long seemed to gather himself, his hands dropping down on his desk. "Know this, Mr. Roosevelt. You are never to be allowed to maintain control over this department again. Is that understood?"

Roosevelt hesitated but knew there was only one answer.

"Yes, sir."

"Now, that's all."

Roosevelt expected more.

"Um, Mr. Secretary, exactly what did I do that was wrong?"

"I have explained myself. You pulled the rug out from under my office." Long paused, shook his head, leaned back in his plush leather chair. "But the president has not ordered me to reverse any of your decrees or orders."

"You mean . . ."

"I don't know what I mean. Your storm of paper seems to be producing results, and even the president is impressed. He has determined that your requests and demands and whatever else you've done should remain in place."

Roosevelt wasn't certain he had heard Long correctly.

"Everything? What about Commodore Dewey?"

Long looked up at him, exhausted eyes, the redness fading from his cheeks.

"Especially Commodore Dewey." Roosevelt was ecstatic, tried his best to hide it. Long ignored that, said in a quieter voice, "Why? What do you know that none of us do that leads you to believe there will be a war? Or do you plan to start one? It's awfully easy, Theodore, to sit up here in this office and order warships and their men to go off and fight. There can be responsibility for that, especially for all the sons and husbands you're putting in harm's way. Do you understand that?"

"Sir, my responsibility is to my country first, before anyone else. As for my own sons, they are too young, and that is the only reason they would not fight. But, sir, I have said this before, and I repeat it now. In the event a war is declared, it is my intention to enlist myself in the army. I am only thirty-nine, sir, and I *will* fight."

IN LATE JANUARY 1898, the American battleship USS *Maine* was ordered out of its base in Key West, Florida, and sent to drop anchor in Havana Harbor in Cuba, what was diplomatically referred to as a "friendly visit." One other purpose was to protect American interests in Cuba, a need arising from the considerable conflict emerging there between Spanish troops and the Cuban populace. On February 15, 1898, at 9:40 PM, the *Maine* erupted in a catastrophic explosion, causing the loss of 260 officers and men. Immediately, Roosevelt and many others in Washington and throughout the military insisted in the strongest terms that there was no longer any reason to cling to "peace at any cost." Still, Congress and a reluctant President McKinley tiptoed through the obvious crisis, until pressure from the more militant members of Congress finally persuaded McKinley to demand Spanish withdrawal from Cuba and to authorize the U.S. Navy to blockade Cuban ports. The results were predictable. On April 23, escalating what had been a fast-moving diplomatic crisis, Spain declared war on the

United States. Two days later, faced with no alternative, and with the backing of Congress, President McKinley finally satisfied Roosevelt's energetic efforts, and the U.S. declared war on Spain.

May 1, 1898

He was finally impressed with his superior, John Long.

Commodore Dewey

War has commenced between the United States and Spain. Proceed at once to the Philippine Islands. Begin operations at once particularly against the Spanish fleet. You must capture vessels or destroy. Use utmost endeavors.

Secretary Long

Long sat back, waited for him to read.

"You see, Theodore? Not everything has to carry your heavy handprints. These orders went out five days ago, under the direct supervision of the president. We're waiting for word as to the results."

Roosevelt leaned forward, seemed to hang on Long's words.

Long paused, stared at him with tired eyes. "It isn't necessary to grade me, Mr. Roosevelt. You are not my teacher, and I am not your student. I hope now you understand that just because you wish something done on your own timetable does not mean the thing will not get done. We are at war. Some, such as you, seem positively giddy about that. I am not. And neither is the president. We have seen war, we have seen the cost, the horror, we are reluctant to look at a sea of young men and order them to go fight and possibly die, unless there is a very damn good reason. I am still not convinced that the Spanish have given us one, but before you spew out venom all over my desk, know that now that the thing has happened, we shall see it through. Commodore Dewey is half a world away, and he knows what we are asking him to do. I believe you met Captain Sampson of the *Iowa*. He has been promoted to rear admiral and has been named to command all naval forces in the North Atlantic. He also knows what to do. It is no longer necessary for you to issue proclamations and requests from this office unless Congress or the president requires it. You seem to forget that we have no definitive proof of just what happened to the *Maine*. It's a great rallying cry for the uneducated, 'Remember the *Maine*,' all of that. Great calls for revenge. Who's responsible for that? The Spanish?"

"Certainly they are."

"How do you know? Our own investigation wasn't clear on who caused that explosion. It's convenient for us to blame the Spanish, as it is convenient for them to blame us. That one diplomat, claiming it was our own crew by their own behavior . . . ridiculous, yes? But what if he's right? Some enormous mistake in a powder magazine, what seems now only to have been a mine explosion from outside. The point is, we don't know. Now, with war declared, we may never know."

"With war declared, it hardly matters."

"To you, perhaps. But there are those of us, including the president, who insist on knowing if what we are doing is justified, moral. If that's not important to you, well, God help you."

Roosevelt wasn't sure what to say, paced a few steps, then back. He could feel Long watching him, said, "Do I understand correctly that I am to continue my work upgrading and modernizing this navy to increase readiness so that we may actually fight this war as efficiently as possible? All under your supervision, of course."

Long let out a breath.

"War changes things. Do your job as you've been doing. It isn't necessary for me to examine every scrap of paper you send out of here. Just try not to start any *more* wars. Do you understand, Mr. Roosevelt?"

Roosevelt couldn't stay seated, the raw excitement of the moment too much for sitting. He moved to the back of his chair, a fiercely enthusiastic nod.

"I do understand, Mr. Secretary. Thank you."

"For what?"

Roosevelt chose his words.

"For allowing me to pursue the best interests of this department and our country."

"We're doing what we have to do. It's the judgment of men, fallible men. I have no idea if we're acting in our best interests, Mr. Roosevelt."

"I don't agree, sir. History will prove that our actions against the Spanish will secure our hemisphere for generations, perhaps centuries."

"If you say so. I am more concerned that Commodore Dewey doesn't get his fleet blown out of the water. You should be too. I'm waiting for word. I'd hoped we would have received some sort of communication by now, but the Philippines is a very long way away."

There was a soft knock, and Roosevelt responded with a jump, moved that way, saw the young officer holding a note.

"Excellent. Let me see that." He began to tear into the paper, realized what he was doing, handed the note with a formal bow to Long.

"Thank you, Mr. Roosevelt. I'm happy to read this aloud, since that's the only way I'll keep you from crawling across my desk. Hmm. This isn't from Dewey. It's from the Spanish, or at least it has been passed along from our consulate in Manila. 'To My Fellow Spaniards: The North American people, constituted of all the social excrescences, have exhausted our patience and provoked war with their perfidious machinations, with their acts of treachery . . . The God of Victories will give us one as brilliant and complete as the righteousness and justice of our cause demands. Spain will emerge triumphantly, humiliating and blasting the adventurers . . . insolence, cowardice . . . vain designs, ridiculous boastings . . .' Oh, for crying out loud. Whoever this fellow is, he loves the sound of his own voice." He handed the note to Roosevelt. "Here. You can frame this. This official does everything here except mention you by name."

Roosevelt read the rest of the proclamation and said, "I suppose this is what you do when you don't have a legitimate cause to fight for. You just insult your enemy."

"Sir?"

A different young man appeared now, yet another piece of paper. Long motioned to Roosevelt, who retrieved the note.

"It's from communications." He felt a cold blast in his stomach, saw the message signed by Dewey. "May I, sir?" Long gave a short wave with his hand. "I wouldn't dare stop you."

Roosevelt read, then began pacing, the words rolling off the paper.

"By Godfrey. He sank the fleet."

Long stood now, held out a hand.

"Give me that."

Roosevelt obeyed, and Long sat again, read, said, "It appears you're right, Mr. Roosevelt. He took his entire complement into Manila Bay and obliterated the Spanish fleet. Our losses were minimal. Good Lord."

Roosevelt heard emotion in the older man's voice, waited for more, but Long put the paper on the desk.

"Send someone out to check on the newspapers. It won't be long before this is headline news. The Hearst people will go crazy with this." He looked up at Roosevelt now. "It appears the first battle belongs to us."

Roosevelt couldn't control his childlike excitement, slapped a fist into his hand.

"Dewey is a hero. This is magnificent. *This is bully!*"

Long didn't seem impressed.

"What this is, Mr. Roosevelt, is narrowing our focus. With the Philippines handled, our concern right now is south. We must put all our energy into the next objective."

"Yes, sir. Cuba."

CHAPTER 27

April 27, 1898
Washington, D.C.

"Are you certain of this?"

"I am quite certain, Mr. President."

Roosevelt stood stiffly, as though standing at attention would demonstrate to McKinley that he was qualified to be a soldier.

"Well, both the secretary of war and General in Chief Miles have signed off on this, so I have no reason to contradict their approval. And I have to repeat to you that the offer they put to you still stands. They feel it might be appropriate that you command the regiment, at the rank of full colonel."

"Thank you, sir. But as I have stated before, Leonard Wood is far more qualified for the command. I am happy to serve as his second-in-command, as lieutenant colonel."

"Hard to dispute your decision, Mr. Roosevelt. But, as qualified as Colonel Wood might be, word has already begun to circulate that the men most likely to join your regiment will do so because of their loyalty to and familiarity with you."

"Sir, all I want is to serve at the front. If required, I would serve as a private and carry a rifle. Regardless, I make no pretense as to my abilities to command. Leonard Wood is far more suited."

McKinley shrugged. "As you suggest, Mr. Roosevelt."

Roosevelt let out a breath of relief, was wondering if the president, as well as the secretary of war, Russell Alger, would insist he command the First U.S. Volunteer Cavalry solely to remove Roosevelt from his thorny position at the Navy Department. The suggestion that Roosevelt command the regiment had seemed to drop out of the sky, as though no one was paying much attention to whether that command or the cavalry unit truly mattered. Roosevelt had other ideas.

LODGE HELD UP his glass, a swirl of brown liquid.

"I salute you, my friend. I was one of many who didn't truly believe you were going to strap on a sword, climb your horse, and march off to war. Not everyone here is sorry to see you go, of course. But there are others ... Henry Adams has wondered aloud if you have simply gone mad."

Roosevelt smiled, a brisk nod toward Lodge.

"Perhaps I have." He was serious now. "I'm doing what I must. Tell them that, all the detractors and those who enjoy a good laugh over their brandy. I know ..." He paused. "I know I might not be completely sure of my motives. But I have pledged to do this for years, and I will honor the pledge. I have been told that this will likely destroy any chances I have for a political career."

Lodge nodded slowly. "Very likely."

"It will be an acceptable price to pay, to launch myself into our country's fight."

"If you aren't killed in the process."

Roosevelt shook his head.

"I won't be killed. They wouldn't dare."

May 2, 1898

"Good Godfrey, what is all this?"

He stepped over a massive cloth bag, then another, saw his aide, the young ensign Sharp, struggling with another bag through the outer door.

"Sir, it's mail. All addressed to you. They're mostly applications to

227

join your cavalry regiment. And the newspapers . . . they're fueling this, pretty sure. I didn't know your unit had a name."

"Neither did I."

"Well, according to the papers, there's several: Teddy's Tarantulas, Roosevelt's Rough 'Uns, Teddy's Cowboys. And a good many more, sir."

"This is outrageous. I'm not in command of the regiment. It belongs to Colonel Wood."

"It doesn't seem to matter, sir. You're the one they're clamoring about. These bags . . . according to the post office, there's over twenty thousand letters here."

"Twenty thousand . . . ?" He stepped over another sack, moved into his office, another sack in front of his desk. He grabbed a handful of letters, sat at his desk, read through a sample.

I would be honored to serve the great Teddy Roosevelt . . .
Please consider my application . . . I can shoot straight and do
well on a horse . . .
I should hope to become one of Teddy's Rough Riders . . .

He stopped, thought, Where do they feel so privileged as to refer to me by a casual nickname that belongs to no one but my family? And *rough riders*? This is not some Buffalo Bill show, some circus. This is serious business, putting men in the field who, indeed, might be some rough-riding men, but they will not be rough in their behavior, or their discipline.

He heard a clamor outside his office, stood, called out to his aide, "Mr. Sharp, what is the noise?"

He was surprised to see Long now, stumbling angrily into his office.

"By Jesus, Theodore, you've started a riot. I came down here to wish you well, offer you a toast of farewell, as it were, and I am accosted by a dozen young men on the main floor who insist I lead them to *you*. This is still the Navy Department, you know. Get these people under control."

Roosevelt sat back in his chair, had never expected this, had no idea that his own enthusiasm for a fight would spread so completely. He glanced at the letters piled on his desk, Mississippi, Missouri, Arizona, Iowa, said,

"I don't know what to do, sir."

"Well, figure it out. If they're to be your men, you have to command them. So . . . command them."

"Quite so, sir."

"Look, Theodore, I just came down here to say that I wish you good fortune, and that this war does not cause us too much anguish. Go, do your job. If you come back whole, likely this desk would be yours again."

Roosevelt stared at Long, thought, Or just as likely not. But he knew this was a moment that he could not let pass. He had to say something to the old man.

"Sir, I hate to leave you. But I hope you understand why I must. It's the same passion that brings all of this mail, that brings those young men to my door. I know that some are thinking me a fool."

"That they are."

"I cannot let that sway me. Opinions matter little when bullets are flying."

"If you say so, Theodore. I have wondered if you are, in fact, out of your mind or are simply behaving in a suicidal manner against all good sense. And yet how absurd that will be if, by some turn of good fortune, you should accomplish some great thing and strike a very high mark. Pay attention to that. Don't just go off with a gun in your hand lusting to kill the enemy. These men want you to lead them. So . . . lead them."

On May 12, Roosevelt left Washington for the regiment's training ground at San Antonio, Texas. Shortly after arriving, he was astounded to see a large sign erected at the train station pointing the way to the fields and camps occupied by Roosevelt's Rough Riders. Horrified at first that this was an enormous breach of military etiquette, Roosevelt sought out Colonel Wood to apologize. In a surprise to Roosevelt, Wood had no issue with the sign and all that it symbolized. Most of these men, from Harvard gentlemen and New York dudes to western ranchers and rugged cowboys, had joined the unit solely because of Roosevelt. Wood had approved the sign himself.

CHAPTER 28

May 23, 1898
San Antonio, Texas

There had been no respite from the heat, and Roosevelt had quickly surmised that the choice of San Antonio as their training ground had been made by someone who understood just what fighting in the tropics might mean.

That person, whoever he might have been, did not, however, choose the uniforms, which were heavy wool, right down to the socks.

He ordered the men off their horses, the river close, the men eyeing him for approval as they tore off shirts and wool jackets, a brief plunge into the lukewarm water, a considerable relief from the raw heat and dust they endured on horseback.

He kept himself on his mount, named Little Texas, made a mental note how long it had been, five minutes, then a quick motion of his hand, the men mounting up again, coats in place, few signs that they had been in the water at all.

"THIS IS ABSURD."

Wood handed him the note. "Perhaps. Read it for yourself. There is a regulation in the books. The men are to be issued winter uniforms, so that by wintertime there will be no shortages."

Roosevelt began to pace, felt the pulsing anger building.

Wood said, "Please sit down, Colonel. You're making *me* sweat."

Roosevelt sat in the rickety wooden chair, couldn't hold it in. "So, we dress the men in deadly clothing now, killing them in the summer heat, so they'll be equipped come January. Has anyone informed the commissary department that we are fighting a war with the Spanish, in tropical Cuba? It isn't any more likely to be cold then than it is now."

Wood seemed to be keeping something to himself, so hard to tell behind the emotionless expression. "You have more influence with men in high places than I do. Contact them."

Roosevelt looked at the order again, still fought to control his temper. "Contact whom? What else is there? How much more stupidity are we asked to deal with?"

Wood retrieved another paper from the makeshift table. "Well, then you'll enjoy this. 'The men are to be trained in the use of the saber.'"

Roosevelt leaned forward, took that paper as well. "Swords? We're to use swords? In the jungle? And if there's no jungle, we'll be in the open. Someone needs to be told that the enemy uses rifles. The Spanish train their soldiers too."

Wood shook his head, a rare show of frustration. "We can use the swords, I suppose, to hack our way through brush, or perhaps cut down trees."

"Please, Colonel Wood, don't just accept these orders. These decrees are being passed down from mindless bureaucrats in the War Department."

Wood stared at him for a moment, then said, "You know anyone who might have the ability to overrule the War Department?"

Roosevelt waited for a smile on Wood's face, not there.

"I know one man who might listen. He doesn't owe me anything, but I believe he takes me seriously. At the very least, he's probably tired of hearing me complain. I'll have a wire sent to Washington tonight. The president ought to receive it by tomorrow morning."

THE MEN SCRAMBLED through the piles of khaki, shirts and pants pulled on, raucous shouts and playful jabs at the ill-fitted. Roosevelt stood back, Wood nearby, other officers standing in a group. Wood looked over toward him, and Roosevelt caught the glance, knew that Wood was impressed, that Roosevelt's wire to President McKinley had had an immediate effect on those "mindless bureaucrats."

Unlike the enlisted men, the officers had the responsibility for purchasing their own uniforms, something Leonard Wood was accustomed to, a practice completely foreign to Roosevelt. But it was a practice he adapted to immediately, and with considerable style. He had ordered his tan uniform from Brooks Brothers in New York. In color and the light weight of material, it matched what his soldiers were now being issued. There were differences of course—Roosevelt's shirt adorned with yellow trim and, most important to him, his hat specially fitted to allow for spare spectacles to be slipped into the brim.

He walked away from the melee, moved toward his tent, which was parked close beside Wood's. He scanned the perimeter of the San Antonio Fair Grounds, what served now as their training ground, saw sightseers peering in along the closest fence. The throng was nothing like it had been a few days before, the training exercises an open house that brought a civilian invasion, thousands gazing intently upon their newly minted soldiers. The drills and routines seemed to be stepped up a notch for the onlookers, none of them disappointed, the newspaper reporters once again taking up the call that these men belonged to the famous Roosevelt. Once more, the one nickname that seemed to stick, despite his own wish that it would go away, was Roosevelt's Rough Riders.

He reached the tent, saw a man coming toward him quickly, short and thin, a stringy handlebar moustache, the uniform of an officer. The man wore a wide smile, mimicking Roosevelt's own.

"Sir, excuse me. A minute, please?"

Roosevelt stopped, couldn't resist the man's obvious energy.

"You're Captain O'Neill, is that right?"

"Yes, sir. Bucky O'Neill."

"I'm doing my best to learn the names of every man in the regiment. I think I have the officers down so far."

"Yes, sir. Thank you."

He was caught by O'Neill's ebullience, saw a great deal of himself in the man's boundless enthusiasm for the job.

"What can I do for you, Captain?"

"Sir, I just want to thank you for what you've done for the men. The uniforms are a real boost, the new rifles coming in are a godsend, and the word is, sir, that you've made certain we don't have to wear those ridiculous sabers."

"You seem to be unusually attuned to gossip, Captain. Don't give me credit for too much. Like you, I'm just looking out for the men."

"Sir, please forgive me, but I know a good leader when I see one. I was a lawman in Arizona, spent time as the mayor of Prescott, and I knew a good many men who were fit and a good many more who were unfit. I come to know the difference."

Roosevelt laughed.

"No introductions are needed, Captain. I heard of you when I was in the Dakotas. For a sheriff and Indian hunter, you're pretty well known. I remember reading your application for command. Your father fought in the Civil War."

"Yes, sir. Fought under General Meagher, the Irish Brigade."

"Well, if I have anything to say about it, you'll get plenty of fighting right here."

"I'm hoping so, sir." He paused, a silent moment between them, Roosevelt looking up at a darkening sky. Finally, O'Neill said, "Sir, forgive me for asking. This isn't something I can talk to my men about. You ever get afraid? Dying and all?"

Roosevelt was surprised by the question.

"Every day. And never. If I've done the right thing and have a clear conscience, I'm ready to go out. If I have to make up for something, well, then I want more time. I suppose that's what makes me afraid, that I've left too much undone."

O'Neill pointed a finger at him. "That's putting it squarely, sir. As a lawman, I've had to put up with my fair share of foolishness, when the risk was death. I survived some pretty dangerous situations, so I'm guessing the odds are against me by now." He laughed. "Before I left Arizona to come here, I took out a pair of life insurance policies, so my wife is accounted for. Maybe that helps the odds in my favor."

"You won't need those, Captain. If we get into this thing, we'll make short work."

"I hope not, sir. I want to fight, and I want a tough fight, so I can say I did it."

"That's why all of us are here. We can say we did it."

THE DAY HAD been hot, the training intensely difficult, the men following Roosevelt now back toward their camps. He wiped the sweat from his eyes, blinked through the salty grit, looked out across the river, a settlement he knew as Riverside Park. One sign caught his eye, rising high on a plank of rough wood, REFRESHMENTS, and another, smaller sign, BEER.

He turned, saw Company A's flag, called out, "Captain O'Neill, forward."

O'Neill came close now, said, "Yes, sir. I have to say, sir, my men are ready for some rest."

"I'm guessing they're also ready for something to drink. Captain, the men are authorized to dismount and find their way to all the beer they can drink. I'll pay for it."

Word spread quickly, a loud cheer engulfing him, the men now in a mad scramble through the shallow water to the park. O'Neill stayed close, said, "Company A is grateful, sir."

"What about you, Captain? Go on, enjoy yourself. Just because you're an officer doesn't mean you can't enjoy the company of your men and a few dozen bottles of beer."

O'Neill hesitated, surprising him.

"I'm not certain of that, sir. Might not be seemly for an officer to drink with his men."

"Nonsense. Enjoy yourself."

"WHERE IN HELL did you get the notion that you are a *good friend* to your men?"

Roosevelt started to speak, but Wood held up his hand.

"This is no carnival, Colonel. You've said that yourself. This is an army at war, and there are rules about that sort of thing. Officers are in command by their discipline and the good training of their men.

Under fire, a soldier must rely on the strength and brains of his officers, and not just because they've been his drinking buddy. We're out there teaching these men to follow their orders without question. What you've done by endearing yourself to them is undermine that discipline. 'Oh, it's all right to disobey. Mr. Roosevelt's our friend.' In my opinion, and the opinion of the army, an officer who drinks with his men is not fit to hold a commission. Am I clear, Colonel?"

He felt a burn on his face, down his neck, the sharp butterflies in his stomach. He was embarrassed, ashamed, angry at himself. He absorbed the chewing out, more temper than he had ever seen from Wood.

"Sir, I consider myself the damnedest ass within ten miles of this camp."

Wood stared at him for a long moment.

"That you are, Colonel Roosevelt. Just don't do it again. Dismissed."

Roosevelt bowed slightly, then threw up a salute, which Wood answered.

"You're inside my tent, Colonel. You don't have to do that."

"I insist, sir. You will not have cause to doubt my fitness for command again. Good night, sir."

May 27, 1898

The unit stood stiffly at attention, the bugler beginning the sorrowful notes no one wanted to hear. Roosevelt stood beside Wood, the other officers scattered throughout their commands, company commanders and platoon leaders all staring ahead as the soft music drifted past them.

The trooper's name was Irad Cochran. At first, his injury was thought to be not all that severe, his horse throwing him in the midst of the usual morning exercises. But Cochran's head had impacted the ground with a sickening crack, and the doctors were immediately aware that the injury was far more serious than they could treat at the encampment. The young man was sent quickly to Fort Sam Houston, and the diagnosis was grim from the start, the wound leading to fever and meningitis. In less than a day, the injury some had thought would pass with little more than a headache had proved fatal. Cochran had died the night he was injured.

The bugler completed his playing of "Taps," and Roosevelt felt sick, kept his gaze forward, knew there was high emotion among the men. There had been other injuries, to be sure, most of them to do with unruly horses. But Trooper Cochran was the first to die. The question rolled through Roosevelt now, a question he had kept far away, shoved aside by the adventure of it all. How many more of us?

Beside him, Wood called out, "That is all. Return to your billets."

The men began to move away, the formation breaking up. But some stayed, and Roosevelt watched them, felt a twinge of alarm. How will this affect them? The training has been rugged and difficult, but in the end the men were learning, becoming one unit, comradeship and pride in their skills increasing. How many of them embraced the notion that they might die or were utterly immune from death? And what about you, Colonel? You've wallowed in their adulation, and no matter how often you protested their nickname, Rough Riders, you rather enjoy that, right? Are you prepared to die?

Beside him, Wood said, "Very difficult, always. We're in a dangerous business, and most of these boys just learned that."

"Yes, sir. I hope it doesn't turn them away from it all."

Wood looked at him.

"You mean, the fight? They'll be all right. The rough boys will help the others. Most of these men have never seen death or blood in the field. But they'll help each other. I saw it when I was out west, the fear and the uneasiness, their backbones strengthened by having a man beside them. No matter if an entire squadron is fresh, no one wants to be the man who runs, who can't take it. They say that cowardice is contagious. I don't believe that. From my experience, it's the other way around. It's bravery that's contagious. No, Mr. Roosevelt. They'll be fine."

He looked out across the field, saw officers speaking to their men, small clusters, doing exactly what Wood had described.

Roosevelt said, "I'm not sure how this usually goes, of course. But we've been training for a few weeks now. That may not be enough, but most of these men look fit, most are handling their horses well, their rifles. But there's an itch in them, that unless we get moving soon, we'll miss out, the war will go on without us. That will make them reckless, damage their morale."

Wood looked at him again, a hint of a smile.

"Is that itch coming from the men or is it in you?"

Roosevelt looked down, a silent moment, said, "We're in Texas, for Godfrey's sake. The war is a great many miles from here. It's time to go."

May 29, 1898

The telegram came from the War Department directly to Colonel Wood, ordering that the First U.S. Volunteer Cavalry was to board the half dozen trains that would carry them to Tampa, Florida. The loading took a couple of days, the trains moving east and south through the kind of land most of these men had never seen. They stared with curiosity at Spanish moss and swampland, alligators and white plantation houses, some untouched since before the Civil War. They passed through towns that had felt Sherman's torch, the tramp of ten thousand boots, the musket fire from both the North and South.

The men were surprised to draw crowds and cheers everywhere they passed, the newspapers leading the way with tales of the exploits of the Rough Riders. Whether those tales had any basis in fact, the reporters seemed not to care, and the troopers responded with waves and calls of their own. Very few of the crowds could distinguish from any other troop train and the ones carrying Roosevelt's Rough Riders, but that seemed not to matter. In every case, the civilians already seemed to regard these men as heroes.

After a four-day journey, they rolled into the freight yards in Tampa, but there was nothing glorious about their destination. The trains were halted at least two miles outside the city, caught up in a traffic jam of supply cars and other troop trains. The chaos was absolute, Colonel Wood ordering his men to billet well beyond their designated camps until space or transportation could be arranged. Eventually, the misery of the confusion was sorted out, the men marching to their correct camps only a mile outside town. Roosevelt had expected to stay with them, as he had in San Antonio. But the army had other ideas. The senior officers were headquartered in the Tampa Bay Hotel, an opulent structure near the heart of the city. Waiting for Roosevelt were the usual crowds of reporters, who had questions about his command and even more questions about the commander himself. As much as he appreciated the attention, he was quick to find that there was jealousy aplenty from other units and their commanders. The newspapers seemed only interested in the exploits, real or imagined, of the Rough Riders and the man who, according to the papers, commanded them. Under the sharp gaze of other officers he didn't know, he forced himself to back away from the glare of so much adulation. For the most part, his efforts didn't work.

Besides the reporters, there was one other temporary resident arriving at the Tampa Bay Hotel. On June 6, Roosevelt had a much-anticipated visitor, an answer to an invitation he had doubted would be accepted. It was one more luxury for a man who seemed to be followed by them. Edith had arrived.

SHE STARED OUT the window toward the vast bay, said, "This is beautiful, Teddy."

"I wish I had time to enjoy that, especially with you. But we received word today to be prepared to ship out at any time. I admit, I am anxious to board that ship. I had thought, truly, that I would miss it all."

She turned to him, her hands on his shoulders.

"Then I am happy I came, if only to be with you a short time. We do not know what will happen."

He thought of Trooper Cochran, the sad notes of "Taps." He had said nothing of that to her and would not now.

"It will be fine. The Spanish are said to be poor fighters with poor weapons. Once we're there, it should be short work."

"You are a poor liar."

"A man is a liar when he doesn't believe what he says. I believe every word. But it is one thing to march off to war. I am in command of near a thousand good men, well trained, well equipped, who respect their commanders. There has never been an army like this in any part of the world who has failed to succeed. I am grateful to be a part of it."

There was a knock, and Roosevelt leaned close to the door. "Yes?"

"Sir, forgive the intrusion. General Shafter wishes to meet you, sir. Right away, if it is not inconvenient. I will escort you, sir."

He turned to her, spoke in a low voice. "When the commanding general calls and sends his aide to fetch you, you had best go."

"Of course, Teddy. Return as soon as you can. I will go down to the veranda. It looks lovely."

He hesitated, knew that she was one of a very few women who had come to visit their husbands. Already there was talk of such impropriety. But he knew she could hold her own, whether or not anyone knew just whose wife she was.

"Enjoy yourself, Edie."

HE WAS ASTOUNDED to see William Shafter, the man easily three hundred pounds, the first thought entering Roosevelt's mind: How is he going to ride a horse?

"Good to meet you, Colonel. You have quite the reputation, here and in Washington."

"Thank you, General."

"I'm glad you and your men are prepared for this journey. These days, if you're not right here, you'll probably miss the whole thing. Your name will look good in the papers, a morale boost for the whole army."

Roosevelt cringed, knew that Wood was standing off to one side, absorbing more of the mythology that surrounded them.

Shafter seemed to be in pain, shifted his weight from leg to leg, said, "I fought in the Civil War, you know. Bloody awful, those days. They gave me one of those medals everybody is so eager to receive. All I did was kill rebels. Just like we expect to do here. Spaniards, of course. Though it is my expectation that once they get a good look at us, they'll scamper away. They were foolish to start this thing. We'll see how long it takes to end it."

Shafter was distracted by another officer, moved away, waddling slightly. Roosevelt slid closer to Wood, said in a low voice, "He's not what I expected."

"He's not what any of us expected. He's gained a hundred pounds in a year, and he limps from gout. He's right about the Medal of Honor. But he wears that medal around his neck, even when he leaves it home. You ask him about that, and he'll talk for an hour. Someone should tell him that the Spaniards know how to dig trenches just like Lee and Longstreet did. I doubt there's going to be much *scampering* by anyone."

"Maybe he should hear that from you."

Wood coughed, a slight laugh.

"No one tells General Shafter anything he doesn't want to hear. He's the commanding general, and if he decides he doesn't like you, you'll sit right here for the duration. No, sir. You and I . . . we're keeping our mouths shut."

CHAPTER 29

June 14, 1898
Aboard USS *Yucatan*

The order to board the transports had first come on June 8, six days before, an impatient General Shafter ordering the ships to set sail, only to receive a contradictory order from Washington. The cause was a panic-laden report of enemy activity, stating that the Spanish had moved gunboats and a torpedo boat into the presumed route of travel, laying a trap for the mostly defenseless transports. Shafter had obeyed Washington's orders to pull the ships back into port. But instead of off-loading the troops, he ordered them to remain aboard the transports, assuming that a new order might come at any time to resume the operation. Certainly, that made sense to Shafter. But to the men, who were trapped on board the ships, the decision was uncomfortable at best and could have been catastrophic. With the yellow fever season fast approaching in Cuba, the logical fear was that every day's delay could mean the army was sailing straight into a cauldron of horrifying disease. But that fear only added to the misery the men endured on the ships. With no anticipation by the commissary officers that the men would be shipbound for an extra six days, the food supplies were woefully inadequate. As it was, Roosevelt's men had learned that, throughout their travels, through San Antonio to Tampa to the USS *Yucatan*, the food had gotten worse at each stop along the way. What rations there were now consisted mostly of unsalted canned beef, beans, and canned tomatoes, along with the usual hardtack and coffee. There was fear as well that some ailment might lurk in the ship's water supply, the freshwater tanks on the *Yucatan* suspiciously smelly, the taste of the water nauseating.

There were ways around these handicaps of course, especially for the resourceful, who understood the value of bribing a cook. While that might have increased the amount of the rations they had to eat, it didn't do much to change the menu.

Roosevelt allowed himself the luxury of a deep breath of the cool air, looked back along the ship's decks, men crowded shoulder to elbow, most of them doing what he did now. He could see the faces, some looking back at him, smiles and waves. He didn't fault them their casual behavior, knew that once they were back on land, the salutes would return.

He smiled to himself, thought of Edith. *I'm so happy she came. It would be a terrible thing if something happened to me and we never had a real goodbye.* In the days he had waited to board ship and then the days on board, Roosevelt had poured out his usual flow of letter writing, missives to every member of his family, especially his children. *I already miss them,* he thought. *My blessed bunnies. How they would have found adventure in all of this, even the most miserable parts.* He smiled. *They'd probably enjoy the canned beef. And then there are the horses, so many men with rifles, and of course this ship.* He laughed now. *What a young boy sees, compares to what is. They will learn reality soon enough, all of them, just as I did. Yes, it would have been nice to have them here, with Edie. Perhaps I could have arranged a suite . . .* He stopped. *No, don't be a fool. You have enough detractors as it is. Don't give them bait . . . and the reporters. You make enough good copy for them already. Here's a headline:* ROOSEVELT TAKES HIS FAMILY TO WAR. *I'd never work in Washington again.*

He scanned the men, was happy to see the officers scattered among them, no one in his command a martinet, none too proud to stand beside the men of his own company, his own platoon. He spotted Bucky O'Neill, saw more Westerners, Curry and Ballard and Brodie, and others, Capron, Hamilton Fish, and Micah Jenkins. He thought of the Easterners, so many college boys, Greenway and Kane and Goodrich. He marveled at how many had come to the regiment from the far west, some from the Dakotas who were eager to serve with the man they knew and others from elsewhere who knew his reputation. He didn't talk about that, not to them or to Leonard Wood. *I came here to fight*, he thought, *not to make headlines, not to make friends. As Secretary Long said, they expect me to lead them. Just do a good job of it.*

The sun was setting, a dull reflection of a distant warship, and he focused on that, recalled the *Iowa*, the pure adventure of such a violent beast. Close by was another, much smaller craft, what he had been told was a torpedo boat, one more layer in the veil of protection. *It looks like some kind of toy*, he thought, then remembered the briefing from the *Yucatan*'s captain, that the torpedo boats had the ability to sink any size ship and then simply scamper away. *Venomous little devils*, he thought. *I'm happy they're ours.*

He heard music, men responding with respectful cheers, then silence. He turned, saw the band gathered at the stern, brass and woods and a great deal of skill. They belonged to the Second Regiment, were orphans of a sort now. The original order had called for the Second Regiment, the Seventy-First New York Volunteers, and Wood's men to be transported on the *Yucatan*, a situation that none of the men or their officers found appealing. Roosevelt had solved the problem by ordering his men to board the ship at the pier in Tampa as rapidly as possible, then hold station against anyone else who tried to board. For reasons the navy would never have approved of, the strategy worked. But the band and a fraction of the other regiments had made it on board, and the band made the most of it now by playing as they would for their own men. It was small consolation to Roosevelt that nearly a third of his own regiment had been left behind, orders that had to be obeyed. More than three hundred men of the original thousand who had trained in San Antonio were forced to stay behind in Tampa. The army's logic was the sort of thing Roosevelt was beginning to despise, someone high above, possibly Shafter, deciding that more regiments with fewer men would spread around the spoils of war to all of them. For Roosevelt and Wood, the selection process had been agonizing, that agony shared by the men chosen to remain in port. He thought of them now, the faces with tears, some red with furious anger, men loosening their tongues in a way that would have brought immediate discipline. But there was no punishment, Roosevelt relieved that Wood had appreciated the anguish of being left behind. Roosevelt had tried to imagine his own feelings if that had been him. He couldn't.

His thoughts were broken by a loud blast from the ship's whistle. The band stopped, heads turning, and Roosevelt looked toward the bow, was surprised to see another large transport straight ahead, the *Yucatan* on an obvious collision course. On the bridge beside him there was a flurry of shouting, a scramble of activity, another blast from the whistle, an officer calling out, "She's at anchor. Prepare for collision. Full to stern. Drop anchor. Now!"

Roosevelt felt the urgency, stared ahead at the other ship, could see the faces there looking toward him, the distance closing now, a hundred yards, less, a loud splash, the anchor dropping. He heard the shouts from below, his own men responding. He stared at the bow, then up again toward the transport, saw the name *Matteawan,* hundreds of terrified faces, more on the *Yucatan.* He gripped the rail, his eyes fixed on the *Matteawan,* a new fear. He let out a breath, thought of the dynamite, hundreds of pounds stowed in the bow of the *Yucatan,* ammunition for the new dynamite cannon they carried. My God, he thought. We'll never know what hit us.

The activity on the bridge was as frantic as before, and Roosevelt did as they all did, stared at the *Matteawan,* the distance closing, a few dozen yards, a voice from the bridge,

"Come on! Grab!"

The ship seemed to lurch, the bow dropping slightly, the distance only a few yards, and then . . . it stopped. He looked into the bridge, saw officers slapping the backs of the sailors, and he called out, "What happened?"

One officer looked out at him. "Anchor caught. Saved us, Colonel. I promise you that."

Roosevelt looked out toward the other ship, less than ten yards apart, men lining up, salutes from ship to ship, breathless talk and cheers. He tried to move, his legs like jelly, his hands still gripping the rail. He saw Wood now, the emotionless man with a rare display of emotional relief.

"The captain said we had a problem with the steering. It's being repaired right now. That was closer than I'd like to come. You can tell your children about this one, Colonel."

Roosevelt shook his head. "Maybe someday, sir. Right now, I'd just as soon forget about ships and put the men on hard ground."

For nearly two days, the scenery off their starboard bow had been spectacular, the shoreline of eastern Cuba bursting with sharp mountains, thick with jungle or bare with thickets of grass and jagged rocks. Roosevelt had marveled at the sight, so very different from anything he had seen on the East Coast, but so very much like what he had experienced out west. The others from that part of the country repeated his praises and asserted that the mountains seemed to mimic New Mexico and Arizona, while some insisted it was Montana. He absorbed the beauty of that, as they all did. But to him, there was so much more. They were that much closer to a landing.

He stood his usual perch, just off the bridge, stared into green mountains. O'Neill stood beside him, said, "Odd to see timber here. I always thought it was tropical jungle, vines and palm trees."

"It is, down low. Those mountains are more than five thousand feet. Healthiest place in the country, probably."

O'Neill laughed, got the joke.

It was another stroke of the laughably absurd from the War Department, estimates on the most effective way for the army to avoid the twin plagues of yellow fever and malaria. Word had come through General Shafter that the best medical minds in Washington had recommended that malaria could best be avoided if, when the troops landed, they immediately climb to an altitude exceeding one thousand feet—and, if possible, much higher. In addition, the troops should be housed in quarters that were thoroughly ventilated and disinfected. As a crowning touch of lunacy to the recommendations, the War Department advised that the soldiers avoid moving about in the sun, making every effort to move outdoors only in the coolest part of the day. It was certain that none of these medical people had ever been in a war.

Roosevelt looked up, the sun fading, a bright orange sky toward the bow. He didn't have to say it. The entire ship knew they were heading west after a quick southerly course, easterly before that, a wide, sweeping course that had rounded the far eastern capes of Cuba.

Roosevelt said, "You would think they would tell us where we're to make our landing."

O'Neill laughed. "My men are saying that General Shafter's afraid of Cuban spies out here on these ships, so he's keeping the big secret."

"We'll find out when they want us to, and not before. Not much else for us to do out here anyway, so tell your men to ask questions you can answer."

He regretted the tone, knew O'Neill could read him well, no need for any frustration to be leveled at this man.

O'Neill looked skyward. "I had one man, Corporal Duncan, ask me if we had any chance of making it out of this mess alive. His words. It's the first time I've heard that kind of doubt. Until now, they're all acting like they're pretty much invincible, like this will be *fun*. Seeing the Cuban coast woke them up. Most were thrilled, we're almost there, most asking if the war was still happening, that same old fear from back in San Antonio that we'd miss out on the whole thing. I've been telling them the truth as I know it. It's hard to look at all those faces and tell them that there's a good chance some won't be going home." He paused, and Roosevelt said nothing, knew that O'Neill had a deeper grasp of questions of life and death than any man in the regiment. After a long moment, O'Neill said, "You ever run away from a fight?"

Roosevelt laughed. "Nope. I never started one, but I learned in the Dakotas that any man who backs away doesn't earn respect. I stumbled into a few places where I had to rely on my fists. Not proud of that . . . well, hell yes, I am proud of that. Why? You worried about backing out of the fight here?"

O'Neill seemed surprised by the question. "Of course not. But we don't know where we're bound or what awaits us. I suppose that's the adventure of it all." O'Neill stared upward, the first stars appearing. "I'd rather think about all the good we can do, what might happen to us. You might leave here promoted to general." He kept his eyes upward. "Who wouldn't risk his life for a star?"

Roosevelt searched the same stars, knew there was more meaning to O'Neill's words than a promotion.

"Colonel Roosevelt."

He knew the voice, turned to see Wood emerging from the bridge, a hint of a smile.

"Yes, sir?"

Wood seemed to pulse with energy, a rare sight, said, "General Shafter has decided to include the army in his little secrets. The landing will be tomorrow morning, the village of Daiquirí. Once on shore, our goal is to move inland, to pressure the city of Santiago. If we are successful, the combined force of the naval blockade and our assault will convince the Spaniards to surrender the city. It might end the war."

Roosevelt felt a great release, drew energy from Wood's enthusiasm. "May I tell the men?"

Wood shrugged. "No secrets now. They should know to be prepared."

Roosevelt faced the wide deck, saw faces watching him, as they always did. He thought of O'Neill, his men insisting this was going to be fun. God help us, but I hope they're right. He raised one hand over his head, clutching his hat, the other on his hip, words coming, a song he had learned in the Dakotas, foolish and playful and entirely the way he felt right now. He waved to them all, gathered their attention, sang out in a loud voice, "Shout hurrah for Erin go Bragh, and all the Yankee nation! By Godfrey, we're going ashore tomorrow. You men, make ready! It's a glorious thing."

CHAPTER 30

June 22, 1898
Aboard USS *Yucatan*

At 3:30 in the morning, reveille had come, and word passed quickly that it wasn't a drill. Staggering topside, gathering in thick masses on the deck, the men could see the outline of the shore, still far distant. For two days, since the Cuban coast had come into view, the direction they sailed had offered the men only a clue as to their destination. With Cuba off the starboard side, more than one man with a keen sense of the compass determined that the target was farther to the west, the city and harbor of Santiago. As the flotilla of transports and their escorts drew closer to their goal, it was clear to all that the navy had already established its presence, American warships anchored outside Santiago Harbor. Immediately, the questions came to him from so many of his men, Roosevelt surmising what most of the officers had figured out for themselves, and what, now, General Shafter had revealed in detail. Those ships had formed a blockade.

As he moved through them across the deck, Roosevelt could feel the pulse of his men, shared the raw excitement, only dampened by the equipment each man was to carry on his back. Their haversacks contained the usual personal articles, plus three days' rations. Strapped over that was a blanket, shelter half, and poncho, along with their rifle with a hundred cartridges. The total load was roughly sixty pounds per man, and no one was too sure just how they were to make it from the *Yucatan* to shore. They were still pretty far to sea.

He saw Wood up near the bridge, pushed through the crowd that way. He patted men on their shoulders, their backpacks, called out, "Prepare to go ashore, men! By Godfrey, this is a fine day."

Wood saw him coming, separated himself from the ship's officers, waited at the top of a ladder. As Roosevelt climbed up, Wood read him, asked, "What's wrong, Colonel?"

Roosevelt was out of breath, said, "I wouldn't say anything to the men. But I smell a problem. We're ready to go, and there's no place or no way to go anywhere."

Wood pointed out toward the shore. "Patience, Colonel. We're about to bombard the town . . . Daiquirí. It's a good idea to soften up the defenses there before we roll in."

"Well, yes, that will delight the men, to be sure. A fireworks show. But it doesn't answer the question how we're supposed to *get* to shore."

Wood put his hands on his hips, stared out toward the other ships, waiting as well. "I'm not in command, Colonel. I do what I'm told. General Shafter has passed the word that we are to disembark as soon as the beach and the town are thought to be secure. We are to make do with what we can find, much like we went through in Tampa. The prize goes to the clever, Colonel. Keep a sharp eye out for opportunity."

"How do we know when the town is secure . . ."

The first artillery piece sent its signal to the rest, and each of the warships joined in, small and large, streaks of fire focused on a village that seemed to be little more than a collection of beachside shacks. The men all stared that way, cheers with each impact, whether they struck a target or not.

Roosevelt watched, heard music from the stern of the transport, the band, a familiar tune: "There'll Be a Hot Time in the Old Town To-night," the men joining in, a jumble of discordant voices, the carnival atmosphere too contagious to ignore.

He watched them, a beaming smile, hands on his hips. They looked up at him, some mimicking him, hands on hips, a wide toothy grin, none with the toothiness to make it work.

The artillery fire ceased now, heads turning back to the beach, a small flotilla of boats sliding that way. Roosevelt knew what his men did not, that it was American soldiers making their first landing on Cuba. Eyes followed them as they reached a pier at the beach at

Daiquirí, Roosevelt could see movement, what seemed to be a large-scale reception. He wanted to say something to Wood, couldn't avoid a stab of fear, forced himself to hear rifle fire. Wood was beside him again, holding binoculars, said, "Here, take a look."

Roosevelt raised the glasses, could see a large Cuban flag, held high above the pier, the boats, and the soldiers.

"There's the answer to at least one of your questions, Colonel. Insurrectos. That's what they call the anti-Spanish. Daiquirí appears to be secure."

Roosevelt heard voices calling him, and Wood pointed, said, "There appears to be a craft off our stern. It seems your presence is required. Would you mind if I tag along?"

Wood rarely made a point of the unbalanced attention, and Roosevelt cringed. "Certainly, sir. I'm not sure what they want."

They pushed quickly through the troops, the men making way.

Roosevelt reached the stern, saw what seemed to be a yacht, a sailor waving frantically. He saw the name on the boat's stern, *Vixen.*

"By George, that's Mr. Sharp."

Wood said, "Who?"

"My aide in the Navy Department. He begged in the worst way for a command, so I got him one. I wonder what he wants out here?"

"Why don't you ask him?"

THE OPPORTUNITY WAS obvious and greatly appreciated. Roosevelt and Wood would board the *Vixen,* while the small boat's captain, a Cuban with a great deal of experience in local waters, would guide the *Yucatan* much closer to shore. To the dismay of the observers on the other transports, none of them quite sure what they were supposed to do next, the First Cavalry began to off-load onto the beach at Daiquirí.

The loading was done with the ship's own boats, other transports moving to the single pier on the beach. He stood on the beach, watching each boat off-load their troopers, most of the regular army troops in blue, his own in khaki.

His nerves were taut, his stomach tight and cold, the unavoidable fear shared by most of the officers that the landing had been too uneventful, no resistance, no gunfire at all. Roosevelt kept his eyes on the nearby jungle, perfect cover for an ambush, the wreckage of the village providing a myriad of cover for an enemy who seemed not to be there at all. He didn't trust that, watched again as his men scrambled across the rickety ruin of a dock, assembling on the wide beach. There was tense silence from most, but there were the shouts, nervous excitement, one man calling out now.

"Sir! The horses!"

He looked that way, one of the transports moving as close as the shallow water would allow, horses hoisted down, then released into the water. Most swam ashore without problem, but the surf had kicked up, sharp waves washing the sides of the small boats, panicked horses still being tossed into the water. Roosevelt had a sick feeling, saw a dozen horses swimming the wrong way, farther out into deeper water. He called out, useless, heard now a bugler on the beach, the call to charge, then again, and he stared in amazement, watched the horses turn in the surf, responding to the bugle call, leading themselves to the shore. Men were cheering now, and Roosevelt searched for the bugler, hidden in the mass of men and horses, thought, Give that man a medal.

"Sir, it's our mounts, coming ashore now!"

Roosevelt saw them, the pair of his own horses, Little Texas and his most recent pickup, Rain in the Face. He watched anxiously as Rain in the Face was hoisted off the deck of the transport, then lowered slowly toward the water. But the surf was worse yet, a massive swell rolling alongside the ship, the horse submerged, disappearing completely. Roosevelt started to run that way, another useless gesture, the horse surfacing again, limp, men pulling the animal back up, loosening the harnesses, a scramble of men on the ship, a quick look at the horse. More horses were harnessed, lowered into the surf, and Roosevelt stared up at the carcass of his own mount, furious questions, helpless anger as the horse was shoved heavily into the surf.

"What the hell have you done? Damn you!"

Faces looked his way, heads shaking, and Roosevelt still felt helpless, furious, the carcass of the animal drifting away. He pushed through the formations of men, but there was nowhere to go, nothing he could do. He saw Little Texas now, in the harness, thought, My God, be careful.

The horse was lowered into the water, a moment of calm, the horse now swimming ashore, Roosevelt running that way, the horse shaking the water away. He wrapped his arms around the horse's neck, called out, to no one but the horse, "Thank Godfrey! I won't let that happen again. Asinine foolishness."

He looked out past the surf again, nothing to see, the carcass gone now, more horses coming ashore, teamsters gathering them into their own kind of formation. The men were coming together in formations of their own, a fleet of small boats depositing the men along the pier, then withdrawing, seeking another load. He saw one group neatly assembled, more coming in on the pier, moving past O'Neill, who was assisting the landing. The new men were Black troops, the Tenth, Buffalo Soldiers, the men guided by O'Neill to their own officers, easing along the rickety ruin of the pier. He watched O'Neill, thought of the man's prediction about a promotion, thought, He's the leader here, he's the one likely to get his star.

There was a commotion on the pier now, the small boat thrust against the pier, rolling over, bodies in the water. O'Neill stood above them, others with helping hands, and Roosevelt was stunned to see O'Neill jump into the surf. More men were running out on the pier, more hands out, the troops climbing up onto the timbers, some with hands pointing down, more men jumping, disappearing in the surf, backpacks and ammunition too much for the nonswimmers. Roosevelt was closer now, saw the Black men coming to shore, soaked, no equipment, the surf pulling it away. He searched frantically for O'Neill, felt a grip of panic. More men jumped, splashing, heads appearing, tall waves shoving the men against the capsized boat, men struggling to save themselves as they sought to save the others. He saw O'Neill now, hands helping him out onto the pier, and Roosevelt moved quickly that way, called out to him, "Did you get them all? Are they all right?"

Other officers were there, the Black soldiers still moving gingerly along the pier, more of them wading up out of the surf.

O'Neill struggled ashore, sat heavily on the sand, deep breaths, shook his head.

"I tried. I saw two of them go down, hands up, and I jumped in. I had a hand, felt them grab me, but it's deep, they couldn't hold . . . I couldn't. Damn it, damn it to hell. The damn Spanish did this, wrecked this pier, so we'd have trouble. Well, we've had trouble. There could be more . . . not sure how many the others pulled out. I lost two. They're gone. Nothing I could do, sir. I fear they're drowned." He called out now, toward the Tenth's officers. "Be careful. Unload 'em one man at a time. This damn pier might collapse. It might as well be booby-trapped. The Spaniards busted it up, burned the timbers. Damn them to hell."

He looked at Roosevelt now, other men easing away, the horror past, the routine beginning again.

Roosevelt said, "Are you all right, Captain? There wasn't anything you could do. My God, I thought you had drowned."

"They were right in front of me, sir. When they went in, they just sank straight away. Damn Spanish. They thought if they wrecked this place, we'd . . . what? Change our minds?"

Roosevelt saw Wood coming along the beach, meeting already with other senior officers. Wood moved close, said, "We lost some people here?"

"Two of the Negro troopers. Drowned."

O'Neill said, "I tried, sir. I felt one hand . . . I couldn't hold him. I'm sorry."

Wood said nothing, looked out toward more of the boats, slow progress, the wrecked pier.

"Their colonel will handle it. Nothing for us to do here. Form the men up by those palm trees. Make sure everybody has their equipment, especially their rifles and ammunition. I have to speak with General Wheeler."

Roosevelt watched him go, a quick trot down the beach. The name punched him. "Fighting Joe" Wheeler. It was a question no one wanted to provide an answer to, at least not to Roosevelt. How does a former Confederate officer find himself in a position of authority in the United States Army?

Wheeler had settled in Alabama after the Civil War. But always the soldier, with the outbreak of this war, Wheeler had petitioned President McKinley for a commission in command of cavalry. For reasons known only to McKinley, the petition had been granted. Now, the aging general commanded the cavalry division of Shafter's Fifth Corps, which included the Rough Riders. Given that a three-hundred-pound major general and a sixty-one-year-old former rebel were in senior leadership positions, Roosevelt couldn't avoid the nagging question of just how this operation was being managed.

By late morning, the men of the First Cavalry had all reached shore and sorted through their necessary gear, awaiting their next orders. By 1:30, those orders came. The First would make camp adjacent to the Tenth, well off the beach in a clearing behind the village. As they waited, still organizing their squads with their officers, the rest of Shafter's Fifth Corps would continue the slow process of coming ashore. By late afternoon, the infantry would be prepared to begin the push toward its first objective, marching through a ragged road that paralleled the shoreline to the town of Siboney. Whether there would be resistance would be solely up to the Spanish.

CHAPTER 31

They had made their camp high above the village, beside a stream, beneath palm trees and thickets of dense grass. On the beach below, the activity continued, Shafter's infantry still engaged in the tedious process of off-loading from the transports, helped by the smaller boats ferrying the men to the beach. Roosevelt could see it all from the heights, thankful now for the favor of Lieutenant Sharp, for what he could only feel was an intervening hand of fate.

He drank from a cup of dense Cuban coffee, a powerful gift from the local insurrectos. He thought of their generosity, men with nothing but the clothes they barely wore, weaponry that was outdated fifty years ago.

He saw an officer making his way through the tents, Captain Muller, of E Troop, one of the New Mexico companies.

"Colonel, one of my men was fortunate enough to capture a chicken. It's a bit scrawny, but Private Prentiss is somewhat skilled in making soup. My men were happy to offer you a portion, sir. We owe you a great deal."

Roosevelt stood with his hands on his hips, could see faces watching him from far beyond the tents.

"Captain, you may tell them that as much as I relish a feast of chicken soup, I'd rather see the feast go to those who will carry the load. We will be marching tomorrow, and I'd rather see full stomachs prepared to meet the enemy."

Muller saluted. "My honor, sir."

Wood was there now, said, "Good decision. The soup might be acceptable, but trying to eat one of these birds is like chewing your boot. I agree with you. Let the men enjoy what they can."

He looked at Wood, knew there was a reason he had come out, had become too familiar with the colonel's habits to know that Wood wasn't just being friendly.

"Something we need to know, sir?"

Wood crossed his arms, seemed to ponder his words.

"The generals are squabbling. General Wheeler insists the cavalry division lead the way. General Lawton believes that privilege should go to the infantry. Lawton's people came off their transports yesterday and marched straightaway to Siboney. According to General Lawton, his men captured the place. That isn't sitting too well with Wheeler. I'm not sure that these generals are more concerned about their men than their pride."

"What about the enemy? No one was home right here. What about Siboney?"

"According to General Lawton, the Cuban insurrectos had a fight with the retreating Spaniards. But know this, Colonel. Just because a handful of Spaniards are lickety-splitting out of here doesn't mean they don't have support. Those people know this land, this jungle, and they're going to be waiting for us somewhere. Whether or not we're to push out in front of the infantry, that's up to General Shafter. But he's out on his transport ship soaking his sore feet." Wood glanced around, a few of the men hanging on his words. "I didn't say that, you understand me?"

Roosevelt saw the same curious eyes, shook his head in their direction.

Wood said, "With General Shafter still out to sea, Wheeler is the ranking commander. That's the main reason why our camp is this far inland. He wanted the cavalry to be that much closer to the trails, to move on Siboney as quickly as possible. Be prepared to march at any time. It could be tough. San Antonio was nothing like this place. Our boys keep talking about how curious they are to be fighting in a jungle. Unless the Spanish have retreated all the way to Santiago, we're about to find out."

Roosevelt saw the small crusty man coming, knew it was Joe Wheeler. He was not much over five feet, mostly bald with a ragged white beard. Roosevelt couldn't help a smile, thought, Does he think we're chasing Yankees?

Wheeler focused on Wood.

"Let's get moving, Colonel. The infantry's sitting in Siboney, waiting for orders from General Shafter. No need to guess what Shafter's going to tell them to do: march. So let's beat them to the punch. Nobody's leaving my boys behind. Put your people on the trail as soon as they can put one foot in front of the other. Sooner is better."

Wood saluted, the word passing quickly to the officers to strike the newly raised tents, no one grumbling the order. Wheeler watched the burst of activity, seemed pleased, another glance at Wood.

"See you in Santiago, Colonel," Wheeler said.

Roosevelt watched him go, said, "He's quite the bandy-legged rooster, a regular gamecock."

Wood said, "Agreed. But somebody gave him the nickname Fighting Joe for a reason. Not sure how much he enjoys wearing a blue uniform, but so far I agree with everything he's done. Let's move, Colonel."

Roosevelt went to his horse, ran his hand over the strange saddle, a temporary gift from one of the war correspondents. In the haste to unload the men from the *Yucatan,* and pressured by the other transports, nearly all of the regiment's gear had been left on board. Included in that was Roosevelt's saddle and a good bit of his spare clothing and bedding. As infuriating as that was, he knew that most of the men were going without their own equipment as well, having only their rifles and ammunition. Of the hundreds of horses assigned to the regiment, including those to be used to haul stores and equipment, only eighteen had made it ashore. It was small consolation that at least Roosevelt had his horse.

He climbed up on Little Texas, glanced at his watch, nearly three o'clock, thought, Nobody said anything about marching after dark, thank God. So, we've got maybe four hours.

THE TRAIL, ROCKY and treacherous, was made worse by the stifling heat that seemed to swallow the men from the thickets of brush on both sides. But the open clearings were worse, a blue-sky furnace, the sun pushing down on the men like the weights they carried on their backs. In a short while, the men began to shed their equipment, blankets and haversacks, extra clothing and even rations—anything that added weight to the efforts. Roosevelt had dismounted, wouldn't be seen to ride while his men struggled on the rough path. As they climbed, the path passed again through dense jungle, narrowing, the men falling back, single file, the march simply a hike now.

They reached Siboney at dusk, walking with heavy steps past surprised infantrymen. But there was no stopping, Wheeler ordering his cavalry to move farther, set up their camps out past the infantry, close alongside their partners on the march, the Tenth.

They pitched tents and lit their fires in a thick grove of coconut trees, the men who still carried their tin cans of rations sharing them with those who needed them. Some men slept without rations, some without bedrolls, the nickname they were hearing from the infantry completely appropriate: Wood's Weary Walkers.

A storm had blown through without warning, flashes of lightning with a thunderous downpour that soaked every man. Even the tents couldn't keep the windy deluge away, many of the men conceding to the soaking. As quickly as it began, it ended, the thunder sliding far out to the east, the stars returning, an odd miracle that most of these men had never experienced before.

Roosevelt suffered the wetness, wouldn't strip down, as so many were doing. Decorum, he thought. The air heats up, at least I'll be cool.

Soon, the campfires came to life again, heavy with smoke, the sticks and dead leaves drying quickly. Roosevelt moved through the camp, slow, muddy footsteps, gnawing on a piece of dried beef, tossed a half-empty cup of coffee into the brush. Nearby, he heard snoring, heard some of the men in low conversation. Officers acknowledged him with silent salutes, no one smiling. He saw O'Neill staring into a fire, looking up now, noticing him. O'Neill stood abruptly, unnecessary formality, and Roosevelt motioned, no, sit. But O'Neill had the energy for both of them, moved toward him, spoke in low, manic words.

"They're waiting for us. I can feel it. This is like chasing Apaches. You can't see them, but you know they're watching you. How much longer?"

Roosevelt led him away from the tents, no need to wake anyone.

"I don't think the army we're chasing is as smart as the Apaches. They'll be dug in on good ground, one of these ridgelines up ahead, but if we attack them and keep at it, they won't stay put."

O'Neill seemed to perk up even more.

"We attack them on good ground, we'll take casualties. We're in their country and they're waiting for us. This is how wars are fought. Somebody has to wait; somebody has to advance. They say the defensive always has the advantage."

Roosevelt didn't need this conversation, not now. But he knew O'Neill had to let it out. After a silent moment, Roosevelt said, "Captain, the Spanish have no advantage at all. Look around you. These men are aching for a fight. I'm guessing the Spanish are tired of theirs. They're a long way from home, and they've been trading blows with the Cubans for years. It's human nature to want to go back to your wives and children. Now, there's us, a new fresh enemy, and those people have to go through this again. They'll fight, but we'll fight harder. I believe that."

O'Neill seemed satisfied with the answer, another silent moment, and Roosevelt said, "I'm going to grab some sleep. Big day tomorrow, most likely. I suggest you do the same."

O'Neill saluted him, said, "I'll probably dream about Apaches."

Roosevelt moved to his tent, close beside Wood, saw that Wood wasn't there. He had an itch about that, knew that Wood had been summoned by Wheeler, but that was some time ago. Planning, he thought. He smiled now, thought of Wood's words. Squabbling between generals. Well, try to get sleep. He needs you, he'll wake you.

"Colonel. Wake up."

Roosevelt rolled over, blinked, saw Wood.

"What time . . . ?"

"Midnight. We have instructions for tomorrow."

Roosevelt was fully awake now, felt his heart beating, Wood's face reflected in a nearby fire.

"Yes, sir."

"Orders from General Wheeler. At dawn, we're to march north, parallel to the infantry. They're taking the road; we'll push up a long ridge on a rough trail. Where our trail joins up with the main road . . . that's where the Spanish are supposed to be entrenched. We have no idea how many there will be. The place is called Las Guasimas. According to General Wheeler, there will be eight hundred insurrectos alongside us helping out. Supposedly, they'll know just where the Spanish are dug in. In the event they don't do what they're supposed to, there's a landmark on the trail, which will tell us where to deploy."

"What kind of landmark?"

Wood hesitated.

"The Cubans say that there is the body of an insurrecto lying in the path."

"A body?"

Wood nodded.

"It seems those people would rather make use of one of their dead than burying him. That's not our affair. The infantry will attack the Spanish position on the right, straight up the main road. The cavalry will hit them from the left. We're taking the word of the Cubans about the lay of the land and the Spanish positions. I'm not completely comfortable with that, but there really isn't any choice. We could advance blind and walk into a disaster. We have to trust them." He paused. "Reveille at oh-five-hundred. Try to get some sleep."

"Thank you, sir. That's not going to happen." Wood backed out of the tent, and Roosevelt followed, saw shadowy shapes beside a nearby fire. He and Wood moved that way, and Roosevelt saw Captain Capron and Sergeant Fish. The men stopped their conversation, surprised by the presence of their commanders.

Capron said, "Excuse me, sirs, but when I see the senior officers talking past midnight, I figure something's up. We're gonna find the enemy tomorrow, right, sirs?"

Wood said, "No point in discussing this with your men, Captain.

Let them sleep. Otherwise, they'll be like Colonel Roosevelt here, ready to do a war dance."

"Well, sir, if we're to meet the enemy, I'd request that you allow me to lead L Troop in the vanguard. We'll make you proud, sir."

Wood said, "No doubt. All right, Captain, the vanguard belongs to you."

Roosevelt saw Capron pump his arms, a hard slap on the back of Fish. Roosevelt shared Capron's excitement, the word echoing through his brain, *finally*. Wood started for his tent now, turned to Roosevelt, said, "Oh, go on. I can feel you about to bust out all over the place. Go do your war dance."

CHAPTER 32

June 24, 1898
Las Guasimas, Cuba

They began the march at six AM, the first leg so steep it put some of the weaker men to the side of the trail. As before, Roosevelt had his horse, but there would be no riding, not in these conditions, and not while his men were struggling on the rocky slope.

As promised the night before, Captain Capron's L Troop led the way. There were four advance scouts, led by Sergeant Fish, with a Cuban insurrecto acting as guide. Behind the advance came another two dozen of Capron's L Troop, then Colonel Wood. Roosevelt followed, leading the bulk of the five hundred men in the force.

In a short time, the wide, rocky trail narrowed, the jungle closing in on both sides. Roosevelt felt the nerves, could see it in the men, that there was no visibility, no way to see the enemy. If there were Spanish troops nearby, there would be no way to know until they opened fire.

Climbing close to Roosevelt were two newspaper reporters, friends, who seemed willing to promote Roosevelt's adventurous spirit. Though Roosevelt wouldn't insist on a public relations campaign, he wouldn't object to some positive articles. Both men, Edward Marshall and Richard Harding Davis, were making the climb with the soldiers and seemed to have no hesitation about marching straight into the enemy. Roosevelt was impressed.

THE MEN CRESTED the hill, clear of the vines and thickets, and Roosevelt drank from his canteen, saw others doing the same. Wood was there now, the stern face Roosevelt was used to.

"The men can have a short break. The infantry boys are down below to the right, and they've got a regular road to walk, so they'll make a hell of a lot better time. We can't hang them out with open flanks, so we can't just sit up here getting a suntan. I'm expecting to get word from their command just what the hell's happening down there."

Most of the men around Roosevelt dropped where they had stood, canteens in their hands. Roosevelt saw their exhaustion, the dirty sweat, thought, Five more minutes wouldn't hurt. Tell the infantry down there to take their time.

He looked to one side of the trail, caught a small reflection. He crawled that way, picked up a curled piece of barbed wire, examined the cut edge. Others were watching him now, and he held up the wire, said, "The wire is freshly cut."

One of the reporters, Marshall, was there, said, "How in the world do you know that?"

"Shiny edge. The rest of it's rusty. This was cut this morning."

One of the troopers came up now, examined the wire. "I been a ranchman all my life. I know fresh-cut wire. You're right, sir."

Marshall said, "The question is . . . why? Why'd they cut down a fence row? Had to make it easier for us."

Wood was there now, examined the wire, said, "I'll take your word for it, Colonel. They might have retreated through here first thing, but, regardless, it means they're here and they know we're here, and, for all we know, they're watching us right now." He mounted his horse, pointed. "There's an infantryman coming up. I hope it's General Young's messenger."

The man was as exhausted as the men around him, put one hand on Wood's horse to steady himself.

"Sir, General Young reports that we have made contact with the enemy down below. General Young has ordered a temporary withdrawal. The enemy is dug into heavy jungle, and he will await your presence before reengaging."

Wood said, "Very good. We'll make the best time we can."

Roosevelt stood now, knew what was coming.

Wood called out, "Rest is over. Let's get moving."

Roosevelt watched as they pushed up to their feet, falling into a column. He heard grumbling, but not much, called out, "Let's go find the Spanish, boys."

He took another look at the barbed wire, could see where the fence had been. Why would they do this, unless this is where they wanted us to come?

He stepped out in line behind Wood's horse, his eyes wandering, the ridge beautiful, flowers and palms. He listened for the birds, mostly unfamiliar, which was always intriguing, but this was no place to take notes. Like the men, he marveled at the wider view: behind them, Siboney and the blue sea; far out to the front, more ridgelines, thick jungle. He looked to the right, down past a deep ravine, another ridge, and beyond that, the road, the march of the infantry . . . *we have engaged the enemy . . .*

He was surprised to see Captain Capron, in a hard run back toward Colonel Wood. Wood waved Roosevelt forward, and he jogged that way, saw manic excitement on Capron's face.

"There's an enemy outpost to our front, sir. I don't think we were seen."

Wood said, "Get back up there, Captain. Don't engage unless they engage you. Tell your men we're right behind them."

"And one more thing, sir. We found the dead Cuban. He's on the narrow trail. Our Cuban guide took one look and did a hoopie-boopie dance and disappeared through the thickets."

Wood said, "Then I guess we're in the right place." Wood turned to Roosevelt, other officers gathering. "Have the men fill their magazines. Colonel, take three troops and deploy on the right of the trail. Major Brodie will do the same on the left. Advance with your men."

Roosevelt turned, pumped his fists, made a low hop, couldn't avoid a childlike excitement, his first real command of troops. He jogged back along the line, spread the word to the captains, then walked out away from the line, waved them off the trail to the right, spread into attack formation. He stood at one end of the line, fists clenched, heart pounding, wanted to shout his lungs out, forced himself into quiet, the same subdued voices as the men. As they pushed along the right of the trail, the jungle rose up again, and he looked across the trail, saw the other senior commander, Major Alexander Brodie, a West Pointer, one of the few regular officers among the Rough Riders. Brodie had deployed his men, looked over to Roosevelt as though appraising him, then offered a wide smile, waved one arm forward. In front, Wood was still on his horse, repeated Brodie's motion, looked at Roosevelt with a sharp nod.

The crash of fire made him jump, the sounds ongoing now, all up ahead in the thicket of jungle. L Troop, he thought. Capron. Godspeed.

Wood ordered Brodie to advance, Brodie's men mostly in the open, a wide, flat plain. Roosevelt stared into the jungle to his front, more firing now, said aloud, "There's no place for us to go. We have to see what's happening." No, he thought. *You* have to see. He looked down the line, anxious men, no fear. He called out in a hushed voice, "Captain Llewellen, Lieutenant Greenway, Lieutenant Kane. Your men move up with me. Captain Jenkins, Captain O'Neill, stay back for now. It's too dense for all of us."

There was no arguing his logic, the fighting invisible, ongoing.

"Forward! Keep low."

The *zing* split the air above him, just above his hat. He flinched, waited for more, heard nothing, the men around him staring hard toward the jungle. He stood straight, saw the men watching him, and Roosevelt made a nervous laugh.

"By Godfrey, they're shooting at me! Let's go return the favor."

He led them through the jungle, straight toward the sounds of the fight, saw some of Capron's men now, mostly prone position, firing at targets Roosevelt couldn't see. He squatted down, the men behind him spreading out, no firing, no targets. The fire from the Spanish sliced through the leaves above him, and he eased closer to a palm tree, peered around, thick brush and trees, felt a thump, the tree seeming to explode in his face. He sat back, wiped at his eye, his ear filled with sawdust.

"Sir, are you all right?"

He blinked through the debris, could see more clearly, shook his head.

"By Godfrey, there's no cover here. We have to keep moving."

The jungle seemed to thin, visibility improving now, Roosevelt leading his men into the open, too open. The bullets came again, and now the Spanish had the aim, a sickening *thump*, one man curling over, then another, dropping backward. Roosevelt scanned the jungle in front of them, one man moving up beside him, aiming at targets that weren't there, the trooper's rifle firing, then a soft grunt, the man falling close beside Roosevelt's feet. He looked down, others moving up, caring for the man, no use. Roosevelt felt a red-faced fury, Come out and fight! But still, there was no sign of smoke, no sign of movement. Damn them!

Behind him, the reporter Davis stood tall, faintly ridiculous in a snow-white suit.

"Colonel, I see them."

"Where?"

"That shallow valley, there. I see their hats moving."

He ached to see, caught the motion now, called back, "Private Green. You were the best shot in training. Prove yourself now. You see them?"

Green crept forward, rested his rifle on a small log. The wait was excruciating, Roosevelt straining to see what had to be a Spaniard's hat . . . and now Green fired, Davis pumping a fist.

"Good shot, young man. You got one."

Roosevelt called to the men around him, "That glade, besides the green thicket. Get them!"

The fire now went out the other way, and Roosevelt focused on the glade and the jungle, saw a mass of movement, a crowd of soldiers scrambling out, some in the open, pulling back.

"Hit them, men!"

The men opened up as one line, the Spanish returning fire, but without much effectiveness. But still, the Spanish Mausers found a target, another crack of bone, a man wounded, a low moan, another rolling over, no sound at all.

As the fight continued, the Spanish began to pull away, and with their knowledge of the jungle, they kept mostly out of sight. Out on the main road, the pressure from the infantry had been even more effective than Wood's cavalry up on the heights. As the day wore on, Wheeler's plan came to fruition, Roosevelt advancing his right flank down to link up to the infantry's left on the main road. The tactic of striking the Spanish from both flanks had worked.

ROOSEVELT LED HIS men back through the thickets, the main trail now a hospital site. He hesitated, didn't want to see this, didn't want to know who was gone. There had been dead and wounded enough in the thickets, men who even now were being retrieved. For the first time, he saw a Spaniard, a dead man brought to the clear ridge. The man was raw-boned, rail thin, had a wide moustache and a clean hole in his forehead.

"We had to chase off the land crabs from this one, sir. Nasty creatures. They seem to circle a wounded man until he dies; then they attack."

Roosevelt had seen them back on the beach and all through the woods, the size of a human hand.

"Good job, trooper."

"Thank you, sir. There's some Spanish mules being brought in too. Their saddlebags have rations of a sort, beans mostly."

Wood was there now, said, "Bring 'em in. That'll make a good meal compared to the misery they hand us."

Roosevelt looked at Wood, saw filthy sweat, just as much as the men around him.

Wood said, "Tell your men to get comfortable. Not sure how long we'll be here. The badly wounded need to go back to Siboney. Major Brodie's wounded, so you'll command both wings for now. Be ready for any orders, any situation."

He motioned to his men to find whatever shelter was there, pointed out toward thickets of palm trees and patches of vines. Already, some were breaking out rations, the men still with backpacks sharing with the others.

Wood motioned him closer, and Roosevelt moved that way, close to the first body, soft-glazed eyes. Roosevelt felt the jolt, saw it was

Sergeant Hamilton Fish. Beside Fish was the uniform of an officer, and Roosevelt forced himself forward, another jolt, shook his head. My God, he thought, he was the first to see the Spanish, he led the way, and he paid for that with his life. It was Captain Allyn Capron.

He stared down between the bodies for a long moment, didn't want to see faces, knew there were others, officers and their men. He wanted to believe that it was enough for him to know that, that he didn't have to see or even know their names.

Wood was beside him now. "I'm not sure if you knew . . . Tom Isbell was up front with Capron. He has seven wounds, but they say he'll live. There're some pretty nasty wounds all around, but most of the men will make it."

Roosevelt said, "Some didn't. I saw it. A horrible sound, and all that blood."

Wood paused, then said, "It's the cost, Colonel. Eight dead, thirty-four wounded. Remember that. War is about cost. The price these young men pay. Maybe they don't know that, but we have to. And no matter how tempting, we can't mourn. Today, we won what somebody will call the Battle of Las Guasimas. But this fight didn't end the war. Tomorrow, or the day after, we'll have to do this all again."

CHAPTER 33

They buried the dead on Saturday the twenty-fifth, the day after the men had fallen. Roosevelt had stood with the rest, hats off, silent, reverently, hearing the words of the chaplain Henry Brown. The singing had come, as it always did, "Rock of Ages," some of the men reciting the familiar lyrics with tears in their eyes.

Roosevelt tried to feel it, to give the men the emotion they deserved, but it wasn't there. As the chaplain's words drifted past him, his mind wandered, always a problem for him at funerals. He cared desperately for his men, but the emotional calls to God, the reliance on religion pushed him away. Another song now, "Amazing Grace," and he mouthed the words, glanced upward, caught movement, a ring of vultures circling, as though protesting the funeral. Among the men, he caught eyes looking back at him, some with red eyes, inquisitive, searching for something, comfort, strength, or some like him, who had pulled themselves away from this particular horror. He couldn't be sure. He didn't want to know.

He couldn't avoid guilt for that, knew the names of the dead even if he wouldn't see their faces. The thought ran through him, a dozen times, My job is to lead the living. I can do nothing for the dead.

As the day ended, the rains came, the relentless soaking that seemed to engulf these men every afternoon. Unlike in Siboney, where there were tents and half covers, here the men suffered mightily with very few covers and almost no rain gear. But the rains were blessedly temporary, the storms passing in less than an hour, leaving behind a new misery: a thick blanket of mud.

Worse than the daily soaking was the lack of decent rations. Back on the beach at Daiquirí, and then at Siboney, the commissary officers were working through the transport and cargo ships, a frantic effort to get the right equipment to the proper units, all the while struggling to send rations into the hills, to feed men none of them could see. All they knew of the soldiers they gleaned from the frequent visits of the stretcher bearers, carrying the worst of the wounded to the ships, or the walking wounded, making their way down the trail by themselves. If there was information to be had along the beaches, it would be provided by the stretcher bearers, performing their duty, a brief word, passing along some kind of information, some urgent request, then returning to the ridges high above.

"WELL, THAT'S OUTSTANDING. By George, outstanding!"

Wood looked up at him from the small camp table.

"Perhaps. I didn't ask for the promotion, but it goes with the job. With General Young down with fever and his second-in-command out of the fight as well, someone, presumably General Shafter, decided I can do the least harm."

"Sir, allow me to salute the army's newest brigadier general."

Roosevelt made a show of the salute, could see that Wood had little patience for the ceremony of it all.

"You know, of course, that with my being shoved upstairs, so to speak, the ranking officer of this regiment is elevated to command of the entire regiment. Congratulations, Colonel. You have been selected to receive the field promotion of full colonel. The Rough Riders, if you wish to call them that, now belong to you."

He assumed this was coming, but he knew better than to feign surprise. Wood would never fall for such theatrics.

"This is wonderful, sir. I will do these men proud—our nation and your command as well."

Wood winced, and Roosevelt knew he had gone over the line.

"Just make good decisions, Colonel. We're going to lose more people before this is over. Take that seriously. They're *your* people."

"Are you certain?"

"Yes, Colonel. I saw the sacks myself, labeled BEANS, pretty as you please."

Roosevelt paced, then said, "Beans. The kind you eat."

"Um, well, I guess so, sir. I'm not sure what other kind there are."

He rocked with his hands on his hips, saw Bucky O'Neill drying his shirt in the bright sunlight, called to him: "Captain, loan me a dozen of your strongest men. I'm not wandering down through this jungle by myself. While you find the men, I'll send word to General Wood that I'm taking a brief sortie downhill. Also, secure me a pair of those Spanish mules." He looked again at the stretcher bearer, the man with the observant eye. "Good work, trooper. You may have saved lives."

He tried to ignore the soaking sweat, knew the men behind him were suffering as well, each of them bearing the weight of their rifle. He led them out of the jungle, stepped into soft sand, scattering a herd of land crabs. He saw the army's large tents in the distance, glanced back at the men, said, "That's the place. Let's do our best to look lie we're supposed to be here."

He led them to the commissary tent, peered in, no one to interrupt him, stepped in royally, said to the officer, "So, you have how many pounds of beans?"

The man seemed surprised, then concerned. "Eleven hundred pounds. Why?"

"I'm here to pick them up. Colonel Roosevelt. First Volunteer Cavalry Regiment. My men are outside, with the mules."

"I'm afraid you can't have them. Those beans are, by regulation, only for officers."

Roosevelt stared at the man for a long second.

"I'll be right back."

He moved outside the tent, winked at the men waiting for him, turned, moved back into the tent.

"Those beans are for our officers' mess. I should have mentioned that."

He saw skepticism now, a man not accustomed to being hoodwinked.

"Colonel, there is no chance that your officers can eat eleven hundred pounds of beans."

"You are surely wrong, sir. There are many officers and they have extraordinary appetites."

"I don't know." Roosevelt saw a distinctive smirk. "I'll have to send the requisition order to Washington."

"That's fine; you do that. But I'll take the beans."

"Colonel, until Washington approves the requisition order, those beans will have to be paid for out of your salary. Without Washington's approval, there's no other way."

"Fine. Take my money. Just give me the beans."

Within the hour, the mules and the strong-shouldered men appeared on the ridge, where the Rough Riders were stunned to see them hauling great sacks of beans, a fresh feast far more desirable than the everyday torture of saltless beef, fatty bacon, and hardtack. Though word spread through the commissary officers about what Roosevelt had done, there was no inquiry from anyone along the beach. Roosevelt's check was good.

ON THE TWENTY-SIXTH, the army began a general advance, closing the gap between themselves and the primary fortifications of the Spanish. For the Rough Riders, it meant an advance of more than a mile. With the mud, insects, and various varmints plaguing the men, a fresh campsite of their choosing was a welcome relief. There was water from a stream and, with an east-facing hillside, sufficient cover from the Spanish lookouts so that they could enjoy fires, both for cooking and drying their laundry.

Roosevelt walked among the men, saw Cubans scattered about,

bartering tobacco and coffee for whatever the soldiers might have to offer. O'Neill walked beside him, said, "Look at these people. Pathetic. They don't seem to be living, just existing, and poorly."

Roosevelt watched a Cuban hand a plug of tobacco to one of his men.

"We can't say how much the Spanish have done to them, Bucky. There's a reason they hate each other. I'm sure, to the Spanish, these people are just in the way, an inconvenience. To the Cubans, the Spanish are slave masters, brutal. They're damn happy we're here fighting for them."

"Are they? Colonel, we were told there were to be eight hundred insurrectos to help out the infantry. They never showed up. None of them. I heard that Captain Capron's scout ran away too. For people who want our help, they have a funny way of showing it."

Roosevelt watched more of the transactions, a bottle of something golden changing hands. Rum, he thought. He said to O'Neill, "Let the men enjoy those spirits for a while, but not when there's a fight. Look, Bucky, I have no idea who these people are any more than I know the Spanish. There's a war here, and the enemy are those people who were shooting at us. Once that stops and the war is over, we'll go home and leave Cuba to the Cubans. That's all I know."

"Sir, you did real well in that fight. I heard you were in the thick. Just wanted to say how the men are real pleased. There were some doubts. But not anymore. There's no bellyaching at all about your promotion, about the whole regiment answering to you. What you did, putting yourself out there, well, the men honor that. They'll follow you, for sure. You know just like I do, sir, that sometimes the high brass, those fellows in the clean uniforms, sometimes those people think there's no harm in it for them, that they outrank death and suffering. Isn't it Walt Whitman who says of the vultures that they 'pluck the eyes of princes and tear the flesh of kings'?"

Roosevelt was impressed, looked at O'Neill. "I'm not familiar with the quote. Where did you read . . . oh never mind. I know better than to ask. I have no doubt that vultures don't discriminate, that generals can die as easily as privates. Generals know that, too. That's why a lot of them stay in the rear. I'd rather be out front, leading. By Godfrey, *I was alive.*"

ON SUNDAY, JUNE 26, the same day Roosevelt had secured the store of beans, great effort had been made down on the beach to secure the army's strongest mule in order to transport General Shafter inland from the beaches. The mule was forced to pull a rickety wagon, the obese, gout-plagued general suffering the ride in the back. Then, after spending four days up along the relative comfort of the breezy ridgeline, Shafter made the decision to inspect firsthand the hills and ridges that stood before Santiago. Once more, the strongest mule was used, a crew of men laboring to mount the general on the animal's back.

The rumor that the men were finally to move set a ripple of joy through the camps. For the Rough Riders, the stream that had suggested clean drinking water was actually downstream from several of the army's other units. With even more units below them, it was essential that none of the men foul the stream at all, and orders were explicit that no one drink the water unless it was boiled.

Several days of keeping to one camp had other problems as well. The flow of rations from the commissary officers became limited yet again. Besides the sacks of beans, the men were relying once more on bacon and hardtack, inspiring all manner of creativity in its preparation. But in the end, it was still bacon and hardtack.

The greatest problem was dysentery, brought about by a diet of mangoes that grew on trees scattered through the jungle, a tempting treat that caused misery. Though the Cubans seemed to thrive on the fruit, the Americans quickly learned that their systems weren't compatible.

Roosevelt's challenge was going for several days without a change of uniform or any kind of bath. The thunderstorms helped, of course, the men able to peel away their uniforms, drying their shirts and trousers around their numerous fires. But the mud never seemed to dry, the creek only usable for wash water. Roosevelt began to worry seriously that if these men did not receive orders to move, sickness might tackle the entire regiment.

"Where is he now? Are we supposed to know?"

Wood looked up at him, shrugged.

"We do what we're told, Colonel. General Shafter finally decided it was time to scout forward. I think they took him out to that good vantage point, El Pozo."

Roosevelt pointed that way. "But we've scouted there already."

"*We* are not the commanding general. Those vantage points aren't scouted until *he* sees them. He has to decide just where we go next, and those hills between us and Santiago are pretty stout. The decisions he makes out here could get a lot of people killed, or they could win the war. I promise you, Colonel, it's not a job either of us wants."

Roosevelt thought about that, tried to imagine the scenario, responsibility for an entire army. By George, that would be a challenge.

Roosevelt saluted Wood, said, "I'd like to return to my camp, write some letters, if it's all right, General."

"*Your* camp. That didn't take long. Good, you're showing confidence. Your men will need that from you, all the time. Just be prepared to pack up and move when Shafter decides it's time."

ROOSEVELT WIPED AT the sweat on his face with a dirty white handkerchief, slipped beneath the canopy of canvas, a wagon cover now serving as the roof of the regiment's headquarters. This is madness, he thought. Our commanding general finally makes time to figure out what we're supposed to be doing, when these men were primed for a fight days ago. Now they're primed for dysentery and yellow fever.

He watched the men, a variety of activities to break the boredom and the misery of the latest thunderstorm. To one side, a line of naked men were tending to laundry hung on a makeshift clothesline. He chuckled to himself. It would be an inopportune time for an enemy assault.

He sat on the camp chair, tried to find the beauty in the canopy overhead, fat leaves and vines draped by the canvas. Better than my small tent, for certain.

A rider caught his attention, the man spotting the makeshift headquarters, dismounting now, moving toward him. The man saluted, said, "Colonel, I'm Lieutenant Yates, from General Shafter's staff. The general has ordered that your regiment, along with the rest of the army, make necessary preparations for a possible advance against the enemy within the hour. The general has just completed a council of war with most of the army's senior commanders, and they are in agreement with the general's planning."

"What planning is that?"

He knew the man had stretched his message too far, more detail than Roosevelt needed to know.

"Um, sir, there is a plan in place to make the best use of our forces against the enemy."

Roosevelt held up a hand. "Never mind, Lieutenant. I'm sure the plan is a good one. The important thing is that these men here shall be a part of it all. I suppose the next time I see you, it will be in Santiago."

The man smiled. "Yes, sir. Indeed."

"You are dismissed, Lieutenant."

The man saluted, was quickly gone. Roosevelt saw the reporter now, Davis, slogging through a wide trough of mud, still in the white suit, though a sizable amount of jungle had attached itself.

"Yo, ho, Colonel. Another hot one. Just came across one of your fellows, who got his hands on some limes. Says it's the best thing he's eaten in Cuba. We should try to locate some more."

Roosevelt looked at the man's pistol, a discreet holster at his belt.

"You actually shoot that thing?"

"During the fight? Most certainly. Can't say I took down the enemy, but I made a good bit of noise."

Roosevelt couldn't help but like Davis, the main reason the man was there in the first place.

"How was your scouting adventure? Shafter approve you tagging along?"

"Shafter hates reporters. The feeling's mutual. I had to keep well back, pretend I was studying flowers."

Davis paced now, hands clenched behind him.

"Theodore, it was amazing. General Shafter was eyeing all manner of possibilities, and admittedly, as much as I dislike commanding generals, to see the lay of the land through his eyes was remarkable. There is a small, well, town, I guess you'd call it, out to the right . . . El Caney. The Spanish are dug in there in great force. Beyond that is a wide ridgeline, the San Juan Heights, which you've seen. There's one larger hill with Spanish blockhouses, more hills to each side, and in front of it all, closest to us, a smaller hill in front of it all. Blockhouses and more entrenchments there, a few haciendas. At the base of that hill is the San Juan River. Shafter says that will give good cover. All over the ridgelines, you can see the Spaniards plainly, dug in, so it's obvious they aren't afraid of what we're trying to do." He paused. "You're about to march. I heard that much. The whole army is to move forward by tonight. The challenge is tomorrow. They're massed, and they have artillery. Our only approach is straight on, and once we're out of the bottom, where the jungle hides us, it's open ground. Climbing those hills will test us."

Roosevelt crossed his arms. "I believe we're prepared for a test, Richard."

"You're smiling. That surprises me a bit, Theodore. Tomorrow could be a bloody catastrophe."

Roosevelt was annoyed at his friend's pessimism. "Or it could be a glorious victory. I have faith in my men, and I believe they have faith in me. We will not lose this fight. I would prefer you agreed with that."

"Quite right. I've just not been in this kind of situation before. Rather intense, I'd say." He pulled a paper from his pocket, handed it to Roosevelt.

"Here, I copied this from General Shafter when he was trying to climb off his mule. It's sad. His own staff laughs at him; then they worry about him tumbling over."

"A map?"

"It's sketchy, a little rough. But it shows El Pozo, where we were, and then the entrenchments and the big blockhouse hill, here."

"I know El Pozo. We've been out there. Took a lot of fire, but it's an excellent vantage point. Santiago's beyond the ridgeline. We just have to get control of those heights, those hills."

Davis leaned closer, pointed. "Yes, that's what Shafter said, that we have to take San Juan Heights. The key to most of the position is that largest hill, with the blockhouses . . . General Shafter called it . . . San Juan Hill."

BY LATE AFTERNOON on the thirtieth, the Rough Riders had been given orders to join the march. But there was very little about the effort that could be called marching. General Shafter had ordered the entire army, some six thousand men, to advance toward the Spanish position using the same rough dirt road, no more than ten feet wide. The predictable result was a traffic jam, made worse by the deepening mud along the way. As before, the troops and their officers, Roosevelt included, had left their baggage behind, along with the greater part of their rations and medicine, each man restricted to three days' worth of salt pork and hardtack.

Well after nightfall, they climbed El Pozo Hill, the men finally allowed their makeshift camp along the edge of a stretch of jungle. The crest of the hill had drawn more than just the lookouts and reconnaissance officers. General Wood was there.

"IT'S NOT RAINING. Thank God for small blessings."

Roosevelt said nothing, saw a scattering of paper on Wood's camp table.

"Maps?"

Wood shuffled the papers, shook his head.

"Maps would make this too easy. These are written orders from General Shafter, his attempt to organize the advance. Since we're all using the same road, crossing the same river, it should be simple. But no one told Shafter that sixteen thousand men take up more space than he figured on."

Roosevelt knew better than to criticize the commanding general, even to his friend.

"We'll be fine. The men are eager for a fight."

"Colonel, every man here is eager for a fight, until the lead starts to fly. Keep control of your troopers. Even the best soldier needs officers he can rely on, and now you have officers who'll want to rely on *you*. They have nowhere else to look."

He wasn't sure why Wood was giving him the lesson in command.

Wood said, "By the way, General Wheeler is still ill, but he wouldn't keep to the rear. He's over past that thicket, raising hell with anybody he feels like. General Sumner's there too. Some well-placed artillery fire could cause this army a problem."

Roosevelt said, "We won't be here after daylight, sir."

"No. I just wish I had a better feeling about our advance. It could be a jumble."

"Well, sir, the best we can hope for is to keep every man pointed in the same direction."

CHAPTER 34

July 1, 1898
Near El Pozo Hill, Cuba

They were up before dawn, packs and rifles, moving into position along El Camino Real, the muddy road that would take them toward San Juan Heights. By six AM, cannon fire could be heard off to the right from the village of El Caney, now the target of the infantry forces under General Lawton. In front of Roosevelt's position, a battery of American artillery had come up, adding long-range fire to the attack on El Caney. Once more, evidence was plain that the Spanish had an enormous advantage in artillery, which used smokeless powder. Unlike the American cannon, which spit out a smoke cloud from black powder, the Spanish guns could fire and remain undetected. The American artillery could only maintain a set position for a few minutes, or else it risked being knocked completely out of action.

The orders so far had been infuriating. Roosevelt itched to move directly against the Spanish trenches and blockhouses on the largest hill straight in front of him. But Wood had told him to maintain his position on the main road. The army, nearly sixteen thousand men, was only now sorting itself out, the result of General Shafter's blunder, ordering the entire force to advance on the single road. With the sunrise, the divisions and brigades had finally become separate units. For Roosevelt, that couldn't come soon enough. From the heights all across the Rough Riders' position, the Spanish were already throwing out massed rifle and artillery fire, casualties mounting on the American side, with no real effective counter.

"COLONEL, THE ROUGH Riders will be the lead unit of the brigade. You'll lead the way."

Roosevelt was only half surprised, knew that even if Wood wouldn't admit it, he favored the Rough Riders above the other regiments.

"Thank you, General."

"Don't thank me until this is over, one way or the other. You might end up cursing me. Now, listen. You're to cross the San Juan Creek at the ford up ahead, then move a half mile farther right. The rest of the brigade will be deployed behind you, back this way. Once in place, you will wait for further orders. Since we're so close to our own batteries, we're certain to draw artillery fire meant for them. Move your men out right now, and once you're across the creek, do your best to keep to cover."

He hadn't seen Wood with this level of excitement, felt it himself. Behind him, his men began to rise, falling into formation, word spreading quickly. Roosevelt looked that way, waved his arm, the bugler picking up the signal, a brief musical order to begin the march.

Roosevelt was pulsing with excitement, added his own voice to the bugle.

"Fall in! Four abreast. Prepare to march!" The troopers were already obeying the order to move, but Roosevelt couldn't hold back, called out again: "Formation, march!"

He moved to his horse now, the orderly, Bardshar, holding the reins. He looked back at Wood, saw the man's faint smile, and Wood called out, "Remember your orders. Cross the river, go a half mile to the right, and halt."

The sound whistled overhead, the blast now straight above them, shrapnel raining across the area. Wood ran to his horse, said, "They've found us. Mount up. Move out of here, now!"

Roosevelt climbed up on Little Texas, and now another shell came, a thunderous blast. He felt a sharp pain on his wrist, pulled his arm in tight to his gut, spurred the horse out of the clearing, farther down the muddy road. He looked at his wrist now, aching pain, saw a fat red lump. He shook his hand, no blood, nothing broken. He pushed the horse down along the road, tried his best to ignore the pain, made himself think of the wounded he had seen. Ignore it! You still have your hand.

He looked up the long, sloping hill, caught glimpses of the Spanish works, shouted out, "You boys will have to do better than that!"

The artillery fire continued to drop in, some of the shells brutally effective, a small group of officers knocked flat, a mass of Cuban insurrectos taking a direct hit, several down, the rest in a mad scramble to safety. Roosevelt moved up quickly to the front of his column, leading the way, and now, behind him, a voice, "What in God's name is that?"

He turned, halted the horse, saw Wood well to the rear, looking out as well. Roosevelt felt a jolt now, saw the balloon, yellow and massive and ridiculous, a basket hanging below carrying two men.

Wood shouted out, "Get that damn thing out of here. That's not reconnaissance—that's suicide!"

But his orders were useless, the balloon floating high overhead, drifting along the muddy creek. Roosevelt rode ahead, his men still on the march, could hear the sounds of rifle fire thumping through the balloon. The ford was up ahead, and he motioned that way, the men in line, following. He pulled up alongside the creek, waited as the first men crossed, the others following in good order, rifle fire ripping past them overhead. He looked back toward the balloon, thought, Every Spaniard here will be taking a shot at that thing. At least it draws some fire away from us.

He realized now that the balloon was drifting with the wind, following the line of the creek, dropping low now, out of control. The basket impacted the brush, capsizing, spilling the two men into the mud, the balloon coming to a stop just above the ground, sinking slowly, still a fat lemon-colored target.

Roosevelt shouted to the passing column, "Move! No stopping!"

He splashed through the creek, moved toward the head of the column, Wood's order in his mind, *a half mile*. He was out in front now, the color-bearer just behind him, Captain O'Neill leading A Troop, the first of the eight troops.

To his left, the firing was increasing, and he watched as much as he could see, blue uniforms, the First Brigade, infantrymen, advancing up the larger San Juan Heights. He felt a rush of envy: By God, they're going into the thick of it. What are we supposed to do to help?

In another half hour, he halted the men, a good estimate of the half-mile distance Wood had ordered. They kept close to the creek, in some places little more than a muddy hole. With the Spanish fire still seeking a target, most of the men were taking advantage of the cover of the creek or the vast thickets of tall grass that spread out toward the hill. But nothing could protect them all from the sun, now fully risen, a baking heat growing hotter still. He felt the sweat down his back, thought, This is ridiculous. We're just sitting here. By the time we're told to do anything, the whole regiment will have heat stroke. Pretty clear that the fight's over there on the larger hill. The horse gave him a taller vantage point, and he could see more lines advancing through the thickets, the First Regular Cavalry, the Ninth Buffalo Soldiers, more infantry coming up behind the Rough Riders.

He called aloud, boiling frustration, "By God, we're here. What the hell do we do now?"

He looked at his men, settled on Glover, one of O'Neill's men.

"Go back, find General Wood or General Sumner. Ask for orders. We're just sitting here baking in the sun and taking fire, and the whole army is around us. There's fighting to both sides. No, don't say that. Just ask in the politest way if we can get ourselves to some place where we can do some good. Make it fast, trooper."

The man scampered away, back along the creek, and Roosevelt looked again at the balloon, thought, He'll have to run right past it, through a shower of lead. Damn stupid reconnaissance officers.

He heard the soft cry, a man hit, then another, the rest hunkering down along the riverbank, more men spreading out into the dense, grassy thickets. He dismounted, cursed, slapped his hands together, angry at every general, those men in clean uniforms. His own men were absorbing a storm of cross fire now, the Spanish Mausers doing their work, inflicting wounds, more dead scattered along the creek, out through the thick grass. He paced angrily, his orderly, Bardshar, holding tight to Roosevelt's horse.

"By Godfrey, where are the commanders? *I need orders!*"

He was truly angry now, winced at every sound of the bullet into flesh. To one side he saw a cluster of men, a pair of young lieutenants. He couldn't hold it in, said aloud, "We'll go on our own, by George. I'll not sit here until we cease to be! If they can't give me orders, I'll make my own!"

He looked again up the hill, saw a muddy, sunken lane leading straightaway, eyed a wire fence leading uphill through a shallow ravine, dividing the hill above him. To one side of the hill he could see the Spanish blockhouses, with the other half mostly haciendas and stone fences. Nobody's up there, he thought, except for the damn enemy. *It should be us.*

There were more wounded men now, and worse, one man shot through the skull, blood and bone. The wounded were tended to, but there was no place to go, the only orders he had not allowing him any flexibility for moving his men. He saw several of his officers moving along the line, trying to focus the men away from the carnage, saw Bucky O'Neill, easing along the muddy bank, smoking his ever-present cigarette, offering his usual reassuring words. Roosevelt smiled at him, yes, that's what a good officer does. O'Neill slipped past him, was speaking still with his men, was getting a cautious warning from several of them, *get down*. O'Neill responded in typical form, exhaling a soft cloud of smoke. "There's not a Spanish bullet made that can kill me."

Far up the hill, the Spanish sharpshooters searched for targets, movement, a splash of color, or perhaps a cloud of smoke. The shot came with a soft whistle, striking O'Neill in the mouth, blowing through the back of his head. Before his knees buckled, he was gone.

Roosevelt stared with a sick turn inside him, closed his eyes, the fury returning, No, damn it all, *no*. He wanted to curse them all, the young officers with their bravado, but he knew it had to be, that all of them, the young captains, men like O'Neill, had to show their men what bravery is, whether or not it gets you killed.

And now, he thought, O'Neill is dead. The man who reads Walt Whitman. He watched O'Neill's men pull his body back into high grass, saw their faces, sad and angry, Roosevelt's feelings precisely. Men were pointing, and he turned that way, a rider, a surprise.

Roosevelt called out a greeting: "Colonel Dorst."

"Colonel Roosevelt. I have orders for you, sir. General Sumner has convinced General Shafter that we should advance on the Spanish positions to our immediate front, the smaller hill. Therefore, you will advance in support of the regulars who are assaulting the San Juan Heights. The volunteer cavalry brigade, which you will lead, will be accompanied on your flank by the Ninth Regular Cavalry, and you will be supported from behind by additional infantry and cavalry. You will follow the Ninth in your advance. Make ready immediately."

Behind Dorst, another horse, and Roosevelt was surprised to see General Sumner.

"Colonel, have you received General Shafter's orders?"

Roosevelt stood a bit taller, offered a salute. "That we have, sir."

"You are flanked by regulars, Colonel, so try to maintain good order with your men. No need to become tangled up."

Bardshar seemed to read his mind, moved the horse close, Roosevelt climbing up. The general moved away quickly, Colonel Dorst behind him. Roosevelt spun the horse, saw hundreds of faces watching him from their cover along the creek, deep in the grass. He felt the heat of the day, relentless, no shade, and he looked again up the hill, waved his hand, spotted the bugler, shouted out, "Advance by troop!"

The bugle sounded, and the men rose up from their cover, their officers forming the lines. They lined up in troop width, but they were too close together, no space between each troop, the regiment moving out in a fat mass. He spurred the horse, rode up into his rearmost line, pushed the horse past the men, holding them back from the men to their front.

"Maintain distance!"

He maneuvered the horse up to the next line, repeated the movement, separating each line from the ones in front. He looked down into a tuft of thick grass, one of his troopers huddled low, the look of terror on his face.

"Let's go, boy. Jump up, fall into line."

The young man seemed paralyzed, others passing by calling the man's name, and Roosevelt said, "Here I am up here on a horse! Are you afraid to stand up?"

He didn't hear the shell, just the result, the young man starting to stand, then tipping forward, a bloody wound on his neck. Roosevelt stared for a long second, glanced up the hill, thought of the Spaniard. *Aiming at me?* It was one more horror, stowed away, and he spurred the horse, thought, We must end this. *It is time to go.*

After several maneuvers on Little Texas, he was out in front of the entire regiment, not where he was supposed to be, but he stared up the hill, the crisscrossing mass of Spanish trenches, could see the Black troops, the Ninth, up in front. They were fully in the open now, the Rough Riders and the rest of Wood's brigade. Roosevelt stayed high on the horse, could see the infantry far out to the left, fighting their way forward on the larger hill. He looked up the hill to his front, could feel the hum and zip of the Spanish fire, gripped the reins, thought, *Over there* doesn't matter. The fight is right here, straight up this damn hill. Men were coming up beside him, and he spurred the horse to keep to the front, aimed the horse straight up the hill, the rifle fire blowing over him like a storm of bees. More men were dropping, but there was no halt, the lightly wounded finding their way into cover, the dead left behind, no help for them at all, not now.

To one side he saw officers, standing, no effort to advance, and he realized now their men were down in the grass, seemed to be seeking cover. He cursed, stopped the horse, saw it was one unit of the Ninth, the men splayed out through the grass directly in his path, in the path of his advance. He moved toward one of the officers, an elderly captain, said, "Captain, we are advancing. You must order your men to climb the hill."

The man looked at Roosevelt with a sneer. "I'm Captain Dimmick, Ninth Cavalry. I have no orders to advance. My men are tired and will remain here until I receive word from my colonel."

Roosevelt could feel a different heat, ignored the rifle fire, a fire of his own in his brain.

"Where is your colonel?"

"I can't say."

"Well, then, I am the ranking officer here. I order you to charge the enemy."

"Until I hear the order from my colonel, I will not acknowledge you, sir."

Roosevelt felt a strangulation coming, could see his own lines bunching up, holding below the resting men.

"Then you will allow my men to pass through."

The captain shrugged, still inspiring Roosevelt's need to break his jaw. He looked back, waved his men into motion, saw the faces on Dimmick's troops, bewilderment, plus an anger of their own. Now, some of them began to stand, rifles up, falling in with Roosevelt's men. Roosevelt turned the horse, resumed the charge, had no idea what the elderly captain was doing now, nor did he care.

He kept the horse moving uphill, his orderly, Bardshar, trotting alongside, exactly where he was supposed to be. Roosevelt looked back to the thickets along the base of the hill, could see more of the regulars, the Tenth Cavalry Black troops, two more regiments of infantry. He felt the power of that, raw strength, a great fist moving up as one. He turned the horse, moved out in front of his own men again. He looked back at his men, saw smiles, a surprise, his men embracing the fight, embracing him. They began to fire back at the Spanish above them, and Roosevelt held up a hand, shouted, "No firing. Advance! Charge them!"

He spurred the horse to a faster gait, pushed down into a small creek, then back up, wide-open grass, the haciendas above, trenches and small blockhouses. He could see the rifles of the Spaniards, their faces, hats, only small targets. He waved again, shouted, "Charge!"

He glanced back, his men making good time, but the horse was faster, and he couldn't hold back, raced higher, Spanish soldiers fleeing the buildings, parting shots, wild and useless. He saw other men out on his flank, officers leading squads from the Black troops, from the infantry, absorbing a scattering of fire as the Spanish retreated. He kept the horse moving, stared at the backs of the enemy, thought of the sabers. Now, I wish I had one. He moved past the last of the buildings, closer to the crest of the hill, saw a barbed-wire fence. He stopped, pulled the horse up, wouldn't jump him over, not after so much work. He hesitated, looked down at the horse, dismounted.

"A job well done, my friend. Good God, you're wounded. Well, Little Texas, I will not run you to death. Be safe." He turned loose of the reins, the horse slowly moving away, said to himself, I doubt I'll ever see you again.

There was a crack of rifle fire, then another, and he ducked, spun around, his pistol drawn. He was surprised to see Bardshar, aiming, another crack, and Roosevelt saw them now, two Spanish soldiers, crumpled over. He looked at Bardshar, a toothy smile. "By Godfrey, you're a keen shot! We should go hunting sometime."

Around him, more men were gathering, exhausted, some with bloody wounds. He saw the Black troops, their white officers, more exhaustion from the men who had made a good fight.

He heard incoming fire still, hard whistles, artillery bursts overhead, relentless, a blending of the brutally accurate Mausers and the Spanish artillery, the shells whose fuses had been calibrated to precise range. The men scrambled into cover, and Roosevelt looked over to the larger hill, the fighting there ongoing as well, the infantrymen struggling to push to the top, the Spaniards well covered in blockhouses and trenches. But he saw the hidden trenches now, much closer, on the face of the hill in his direction. Around him, the Rough Riders and the other infantry and cavalrymen were returning fire as best as they could, but the Spaniards were too well protected to be driven away.

Roosevelt paced, his eyes locked on the Spaniards, the open grassy hill rising up from a shallow ravine in between.

"Sir! Look at this!"

Roosevelt didn't want the distraction, but saw Captain Llewellen waving toward him. He threw a glance back toward the Spanish, then jogged over to where men were gathering, cover behind a small building. He saw now, just past the walls, an enormous iron kettle.

"What in the world . . . ?"

One of the men spoke up.

"It's for making sugar, sir. This has to be a sugar plantation."

The rifle fire still whistled past, one man struck in the stomach, a hard groan, others tending to him.

Here we are again, he thought. No one thought we'd get this far, so now we just sit around and take fire. He looked again at the huge kettle.

"You boys should put this to good use. It makes excellent cover." As he spoke, a round impacted the kettle, a loud ping, then another. Men began to gather, his own and some of the black troops, men who seemed as anxious as he was to finish the job they started.

"Sir, look. Coming up the hill. It's General Sumner."

Roosevelt was becoming more impressed with Sumner, a

commander who had no apparent fear of dying. That will endear him to his men, Roosevelt thought. Hellfire, it endears him to *me*.

"Colonel, fine work. But we need to sort out the units. We had six regiments swarm all over this hill, and you can imagine what confusion there is. Begin to sort out up here, gather up your own men."

"Sir . . . forgive me, General, but there's still a fight on the larger hill. I believe we should help out as we can, by assaulting those closest trenches. They're giving our men a fit with their fire."

Behind Roosevelt, a volley of rifle fire, his own men taking aim at the Spanish works on the larger hill.

Sumner said, "Order that to stop, Colonel. Our own men are drawing close to the Spanish positions. I don't want any unfortunate accidents."

There was a new sound, a steady drumbeat, the men trying to focus, the sound unfamiliar. One man called out, "It's Spanish machine guns!"

Roosevelt slapped his hand on his thigh, said, "No! It's Gatling guns! Lieutenant Parker's battery. Four of them. Listen to that sweet sound."

Roosevelt tried to see some sign of the guns over on the larger hill, too far away, too much cover.

The men opened up a rowdy cheer, and Sumner said, "The Spanish are starting to withdraw from their blockhouse, their main entrenchments. That fight won't last much longer."

Roosevelt said, "Pardon me, sir, but there are trenchworks right over this ravine out here. That's where this fire is coming from. Please allow my men to take that entrenchment."

"Fine. Get the job done, Colonel. No firing at the main blockhouse, that's all."

"Uh, sir, we won a pretty good fight up here. Do we know what this hill is called?"

Sumner shook his head, looked around, said, "Hell of a kettle. Unless somebody comes up with a better idea, I'll make sure the army calls this place . . . Kettle Hill."

THE MEN CONTINUED to cheer the four Gatling guns, a steady, rhythmic firing the Spanish on the big hill were finding difficult to withstand. Roosevelt watched them slowly pulling away, the American infantry closer still, a rough and bloody fight. On Kettle Hill, the ground fell away in that direction, and beyond the shallow, grassy depression, the Spanish were in force along a set of entrenchments.

He ignored the cheering behind him, raucous and loud, his eyes on the wire fence that ran through the shallow ravine. He glanced back, shouted through the din, "Let's go, men. *Charge!*"

He led the way, ran out through thick grass, downward. Immediately, the rifle fire began, sharp whistles past his head, slicing through the grass around his legs.

He reached the wire fence, jumped across, started up the rise toward the entrenchments, only a few hundred yards, sweat and hard breathing, pushing through the grass, more rifle fire. He saw one of his men to one side of him, then another, thought, Go, you'll be faster. He slowed, thought, Let them lead the way. You're just slowing them down. He stopped, expected the charge to pass by him, stared with disbelief. There were five men.

"Halt. Take cover. Where is everybody else?"

The men looked at him, concern and puzzlement, one man, Clay Green, "We heard you, sir. Not sure anybody else did."

He was furious, his fatigue replaced by ripe anger. The firing came again, the Spanish finding their aim, Green suddenly rolling over, blood on the man's back. Now, another man, Winslow Clark, a leg wound.

"Damn it all. I'll go back and get the others. You stay here, and stay down."

He took a deep breath, wiped at the sweat on his face, hopped up, scampered hard through the grass, down, then over the wire fence. On the hill above, he could see men watching him, some beginning to cheer. He was not in the mood for cheering. He reached them now, more cheering, and he tried to catch his breath, waved his arms, quieting them.

"What the hell do you men think you're doing ignoring my order to charge?"

He waited for a response, saw confusion, a handful of men speaking out, "I didn't hear any order, sir."

"We didn't see you go, sir."

"Sir, if you tell us to go, lead on, and we'll follow."

He bent down, hands on his knees, tried to hold on to the anger, but he knew they were telling the truth, the cheering for the Gatling guns drowning out everything else. He smiled at them, wide and toothy, said, "Boys, I mean to charge that enemy entrenchment that's giving us all so much grief. I would very much like some help. Might the regiment, and perhaps the entire brigade, accompany me?" No one spoke, all eyes on him. "Good. This time, when I say charge, you will obey. There's an enemy out there. Let's do away with him."

As General Sumner expected, and Roosevelt discovered, when troops are mingled, and one unit gets the order to charge, no one stays behind. To Roosevelt's delight, a number of the Ninth Black troops fell in beside the Rough Riders, along with troops from the Seventy-First New York and both the First and Third Regular Cavalry, all of which added a great deal of power to the blow he was attempting to deliver.

He kept up with the younger men as much as possible, but long legs and stamina won out, many of the troops pushing past him. The fight was brief and decisive, the Spanish wilting away under the power of Roosevelt's charge. He reached one trench, hands on knees, catching his breath. His men streamed past, most moving out to the left, toward a small blockhouse, another line of trenches. He stepped over the first trench, saw the dead, blue-and-white uniforms, Spanish regulars, almost all with small, tight holes in their heads. Of course, he thought, that's all we had to shoot at. If a man was hit, he died. He moved away from the trench, eased out toward the right, small buildings, another smaller trench. He saw movement, two men leaping up, the sharp crack of their rifles, wild aim, and Roosevelt pulled his pistol, fired, wild himself, but the second shot was measured, calm, the Spaniard going down on his face. Roosevelt looked at the man, stepped slowly forward, still watched for the second one, the one he had missed.

"He's gone, sir." He turned with a jerk, saw his orderly, Bardshar, his own pistol ready. "You got him good, sir. Nice shooting. Didn't know you could hit anything." The man giggled, an odd reaction, and Roosevelt knew he was from New Mexico, wouldn't know much about Roosevelt's ability with a firearm.

He walked close to the dead man, saw the hole through the man's chest and back, flowing blood. He couldn't look away, as though this were the entire fight, the day's battle down to two men, a wild rifle shot and a deadly pistol. He felt himself shaking slightly, cold inside, looked at the man's rifle, the deadly Mauser. What choice did I have? This is why I'm here, after all, the hurly-burly of a battle.

Beside him, Bardshar said, "Haven't seen that pistol before, sir."

"Haven't had to unholster it before. It's a gift. It was on the battleship *Maine*, salvaged and given to me. Funny, all that talk about the *Maine*. I haven't thought about the ship once. Guess I'll never forget her now."

He forced himself to turn away, rifle and pistol fire scattered still over the crest of the hill, his men swarming through every structure, driving the Spanish away, or shooting them down. He moved out into the grass again, could see the troops all across the peak of the larger hill, their goal, the largest Spanish blockhouse, now in American hands.

Roosevelt looked back to the sugar plantation, men occupying that hill, improving the trenches, the men around him now doing the same. Beyond the entrenchments, the men had begun to wander up and over the crest of the hill, but the firing came again, the Spanish retreating to their next defensive position. The officers moved the men into cover, yet again, and Roosevelt kept back, knew it was dangerous to go wandering too far forward past the crest of the hill. Too many of his men were already out there, oblivious to the fire, braving the marksmanship of the Spanish. He tried to think about that, to think about anything to take his mind away from the Spaniard. Victories make men cocky, he thought. And men will take wounds and worse because of it. But it's my duty to lead them, to be in command, even if I have to suffer the sluggish and foolish who anchor themselves firmly behind the lines.

He stepped slowly, using bits of cover, men along the crest hunkered down, shovels working, low talk, the occasional cheer. He climbed the last bit of hill, the ground to the west all clear of troops now, the sunset sweeping across open grass. And beyond, a sight that startled him. It was a city, large and small buildings, white walls, and beyond, warships in a harbor. It was Santiago.

CHAPTER 35

The smells were everywhere, with no way to escape them. He stepped past the longest Spanish trench, studied what lay below, the uniforms, hats, blackening faces, the sickening wounds, precise and deadly, caked now with dried black blood, the flies as thick as the biting gnats. Down across the face of the hill, where his men and so many others had climbed through the deadly storm, the bodies were scattered along with the carcasses of horses and mules, the burial details just now going to work. The wounded had mostly been taken away, back to the largest field hospital east of El Pozo, the few army doctors and the men and women from the Red Cross struggling with the sheer number of patients. Down closer to the beaches and buried deep in the jungles, the bodies there were already set upon by the land crabs and black vultures, sights that none of the living could stomach.

Roosevelt had ordered his men to dig in along the heights, the Rough Riders flanked now by a sizable force of Shafter's army. But the fight was not yet over. To their front, Spanish sharpshooters and snipers did their work, still inflicting casualties on a force that believed they'd won a victory. The Spanish had made one weak-hearted attack, their only attempt to drive the Americans away from San Juan Heights. But the energy and the high ground now belonged to the Americans, the Spanish attack ending as soon as the first volleys were fired. Now, they seemed content to pick at the Americans, the careless on Roosevelt's side of the line paying the price.

He had no training in trench warfare, assumed naturally enough that a trench was simply a ditch, deep enough to hide a man, wide enough to allow him movement. There were no traverses, no bomb-proof or intersecting trenches allowing the men to slip unnoticed behind the lines. As a result, the Rough Riders were kept low throughout the long furnace-like days, free to move only after dark. He had quickly dealt with that problem by dividing his men into shifts, squads of men scrambling rapidly forward, seeking the cover of the trench before the Spanish could find their aim. Then, when the calm returned, the men being relieved would scramble away. It was a clumsy system, but for the men suffering in hundred-degree heat, squatting in the mud of their own urine, any change was welcome.

The army's rations had finally come forward, but the variety was dismal, the usual fat bacon and hardtack. Roosevelt had authorized his men to scrounge wherever possible, and the result had been a rare treat for men who were used to no treat at all. The Spanish had abandoned stores of their own, including pots of beef stew and roasted potatoes, hard bread, and vegetables. Though the quantity wouldn't provide a full meal for them all, the men parsed out the bounty in equal portions. They might not have been fully sated, but their morale was vastly improved.

For the lines of troops now anchored at the San Juan Heights, time had slowed, the short time after their great victory now evolving into a siege against the city of Santiago, as well as against the Spanish troops in the jungles down below, who seemed to have nowhere else to go. That changed completely on July 3, a rolling thunder of a fight that erupted out at sea, just beyond the mouth of Santiago Harbor. The fight was brief and one-sided, and when it was over, the American warships had decimated the Spanish fleet. The great power that the Spanish were depending on to secure their position in Cuba was no more.

What remained was to negotiate the final peace, what should have been a simple matter given the defeat of both the Spanish army and navy. But the Americans underestimated the Spanish need for saving face. In the end, surrender was to be called "capitulation," and the Spanish troops agreed that they would lay down their arms only after a harmless bombardment by the American ships, exploding shells high above Santiago, so that the troops could return to Spain claiming they had capitulated only under fire.

On Sunday, July 17, the Spanish signed surrender documents ending the war in Cuba.

HE STOOD TALL, baiting any sharpshooter who might still be below, testing whether the peace, in fact, existed. Beside him, Wood said, "They're gone, you know. Oh, some will stick around, deserters mostly, who'd rather stay here than go home to Spain and be spat on. We're not sure yet what to do with the prisoners. There are a few thousand of them, and General Shafter is dead set against just releasing them to go home and fight again. That decision will be made by others. I'm glad for that. Nothing good comes from penning up four thousand angry soldiers."

"This whole *shame* business. They really feel that way?"

Wood shrugged. "So I'm told. This was a double shame for them, losing most of their navy and a big slice of their army. Losing Santiago, losing Manila. No amount of government propaganda can fool those people into pretending they won anything. We chased them right out of this hemisphere. And they've been the strongest colonial power here for four hundred years."

Roosevelt looked down at the earthworks, his men mostly looking back at him.

"I guess I don't know much about the Spanish. But I'm not too happy with how it all played out. I feel like we gave away the store. This ended with a whimper, not a bang. And I'm not certain they've really quit. We should be on our toes."

Wood seemed surprised.

"You'd have had us massacre every one of them? No, Colonel, it's over. And you have new orders. You are to march your men down to the low ground west of El Caney and take up position facing west. I don't think you'll have any kind of problem, but pay attention. There could be a few die-hard. snipers in those jungles. And I assume you received word of your latest promotion?"

Roosevelt stared at him, felt a jump in his gut. "No, sir."

He waited for the words, and Wood took his time. "I've been named governor-general of Santiago. I'm not exactly sure why. Maybe they feel that a doctor could be useful in this mess. In my place, you're to command the First Brigade, Cavalry. No rank promotion yet, but that might come later. The army has too many generals as it is. Congratulations, Colonel."

Roosevelt shook Wood's hand, felt like breaking into his fabled war dance, clamped it down, tried to show Wood some decorum.

"Thank you, sir. I'll not let you down."

Wood gave a half smile.

"Maybe. Maybe not. You've been better at caring for your own men than paying much attention to generals. How many men did you lose?"

The question surprised him, a dark cloud over his private celebration.

"We took four hundred ninety men up those hills. Suffered eighty-nine casualties. Since then, the sickness . . ."

"I'm not interested in 'since then.' This army is in a bad way, and somebody in Washington is too busy counting paper clips. Some units, including yours, are at half strength with malaria or dysentery, and the medical people are scared as hell that yellow fever could break out at any time. This whole force could dissolve right into these jungles. A good day for sand crabs."

AFTER FOUR WEEKS on the heights, Wood's prediction was becoming dangerously real, what could become fatal for hundreds, if not thousands, of the troops. Roosevelt agonized over the health of his men as much as did any commander in the field, and he was both surprised and grateful that on July 29 he received an order to report to a meeting of the senior commanders. The purpose was to find some way to bring the campaign to a close before illness did it for them.

July 29, 1898
HQ—U.S. Army Fifth Corps

He was appalled by Shafter's appearance, the commanding general reclining in an oversize bamboo chair. The man seemed to reek of pain, every part of him moving stiffly, or not moving at all. Around Shafter, the others sat on the ground or in one of a handful of camp chairs. One chair held Shafter's second-in-command, General Wheeler, and Roosevelt studied him, the man seemingly recovered from a dangerous illness of his own.

Shafter waited for the men to sit, said, "First, I will congratulate Colonel Roosevelt. He has been promoted to brigade command, for the First Brigade of cavalry. Fine work. Keep it up."

Roosevelt started to respond, had wondered if Shafter even knew who he was. But there was no pause, Shafter going on.

"And one other promotion of a sort. General Wood has been named by the president as governor-general of Santiago, to serve here in a diplomatic as well as military capacity. A round of huzzahs for General Wood."

The men responded with feigned surprise, the appointment known about for a week or more. They responded as ordered by Shafter, a healthy cheer toward Wood, who acknowledged with a nod.

Shafter's mood seemed to change, a deep scowl.

"The health of this army is in a bad way. We all know this. The question is, what do we do about it?"

Roosevelt was bursting with opinions, glanced around, saw Wood watching him, a subtle shake of his head. Well, fine, he thought. I'm the new man here. Keep your mouth shut.

To one side, Wheeler said, "Put a damn letter together, signed by all of us. Send it to the secretary of war, or General Miles, or the president—or all three. Tell them there's very little reason for us to be here. Tell them if we don't recall the army out of Cuba, we will be subject to absolute and objectless ruin. Right now, we're at half strength, and getting worse every day."

Across from Wheeler, another man spoke up, clearly horrified by such a suggestion.

"General, with all respect, this army has a job to do, to solidify our relationship with the Cuban people, to prevent any kind of unexpected uprising, to guard against a new invasion from the Spanish."

Wheeler leaned forward, his cane under his chin.

"How do you think the Spanish are going to get here? Rafts? And

I would say that our relationship with the Cuban people is on pretty solid ground these days."

Shafter put up his hands.

"I know how you two feel. Anyone else?"

Roosevelt couldn't contain himself, Wood's admonition or not.

"Sir, someone must write a formal letter as stated by General Wheeler. I would be happy to create such a document, to be signed by you all."

Roosevelt was stunned by a sudden mumble of backtracking from the others.

Wood spoke now. "The problem, Colonel Roosevelt, is that there is hesitation among this group for risking offense against Secretary of War Alger, or even the president. It could be costly to one's career."

Roosevelt was speechless, stammered through a mumbled protest. Shafter looked at him for the first time, said, "I agree that a letter should be prepared by Colonel Roosevelt, which we shall all sign. Career be damned. We're losing an army down here. Colonel, write a letter."

We, the undersigned officers . . . are of the unanimous opinion that this army should be at once taken out of the island of Cuba and sent to some point on the northern seacoast of the United States. That the army is disabled by malarial fever to the extent that its efficiency is destroyed, and that it is in a condition to be practically entirely destroyed by an epidemic of yellow fever, which is sure to come in the near future. This army must be moved at once, or perish. As the army can be safely moved now, the persons responsible for preventing such a move will be responsible for the unnecessary loss of many thousands of lives.

ON AUGUST 3, 1898, the letter was received by President McKinley, Secretary of War Alger, and most major newspapers. The response was rapid and fierce, and not quite what Roosevelt had expected. What became known as the "round-robin" letter produced outrage against Washington from the public, and that outrage, in turn, was focused by Washington on Roosevelt. But both the president and the secretary of war quickly realized that the improper condemnations contained in the letter were accurate, the kind of blame no politician was willing to accept. And so the letter served its purpose. Almost immediately, orders were issued withdrawing American troops out of Cuba.

On August 7, 1898, the Rough Riders boarded the transport USS *Miami,* and sailed for home.

CHAPTER 36

August 10, 1898
At Sea—USS *Miami*

He had been reluctant to approach General Wheeler, something cold and ornery about the man, nothing to encourage friendship. But he approached him now, understood that he might never actually see the man again. Despite his lofty rank and his illness, Wheeler had been an important part of an experience Roosevelt would embrace for the rest of his life. At least now, with this one opportunity, he could talk to the man.

The old man was leaning precariously on the cabled railing, his cane propped up beside him, a familiar stance. Roosevelt eased closer, said, "Good afternoon, sir. Sorry if I'm bothering you."

Wheeler looked at him as if for the first time, then said, "I hate the ocean. Miles and miles of nothing at all. Navies fight each other by dancing around in an infinite world. Nobody faces off, man-to-man, standing tall in the face of the enemy. The smart sailors are the ones who keep below the horizon, shelling their enemy from too far away to see. Damn fool way to fight a war."

There was no room for a response, Roosevelt daring to prop himself against the railing a few feet away. He focused on the vastness of the open sea now, shared none of Wheeler's distaste. A cloud of salt spray drifted past, kicked up by the bow of the ship, and he reveled in the clean perfection of that, so very different from the putrid and foul water that his men had endured throughout their seven weeks in Cuba.

"So, how'd you like being a colonel?"

The question surprised Roosevelt, and he looked at Wheeler, saw a

301

hint of a smile through the grizzled white beard. The response came to him: so, how do you like being a general? But he wisely kept that to himself.

"It has been a magnificent experience, sir. Commanding these men, serving them in return, caring for soldiers in the field, fighting a deadly enemy. Risking death is not something I ever expected to enjoy, but, by Godfrey, I did." He paused. "Does that make me a good soldier? Or am I just off in the head?"

Wheeler laughed now, another surprise.

"Not sure if I ever enjoyed being close to death. But I respect it. If you're going to lead troops, you have to expect it too. Sometimes there is a great deal more death around you than you would ever have believed. The bodies of soldiers, no matter which side, are a grotesque symbol of man's viciousness." He paused, rubbed a wrinkled hand through his beard. "But by God, I did love it. Fighting Yankees. Well, Cubans too. Yankees more. This damn Cuba is a godforsaken place, a horror of a battlefield. If you didn't get knocked down by malaria, you're liable to be gobbled up by flesh-eating crabs bigger than your hand. No, sir. You can have Cuba and everything there."

Roosevelt felt lost, was utterly charmed by the old man, but knew, by rank, he had to keep his distance.

"Yes, sir. I would imagine the Civil War was a terrible experience."

"Don't snuggle up to me, boy. It was magnificent and it was horrible, and you'll never know why. I don't talk about it much. Makes the blue bellies in Washington nervous, like I'm gonna start it up all over again. Wouldn't much matter. We'd lose just the same."

A long silence set in now, Roosevelt trying to focus on the serenity of the water, Wheeler's strange words bouncing through him. After a long minute, Wheeler said, "You'll be hanging up your spurs, right?"

"Yes, sir. I was part of the volunteers, so the army . . ."

"Good God, Colonel, I know what the army does. Half the time, I make those decisions. Shafter thinks he's in charge. Well . . . just leave that alone. I know your group is to be sent home, with the grateful thanks of a proud nation. That's usually how it goes. You did fine work, and there's talk of a medal for you. That's okay with me. I'm too old for medals. How're your men holding up?"

Roosevelt was happy for a topic he could address.

"Many of the sick are getting better. It helps being away from Cuba. This sun and salty breeze are clearing away most of the malaria. The wounded have been treated well, and a good many of them are getting around on their own."

"You'll be in quarantine, you know. When we get to New York. Maybe a week, maybe less."

That hadn't occurred to him.

"Well, yes, of course. I understand. That should strengthen the men even more."

Wheeler looked at him again, removed his hat, ran his hand over a bald scalp.

"It's not for the men, Colonel. It's for the people, all those cheering mobs who will welcome you. It wouldn't do to infect half a thousand people with army crud."

Roosevelt nodded, struggled for the right words, a rarity.

"What will you do now, sir? Retire?"

"Hell no. I'm a congressman even now. Did you know that? Voters in Alabama have no common sense. They keep sending me to Washington. But I'd rather wear a uniform, even a blue one. That's a decision that'll smack you in the face before long."

"Not sure I know what you mean, sir."

"Wise up, Colonel. You're a damn fine soldier, and you're not a soldier at all. That makes you a hero as a civilian. Don't play naive with me. I know enough about you to know you've got ambition, that when it comes to politics, you're a bull in a china shop. It's fun, right? Well, you're gonna have your pick of what you want to do next. Make the most of it. Just . . . when you say goodbye to your men, make sure you don't forget it was them who put you up on this throne."

August 15, 1898
Camp Wikoff, Montauk, New York

The greeting from the crowd had been more raucous than even Joe Wheeler had predicted, a vast horde of well-wishers along the pier, and, to no one's surprise, the majority of them were calling out Roosevelt's name. He led his men down the gangway to bursts of band music, most of it ignored by his exhausted men, until the one refrain drifted over the crowd, men stopping to listen, caught off guard, all of them understanding why, just where their next stop would be. It was "Home Sweet Home."

Once ashore, Roosevelt led the men on a mile-long walk, a struggle for the sick and wounded, but few wanting to show just how weak they really were. They marched to their designated camp, where they would rest idly in quarantine, one small part of a picturesque plain the army had named Camp Wikoff. The unit was far from alone, the five-thousand-acre facility set to house more than twenty thousand troops. With two hospitals, the facility was preparing to care for those men still carrying the ailments contracted in Cuba, although in many cases those diseases had been aggravated by malnourishment, a combination that caused deaths long after the rifles had stopped firing.

As the Rough Riders set up camp, they had one unexpected surprise. From their camps in Tampa, some three hundred members of the regiment had arrived, the men who had been left behind. Despite the assumption from some that there would be resentment and friction between the two groups, Roosevelt was grateful to see that the opposite was true, the Tampa men welcoming the enfeebled combat veterans as their own. The only obvious difference between the two groups was their appearance. To a man, the Cuban veterans were significantly underweight.

With the quarantine completed on August 19, the Rough Riders moved to a more permanent site at the camp. Almost immediately, word was passed down that the unit was to be mustered out of the army in early September. Roosevelt granted five-to-ten-day furloughs to those who requested one, most of those men flocking to the partying atmosphere of New York City. One of those who took advantage of a brief furlough was Roosevelt himself. On August 19, he went home to Sagamore Hill.

THE CHILDREN CAME first, a rollicking explosion of hugs and peals of laughter. Even Alice seemed unable to contain herself, the fourteen-year-old hugging her father with tears and laughter all her own. When the children and their father were finally exhausted by their revelry, Roosevelt had focused on the patience and the perfect loveliness of his wife. With the children looking on, she embraced him, the children standing back, only one, Alice, uttering a soft teasing sound.

Edith released him, said, "Children, go find something to do. Your father and I must talk."

He motioned to them all with his hand, scoot, saw the pouting frown from Alice, her typical expression, but like the smaller children, she obeyed. With the parlor now empty, Edith held him by the arms, said, "You are a sack of bones. You must have lost twenty pounds, if not more." She smiled at him now, squeezed his arms. "Welcome home, Bones. We must begin fattening you up again."

He felt strangely weak, put his hands on her shoulders.

"The weight will come back. Too much good food around here. But, by God, Edie, I have survived. It was the greatest challenge of my life. I don't think that entered my mind until this moment. I could have lost all of this, all of you. Or, well, you could have lost me."

Edith released him, moved to a small chair.

"It was what you had to do. I know that. I wasn't terribly happy about it, but I know you, Teddy. You have mountains to climb, and no one can stop you."

He smiled.

"I climbed this one at the head of some extraordinary young men. We won a victory, an enormous victory against any odds. We took a hill that was fortified by dug-in troops who had better guns. And we did it. By God, we did it!"

He realized he was shouting, felt his breathing, the weakness again. Edith was staring at him, the smile now concern.

"Teddy, did you see all those people at Oyster Bay? I thought we had kept your furlough here a secret, but there must have been a thousand or more waiting for you at the train station. I fear we shall not enjoy much privacy from now on. All because of your hill."

He could see the frustration in her face, didn't want that, not now.

"What do I do, Edie? I can't ask them all to just leave me alone, now can I?"

"So, reporters keep asking me if you're going to run. As if I know what you will do."

He had wondered how this would go, her response to the approaches being made toward him to run for governor of New York, the serious energy aimed at him from senior members of both the Republican and Independent parties.

"I haven't decided. But is it wrong for me to accept what the people want?"

She shook her head, stood again, went to him, hands around his waist, pulled herself against him.

"If it is what *you* want, then it will suit me as well. But don't do what you do so often. Don't be in a rush. Think about it, all of it. Those people out there, they won't let you be, not even for a moment."

"I'm afraid, Edie, they won't leave me alone even now. And I would rather lead my regiment in a dozen great fights three times over than serve as the governor of New York. I'm a *hero,* by God. I can't explain what that feels like. But I do enjoy it. No, it's more than that. *I love it.*"

HE RETURNED TO Camp Wikoff on August 25, the reports swirling around him that the Rough Riders were to be mustered out of service in a matter of days.

They had all been surprised when the gilded carriage rolled through the entrance of the camp, Roosevelt sitting on horseback as the carriage pulled to a stop. Behind, more carriages, men with cameras on tripods, reporters with their pads of paper. President McKinley had broken protocol, had stepped down from the carriage and gone to Roosevelt, a hearty handshake, Roosevelt as surprised as the president's entourage. It was Roosevelt who was still gathering headlines as the man stirring up the public with the round-robin letter. As the president made his rounds through the camp, the Rough Riders performed exactly as Roosevelt had hoped. Instead of the formal cheer usually reserved for high officials, the men broke down into raucous and rowdy whistles and hoots, surprising the president and his entourage even more. It was up to Joe Wheeler to explain to McKinley just who these rowdy troops were.

"Sir? Excuse me. Would you mind stepping out here?"

Roosevelt looked up from the annoying paperwork, saw Colonel Brodie, said, "Right now? Colonel, there's an enormous amount of work to do to get the boys mustered out."

"Please, sir. Just a moment."

Roosevelt pulled himself to his feet, still felt the weakness in his legs, the looseness of his trousers.

"Who's fighting now? You've been promoted too, you know. Can't you take care of it? Don't they know it's only a few days? The least they can do is be cordial to each other."

He stepped out of the tent, was surprised to see the entire regiment arrayed in a hollow square. The men were facing inward, the center of the open square occupied by his officers.

"What is this, Brodie?"

"It's for you, sir."

He saw now that alongside the formation of officers was a canvas-covered object propped on a table, hidden from view. Good Godfrey, he thought. What is happening?

Brodie escorted him to the center of the square, and he eyed the men through the glasses anchored on his nose, scanned the entire group.

"It's hot as blazes out here. I don't expect formations like this. Not anymore."

He saw one of his troopers step forward, the man hesitating, clearly nervous, and Roosevelt said, "Private Murphy, you have something to say?"

"Yes, sir. This here is a very slight token of the admiration, love, and esteem in which you are held by the officers and men of your regiment. Sir."

Murphy went to the table now, and Roosevelt could see the man shaking, saw tears on his face. He watched as the young man slid the canvas away. Murphy stood back now, said,

"The entire regiment pitched in, sir."

Roosevelt was frozen, fought to hide the overwhelming emotion of the moment. He stepped to the table, reached out, his hand gliding softly over the bronze figure.

"This is Frederic Remington's work. *The Bronco Buster*. It's magnificent." He couldn't stop his own tears now, heard sobbing from several of the men closest to him. He gathered himself, took a deep breath.

"I really do not know what to say." He paused, heard a glimmer of laughing. "However, I shall make the attempt. Nothing could possibly happen that would touch me and please me as much as this. Had this come from only the officers, I would have been deeply touched. But coming from all of you, I appreciate it tenfold. This comes from those of you who have shared the hardships of this campaign, who shared your hardtack when I had none and who gave me your blanket when I had none of my own. You men are a peculiarly American regiment, and to receive your gift touches me more than I can say." He paused, wiped at his eyes. "Let us never forget those whom we left behind in Cuban soil, and those who died in the hospitals right here. Let us not forget that it was not only wounds but disease that struck them down. They must be with you even now, and forevermore. I cannot mention every name now, but those of Fish and Capron and O'Neill will serve. They were all men who died in the pride of their youthful strength." He put out a hand again on the sculpture. "This is something I shall hand down to my children, and I shall value it more than the weapons I carried through the campaign."

He saluted them now, said, "I will shake your hands, each and every one. Very soon we shall go our separate ways, and I intend to remember each face and each name."

A handful of men called out, their cry obviously rehearsed. "Three cheers for the next governor of New York!"

The cheers came now, the nine hundred men raising their hats, still the tears. He wiped his eyes again, the men lining up by troop for his promised handshake.

He met them all, recalled most of their names, shared silent tears with many. As they passed, they continued to linger, some finding their words, all of them knowing what lay ahead, one more hearty meal, their pay, laying down their rifles, finding their way home.

He completed the handshakes, looked again at the sculpture, the cowboy struggling to handle the bucking bronco. Such is life, he thought. Mine, theirs. We must all learn to handle what comes next, no matter the struggle. He looked at the regimental colors, full of the breeze that swept past. All things must pass away, he thought. But these were beautiful days.

PART IV

WALK SOFTLY . . .

There is no more "natural right" why a man over twenty-one should vote than there is why a Negro woman under eighteen should not.

—THEODORE ROOSEVELT

Nobody likes him . . . but the people.

—JAMES BRYCE,
BRITISH AMBASSADOR

CHAPTER 37

"Haven't you had enough, Mr. Hagedorn?"

"Actually, no, sir. Begging your pardon, but this book will not be a twenty-page pamphlet." He paused, and Roosevelt saw the man pulling his words back, fighting for patience. "Thank you, sir, for allowing me to come back. I know your family is preparing for the New Year, so I'll try not to linger. I don't want to be in the way."

"You're a writer, Mr. Hagedorn. You're *supposed* to be in the way. And don't worry about the New Year's business. I stay out of that, as much as I can. When they want me at the dinner table, I'll go. Even this year. I've never been too sick to dig into a feast."

"If I may ask, sir, how are you feeling?"

"I'll not discuss that. There are a great many people out there suffering from this god-awful influenza, and so far it has avoided me. Whatever else I'm carrying around, it's not the flu. So, I don't need coddling. Just ask me questions until I run out of steam. Then go home."

He saw Edith at the door now, the scolding frown.

"Oh, go on, Edie. I'm doing just fine. Mr. Hagedorn has a job to do, and I had an acceptable nap this morning."

She moved slowly in, stopped beside the younger man.

"Mr. Hagedorn, do try to be brief. The doctors insist that his strength not be taxed."

She moved back out toward the door, one last glance at him,

managed a smile. She knows, he thought. I must have this, the writer, the biographies. I must know that the people still care.

He saw Hagedorn fumbling with his pad of paper, could tell he was itching to begin.

"Don't ask me about the damn Medal of Honor."

Hagedorn seemed surprised, but he took Roosevelt's bait.

"Um, sir, what about the Medal of Honor?"

"They didn't give it to me. I earned it too. My entire regiment insisted, and half the generals in Cuba put me up for it, especially Leonard Wood. But I stepped on toes, one of my greatest talents. Angered a few of the wrong people. I came home from Cuba the most popular man in this country. I heard that everywhere I went. Well, in Washington people who aren't as popular don't appreciate that. They growl about it, and figure out a way to get their pound of flesh. In my case, they denied me the Medal of Honor. I heard that Congress would have approved it overwhelmingly. It was the secretary of war who refused to endorse the recommendations of all those generals, the men who knew what they were talking about. Now, that man, Alger, is gone, but the fire is out for giving me any kind of award. Attention is rightfully being paid to those heroes who are even now coming home from Europe. We've had a far worse war over there than we had with Spain. The Great War has been a horrible, horrible thing. So, it seems petty, even selfish of me to expect that the government should remember what I did in Cuba. Still . . . I'd love to have that medal. This will sound very egotistical, but I am entitled to the Medal of Honor. I want it. By God, I earned it."

He had worn himself out, stopped for a long moment, saw Hagedorn staring at him. He looked away, staring toward the window, a cold, clear day, bare trees, the few remaining birds standing out on the limbs like small flowers. He knew Edith had heard him, thought, She's probably right outside the door, watching over me in case I do . . . this. Exhaustion. But dammit, I wanted that medal. Still do.

Hagedorn scribbled something on his pad, said in a low voice, "I'd arrange it if I could, sir."

Roosevelt looked at him, shook his head.

"You're supposed to be impartial. Keep your head above the fray.

Your kind has had to do that with me for decades, keep your heads above the chaos." He paused. "I rather thrive on chaos, especially when I can push it onto someone else. Politics lends itself quite well to chaos. If everybody agreed on everything, if everybody trusted everyone else, nothing would get done. Makes no sense, I bet, eh? But it's chaos that forces deals to be made, agreements to be forged, usually in some sweaty, smoky back room. You want to prevail in politics, you stay just a bit outside the chaos, let them come to you. That's how I got to be governor. I stepped off that ship at Montauk, and those cheering people would have anointed me king. But the position wasn't open. Instead, the word starting flooding through every hall of every political building that I'd win the election for governor, hands down. I believed that myself, but I couldn't let on. Good lesson, Mr. Hagedorn. Listening can sometimes be better than talking. I'm not the best example of that, I admit. But I waited, and sure enough, the visitors came, fancy suits and happy handshakes. I let them dangle a bit. I had both the Republicans and Independents chasing me. The Rough Riders hadn't been mustered out a week when I agreed to run as an independently minded Republican. It was perfect. Except for the Independents. I didn't expect them to spit such venom in my direction. They called me a dough face, for God's sake. I'm still not sure if that was mere disrespect or some sort of joke. I was hardly overweight."

"I heard you campaigned as a Rough Rider, hat and spurs, your old uniform."

"Bunk. The Republican Party machine was too scared of me to have me go dancing about like some kind of toy puppet soldier. I mostly stayed right here and let the newspapers and the bosses do the talking. That way, when I chose to open my mouth, people paid attention. There's a difference between talking too much and talking all the time." He smiled. "Even if you're entertaining, like I am."

"Do you stay in touch with many of the Rough Riders?"

"Some. I consider those men lifelong friends, no matter if I hear from them or not. You have no idea what it means to make a train stop in some godforsaken rail depot, and here comes a fellow with his hand out, a familiar face. That's bully, absolute bully. I give those fellows my time everywhere I go. Every one of those men was a natural fighter, men of courage, intelligence, and physical prowess. Not a finer group of human beings anywhere. And they taught me that."

"You fought along with the Colored troops . . ."

"The Ninth and Tenth Cavalry. Some were Buffalo Soldiers. As the fight was confused, some of those men became mixed up with the Rough Riders, and let me tell you, they were as fine a group of troops as my own. I take nothing away from them."

"Sir, there are some who say the Colored troops should not be, that the army should always stay white."

"Some of the Rough Riders were Indians, young man. Remember that. And I respect them as much as anyone in my command. I never considered the race of the Colored troops to be a detriment to their fighting ability. They proved their courage and their skill as soldiers. They did have white officers, of course. The Colored troops seem to have a peculiar dependence on them. One difference, I suppose, is that the Colored soldiers don't make especially good noncoms, sergeants. Now, I did witness a good many of the Buffalo Soldiers taking charge of the field when their officers were struck down, and they did that with as much heart as any of my men. But I would say it's not fair to expect that."

He watched Hagedorn writing furiously on his pad, felt a twinge of caution. God, I'm giving him my life story with warts and all. Now, I know that Edith isn't lurking out there around the corner. She'd have been in here in a flash to shut me up.

"When you came home and ran for governor, you won in a landslide, right?"

"Where do you hear this sort of fiction? Never mind. Here's the facts. I won by about eighteen thousand votes. Hardly a landslide. That taught me a lesson right off the bat. I was beloved by a majority of the voters, but I was most certainly not beloved by the rest of them, nor by the state legislature. You don't bully your way through those gentlemen unless you have an overwhelming mandate, which I didn't have. So, naturally, I charmed them, until they did mostly what I asked for."

He paused, took a long breath, felt himself sweating.

"Might we continue, sir?"

Roosevelt saw Edith slipping in quietly, the usual scowl, easing up beside Hagedorn.

"You're perspiring again, aren't you?"

He tried to control his breathing, nodded, avoided her eyes. "Only a little. This fellow gets me riled up about all sorts of things. He wears me out."

Edith stared at him, the unspoken question, and Roosevelt said, "No, really, I'm fine. Let's allow the man another hour or so. Then, maybe he can come back tomorrow."

She crossed her arms. "Teddy, tomorrow is New Year's Eve."

"Well, hell, he doesn't care. He's young and ambitious, and he needs this interview to show his editor he'll have another book. Right, Mr. Hagedorn?"

The young man seemed uncomfortable, caught between two storms. "Yes, sir. That would be fine, sir. Thank you." He looked up at Edith now. "Mrs. Roosevelt, I shall be aware of his condition. I promise."

Roosevelt could see that she wasn't convinced. "Edie, go on. Everything's fine here. He promises."

She couldn't hide a laugh, shook her head. "I'll bring some lemonade. Not too sweet, not too sour. That's *my* promise."

She was gone now, and Roosevelt sat back, felt enormously tired.

"It's hard. Growing older has a dreadful price. I so enjoy speaking, charming any audience just as I charmed the New York Assembly. But it takes fuel, and I regret to say that I'm running low. I thought I could hide from you what's happening to me. Edie didn't believe I could. And she's right. I can't hide it." He took a deep breath. "I don't want you to write that I gave you all of this only because I'm sick. I'm asking you that, and I hope you'll respect it. No one will want to read about me growing frail, I promise you that. I can't stop what you scribble down there, but I can offer you some important advice. Write what people want to hear, especially about me. Reality can be ugly. You won't do yourself any favors if you write a sensational book about my problems, my ailments. I hope you trust me on that."

Hagedorn had stopped writing, stared at Roosevelt with sad eyes. "I don't want you to be sick, sir."

"Neither does anyone else. Most people don't want to hear about politics either, but here we are. Let's stay with that."

"Yes, sir. I understand. So, what would you say was the basic theme of your term as governor?"

"*Roosevelt Fights Corruption.* That sums it up. No, I don't want to dig any further into that. Some of those people are still around."

"Sir, my editor says that it's a great mystery how you became vice president, since you were doing so well as governor."

"Your editor doesn't read much, does he? Never mind. Being governor was tedious at best. Too many bridges to fight your way across. Sometimes that's fulfilling, sometimes it's just work. Unpleasant work. And sometimes the bridge drops out from underneath you. But don't get me wrong. I was fully supporting McKinley for his 1900 reelection, and maybe I did have some ideas about running for president in 1904. But a great number of people in the Republican Party starting tossing my name out there as a candidate to replace McKinley. I wasn't happy about that. I stated publicly, for the record, that I was not a candidate for the presidency. But the people, the crowds. It's infectious, Mr. Hagedorn. They cheer your name and you begin to think that anything is possible. Apparently, McKinley felt the same way, that I might be popular enough to shove him out of the way. It was Lodge, Henry Cabot Lodge, one of my oldest friends. He suggested that if I wanted to appear the loyal Republican, and still open the door for 1904, that I consider becoming McKinley's vice president. I wasn't pleased with that idea. I had my eye rather on the War Department, secretary of war. That fellow Alger was retiring. No one wept tears for that. I thought I could do some good there. But the president was nervous that I'd get in there and toss too many old generals out the window, so he wouldn't give me the job."

"Sir, President McKinley already had a vice president."

"Your ignorance is a gift to me, son. Makes my brain work harder. Vice President Garret Hobart was only fifty-five, looked older, older than me. In 1899, a year before the election, he died. He didn't have a say in the matter. Left McKinley with a decision to make. I truly didn't want the job, despite my friend Lodge pushing me. But a tide turned in New York, scandals erupting that some of the power people didn't want made public, and didn't want me to meddle in. Things in Albany began to smell, especially when I began to see how many of my loyal supporters in the legislature suddenly wanted me to be gone. I stirred up too much soup, apparently. I always enjoyed what I did there. But I might have been the only one."

He stopped, coughed through his growing hoarseness.

"I didn't want the job, vice president. It's a burial party, a job where there is usually nothing to do. And I knew there would be so many things I'd like to do. That's how I felt. But by the time of the Republican convention, the pressure was relentless. So many, from my friend Lodge to so many others, insisted that I accept the nomination." He paused, smiled. "I rather liked that. It's quite a joy to inspire so much affection from so many. But it wasn't unanimous. Other names were tossed about, handed on silver platters to McKinley. He was infuriatingly mum on the whole process. In the end, he agreed to accept the will of the convention. That *will* turned out to be me. Admittedly, most people were pretty positive about that. One most assuredly was not. My wife."

Hagedorn looked up from his pad.

"Mrs. Roosevelt didn't want you to be vice president?"

Roosevelt chuckled.

"No, she did not. I'd call her in here to verify this, but she'd probably launch into me all over again. Let's leave her be for now. She thought it was the wrong job for me, that I'd be miserable. So, she'd be miserable. Even she admits it didn't turn out quite like she imagined it."

"So, did you enjoy being vice president after all?"

Roosevelt stared at him, wasn't sure if the question was serious.

"As I said, I didn't have much to do. There is some luxury in that. My sister Corinne's son, my nephew, came down with diphtheria. Awful thing. But I was able to leave my office and visit them at a moment's notice. If I were to do that as governor, someone in the press would always roast me for it. This time, nobody even knew I was gone. There were occasions that I even took the time to do some hunting—one trip to Colorado, for example." He leaned forward, as though imparting a great secret. "I killed a cougar with my knife. Do you know anyone else who can make that claim?" He leaned back again, shook his head. "I don't talk about that much. Edith is tired of hearing about it, and the rest of the world, well, they wouldn't believe me anyway." He paused, thought a moment, felt a twinge of seriousness, wondered how far he should go. "There was one trip . . . a pleasant jaunt up into Vermont." He stopped. "That's not entirely true. There was little about that trip that was pleasant. I certainly welcomed the excursion, looked forward to meeting supportive audiences. But . . ." He paused, surprised himself with a flood of emotion. "Nothing stays the same, young man. Nothing."

CHAPTER 38

September 6, 1901
Isle La Motte, Lake Champlain, Vermont

He was thoroughly in his element, one more speaking event to an audience that seemed to gulp down his every word. After a long, satisfying luncheon, the outdoor picnic atmosphere was winding down, several hundred people having eaten their fill, all of those waiting for the magnificent opportunity to shake hands with the vice president of the United States.

For most of the afternoon, he sat among them, enjoying the decadence of fried food, baked casseroles, and sugary treats, cheerily wowing those nearest him with stories of great excursions out west or his adventures leading troops in Cuba. On cue, he was escorted from his chair, following along to the elegant home of Vermont's former lieutenant governor Nelson Fisk. Inside, a select number of the partygoers would be called into a receiving line, where Roosevelt would treat them to a handshake and a brief second of conversation.

Fisk and a member of his staff escorted Roosevelt through the perfectly manicured lawn, close to the grand entrance of the house. Roosevelt rubbed his belly, saw the former lieutenant governor's secretary, a squirrel-like man named Goolsby.

"I say, sir, whoever arranged the food for such a gathering deserves an award. It was dee-lightful. If you ever plan to do this again, I would hope for an invitation."

The man made a short bow, obviously flattered.

He heard a telephone ringing from inside, and Fisk moved that way with a brief apology. Roosevelt watched him leave, then smiled out across the lawn to the expectant crowd, the people returning his good cheer. He flexed his right hand, thought, There'll be a lot of handshaking. Look out for the big fellows. They tend to have the most painful grip.

"Mr. Vice President?"

He turned to the voice, saw Fisk motioning him into the house. Roosevelt was curious, a hint of alarm, but he obeyed the request, moved inside. He followed Fisk into another room, the former lieutenant governor wordless, grim. Fisk picked up the receiver, held it out to Roosevelt.

He handed Roosevelt the phone, backed out of the room, closed the glass doors.

"Yes? Yes, this is the vice president." The words flowed toward him in a torrent, his breathing quickening, a tight grip on the receiver. "Is this certain? The details are authentic? Do you have the facts straight?"

His voice had grown higher, louder, a tight shrillness, but the voices on the other end of the line were definite, details gathered with care.

"All right. I will leave for Buffalo immediately."

He put down the receiver, felt a shiver, saw faces in the next room, staring at him self-consciously through the glass door. He pulled open the door, looked at Fisk, then his secretary, the few others in the room. At the outside door, the crowds had moved closer, but a guard now locked the door, the mass of faces curious, concerned.

Fisk said, "The doors of the house are all being locked, Mr. Vice President. No one will enter. I have informed my immediate staff and my family, no one else. Do you believe this news is authentic?"

"It is verified by more than one report. President McKinley has been shot. Some anarchist confronted the president in Buffalo with a pistol wrapped in something, a bandage perhaps, shot him twice at point-blank range. The man was captured. The president is right now undergoing surgery. There is no confirmation yet as to his condition."

He felt suddenly helpless, vulnerable, uncertain what to do.

Fisk said, "I will arrange a train to take you to Buffalo. It is of course appropriate that you be there with him."

"Yes, certainly. The president's secretary said the same thing. Thank you. I should leave immediately." He looked out through the glass toward the crowd, the smiles replaced now by concern, the people sensing already that something was wrong. "We must inform the people what has happened."

"We will see it is done. For now, we'll get you to the train station."

September 13, 1901
Lake Colden, Adirondack Mountains, New York

Of the two bullets that tore into McKinley, only one had caused serious damage, ripping through the president's stomach. Though the surgeons could not remove the bullet, McKinley seemed to recover rapidly, strengthening more each day, so much so that after four days, Roosevelt was advised to leave Buffalo. It was as much a symbolic gesture as a practical one, a demonstration to the American public and the newspapers that all was well. Despite Roosevelt's hesitation, McKinley's staff prevailed on him, and the vice president made a loud and pronounced show of taking his family into the mountains of upstate New York for a brief vacation.

He had insisted, and Edith had agreed to come along, accompanying him into the mountains along with ten-year-old Ethel and eleven-year-old Kermit. It was a rare treat for both children, Roosevelt insisting that they had become old enough to experience the joys of the natural world. Despite protests from the two youngest left behind, Roosevelt fought his own temptation to bring them as well, bowing to Edith's admonition that a three-year-old and his seven-year-old brother were not quite ready for rock climbing. And it was rarely a question if seventeen-year-old Alice would make the trip at all. The invitation was there, Roosevelt longing to have his daughter participate in the kind of outdoors excitement he enjoyed. But the girl seemed to much prefer the company of fawning young men, especially if photographers were present.

They spent two nights in a pair of cabins, the Roosevelts accompanied by a handful of friends and two park rangers, who served as the vice president's guides, if not his security.

HE WOKE EARLY, slipped outside into a cold, foggy mist.

The weather had chased his family and most of the others back down the mountain, one of the rangers leading them safely to a dry place. Roosevelt had insisted that the climb go on, the other ranger, a beefy man named Parker, leading the climb through mud and wet leaves.

Roosevelt stopped, winded, the ranger glancing back at him, pretending not to notice. Roosevelt pointed up to one side.

"What's that big rock up there? Impressive."

The ranger followed his point, said, "Doesn't have a name. Wonderful outlook, though. Maybe not today. The light rain might clear up by lunch, but it ain't likely to be a good morning for sightseeing."

Roosevelt stood straight, took a deep breath.

"I'm going up. No need for you to follow. I'd rather do this alone, if you don't mind."

He sought firm footing, pulled himself up to a great flat rock, the surface cold and slick. He stared out, nothing to see but fog, thought, My God, I'm on top of the world. I wish Edith could see this. Well, there's not much to see. But it's out there, all of it, the whole of New York and New England. How many more times will I do this? I'm forty-two, and my legs will lose their power soon. Not too soon, I hope. Vice president of the United States. Good God. Is that the end of any kind of adventure? Tending the store while the president does his business. All I am is a spokesman, a supporting staffer. Everything I do is designed to put the president in the best light. He thought of McKinley, prone in the hospital bed, heavy bandages, the man managing a brief smile. Strong as an ox, they say. That's good for the country, for certain. My time will come, so I'm told. But I'm down a dark hole, no one noticing, no one especially caring where I am, what I'm doing. I climb rocks. By George, I climbed the Matterhorn once. Now, this kind of place is my Matterhorn. A park ranger to watch over me.

He looked down, saw the ranger waiting patiently on the trail below.

"I'm coming down."

"Certainly, sir. Do be careful."

The words stabbed him, and he slid his way down, small rocks and mud, thought, That's my job these days. Be careful.

"Where to now, sir?"

Roosevelt shook his head, motioned a hand down the trail.

"Let's move down to the lake."

"Lake Tear of the Clouds, sir?"

"Yes, that's it. A lake still looks good in the rain."

They descended on the trail, a break in the clouds, a brief glare of sunlight. But it didn't last, the clouds closing in again, more of the heavy mist. After a long hike, he saw the lake to one side, the glass surface, a cloud of fog drifting past.

"It's near one thirty, sir. Would you care for lunch?"

The ranger opened his pack, held out a paper bundle, sandwiches he knew had come from Edith's hand.

"Sure. It's ham, I would guess."

The ranger smiled.

"Your wife's a fine chef, sir."

He looked at the sandwich, thought, Doesn't take a chef to do anything with ham. Probably why she left, so she could eat real food somewhere.

They sat, what passed for a dry, rocky surface, Roosevelt chewing the ham.

"Sir. That's Horace. Moving up here pretty quick."

Roosevelt saw the second ranger, jogging heavily up the trail. Now, he saw the paper in the man's hand, yellow, a telegram. He stood up, watched the man coming closer, felt an odd stirring in his gut, a creeping cold in his chest.

The ranger reached them, breathing heavily, held out the telegram, said, "Sir, this is for you. They had a dickens of a time reaching you here. We received it just a short time ago. I got up here as quick as I could."

Roosevelt took the paper, hesitated, saw both men looking at him, keeping silent, as though understanding that this was important. He tore into the paper now, adjusted his glasses, read. He let out a long breath, still the cold in his chest, said in a low voice, "The president is dying. This says there is *absolutely no hope*. He's dying." His breathing grew stronger, deeper, a burst of butterflies inside him. "Good Godfrey. I'll be the president of the United States."

CHAPTER 39

September 22, 1901
Washington, D.C.

He had taken the oath of office in Buffalo, at the home of a friend, a grand old mansion decorated with vast curtains of funereal black, adding a grisly air to what was already a dismal scene. The inauguration ritual was witnessed by a modest crowd, including six members of McKinley's cabinet, now Roosevelt's own, mumblings already abounding about who might remain in office to serve the new president. For days after, through the journey by train southward to Washington, the cabinet members and others, close in loyalty and friendship to McKinley, observed the youth of the new president with both optimism and dread. Once in Washington, the official visits began, the dread giving way more to the need to accept this energetic man with all his outbursts, to accept that this man now at the top might be different.

He had waited to occupy the Executive Mansion until Mrs. McKinley had vacated, on her own terms, in her own time. For several days, he had been a guest at the Washington home of his sister Bamie and her husband, Commander William Cowles. The marriage had been a surprise to Roosevelt, who had embraced the foregone conclusion that Bamie would never marry. It was a selfish and self-serving attitude from Roosevelt himself, which he now acknowledged. Bamie was, after all, not destined to be the caretaker for the rest of her family.

Cowles was a rotund man, presumed by the Roosevelt family to be a good second half to the feisty and headstrong Bamie, despite the fact that Cowles showed almost no deference to his illustrious brother-in-law, even as Roosevelt had stepped into the presidency.

As Mrs. McKinley vacated the mansion, Roosevelt requested minor changes to the living areas, and the contractors took charge, followed quickly by the mansion's newest occupant. On September 22, Roosevelt bounded up the steps of his new home, very aware that his excitement for the moment far outstripped his need for solemn decorum. But for a minimum of staffers, who kept downstairs, he toured the mansion on his own, marveling at the views out each direction, examining the various paintings of former presidents, marveling again at each of the well-appointed rooms.

The first night's dinner had been a family affair: sisters Bamie and Corinne and their husbands filling the long table. The most notable absence was Edith, still at Sagamore Hill, handling the details so necessary for a lengthy absence. He had missed her profoundly, his two sisters sensing that, as they always could.

THE ROOM WAS dark, no one to disturb him, and he stared out toward specks of light, spread all across the city, the homes of those he would now serve. The dinner had been exceptional, and he put a hand on his stomach, thought, is that why so many presidents are so round? He looked at the bed—again, his bed—could not escape the images of who might have slept there. If not the bed, he thought, the room. Lincoln. My God. Three presidents killed in office. What does that say about us? This lunatic, Czolgosz, killing McKinley. They say McKinley had his hand out, a gesture of openness, a symbol perhaps: yes, I'm your president too. And the man shoots him. Am I to be worried about that? Avoid crowds, rely on so many guards and policemen? I can't. I won't. I'm not king, for God's sake.

He walked to another window, saw a hint of reflection in the glass, his own spectacles. He thought of his father now, the great man. Do you see me? he thought. Can you know what has happened, where I am? He had little confidence in all the religious talk, afterlife, ghosts and spirits. But . . . you're here; I just know that. He smiled. Yes, and it is your birthday today. My first night in this place. Is there meaning in that? Perhaps you came in with me, and so you will watch, and so I will do the job as you would.

He had a different flash of thought, unavoidable, but he pushed hard, tried to avoid it as he always had. She would love it here, he thought. No, it cannot be. She cannot flow through here like some annoying apparition. Dear Alice, stay gone, please. I have so much to do, so many people watching everything I do, every mistake, every twitch of my cheek will have meaning.

He had a wave of depression now, looked again at the bed. I miss Edith; I miss my children. I know it will only be a couple of days, but still, I need you all to help me make this a home. He had a thought, looked away from the window. I'm changing the name, immediately. They showed me the letterhead, clumsy and grandiose. THE EXECUTIVE MANSION. Lincoln called this place the people's house. I suppose that cannot be, not after three dead presidents. But I shall defer more to Lincoln than all who have come since, so many of those who relied on aloofness instead of forging a link with the public. I will order new writing paper, much simpler, much more accurate. The people do not need a "mansion." This place shall be called the White House.

"I TOLD YOU there would be no wall, no barrier. You are welcome here any time *I* choose." Roosevelt laughed.

Lodge smiled as well.

"Well, then, might I even sit down, Mr. President?"

"Of course, Senator. What may I do for you?"

"You're the president. You can do a great many favors for anyone you choose."

Roosevelt was serious now. "I do say, Cabot, McKinley's chair fits rather well. I seem to be more comfortable in this job than I had expected."

"It's not McKinley's chair."

"Quite right. That is taking me a bit of time. I had been in this office a good deal, when I was standing over there. Now, I'm in charge. Bully for that."

Lodge seemed cautious, said, "My friend, be careful saying things like that. The *people* are in charge, at least when you're in public."

Roosevelt felt chastened, said, "Well, yes, of course. But you're my friend, Cabot. I have to be able to talk to you in earnest. You and Elihu Root. I'll not likely get a knife in the back from either you or the secretary of war."

Lodge smiled again. "Thank you for the compliment. I thought it might be useful for you to know what some of the less congenial members of Congress are saying. Senator Hanna, for instance."

Roosevelt frowned at the mention of the name. "Hanna was very close to McKinley. The president's death nearly did him in." Roosevelt sniffed. "At his age, it won't take much."

"Easy, Teddy. It's one thing for him to complain privately that we now have a cowboy as president. But he's an old-line conservative and a powerful man, ill health notwithstanding. He can still line up the delegates, especially from the southern states. Should you have any thoughts of running in 1904, he could be essential."

"What do you suggest?"

"Take it easy with the bluster aimed in his direction. I can blunt his sword in the Senate, for the most part. But he won't leave you alone. He told me that the best he could hope from your presidency was that you stay McKinley's course, leave well enough alone. I doubt he'll support anything you do to stray from that."

Roosevelt absorbed the advice, shook his head. "I can't fear him, or any other opponent. The stock market has been up since my inauguration. I don't know a damn thing about stocks, but I know a vote of confidence when I see one. Stay the course? We're into the twentieth century, Cabot." He thought of Hanna, the crooked old man, shuffling along with his cane.

"Henry, I'm forty-two years old, the youngest man ever to sit in this chair. When I was on McKinley's funeral train coming down here from Buffalo, we passed through hundreds of miles of farms and small towns, cities like Harrisburg and Baltimore. Those places are growing, prosperous, and it's up to me to push that along. Hanna has no grasp of what this country needs, only what it once had. At one stop, I saw a crowd of old soldiers, gray beards and old blue uniforms. They were calling out to McKinley, calling him 'Major,' like they were still at Antietam. Those old men have no idea who I am, have no idea what it means to be advancing this country forward. What I want from you are ideas and support. I might not agree with everything you ask of me, but if it's good for the country, if it will move us forward, I'll damn well try."

October 16, 1901
The White House

The man arrived precisely at eight o'clock, the guards eyeing him carefully as they passed him inside. He was nervous, uncertain, but hid it well, understood the importance of the moment, observed every detail, the smell of fresh paint, faint cracks in the plaster walls, the uncomfortable glare from more than one of the guards. He was accustomed to that, had suffered indignities his entire life, had worked himself up to a place in the academic world where even white men paid attention. That was an accomplishment, to be sure, but it didn't mean as much to him as what he had come to represent: a Black man in a white man's country creating opportunity for other young Black men to do as he had done, to stand tall without fear of being knocked down. His name was Booker T. Washington, and he had been invited to have dinner with the president of the United States.

ROOSEVELT PUT DOWN the napkin, the signal for the servants to clear away the plates. He offered a glance to Edith, who responded appropriately, made her brief farewell. He fondled the coffee cup, sorted through a lengthy monologue he had rehearsed earlier, but it didn't feel appropriate now that he had met the man, now that he had dined with him.

"They spoil me here, you know. Supposedly, the president has everything, every desire at his beck and call. That's hogwash, of course. What is most available to me, on a daily basis, are people who find me disagreeable, who disagree with any statement I make or any program or piece of legislation I try to put forward. When I was a member of the New York State Assembly, I fought to be heard. Now, I am heard too often for some tastes." He stopped, smiled, looked at the man's face, studied him, as he had studied him throughout dinner. "You may feel I'm heard too often right now."

"On the contrary, sir. You are the president of the United States. The podium shall always be yours."

"Perhaps. I am told that by having you here, I have destroyed any chances I might have had for a second term of office."

"I hope not, sir."

Roosevelt took a long breath, wondered just where this road was leading.

"I am told you were born a slave."

Washington kept his poise, seemed to search Roosevelt now, probing discreetly for the deeper meaning.

"Quite so. I was born a few years before the Civil War, in Virginia, to a slave, and in my earliest years, I was a slave myself. I learned a great deal, even as a young boy, about the injustice pressed upon the Negro in our country. I have made it my goal to help those of my race who might otherwise have no opportunity to succeed in a white world, much as I have been extraordinarily fortunate to succeed."

"I know of Tuskegee, of course. Are there other ways you believe you can absolve the chasm between our races besides education?"

"Mr. President, education comes first. No man can make his stand, can find his place in a civilized world, unless he understands that world. Beyond that, I would only say that I believe in a working relationship with men of all colors. I accepted your kind invitation to this pleasant evening only because I believe you to share my feelings. There are some in the Negro community who feel that confrontation and protest would be the most effective way to bridge our divide, to bring our grievances, as it were, to the white community. I do not agree."

Roosevelt felt overwhelmed, was beginning to understand that this dinner held consequences for both men that perhaps neither had foreseen.

"I should be frank with you, Dr. Washington."

"I would respect nothing less, sir."

Roosevelt thought a moment.

"In my cabinet right now sit side by side Catholic and Protestant and Jew. Each man is there because, in my mind, he is fit to exercise on behalf of all our people the duties of the office he holds. In the same way, the only wise and honorable thing to do is to treat each Black man and each white man strictly on his merits as a man, giving him no more and no less than he shows himself worthy to have. Your work, your efforts on behalf of the Negro are essential to the white race as well. We shall all end up going up or going down together. Your efforts in uplifting your part of our great human community have helped uplift all of us."

Washington seemed to weigh Roosevelt's words, then said, "Sir, from where I sit, deep in the South, there is no spirit of togetherness. We are definitely not one people. My efforts toward educating the Negro have met with considerable resistance. Politicians seem to be especially hostile. The newspapers can be especially incendiary, and thus dangerous. You yourself have stated that the Negro is an inferior creature who must be coddled into advancement."

Roosevelt looked down. "Men must be allowed to evolve. As the Negro is evolving even today, so too have I. I admit to being hesitant to suggest the Negro and the white man stand flat on the same field. But the Negro is advancing, as the white man did before. I hesitate, of course, to group an entire race together. Any man who advances himself should be rewarded with every privilege to be found in our democracy. You are a perfect example, sir. By your own hand, you survived the chains of your mother's bondage and rose to an exalted place in the academic hierarchy of this country. You deserve every accolade. Indeed, you are *here*."

Washington smiled now. "There are things we shall disagree on, Mr. President. I do not condemn you for seeing our world through a white man's spectacles. Perhaps one day *you*, sir, will evolve to even greater enlightenment, where we might stand on that same level field."

Roosevelt absorbed the slight edge to Washington's near insult, smiled now. "I wonder if you would consent to becoming an advisor to the president on matters to do with race."

Washington nodded. "I am honored. However, I would caution

you that no man in *my* position has ever held any such role to a man in *yours*. Be prepared for considerable hostility to come toward you from the southern states, and particularly the southern newspapers."

"Newspapers do not concern me, Doctor. They're just words written by scared or angry men who use anonymity as a shield. But in the end they're just words."

THE NEXT DAY, after word had spread of Booker T. Washington's dinner with the president, the *Memphis Scimitar* reacted thus: "The most damnable outrage which has ever been perpetrated by any citizen of the United States was committed yesterday by the president . . . No Southern woman with a proper self-respect would now accept an invitation to the White House, nor would President Roosevelt be welcomed today in Southern homes. He has not inflamed the anger of the Southern people, he has excited their disgust."

Numerous papers offered similar condemnation, with visceral attacks against Roosevelt and even his family. On that score, Dr. Washington had been right.

Within the next week, Roosevelt was scheduled to attend an event at Yale University, in New Haven, Connecticut, accompanied by his daughter Alice. Expecting a raucous crowd, Roosevelt prepared himself for a long day of backslaps and handshakes. It was the Secret Service who changed the routine. Fearful of some violent outbreak, a result of the president's association with a Black man, the public would be held at bay. For the first time in his public life, Roosevelt had to greet the crowds from a distance.

CHAPTER 40

December 15, 1901
Washington, D.C.

He pushed hard up the big rock, one of his favorite obstacles, slid down the far side, then jumped into the soft leaves below. He didn't stop, ran quickly to the great fallen tree, jumped over, one foot catching a small limb, tumbling him to the mud. He laughed, ran again, high, sloping ground, more rocks, close to the river. He felt his breathing now, sharp and cold from the air around him, looked up away from the water, saw carriages on the wide avenue. He didn't hesitate, ran that way, climbing again, his legs slowing, pain in his lungs, reached level ground, stopped, more carriages, a pair of motorcars, no one noticing him. It was getting darker now, late afternoon, and he looked out toward the city, lights coming on, headlights on the motorcars. He waited for a gap in the traffic, ran quickly across the street, his breaths in sharp rhythm with his footsteps. He saw the White House now, windows lit, one tall tree bathed in small lights, Christmas colors. He jogged up the wide lawn, a guard noticing him, a formal salute. Roosevelt ignored the man, kept up the pace, a guard at the main entrance snapping to, opening the heavy door, Roosevelt jogging past him inside. He stopped now, laughed, his usual reaction, bent down, hands on his knees. And now he heard her voice.

"You fell down again. We'll have to wash your clothes before someone sees you." She paused. "Was it fun, my dear?"

"It's always fun. The shame of it is, no one can keep up with me.

I fear the Congress is populated by the most flabby excuses for manhood I've seen. They won't even accept my invitations anymore."

Edith was smiling at him.

"Then you must continue to prey on the uneducated, the out-of-town visitors. Or, perhaps, just those men who are too afraid of you to refuse the offer. Although, why you insist on abusing people so, I have no idea."

He took a long deep breath, blowing the cold air away.

"Edie, they are perfectly welcome to abuse *me,* if they can. Just ask Leonard Wood. One day he'll return from Cuba, and when we return to the park he'll leave me behind."

Her mood seemed to change, and she looked away for a long moment. He knew what to expect, something coming that might be unpleasant.

"Edie, shall we go into the Green Room? We can sit for a while."

She looked at him again, dark eyes. "I don't wish to sit. I wish to go upstairs to our private residence. We have a problem, Teddy. We have five children. There simply isn't space for this family."

He had heard this before, from her first days in the White House. "Well, then, perhaps we should adjourn upstairs, if that will make you happy."

"What will make me happy, Teddy, is redoing this house. I don't need privacy to discuss this. Everyone among your staff knows how I feel. There is no reason why some of your official offices have to be on the same floor as our home. I would like permission from you or whoever grants such things to remodel the top floor, to make it a more suitable residence. Then we might have privacy, Teddy. We don't need your assistants and messengers walking past our bedroom door all hours of the day and night. And we certainly don't need newspapermen wandering about, digging their noses into our personal affairs."

He glanced around, saw faces in the next room, trying not to appear nosy.

"That would require money, Edie, possibly a great deal. The funding would have to come from Congress. Do you have any idea of the cost?"

She crossed her arms, a hint of a smile. "While you spend your afternoons galloping all over the forest, I have spoken to an architect,

Mr. McKim. He estimates the entire project will cost approximately a half million dollars."

He stared at her, his mouth slightly open. "Really?" He looked around, saw his assistant secretary, William Loeb, peering in from the next room. "Mr. Loeb, here please. Tell me, how do we go about securing a half-million-dollar appropriation to remodel the White House?"

Loeb looked at Edith, and Roosevelt could see that this was a topic they had already discussed.

"Mr. President, the first step . . . possibly the only step, is to go to Congress, the Appropriations Committee, and ask for it."

"THIS ENTIRE PHILIPPINES matter is something of a mess—for the army, for the War Department, and very likely for you."

He stared at Root, hands under his chin.

"You're the secretary of war. You're supposed to be on top of things over there. How did this happen?"

"General Miles has been given access to letters between the commanders in the Philippines and myself, letters that make plain there have been atrocities by American soldiers against certain tribes of the Filipino people. We have known about this for some time and are taking steps to punish the guilty parties."

"Well, I'm relieved to hear that. I don't wish to be labeled as the president who enjoys torturing foreigners."

"What I don't understand, Mr. President, is why Nelson Miles, the general in chief of the army, would hand over this kind of information to Congress. What is he hoping to gain? This is all on his watch as well as mine."

Roosevelt thought a moment, the logic of the entire event becoming clear.

"Is it true that he is handing these communications to certain congressmen who oppose me, all Democrats, correct?"

"It seems so, sir."

"That's it, Elihu. Nelson Miles is ingratiating himself to those men because he has every intention of running for president in 1904. If the newspapers get all of this, he can parade himself around with his grand uniform and his chestful of medals and claim to be not only a great hero of the republic but a man above reproach, a man who will clean out the dirty laundry of the War Department."

Root shook his head. "Mr. President, I have nothing to hide. We have some very bad people running things in the Philippines, and I assure you we're ferreting them out as we speak."

"How does that happen? Is the Philippines so very different from Cuba? In five months, Leonard Wood is preparing to hand over control of Cuba to the Cuban people, a government that at least seems to know how to be a government. But here's the point, Elihu. Wood is a doctor. He understands medical problems and has greatly improved the health of the Cuban people. That place is free of yellow fever for the first time in two hundred years. He has cleaned up some of the worst sanitation horrors in Central America. So, what is so different about the Philippines?"

Root pulled a paper from a small valise.

"There is no *doctor* in command there. The native tribes we have been fighting have proven to be a vicious lot. Atrocities abound, graphic and horrible. I have descriptions if you wish to see them."

"Another time perhaps."

"Well, sir, our troops have in some ways responded to those atrocities in a tit for tat, as it were. When faced with uncivilized warfare, men are apt to become uncivilized themselves. I'm afraid that's what has happened. And it's those examples that General Miles is handing over to Congress. I have no doubt that, sooner or later, one of those congressmen will seek to ingratiate himself to a newspaper reporter."

"Is there nothing I can do to stifle General Miles? I am, after all, his superior."

Root fumbled through his valise, said, "I beg your patience, sir. I'm old. It takes me longer to get to the point. Yes, here it is, a memo passed along to me by the Navy Department. It seems that General Miles has spoken out inappropriately about a naval matter, a legal dispute between two admirals. I was intending to remind him that he has no business engaging in any matter involving the navy."

Roosevelt felt himself rocking in the chair. "No. Let me do it."

The scolding message went to General Miles from the War Department, endorsed by the president. Chastened, Miles immediately journeyed to the White House to either explain himself or apologize for his indiscretion. In a stroke of bad luck for the general in chief, Roosevelt was hosting a large reception, including members of the press and several private citizens. For Roosevelt, it was his ideal setting.

He saw Miles coming, even the man's informal uniform emblazoned with more decoration than Roosevelt had ever seen. He set down a glass of champagne, glanced at Edith, who seemed to know what was coming. Miles approached him now, and Roosevelt cleared his throat, offered the general no room for comment, said in a loud voice, loud enough for all around him to hear, "I will have no criticism of my administration from you, or any other officer in the army. Your conduct is worthy of censure, sir."

Miles seemed shocked, ignored the hundreds of eyes watching him. He backed away now, said, "You have the advantage, sir."

Miles left as he came, and Roosevelt felt his hands shaking, retrieved the champagne glass, saw a slight horror on Edith's face. It's all right, he thought. I am, after all, the commander in chief. Of course, Miles has no real idea why I was dressing him down. But if he believes that it's all about the Philippine matter, I might just have convinced him to sit on his hands.

He raised his glass, a broad, toothy smile. Others joined in, the shock of his outburst wearing off. He called out in a loud voice, "Let us salute the coming of Christmas!" He looked toward Edith, saw her smiling now, knew she couldn't help it. He aimed the next toast her way, called out again, "But I do love being president!"

Christmas Day, 1901
The White House

The music was loud, his voice louder, both hands holding the hands of his daughter Ethel, swinging her in a wide circle, her feet airborne.

He set her down gently now, a quick hug of the exhausted girl, called out with a wide grin: "All right, who's next? No? All right then, I'll go it alone."

He began to dance, a tornado of energy, the children now joining in, Edith dancing more discreetly, staying just to one side, away from the chaos. The guests joined in with him, none with quite the stamina for the dance, Roosevelt more manic still, egged on by all the children. He saw Alice, aloof, and he pointed her way, said, "This season's most eligible and beautiful debutante. You must learn to dance. Maybe even smile!"

She moved forward, seemed to accept the inevitable, joined in alongside Edith, holding her dress slightly above the floor, showing off the gracefulness of her dance steps, but keeping distance from the greater storm. He acknowledged her, called out, "What grace! What beauty! My oldest child!"

He returned to his own fever pitch now, turning circles, his feet moving in a frenzy. To one side, clapping with the others, he saw Senator Lodge, called to him now: "Cabot, join in!"

Lodge broke into a rare smile, nodded in acceptance, slid carefully onto the dance floor, no match for Roosevelt. But Lodge tired quickly, begged for a moment's rest, moved out alongside a laughing Edith, the two of them surrounded by the smaller children. Lodge leaned closer to Edith, another smile, said, "It is apparent to those of us who love him that the president is *six*."

CHAPTER 41

January 19, 1902
The White House

He was surprised by the visit of Mark Hanna, the Ohio senator seeming more sickly and pale than Roosevelt had seen before. But Hanna's energy was in his purpose, and he clearly had a purpose. Just what that was seemed a mystery until Hanna lowered himself painfully into the chair across from Roosevelt's desk.

"Did you happen to see my press release, Mr. President?"

"I saw that you have advocated for the Panama route against the one through Nicaragua. Your voice carries weight, so I must ask why you have made that choice." And why, he thought, have you come to see me in the first place.

Everything Roosevelt knew about Hanna told him that Hanna was most assuredly old-school in Washington and, like William McKinley, prone to the straight and narrow, doing things the way they had always been done. And most important, Hanna had never seemed to regard Roosevelt with an ounce of respect. There was even talk that Hanna would seek the party's nomination for the presidency in 1904, though, as Roosevelt could see now, Hanna was hardly healthy enough to withstand a campaign.

Roosevelt felt an opening, as though Hanna was testing him, said, "I myself have believed the Panama route was best, but Senators Morgan and Tyler have been quite vigorous in pushing for Nicaragua. So, why should I support Panama over the alternative?"

Hanna sneezed, blew his nose into a wad of handkerchief.

"Excuse me, Mr. President. I've been saddled with the nuisance of a cold for a week now. Senator Morgan . . . well, I'll leave that opinion to others. Not my favorite man. Tyler's from Alabama. Anytime there's a sniff of some new market for cotton or coal, he embraces it like a bear to its cubs. I won't suggest any further motives that Senator Tyler might have for shoving the Nicaragua idea down our throats."

Roosevelt smiled carefully, knew it was Hanna's way to make a vicious accusation without actually saying anything. Roosevelt had been the victim of that sort of strategy for months now.

"So, Senator, tell me why I'm correct to like Panama."

"There are a dozen reasons, starting with the reality that the French have already begun the project and left behind a good-sized ditch we could enhance and improve upon. They spent twenty-five years on their project, and it finally fell to pieces because they didn't have the right engineers for the job. We have the engineers, and we now have a head start, thanks to the French ditch. The Panama route would be nearly one hundred forty miles shorter than the route through Nicaragua. There would be fewer locks and a straighter route. It would require thirty-three hours to make the journey through Nicaragua. Through Panama, twelve. Most importantly, as far as most of the public is concerned, would be the cost. The route through Nicaragua would require forty-five million dollars more to construct than the route through Panama. And one more thing. Nicaragua has a big damn volcano, called Momotombo, that blows its top every now and then. That kind of natural disaster could greatly impede operation of any canal there for months, if not years."

Roosevelt had already weighed the various lobbying efforts, understood Hanna's proposal already. He also knew that Hanna enjoyed being the heaviest weight in the room, full of strategic advice. Roosevelt smiled again. "So then, what should we do about this?"

Hanna seemed to energize further. "We make a report to Congress, explaining our reasons. You keep your name off the report, though anyone with a brain will know it's your program. There will be some opposition, besides Morgan and Tyler. I believe most of those people can be persuaded without too much difficulty. The Isthmian Canal Commission has done their research and can respond to any of the questions you and I might not like. Also, there is a Frenchman, fellow named Bunau-Varilla, here to lobby French interests. He is likely to be the conduit for the United States purchasing French rights to their existing material at the canal site, plus the property rights that the French had already negotiated from the governments there."

Roosevelt stared at Hanna, wondered if there was more left unsaid.

"Are you certain that if I back this bill, Congress won't just hand me my head?" He stopped short of the next question to rise up in his mind: Why should I trust a man who has opposed me every step of the way?

Hanna seemed to know what Roosevelt was thinking.

"I can never be certain just what Congress will do about anything. All we can do is make the stronger argument and lobby like hell to push it through." He paused. "Mr. President, I have never been certain just how strong the base is on which you stand. You have been in office for barely five months, but you haven't yet embarrassed this office or yourself. There are some who are surprised by that."

"Senator, I'm certain that's true."

Hanna looked hard at him now, leaned forward with a wrinkled hand on Roosevelt's desk.

"I once told you to stay the course, not to deviate from McKinley's path. You mostly ignored me. But I'm man enough to admit that, so far, you've been right. Mostly. I will continue to fight you when I feel it's important. But I will support you just as well. This canal bill is worth fighting for."

THE DEBATES AND opposing arguments in Congress for the exact route of the canal were intense and grueling, and very soon, with no resolution in sight, the canal bill slid off the legislative calendar, shelved for another day. But Roosevelt made certain it would never fade away completely. After intense debate by those congressmen for and against the treaty, those who, like Roosevelt, saw clear value in the Panama route finally had their day. In June 1902, Congress passed the Panama Canal Act. But the work wasn't complete. The final negotiations for the rights to the Panamanian route required nearly two more years of difficult negotiations between the United States government and their Colombian and Panamanian counterparts. Finally, on November 18, 1903, the twenty-six-point treaty was signed with the Panamanian government. Construction began in May 1904.

For Roosevelt, the battles continued. Throughout the Industrial Revolution, the men at the top of banking, commerce, and railroads had operated with a steady hand at their own controls, with mostly smooth sailing, thanks to the blind eye of several presidential administrations. However, on February 20, 1902, Roosevelt's attorney general, Philander Knox, filed a lawsuit, invoking the Sherman Anti-Trust Act against an entity now called the Northern Securities Company, alleging that a monopolistic trust had been created from the merging of two great railroad lines, the Northern Pacific and the Great Northern. That combination would now control virtually all the railroad traffic throughout the western United States. It was a ripe target for Knox to launch his suit, and for Roosevelt to make good on his reputation as a man intent on breaking up monopolies and overreaching trusts.

Though most Americans had begun to trust Roosevelt and took these actions in a positive light, Wall Street most definitely did not. As news broke of the antitrust suit, a general panic swept through the stock exchanges, concern about just where Roosevelt and his trust-busting hammer would fall next. Stock prices plummeted, only to be rescued by a sudden buying binge by financier J. P. Morgan, who happened to be one of the men mentioned in the Knox suit. Fueled by Morgan's obvious anger at the lawsuit that threatened his convenient arrangement for the railroads, much of Wall Street joined voices in their loud denunciation of President Roosevelt.

Even a visit to the White House by Morgan fell flat as an attempt to bring *reason* to Roosevelt's intentions. Whether anyone on Wall Street believed that Roosevelt had stepped into something beyond his grasp, the president didn't care. He had a cause, which even Congress seemed to rally behind. After an era of corporate mergers and backslapping dealmaking, Roosevelt had suddenly shined a light where darkness had prevailed for decades.

Spring had rolled over Washington, colorful gardens and fields of budding trees. He sat with Edith on the White House's great columned portico, teacups and cake, watching whatever might pass by on the street in front of the White House. It was late, the last hour of daylight, the time he always devoted to her.

She frowned at him now, something he was used to.

"Teddy, are you seriously going to have more cake? You know, you've had three pieces."

"I'm not counting. But, yes, since you ask, I want more. It's quite good, and I still feel some space in these trousers. It can't hurt to fill them up. Makes it easier on my suspenders."

She shook her head, laughed.

"I'm surprised you still need suspenders."

She turned, called out, "Louisa, could you please bring the president another slice of cake? Smaller this time."

The woman appeared, added the cake to his plate.

"Is there anything else, ma'am?"

"No, thank you. He's had plenty. He forgets there will still be a dinner, a large number of guests, as always. You're excused, Louisa."

Roosevelt stared out at the wide street, said, "You know, I don't miss dust. Pavement is a marvel. If they had been able to pave those streets in Medora, the place might have attracted more settlers. You had to wash the grit out of your mouth every time you rode a horse anywhere at all. Probably still do."

"You hardly need pavement to ride your horse around here. Honestly, I do wish you would leave your pistol here. It's bad enough how you frighten the hikers in Rock Creek Park by galloping past them. Shooting at everything you consider a target is really not necessary. Accidents can happen. And besides, how much big game have you brought home from that park?"

He sniffed, knew she was just digging at him.

"If I can hit a tree stump at fifty paces as I ride past, it only means that when the time comes, I'll not miss something more useful. It's keeping my eye sharp. And besides, the hikers have learned to stand aside."

He had given her another opening to jab him for his nearsightedness, waited for it, but she said nothing, then made a small grunt. He looked at her, saw pain in her face.

"What is it? Are you all right?"

She put her hand on his arm, took deep breaths, said, "A sharp pain, in my stomach. It's gone now."

"Are you sure? We can summon the doctor."

"Teddy, it's fine. The pain's gone. It happens every now and then."

He couldn't keep a hint of panic out of his voice.

"How often? Are you sure you're all right?"

She tapped his arm now. "Yes, I'm fine. Look, out there, the motorcar. Isn't that one of those new Ramblers?"

Roosevelt still looked at her, heard the car now, glanced that way.

"I think so. Perhaps we should go inside. For you, and the baby."

She understood his concern, Roosevelt hovering over her ever since she had known she was pregnant. It had been the same before, all five times, and he made no apology for his concerns, tried not to dwell on just why he was so afraid.

"I've had enough cake. I'm sure I have work to do, someone waiting to see me. You should go inside."

She surrendered, stood, and he watched for any signs of unsteadiness, gave her his arm. Across the wide lawn, two of the boys were playing at something that seemed to be fort building, ripping up a small section of White House greenery. He wanted to call out, bring them in, but he let it go, focused instead on Edith, escorted her back inside.

May 9, 1902

He sat in his office, shuffling through the annoyance of papers, a handful of bills passed by Congress, none of it mattering to him. Why do they take so long, he thought, to do every blessed thing? The Capitol hosts one gigantic argument, every day of every session. One minute they profess to support my initiatives; the next, they're ignoring me completely. Men like Hanna come here and preach loving platitudes and then go to the Capitol and curse my name.

He shoved the papers aside, stood, walked to the tall window. He heard hammering now, high above, the carpenters performing Edith's renovation work. The noise made little difference to him, the inconvenience to their residential area a greater problem. It won't be too long now, he thought, and we can all leave for Oyster Bay. The children will prefer that, certainly. That's probably better than Quentin trying to dig a gold mine in the White House gardens. I should use a firmer hand with the boys, but by Godfrey, I do enjoy them, all of them, even the pouting Alice. It's no secret that when I pay her more attention, the pouting stops. So, pay her more attention. Pay them all more attention. It will give me more training for dealing with congressmen.

There was a sharp knock.

"Yes, come in."

He was surprised to see Isabelle, Edith's secretary, saw a look of sadness.

"Yes, what is it? Something wrong?"

"Sir, please come. I'm so sorry, sir. Dr. Hewitt is here. She didn't wish to disturb you. But now . . . sir, Mrs. Roosevelt has suffered a miscarriage."

He rushed past her, to the stairway, bounded up, saw a wad of bloody sheets, saw Edith now, lying on the bed, the doctor beside her, a pair of servants to one side.

Hewitt turned to him, grim, serious.

"She is resting. It was difficult, but she's through it now. I'll check her for infection for the next few weeks. There isn't much more for me to do right now."

"My God. What can I do?"

The doctor looked at Edith, then put a hand on Roosevelt's arm.

"See to your wife. That's what she needs right now more than any single thing."

They sat again on the portico, watching the autocars, the carriages. He saw the younger children coming out from beyond the corner of the house, all five, some kind of noisy chase, certain to require the laundry. Beside him, Edith laughed, a surprise, the first sign of joy he had heard from her since the miscarriage.

He looked at her, said, "It's a lovely day. Summer's here, certainly."

He wasn't sure of her reaction, but she smiled at him, held out her hand, said, "Yes. It's all right, Teddy. I have been brooding on this for a while now. We have a lovely family. I wasn't meant to bear another child. I'm forty years old. It just isn't done, for good reason. The doctor never said that, but I could see it in his face. He said it would take a few weeks for me to recover. When I look at you, I realize I have children enough, Alice and those five out there, and certainly you. You, my child, require more care than the rest."

He wasn't convinced, had seen weeks now of depressed worry, as though Edith had lost more than the child.

"Are you certain you're doing all right? Is there anything I can do, anything you'd like to do?"

She looked out toward the children, said, "We should go to Sagamore Hill. It will be good for all of us, even you."

He nodded, energized by the thought. "Yes. Congress will adjourn the end of June, so there will be no legislation I have to be bothered with. Oh, I wanted to tell you. I wasn't sure you would . . . if it was the right time."

"Tell me, Teddy. You look like you're about to burst."

"The National Reclamation Act. It's the one bill I've been pushing on those tree trunks in Congress, and they finally approved it. I signed it this morning."

"Tell me again . . ."

"It provides funding for the National Geological Survey, for an enormous force of civil engineers to survey and create water-management tracts throughout the western states. One of the greatest problems facing the ranchers when I was out west was water—finding it, securing it, providing enough of it for everyone. The act should do exactly that, funding the construction of aqueducts and dams to supply water where none is now." He laughed. "Even Mark Hanna got behind it. The only voice against it was that congressman from Illinois, Joe Cannon. His entire career seems to rest on one motto, Not One Cent for Scenery. Well, he can cut down all the scenery he wants in his own backyard. The rest of the country will be just fine. After two weeks of wading through bills sponsored by no one I know, finally, *finally*, I signed one that mattered to me."

She clapped her hands, smiled at him. "Wonderful, Teddy. You see? This is why you're president."

He stood, looked out toward the city, hands on his hips.

"Yes, Edie. This is why I'm president."

CHAPTER 42

July 30, 1902
Sagamore Hill, New York

"Papa, I am bored. Bored. Bored. How much longer am I to be imprisoned here?"

He looked up from his book, always saw her mother's face in hers, looked away, still could not call Alice by her name.

"Baby Lee, you are a part of this family. We are enjoying a restful vacation here, and you are a part of that. What is so frightfully awful about spending time up here with the rest of us?"

Alice moved across the room, sat in a huff, her chin in her hand.

"I'm happy to be with the family, Papa. It's just . . . well, after I had my coming out, I heard that I was the most beautiful debutante of the season. I naturally expected all manner of worthy suitors coming round, each one outdoing the other to impress me. That is supposed to be the way, so I'm told. Instead, the only men around here are your Secret Service guards, and they are frightfully dull."

He put aside his book, resigned to the task.

"My dear, I am no happier about the guards than you are. I would shoo them all away if it was allowed. I don't have much choice in the matter. No one wants to see another McKinley. I'm perfectly happy to rely on Big Bill all by himself to take care of any trouble that might threaten us, and, as well, I am perfectly satisfied with taking care of myself."

She still sulked, said, "He's a strange one, if you ask me. I didn't know British men could become so enormous. And he's so old, and yet when I try talking to him, all he wants to do is play with Quentin."

"My dear, first of all, he's Scottish, and he's not much older than I am, so I take your comment as an inadvertent insult. No matter. Big Bill Craig is the one Secret Service man I would rely on in a desperate situation. I'm hoping he will teach me in the use of the broadsword. He's supposed to be quite good at it. Now, do you have any further complaints?"

She seemed to perk up, said, "I should go to Newport. There are some truly wonderful events happening this month. The invitations have positively flowed across our steps."

He was getting annoyed, fought it, exercised more patience with Alice than with any of the other children.

"Baby Lee, you are eighteen. You're not going off to Newport or anywhere else by yourself. Just accept that we are your family, and our time here is for you, as it is for us."

He heard the knock, firm and quick, guessed it was Big Bill. "Yes, enter."

The man came in, enormous, dapper, a telltale bulge beneath his coat. He made a nod toward Alice, said, "Forgive me, sir. My apologies, young miss. Mrs. Roosevelt said I could find you here. I'm just reporting that the men have been spread out in a perimeter around the house, as is proper. Anyone approaches, they'll need a good reason why."

Roosevelt couldn't help but like the big man, even if he thought the security measures were vastly overblown.

"Thank you, Bill. I'm just reading my book, and Miss Roosevelt is seeking something better to do. All is well. I must ask . . . Miss Roosevelt says that you enjoy Quentin's company far more than you do the rest of us. What can a four-year-old offer that the rest of us cannot?"

Bill looked down, seemed embarrassed. "Sir, your young son and I share a common hobby. We rather enjoy cartoons, the comic magazines."

Roosevelt looked at him, a smile now forming. "Well, that was not expected. But, by all means, as you have time, enjoy your hobby. I know Quentin does."

Bill made a quick bow, left the room, and Roosevelt turned to Alice again, still the sulk.

"Look, my dear, I can't do much to erase your boredom. I have serious issues coming across my desk nearly every day. This was supposed to be a restful vacation, but I find it anything but. Now, please. Perhaps you can find a hobby, like your little brother."

AMONG THE MANY presidential concerns that consumed Roosevelt that summer was a strike among anthracite coal miners. As the months passed, concern grew that, with winter approaching, the lack of coal threatened to cause serious hardship across the entire Northeast. The strike had begun earlier that year, nearly one hundred fifty thousand miners, along with a hundred thousand supportive laborers, walking off the job, mostly in the coalfields of eastern Pennsylvania. For weeks, Washington and the president had paid little heed, confident that the strike would soon be resolved. The conflict pitted the miners, led by United Mine Workers president John Mitchell, against a consortium of mine operators, led primarily by railroad and coal operator George Baer. Over the months, the two sides had grown more determined to hold their own position, the miners believing that by the end of autumn, cold weather would test the operators' resolve. The operators insisted that the miners would weaken on their own, mainly because of a lack of income. So far, neither side had blinked.

For the most part, the strike had been civil—loud voices but not much else. On July 29, that changed, a violent confrontation over an imported mine worker, one man ultimately killed, with dozens wounded by panicking police officers.

HE LOOKED UP, another interruption in his reading, the door opening, saw George Cortelyou, his personal secretary. Cortelyou was nearly Roosevelt's age, with considerable experience in Washington, and the job he held now was the same as he had under McKinley. It was normal for Cortelyou to visit Sagamore Hill most mornings from his temporary lodging in Oyster Bay, imparting the day's mail and other necessary events. Roosevelt ignored the frown on the man's face.

"Good morning. So, when are we announcing the Supreme Court pick?"

Cortelyou seemed to snap awake.

"Oh, yes, Mr. Oliver Wendell Holmes has been informed, and this afternoon, the newspapers will have his name. What we are already hearing from your friends in Congress is that he is an excellent choice for the vacancy. He should be confirmed without difficulty."

"Excellent. Dee-lighted. I keep doing things right, and they might start to like me a bit more."

"Sir, there is a problem. We received a wire, passed along from Governor Stone of Pennsylvania."

"Stone. Don't know him well. All right, read it."

Bloodshed ran. Stop. Riot in this country. Stop. Property destroyed, citizens killed and injured. Stop. Situation beyond my control. Stop. Troops should be sent immediately.

Cortelyou held out the telegram.

"The governor has dispatched the Pennsylvania National Guard to reclaim order. He says that it isn't necessary for the federal government to do anything yet. If you'd like to see his message, sir."

"No. Good God, what are those people trying to do? Two sides to a single argument, and they'd rather let it go to bloodshed than solve their problems." He thought a moment. "I could fix this. I know damn well I could."

"Sir, you can't. It's a private matter. Government can't become involved."

"I didn't say government. I said me."

For the next several weeks, the violence in the coalfields seemed to subside, as though, by the violence alone, the workers and their opponents were shocked into a temporary withdrawal. With events calming down, Roosevelt took advantage in the lull to begin a lengthy speaking campaign, beginning with rail stops throughout much of New England. It was a way of testing the affections of the public, as well as taking credit for the nation's current prosperity, tossing out the bone that although most were prospering, many were not. Roosevelt would suggest in strong language that the injustice must be solved, which might mean massive reform of the nation's trusts and conglomerates. It was a carefully thought-out strategy, one that had served him well before: embrace the good, condemn the bad. Although, under some pressure from the influential senators in his own party, including Mark Hanna, Roosevelt was forced to temper his words so as not to anger too many members of Congress, whose votes he might need to pass all manner of programs he was beginning to champion.

There was one concern, held less by Roosevelt than by his security detail. The speaking journey would coincide closely with the one-year anniversary of William McKinley's death. If the president gave that no attention, Big Bill Craig certainly did.

September 3, 1902
Pittsfield, Massachusetts

His train carried him from Connecticut to Rhode Island to Maine, Vermont to New Hampshire to Massachusetts, stops in each state, small towns and large. He had known they would welcome him, boisterous crowds at every stop, cheering on his words or just shouting his name. He fought against exhaustion, kept himself energized from the energy of the crowds, soothed his tender throat along the way, the intervals between towns.

They reached Pittsfield at midmorning, the final stop, Roosevelt prepared to greet the crowd there with smiling exhaustion. He stepped down from the train, a hearty handshake from Governor Crane of Massachusetts.

"Sir, welcome. It has been suggested that on such a glorious day as this, we take advantage of the weather and use a carriage, open-topped, allowing you to wave at the people lining the route. There will certainly be those. The venue is already packed with your audience."

Roosevelt glanced skyward, nodded. "Yes, dee-lighted. Let's take the carriage. Winter will be here before too much longer."

They stepped up into the facing rows of seats, Roosevelt beside

Crane, Cortelyou across from him. He watched Big Bill Craig, nervous always, eyeing the surroundings, thick woods across the tracks. Craig stepped up now, a nodding glance to Roosevelt, sat down beside the driver, the man holding the reins.

THE CROWD WAS exactly as so many before, raucous cheering, a chorus of schoolchildren singing something cheerful, flowers strewn about his platform, the crowd receptive to his words, the final send-off, long minutes of unstoppable applause. He offered them his final bow, raised his Rough Rider hat, his own tradition, more cheers for that. He stepped down from the platform, weakness in his tired legs, one hand holding the railing, steadying himself, the weariness overwhelming. The governor was there now, smiling, another handshake.

"Mr. President, that was inspiring. They truly love you. I wish I could generate that much enthusiasm."

Roosevelt summoned the strength for another handshake, said, "One more stop, then?"

"Yes, if you don't mind. The local country club. There are a number of deep-pocketed donors who have made arrangements to meet with you. It won't take long, I assure you. You must be tired, truly."

"Never. Let's go to your country club."

They climbed up into the carriage, same as before, Big Bill sitting up beside the driver. Roosevelt sagged on the seat, forced his back straight, waved at a small group of children holding flowers.

He saw the trolley tracks, a wide curve running parallel to the road, the tracks then cutting across. He looked at Cortelyou, who seemed as tired as he was, but Cortelyou was deep in thought, and Roosevelt appreciated that, his secretary minding the store even as he traveled with him.

"Well done, sir."

"Thank you. It will be good to get back to Sagamore . . ."

"My God! Look out!"

Roosevelt looked up, Big Bill turning, facing back, wide eyes, a glance at Roosevelt, a sharp rumbling now coming from behind the carriage. And now the impact, Roosevelt tossed skyward, falling out to one side, hard on the ground, sharp pain, his leg, the side of his face. He struggled to stand, saw the wreckage of the carriage, saw Cortelyou, thrown clear, moving slowly, picking himself up. Roosevelt moved quickly to the trolley. Along one side, the massive car had crushed what remained of the carriage. He searched frantically, called out, "Is everyone all right?"

He saw the governor now, staggering, brushing himself off, looking at Roosevelt with breathless relief.

"Are you all right, sir?"

Roosevelt felt the sharp pain in his leg, ran a hand along his jaw, tender pain.

"I'm a little beat-up, but I'm here." He looked at Cortelyou, who said, "I was thrown clear, it seems. I'm all right."

"What about the others? See to them."

Cortelyou said, "The coachman, sir. He's here. I fear he's unconscious. There's blood."

Roosevelt moved that way, saw men running toward him, a police officer, heard Cortelyou, "Oh dear Lord. Sir! *Sir!*"

He saw Cortelyou staring down beneath the trolley, a vast carpet of blood, exposed bone, a man's coat ripped apart.

He stood back, closed his eyes, tried not to see the horror. It was Big Bill.

He felt frozen, then looked toward the trolley, saw the operator, dapper uniform, no expression, and Roosevelt felt himself moving that way, balled his fists, stopped in front of the man, who seemed not to flinch.

"Were you not in control?" The operator stared at him, speechless. "If you had control, it's a goddamn outrage!"

The man showed no emotion, said, "I didn't do this on purpose."

Roosevelt felt his fists harden, his fingers digging into his palms, raised both hands, would kill this man, strangle him, and he drew back one hand, would strike the man as hard as he could. Police were there now, the man pulled back, handcuffs, taken away. Roosevelt was breathing heavily, heard Cortelyou behind him.

"They'll deal with him. You're the president, sir. Everyone will know what you do. You must just withdraw. It's so very fortunate you were not killed."

Roosevelt loosened his hands, the anger giving way to sorrow, the familiar feeling, death, loss, grief. He looked again at Craig's body, men now gathering, doing the necessary job.

He eased himself away from the trolley, saw now that a huge crowd was gathering. A carriage appeared, then another, more police, men spreading out, security, many more staring at him, appraising.

"I'm all right. It's all right." He looked again at Craig's body, said in a low voice, "Poor man. Poor man. I must tell my children."

He saw Cortelyou motioning him toward a carriage, started that way, felt a sharp pain in one leg, blood in his mouth, saw the people staring at him, concern, desperate to help. He offered a brief wave, moved to the carriage, tried to climb up, the pain in his leg like a sharp knife, said to Cortelyou, "I fear I need some assistance."

CHAPTER 43

October 3, 1902
Washington, D.C.

The serious bruise on his lower leg had become something worse, an open wound that had festered into a fluid-filled tumor. One surgery led to two, the tumor drained, dressed, then drained again. Finally, the surgeons resorted to the more extreme measure, removing the tissue down to the bone itself, leaving the bone revealed to allow a complete healing to begin.

With the surgeries complete, Roosevelt could return to his duties. His only concessions to the injury were allowing Edith to mother over him and using a wheelchair.

He had become as frustrated as most of the public with the intransigence on both sides of the coal strike. As fall inched toward winter, the outcries were growing. Although it was not his place as president to arbitrate the differences or to command the strike to a settlement, still he chafed at the idea that he could do nothing at all. Chafing was not something he could tolerate for very long. He made the only legal move he could make, that of a private citizen willing to stand in the center of the conflict and possibly bring it to a conclusion. If he couldn't actually dictate anything to do with the strike, there was nothing improper about the president of the United States offering an invitation for the men from both sides to gather for a meeting. Roosevelt had one definite advantage in such an offer: No one could refuse a formal invitation from the president without seeming disrespectful, if not rude. And so they came.

With the White House still under an umbrella of renovation, Roosevelt had taken up residence in a home just down the street. As the time drew closer for the guests to arrive, Roosevelt began a preliminary meeting with Attorney General Knox, along with his commissioner of labor. Within an hour, the rest of the invitees arrived.

What followed were long days of wrangling, wrestling, and shouting, and even when voices weren't raised, the tension and tempers were often at breaking points. Yet through it all, Roosevelt held sway, with taut reins on the emotions and illogic of both sides. To his enormous surprise, financier J. P. Morgan inserted himself, creating another conduit into the deepest intentions of the coal operators, then coming to Roosevelt with solutions that at least melted the ice. With Morgan's assistance, the talks began to flow more smoothly, the failures smaller, successes large. After two weeks, the strike had been settled.

Ignoring the ongoing discomfort in his leg, Roosevelt gratefully welcomed the outpouring of adulation his actions had caused. In a presidency of successes, this might have been the greatest of them all, and Roosevelt was never one to ignore the cheering of the great crowds. Though not in his planning, the conclusion of the coal strike played directly into his hands in another way. November 4 was midterm election day, the general expectation being the resurgence of the Democrats in both houses of Congress. While they did, in fact, make gains, the Republicans were enormously relieved to maintain a majority in both. In the press and in government offices around Washington, there was no doubt that Republican successes had come solely because of Roosevelt's settlement of the strike. More important to Roosevelt was another election two years away.

WORK ON THE newly refurbished White House had nearly been completed, but the place was not comfortable enough to suit its tenants, with carpenters and painters still working around the clock. As well, Edith was deeply into the selection of furnishings, from draperies and tablecloths to cushions and upholstery. Roosevelt had witnessed her passion, the strictness with which she handled the workers, the attention she poured into every detail of the decor. For Roosevelt, the ongoing labor was a fine excuse to leave, to accept a surprising invitation from Andrew Longino, the governor of Mississippi. Roosevelt accepted the opportunity to embark on a hunting trip in the Delta region of that state hosted by plantation owner Huger Foote. The hunt was to be as discreet as possible, and Roosevelt had wondered if his hosts weren't even more concerned than he was about his presence in a state where he was mostly despised. If his hosts didn't mind his visit, no matter how racially charged his presidency had become, Roosevelt would take advantage of the chance to make one more hunt. The target this time was bear.

HE HAD MADE every effort to keep the location of this adventure secret, but with reporters always lurking about, it was a near impossibility. Still, rural Mississippi's Delta country close to the Little Sunflower River was remote enough that few were likely to follow him to the hunting camp, especially with a phalanx of security officers provided by his hosts. But Roosevelt was never one to shy away from the opportunity to tell a tale, and despite the concerns of his own staff, particularly George Cortelyou, three reporters were allowed access, one per day. At least if the hunt was memorable, someone would be there to write about it.

The train consisted of the engine and a single private car, a comfortable, if not obvious, way for him to travel. He sat across the aisle from Cortelyou, who never seemed to look up from his pads of paper. Roosevelt rocked with the train, stared dreamily out across vast cotton fields dotted with round cypress ponds. Between the fields were more cypress, great mossy swamps, reminding him of the train ride once before, the journey with his Rough Riders from San Antonio to Florida.

"It's beautiful and ugly at the same time."

Cortelyou looked up from his papers, glanced past him out the window.

"Yes, sir. Plenty of both. That might apply to the people as well."

Roosevelt rubbed his chin.

"I've thought of that. The governor, the fellows who invited me, could be asking for trouble from their neighbors. There are still newspapers all over the South that feel the need to call me obscene names. They just don't want to let go, to admit or understand that their old ways do not apply anymore. The Negro is unchained permanently, and assuredly he is making his way into the modern world. Those fellows, right out there in those houses, they want to stop that, pretend they can enslave the Black man, stop his progress, just because it used to be."

"I've been nervous about this trip, sir. Somebody you just described might react to you being here with violence, either against you or . . . well, who knows?"

Roosevelt looked at him. "Lynchings?"

Cortelyou nodded. "It's a real possibility. I've heard that some people down here would kill a Negro just for sport. It rather turns my stomach."

Roosevelt looked out the window again, the train slowing.

"I know. I'm not sure what I can do about that, if anything. You can't send the National Guard out to every small town to protect people. You have to change attitudes, the entire culture, not just the behavior of a few Lily-Whites. I'd love to have a conversation with Abe Lincoln about this."

"At least, sir, you have Booker T. Washington."

The train continued to slow, then stopped, his security guards jumping onto the platform, nervous men spreading out in a loose arc, holding back the hosts Roosevelt had not yet met.

November 14, 1902
Near Smedes, Mississippi

They called him Colonel, a meager attempt to maintain secrecy. But Roosevelt had tossed much of that away by inviting the newspapermen. Still, he rather enjoyed the title they insisted on giving him.

It was early in the day, but already the sweat was in every part of his clothes, running from his forehead into his eyes. He wiped with a sleeve, stared impatiently at the hounds milling about, seeking out a scent. It's been five days, he thought. They keep telling me there are bears about, but you couldn't prove it by me. I can't believe they'd purposely hide the creatures from me. Maybe the bears have heard of me, my fearsome reputation, and they've all left the county.

He tried to find the humor, but there was nothing funny about the misery of the swampland: mosquitoes and water moccasins, and an apparent lack of bears.

The misty silence was broken by the howl of a dog, then another, the energy increasing, the dogs moving off quickly into the thickets. He shared their excitement, the other men going to work, bringing up his horse, Roosevelt mounting up. His host, Foote, led the way as they pushed through the brush, a desperate attempt to keep up with the dogs. But the thickets were impenetrable, the horses holding back, the dogs making distance.

Behind Roosevelt, a sharp voice: "Go right, Colonel. There's a bay, a clearing. I'll try to turn the critter and get 'em to run past you."

The man waited for the others, then led the way, Roosevelt and the others following. After a hard ride, they reached the open bay, framed by cypress and tall pines, tufts of thick grass, a small blackwater pond.

Beside him, Foote said, "We'll hold up right here, Colonel. My man Collier's the best there is at handling dogs. He's dropped more bear than anyone in the state. If that bear can be turned, he'll do it."

Roosevelt tried to ignore the relentless sweat, the steady drone of mosquitoes.

"I appreciate your men holding off on taking a bear. It was my only requirement that I take the first one. Had I known five days would pass, I'd have loosened up my rules."

"You're the president, sir. You make all the rules you want."

Roosevelt burned with the question, Just how do you feel, how do the others feel about Collier, a Negro? He kept it to himself.

Time passed, the sun higher over the trees, Foote leading him to a shady cluster of blackjack oaks. They kept in the saddle, Foote cautioning him that a bear might appear at any time. After so much misfortune, Roosevelt knew he didn't want to get caught wandering aimlessly through the thick grass. After what seemed like hours, Foote said, "Colonel, we might as well head to camp. My man Holt Collier's as good as any man in this state at tracking a bear. I'd put that Negro up against any white man in every part of these woods. Count on that. If Holt hasn't pushed that bear this way, the critter vanished. It happens."

Roosevelt was resigned to another failure, pulled the reins, turning the horse. Once more, Foote led the way, the woods closing in on a tight, narrow trail. Foote pushed the horse harder than usual, and they covered the ground to the camp in a short time. The others were gathered around a coffeepot, a pair of Black men working over a campfire, preparing lunch. Roosevelt eyed his tent, thought, Not much to do now but take a nap. Too hot for these woods. Maybe lunch . . .

Another Black man galloped in, called out, "Y'all come on. The horns are blowin'. Collier's got a bear out yonder, the water bay, out where you were. He says to bring the Colonel."

Roosevelt was back in the saddle, followed the man quickly, Foote just behind. He ducked low, the horse passing beneath vines and low limbs. Roosevelt felt the excitement growing yet again, another chance. They reached the bay, and he saw Collier standing near a half-grown, unconscious bear, the animal's neck bound with a rope tied to a nearby tree.

Collier called out to Foote, "Sir, he got one of the dogs, Little Sue. I couldn't stop that. I busted the bear's head, but he's not full dead. Here you go, Colonel. All yours."

Roosevelt dismounted the horse, stared at the bear, nothing like what he had hoped for. He reached for his rifle, stopped. He felt vaguely sick, a new experience, turned away.

"I'll not shoot it. There's no sport here. Somebody put it out of its misery."

THE PRESENCE OF the newspapermen had seemed to be a waste of time, both for them and for Roosevelt and his weeklong lack of adventure. But while he was still in the Mississippi swamps, the story reached the newspapers that the president had refused to slaughter a wounded, helpless animal just for the sake of the kill.

It was *The Washington Post* that turned the story into a cartoon, Roosevelt the sportsman refusing to shoot a helpless bear. With each successive cartoon, the bear became far less fierce, and far more cuddly. The seed had been planted. Within weeks, a Brooklyn candy store owner, Morris Michtom, saw an opportunity and began to manufacture stuffed, fur-covered bears. Once Roosevelt had returned to Washington, the enterprising Michtom contacted the president for permission to use his name, which Roosevelt granted. The toys became an instant success through the Christmas season and beyond. They were called, of course, Teddy's bears.

CHAPTER 44

January 11, 1903
The White House

"Oww! All right, take that!" Wood held up the stick, swung the lower half toward Roosevelt, striking him in the leg. "That's what happens when you don't follow the rules."

Roosevelt was breathing heavily, held his own stick out, a menacing pose. "What rules?"

Both men laughed now, and Wood said, "You know, if you'd have fought the Spanish the same way you play singlesticks, the war would have been shorter still."

Roosevelt bent low, still laughing. "Thank you, General. I'm dee-lighted by your compliment. Shall we have another go? I promise, I will make every effort to withdraw and reset each time I whack you."

"No, that's it for me. The problem, Mr. President, is that you're too excited by this game. You strike a good blow and you can't wait to do it again. That's why there are rules. I don't relish being beaten to a pulp."

Both men unhooked their padding, the chest protectors and padded helmets, Roosevelt tossing his to one side.

Wood stretched, felt his arm. "There's one bruise for sure. You must know that I'm intimidated by the presence of your Secret Service guards, right downstairs. Should I pound you a bit more, I'm liable to find myself in handcuffs."

Roosevelt rubbed bruises of his own. "I've challenged those fellows to a match as well. They turn me down. Goes against their instincts to beat up the president. I have to settle for you."

Wood sat now, out of breath. "Let's not forget, there was one time I punished you so much your arm was too sore to shake hands."

Roosevelt laughed again, then feigned seriousness. "I fear you exaggerate, General. I was merely giving my right hand a rest so the left wouldn't feel neglected."

Wood looked around now, said, "Edith did a remarkable job, you know. It's all I hear these days, from congressmen to reporters. The White House is a true showplace, a palace and a home at the same time."

Roosevelt sat as well. "It's not a palace. I'm no king. It's something the American people can be proud of. I assure you, I'm proud of the woman who approved the choices. And the architect, of course. They scraped away over eighty years of crust from these walls and floors. There were places where you had to step past a hole in the floor or you'd break an ankle. Have you seen the new portraits? She insisted, and I dared not disagree, that some of the First Ladies should adorn these walls, not just their husbands. I have to admit, I'd never before seen the portrait of Dolley Madison. Entirely appropriate."

"The place just seems . . . larger somehow."

"Credit the architect. Remove the clutter, brighten the place up. My office is wonderful now, large enough to entertain, well, whoever requires entertaining. Upstairs here, we've now got seven bedrooms, enough for the children, or if they're not present, we can house guests. I feel as though this place is much more to what President Washington had in mind."

Wood crossed his arms, looked at Roosevelt with the barely hidden smile. "You know, I always suspected you would turn the tables, and someday become my commanding officer. I just didn't think it would happen so quickly."

He had been surprised by the request for a visit from Anselm McLaurin, one of the senators from Mississippi. The subject was surprising as well: the postmaster of the small town of Indianola, Mississippi. Her name was Minnie Cox, and she was Black.

"I should tell you, Mr. President, that I am not a party to any kind of intimidation or some such. However, such things do occur."

Roosevelt could feel the oil oozing from the man's slow drawl, said, "I have asked the postmaster general about her. She ran her post office in an extremely efficient manner, was well regarded in her community, and there were no official complaints. She was generally admired. I do not see why anyone would have a problem with her, Senator."

"To use a colloquialism, Mr. President, a number of local citizens there felt she was becoming . . . *uppity*. As a result, some of the local people felt they should persuade her to resign her office. Mrs. Cox is an intelligent Negro, and I believe she did the right thing by paying heed to the threat. To put it bluntly, sir, it was suggested that if she did not leave Indianola permanently, her neck would be broken. I believe she has left."

Roosevelt looked down at the paper on his desk, Minnie Cox's notice of resignation. He tried to absorb the senator's tone, wondered just where he stood.

"Thank you for enlightening me, Senator. Please be advised that I am not accepting Mrs. Cox's resignation, and I will see that she continues to receive her full salary. This woman is being threatened by a brutal and lawless element purely on the grounds of her color. I will no longer tolerate this kind of outrage."

McLaurin seemed prepared for such a statement.

"I'm sorry to say that I cannot control the impulses of my constituents. I merely came here to report to you what I know to have happened. You can of course appoint a successor to her office in Indianola. They require a new postmaster."

Roosevelt looked past the senator, saw his secretary in his own office.

"Mr. Cortelyou. Might you bring me a map of Mississippi?"

He waited patiently, knew that Cortelyou had most likely heard their conversation, might have anticipated just what Roosevelt needed. He had no real idea just where Indianola was. A long minute passed, McLaurin trying to appear at peace in the president's office. Cortelyou appeared now, a roll of paper, a brief nod to the senator.

Roosevelt said, "Place it right here, George. Is it detailed?"

"Quite, sir."

Roosevelt studied a moment, nodded, offered the senator a smile.

"I realize you cannot control these kinds of events. Neither can I. However, I can react to them." He folded his hands over the map, a hard stare at the senator. "It seems that I just cannot find a suitable replacement for Mrs. Cox. Thus, I am ordering the closure of the Indianola post office. The good citizens of Indianola will now have their mail delivered to Greenville. That should be no inconvenience for such enlightened people. Greenville is but thirty miles away."

February 11, 1903

"I regret, sir, that you are being castigated vigorously by a good many southern newspapers. I'm not sure what this will do for your chances come election time."

It was the first time Cortelyou had mentioned a possible Roosevelt candidacy, a poorly guarded secret.

Roosevelt moved papers on his desk, held up a single sheet.

"Not everyone hates me. Here, a Reverend McGill in Tennessee. He writes in some publication there, 'the administration of President Roosevelt is to the Negro what the heart is to the body. It has pumped life blood into every artery of the Negro in this country.' I have to believe there are a great many people who share that view."

"The Reverend McGill is Black, I believe."

Roosevelt looked again at the paper.

"I thought that might be the case. Still, I accept this as a valuable sentiment. The Lily-Whites across the South will have to accept that we are in a new century. I will not tolerate blatant racism from anyone over whom I have any authority. If that costs me every white southern vote, so be it. I have faith that the majority of the electorate has sufficient decency to accept the modern standards of behavior."

"You have a greater faith in the Lily-Whites than I do, sir. I hear some of the things Senator Tillman says about you . . . it defies good manners, not to mention respect for the position he holds."

Roosevelt sat back in his chair, tried to relax.

"Senator Tillman is a cross we have to bear. I'm quite sure he is beloved in South Carolina, and for *him,* that's all that counts. I believe he's the perfect definition of an obstructionist. He obstructs me at every opportunity. It's just part of the job, George. After all, there are a couple hundred congressman up on Capitol Hill who despise me, though maybe not as much as Senator Tillman. Their job is to do anything in their power to derail every piece of legislation I send them, no matter how intelligent and useful those bills might be. By the way, the bill now in consideration to create a new Department of Commerce and Labor . . . I need an answer from you. You're my choice to run the thing."

Cortelyou seemed to blush, looked down.

"I am honored. You had mentioned that before, but I just wasn't sure you were serious. You are somewhat . . . excitable."

"I am definitely serious. You're the man for that job, and that's all there is to it. Once Congress passes the Commerce and Labor Act, it will become official. They still have to confirm you of course. That shouldn't be a problem. Even Senator Hanna likes you."

"Will you name Mr. Loeb to fill my place?"

"Of course. He's earned it."

"I agree. Thank you. Now, forgive me, sir, but we have quite the agenda today, and so far Congress has only passed a portion of the bills you're championing. You appear to be winning your fight to add the four battleships to our naval forces. There is little sentiment against your efforts to enlarge the armed forces, particularly the navy. But someone will yet make a fight about it."

"Of course they will. Go on."

"Your Commerce and Labor Act bill is not a sure bet. There is fear that the bill gives you the power to judge whether monopolies are monopolies. There is fear that your power over government oversight of corporate financial dealings means those documents could be laid open for public scrutiny, at your whim. In addition, there are four antitrust bills that are being held up by the usual blockaders—Senator Hanna, of course. And just this morning, the *Post* reports that John D. Rockefeller has come out against the primary trust bill. He does garner the headlines, sir. It appears that the brick walls are being built to stop many of your programs."

Roosevelt let out a breath.

"Mr. Rockefeller has just done us a favor. He is the face of corporate greed and monopolizing in this country. That's exactly how we will strike back, protecting the American worker, the individual against the vast corporate empires like Standard Oil. The congressmen who side with the corporations will look ridiculous. I can grab a few headlines of my own. And if the Congress doesn't choose to follow along, I have weapons for that too. They're set to adjourn in a week, but I have the power to call them back into special session. I will do so, making clear that no one goes home to the warm bosom of their constituency until they exercise some common sense and pass my legislation."

His voice was carrying into the hallway, and he saw the faces of his staff, some daring to peer into his office. He saw Loeb now, the man seeming to sense an opening to come in. But Roosevelt saw emotion on the man's face, said, "Tell me what's happening, Mr. Loeb."

"Excuse me, sir. One of our messengers just returned from Capitol Hill. There is another filibuster ongoing in the Senate—against one of your race-reform bills. Senator Tillman went into quite a rant, sir. He claimed that support for any racial-reform legislation will be completely eliminated from consideration by any committee, or he will die trying. He reminded the Senate that . . ." Loeb hesitated. "He says that you should be aware that, in his words, 'we still have guns and ropes in the South.'"

"Easy, Mr. Loeb. Ben Tillman has a knack for hyperbole. Someone should remind him that the Civil War ended forty years ago and his side lost. If President Lincoln had lived, these very bills would have been sent to Congress long before now. And Lincoln would have seen them passed. Well, now it's my turn."

AFTER ENDURING THE special session, and pushed hard by Roosevelt, Congress finally adjourned after giving Roosevelt most of what he wanted. For the men on Capitol Hill, many accustomed to exercising a unique kind of power over the workings of government, Roosevelt had proved that he had no tolerance for being bullied, that he was just as capable of pushing back as he was able to slough off even the most grotesque insults. The motto he began to employ was one he had adopted from folklore, which could be applied to nearly all of his political wranglings, as well as his approach to foreign policy: Speak Softly and Carry a Big Stick.

CHAPTER 45

April 7, 1903
Mandan, North Dakota

His journey began the week before, a seven-car train that housed the kind of presidential luxury he had never before imagined. He was not alone, of course, the train designed to house a fleet of reporters, as well as several members of his staff and a handpicked squad of Secret Service agents.

The journey was hardly a vacation, even if he tried to describe it that way. The itinerary had been laid out carefully, whistle-stops in small towns, carefully arranged speaking events in the cities. As much as he would miss his family, there were those he would not miss at all, the nine-week trip taking him far from the tedious wrestling matches with Congress. Now, with Congress in adjournment, he sought an adjournment of his own. The speeches were a different kind of work, but he sought out and was gratified to receive the energy of the people, the unheard and unknown citizens of dozens, if not hundreds, of towns, people with no one to hear them except him. If so many speaking events tired him out, he never let it show. The audiences along the way renewed both his energy and his spirit. As the train worked its way west, the towns became dustier, the people more raucous, but everywhere were the smiles and cheers, generous offerings of gifts, songs sung by small children, bouquets of flowers tossed his way. It would dismay many in Washington to see the affection shown him, especially those who believed Roosevelt should be cast aside in the election of 1904.

His speeches were broad and simple, positive messages of all the good he had tried to accomplish, all the work still to come, so much of that sure to benefit the people who came to hear him. At every opportunity, he trumpeted his new and beloved war cry, *speak softly and carry a big stick*. In every town, the newspapers took up that cry, eminently printable, a headline people tore loose to hang on their walls. He never offered an explanation just what the adage truly meant, but he didn't have to. The interpretation would be made by each one who heard it, whether he was talking about breaking the big corporate monopolies and trusts, punishing his most virulent opponents, or bringing rogue nations into line. No matter. The applause and cheers were just as loud.

On April 7, his train arrived in Bismarck, North Dakota, a city straddling the Missouri River. West of the river lay a small town, likely one day to be engulfed by the larger. It was Mandan, and there waited two familiar faces from his days in the Badlands. They were older now, but no less enthusiastic to see him: the Ferris brothers, Sylvane and Joe.

HE ESCORTED THEM up off the dust of the rail siding, climbing to the small porch at the rear of his car.

"Get ready, boys. This is what those people in Washington insist on doing for me."

The door was opened by one of his guards, a lean and surly man who took nothing for granted. He stared at Roosevelt, as if to detect some signal that there might be a problem. Roosevelt knew the routine.

"It's all right, Clete. These are old friends. I'd trust them as much as I trust you."

The guard withdrew, made his way out the far end of the car. Roosevelt turned to the two men, held his arms out wide.

"Well? What do you think?"

Joe pointed ahead. "Bedrooms?"

"Bedrooms, a kitchen, dining room, and two bathrooms, in case I get bored with just one. Come, let's go into the stateroom. Huge windows. You can see the whole world pass by."

They followed him, and he suddenly felt a strange sadness, tried to push it away. He sat now, a plush velvet chair, pointed for them to do the same. They sat slowly, self-consciously, and he studied them, so familiar but not. They seemed much older, more worn out, and he glanced at the window, saw his own reflection, thought, Me too, I suppose.

"So, how are you both? How is Medora?"

Sylvane said, "A good bit different. It's grown. It's strange now that the marquis died. His mansion is pretty much a wreck. There's cattle to run, but it's all fenced off now."

Joe said, "It would probably seem a good bit calmer than what you recall. Not too many fellows going off on the shoot anymore. A lot of new people moved in, women and children, and a lot of the old folks are gone."

Roosevelt had no response, and Sylvane said, "We brought your old pony, Manitou. Thought you might like to take a ride with us. The Badlands ain't changed. That's about the only thing."

His depression was growing, and Roosevelt said, "I'm sorry, boys. I can't do that. The security people won't allow it. Sorry."

He could feel the awkwardness, the two men with very little to add. He felt enormous affection for both, but could see he had almost nothing in common with them, began to wonder now if his love for this land and its people had been some kind of illusion.

"Well, tomorrow morning, the train heads over to Yellowstone. It's been years since I was there. I have a new power now: to protect those places like that that need protecting, so that the big ranchers can't just go in and take what they want. No barbed wire there, not if I have my say."

Joe nodded in agreement. "That's good, I suppose. It might have been good if you could have done something here, before the fences went up. Irrigation ditches too, everywhere. Things are green that used to be gray. It's said that, before long, the Badlands won't even exist."

Sylvane said, "That ain't true. Nobody can make much of a go of farming in this place. Medora won't never be Bismarck."

Roosevelt heard voices behind him, knew the reporters were getting restless, would seek out their daily dose of what was on his mind.

"Well, boys, I'm dee-lighted to see you, both of you. I wish I had more time, but, well, they insist on calling me the president of the United States. That's something, isn't it? No one out here had any idea something like this would happen."

Joe said, "Not true at all, sir."

Roosevelt stood now, the clear signal. The two men followed, and he led them through the car to the porch in the rear. He gave them both a strong handshake, felt a sudden wave of emotion, saw the same in them, gripped each man by the shoulder, no words. They climbed down, and he stood in the doorway, saw a small crowd gathering, some pointing along the train, more enamored of that than they were its inhabitant. At the bottom of the steps Sylvane turned, looked up at him, no smile, said, "It's good to see how well you've done, sir. It wouldn't have done for you to keep your place out here. It would have sucked you dry, and I can't think of anything that'd be worse for you. You outgrew us. That's it. You outgrew us."

Roosevelt didn't respond, made a lame attempt at a wave, the two men moving away, across the tracks. He backed into the car, closed the door, saw faces at the other end, Loeb and others from his staff, held up his hand, *not now*. He kept his stare out the rear window, the track leading the way west, a water tower, the wooden platform, the crowd of people growing, swallowing his friends. He thought of barbed wire, the land turning green. Maybe Sylvane is right. This place isn't for me, not anymore. It's the past. I did love it, though. Or maybe that was illusion. I love the memories, even if some of those things never really happened.

He heard cheering now, a group of men uniting their voices, calling out to him. He took a deep breath, opened the door, stepped out with a beaming, toothy smile.

"Dee-lighted . . ."

April 8, 1903
Yellowstone National Park

He shook the old man's hand yet again, couldn't keep from staring at him, the balding head, lines in the man's face, piercing eyes.

375

"Mr. Burroughs, it is my honor, sir. I am dee-lighted to meet you. Are we ready for an adventure?"

Burroughs laughed, smiling through the snow-white beard, said, "I'm hoping to show you something you haven't seen before, so that you'll appreciate it as much as I do. I need you to understand that. I'm just an old voice calling out from the wilderness. You, sir, have power."

Roosevelt felt suddenly intimidated, an unexpected response, looked past the man, trying to gather his thoughts. The entrance to the park was still bathed in snow that coated the tall timber, great drifts beyond. He looked at the second man, the park's superintendent, John Pitcher. After another handshake, Pitcher said, "Mr. President, as you know, the park is not yet open to the public for the season. There is a good bit of snow you'll have to traverse. We are somewhat hesitant about you doing this, but Mr. Burroughs has assured me that he will watch over you."

Roosevelt had no doubt that John Burroughs would do exactly that. He turned to his entourage gathered beside the train, announced out loud, "You boys from the newspapers will just have to wait, I'm afraid. Not even my staff will accompany me. I expect to be gone for two weeks, and I assure you when I return, there will be no animal carcass with me, no sets of antlers. This journey is only to absorb and enjoy what Mother Nature and Mr. Burroughs can show me. There is no more valuable resource in our nation than these wilderness places. But if I'm going to champion their preservation, then I must know what I'm talking about."

To one side, a squad of cavalry stood in formation, and he turned to them, inspiring a salute from their captain. He returned it.

"Normally, I wouldn't be needing you boys, but my staff and the park superintendent here insist. At least I am allowed to leave my Secret Service boys behind. I'd like to believe I'm comfortably at home in the wilderness. If I should fall into some hole, I suppose you boys can retrieve me."

There was a ripple of laughter, mixed with a hum of concern. He knew he was overdoing it, looked again at the superintendent. "I assure you, sir. There will be no hunting, and no foolishness. I'm here for

376

rejuvenation and to gain even more respect for this place than I have had before."

Pitcher made a short bow, said, "We shall enjoy a spectacular time, sir. I hope to prove a capable guide."

Roosevelt moved toward the horse, a welcome loan from the park, climbed up, watched as the aged Burroughs was helped into a supply wagon. Roosevelt watched him, felt suddenly anxious for the man, thought, All of this is for me. But I must see to it that he is cared for. He's a treasure. Don't abuse that.

HE FELT LIKE a child, pulled himself up the great tree, hand over hand, his feet anchoring solidly on the thick branches. He continued upward, the thicker branches finally thinning out, the tree opening up to a view he had hoped to see.

"By Godfrey, I can see mountains for a hundred miles!"

Burroughs sat still in the wagon, laughing quietly, said, "You get to the top of that next mountain, and you can see farther than that."

Roosevelt jerked his head to both sides, tried to absorb the entire scene, called out again. "I can see the hot springs, the steam. We have to go there!"

Pitcher sat on his horse beside Burroughs, called back, "We will, sir. Next stop. We'll camp near the larger spring."

Roosevelt climbed down with more strength than he had going up. He jumped the last six feet to the ground, couldn't control his energy, hard breathing in the cold air.

"This is bully, sir. I knew this was a beautiful place, but with so much snow, it is truly spectacular."

Burroughs was smiling at him, as though carrying some secret. Roosevelt went to the horse, mounted up, Pitcher and the cavalrymen riding forward to lead the way. One of the soldiers drove the cart, Burroughs beside him, and Roosevelt stayed alongside. They made their way through tall timber, then into the open, a trail disguised by the snow. He rode quietly, awed by everything he saw: a wolf darting away up on a wide hill, a small herd of bighorn sheep pawing their way through the snow. He absorbed it all, had fleeting fantasies of shooting something, but pushed that away. There was a time for that, and it was not now. He knew Burroughs would have none of it, the man renowned for his strict conservationist views. But Roosevelt knew how respected Burroughs was, the man who had stood up against ranching and mining interests for years, crying long and loud about the value of wilderness.

He looked toward Burroughs, who seemed to droop, showing signs of some sort of sickness.

"Are you all right, sir?"

Burroughs looked at him, an encouraging wave of his hand. "I fear I'm catching a cold. I don't often come out here when it still feels like winter. But never mind. I might stay behind for a day or two, to recover. Tell me, Mr. President, what do you really think about our little park here?"

"I have been here before, sir. About fifteen years ago, around the time we organized the Boone and Crockett Club. I know the value here, and before too much longer I intend to push hard against the Congress to authorize me to designate any of these kinds of lands for federal protection. Any thick-headed senator who objects, I'll just bring him out here, show him a herd of bison or a flock of geese, the elk we passed a ways back. I'll show him the beauty of the hot springs and then let him explain to me how he intends to run a railroad through this place. No sir. This place must survive, for my children and theirs. Any movement to preserve these lands is a democratic one, of benefit to rich man or poor. Every citizen should visit here, and I will do all in my power to see it so."

AFTER ROOSEVELT'S TWO-WEEK odyssey in Yellowstone, the rail journey continued, winding through the West and Midwest with a blur of speaking engagements to more adoring crowds. But Yellowstone was not the only natural treasure he would visit. The train made a stop near Yosemite, where Roosevelt toured with naturalist John Muir. Soon, he visited the great redwoods in Northern California and, for the first time, Grand Canyon, where he offered the same message he would im-part to anyone who doubted the value of such places or his particular dedication to their preservation: *Leave it as it is. The ages have been at work on it, and man can only mar it.*

CHAPTER 46

Washington, D.C.

Throughout his summer idyll at Sagamore Hill and into the fall months of 1903, Roosevelt's duties continued to be all-consuming and, in some cases, thoroughly annoying. The Panama Canal issue had still not been settled, rugged negotiations ongoing with the government of Colombia, Panama merely an offshoot of that South American country. But the break finally came with assurances by the Panamanians themselves that secession from Colombia, separating them from the corruption of the Colombian government, would pave the way for a final treaty. At long last, the construction on the canal could begin unencumbered by the morass of politics.

It was a standing joke among Roosevelt and his family that each morning Edith would insert into his pocket a twenty-dollar bill to get him through the day. By evening, the bill was usually gone, Roosevelt insisting to her that he truly had no idea where it went. That befuddlement carried into his understanding of fiscal policy, the workings of his Treasury Department as well as Wall Street, the special child of men like J. P. Morgan. But the specter of currency reform had loomed large, necessary steps to calm a summers-long panic on Wall Street that threatened to spread across the nation. Relying on those who understood such things far better than he did, Roosevelt enacted reforms that, for the time being, satisfied the large banks and their customers.

His foreign policy efforts had frustrated him as much as anything he had taken on as president. Russia was becoming especially troubling, reaching dangerous tentacles into Manchuria, threatening to do the same in Korea, with Japan reacting to Russian aggressiveness with a growling militarism of its own.

In a more positive vein, negotiators in England, including his friend, Senator Henry Cabot Lodge, had hammered out an agreement with the British, finally mapping with precise lines where the actual border lay between Alaska and northwestern Canada.

To add to Roosevelt's aggravation, a scandal had erupted within the Post Office Department, charges of corruption and bribery that, if ignored, might threaten his presidency. As newspaper stories trumpeted the crimes, Roosevelt dispatched his postmaster general to dig deep, ferreting out the culprits and restoring the public's trust in their post office.

To his surprise, the well-entrenched leaders of the major labor unions had become restless, attacking him for his stand on the right to work of all government offices. He hadn't understood until now just how deeply the union bosses were invested in protecting their own power, just as the corporate heads were protecting theirs. But he held his ground in the face of withering criticism from various newspapers, and still he championed the common man's right to work where he chose, without kowtowing to any union. He knew it was a quixotic attempt at changing the culture of the labor market, but he could control one piece of it and continued to support every man's right to a job in Washington. By the end of the year, the voices of big labor seemed to calm down, as did angry voices on Wall Street. Those who despised him in the Senate, of course, had no intention of calming anything.

As the year came to a close, Senator Mark Hanna seemed to marshal his forces, both in his home state of Ohio and across the country, laying groundwork for his own run for the presidency. He was backed by a number of newspapers, a formidable group of congressmen, along with nearly everyone on Wall Street. In the off-year election in both New York and Ohio, Roosevelt's loyalists were given a serious drubbing, and even the mayor of New York, Roosevelt acolyte Seth Low, went down to defeat. Roosevelt had assumed that the wild success of his foray through the western states was a clear sign that his nomination and subsequent election to his own term in 1904 was all but assured. Now, with the grumblings from both Wall Street and his own party, he began to fear that a Mark Hanna candidacy was assured as well.

February 1904

He ignored the cold, swatted the ball with his awkward motion, watched as Lodge stiffly returned the ball with a grunt. Roosevelt swatted again, missed completely, the ball bouncing away behind him. Lodge stood with his hands on his hips, a stare of smug satisfaction.

"That's it, old boy. This day belongs to me."

Roosevelt wasn't satisfied at all, said, "Edith didn't have this tennis court built just so I can lose to a doddering old fool. One more match."

Lodge shook his head.

"No need for insults, Mr. President. I might be your senior, but I won because I'm in youthful trim. You've gained quite a bulge around your middle."

Roosevelt put a hand on the roundness of his stomach.

"I rather enjoy food. Edith says it's my great downfall. That doesn't stop me from eating. One problem with being president, though. They give you whatever you want, in whatever quantity you wish. I rather enjoy that, actually, no matter the poking from my wife."

Lodge came around the net, said, "Might we go inside? My joints are stiffening up."

Roosevelt playfully tested his knees, felt a sudden bolt of pain from his damaged shin, a meager attempt at hiding it. Lodge stared at him, said, "I saw that. It bothers you still."

Roosevelt had no reason to hide anything from his friend.

"Not always. But it's there. They say it will need no more attention, no surgeries. But the pain comes back often, reminds me that I'm not as young as I want to be."

HE HAD CHANGED clothes, ignored his need to bathe, Edith reminding him that the president should not impact his visitors with his body odor. But the day promised to be busier more with paperwork than high-hatted visitors. Regardless, the tennis match with Lodge was a luxury he cherished.

He rifled through the stack of papers on his desk, placed there neatly by his new secretary, William Loeb. There was an assortment of bills, passed by a strangely complacent Congress, though nothing among them was especially controversial.

Loeb was there now, pretended to ignore Roosevelt's casual dress. Roosevelt shoved the stack aside, said, "Who's coming in today? Anyone besides Cortelyou?"

"Sir, George should be here in a few minutes. But then you have an appointment to receive the assistant foreign minister of France. That's in one hour. Then one of your Rough Riders after that."

Roosevelt sighed.

"George won't care, but the Frenchman will expect me to be dressed properly. I should change clothes. Is this an important meeting, or is the Frenchman just paying his respects? I'd rather spend time with the soldier, no matter who he is."

"Monsieur Roissy is here to talk about Russia. As you know, sir, they're allies. I believe he's coming here to remind you of that."

"So, he wants to complain. That's usually the case when people are pushing hard for their own interests. But, fine. I'll make the best of it."

Roosevelt knew that Loeb was well aware that he actually enjoyed sparring with foreign dignitaries, even if their presence was merely an informal visit.

"What else? Lunch?"

"Lunch with your wife. I assume that's acceptable."

Roosevelt laughed. "It had better be. Good, that will be a nice change from the parade of well-wishers and all those people with their hands out."

He heard a commotion in the corridor outside, Loeb turning as well, a small creature scurrying past the open doorway. Loeb made a small sound, and Roosevelt waited for more, saw his son Archie running past in pursuit.

With a hint of alarm, Loeb said, "Which one was that, sir?"

"That was Archie, my second youngest."

"No, sir, the animal."

"Oh. That was Josiah, the badger. I call him Josh. You recall, he's the gift I received on my trip through Kansas. He was but a pup then, but he's grown into full-blown badgerhood. He can be a bit ornery too. Likes to nibble on legs. Well, you know."

Loeb seemed to flex, a slight shudder. "He did inflict a good-sized wound on my calf, sir. We should keep him away from the more important visitors, especially the women. It wouldn't do to have him dig his way under someone's gown."

He saw Archie again, the badger safely clamped between the boy's hands. The boy stopped at the door, said, "Sorry, Papa. He got away again. I'll put him back in his cage."

"You do that, Arch. Where is Pete?"

"I saw him upstairs, with Quentin."

Roosevelt looked at Loeb now.

"Now, there's a biter. For a bull terrier, that dog has no manners at all. I fear one day he might nibble on the wrong leg and start a war. But I would say, of all the critters roaming around this place, Pete's my favorite."

"Yes, sir. I know that, sir. I must say, there is a good amount of wildlife hereabouts. Can't say I've ever heard of that before, not in the White House."

"The *wildlife* are in cages out there. Wouldn't do to have a lion mingling with the zebra, wandering across my tennis court. The rabbits wouldn't fare well either. But the little ones are pretty much free to do as they please, and there haven't been any death-defying incidents yet. Have you seen the one-legged rooster? Who ever thought a rooster would have a personality? Hops around like he owns the place."

"Yes, sir, I know. I've heard him."

"The children know to keep their beasts mostly to themselves. But Alice . . ." He shook his head. "She carries that damn snake around, lets it crawl all over her, wherever it pleases. I know she likes the attention, but it's probably not the best way to appeal to a potential suitor. I wish I could persuade her not to smoke cigarettes. She seems to enjoy the company of cigar smokers and brandy drinkers more than she does the young men of her own station. Very strange. And somewhat embarrassing."

"Is there no way you might control her a bit, sir? There could be some embarrassments beyond this office."

"Bill, I can spend my time overseeing her activities, or I can be president of the United States. Do you have a preference?"

Loeb smiled.

"I understand your point, sir."

He heard a knock behind Loeb, was surprised to see Cortelyou.

"Mr. President, excuse me. A messenger outside handed this note to me, since I was on my way here. It seems that Senator Hanna has been stricken ill. They say it is typhoid fever. And it is quite serious."

Roosevelt sat back, stared at Cortelyou.

"Good Lord. I must go there at once. The Arlington Hotel, yes?"

Cortelyou said, "Yes, sir. But the message says he is not allowed any visitors. Perhaps in the morning."

"This is enormous. I'm sorry, but both of you should leave, for now. I have to think about this, decide what to do, what's appropriate. As much as I've had to lock horns with that man, and as much as he has fought against me so often, we need him. Washington needs him, maybe the whole country. I have feared him, and perhaps I fear him now. He simply cannot fall ill, not now. We have too many battles yet to fight."

ROOSEVELT WAS NOT able to see Hanna, the doctors insisting the senator be kept isolated. For more than a week, Hanna's condition steadily deteriorated until, on February 14, Hanna's heart finally stopped.

The shock of Hanna's death seemed to paralyze Washington, the sudden loss of the man's powerful influence leaving a vacuum that not even Roosevelt could fill.

CORTELYOU SEEMED TO wait for the right moment to speak.

"Sir, I have a request."

Roosevelt looked up from his desk, said, "Who else is sick?" Roosevelt was sorry for the question. "Apologies, my friend. These are dark days. I feel as though I have lost my sparring partner. What's your news?"

"One of the labor unions in Chicago is seeking a meeting with both of us. I'm sorry now that I brought that here. It's not a major priority, certainly not now."

The words drifted past him, and Roosevelt said, "Whatever you say. I'll deal with them later. There's no strike, is there?"

"No, sir. Just basic grievances. I shouldn't have bothered you. I'll handle it."

"Yes, good."

There was a silent pause, and Cortelyou said, "Are you all right, sir?"

Roosevelt focused on him. "Some things I simply can't ignore. I came into this office because William McKinley was murdered. Now, I might be elected because my only serious competition has died. I have been seriously worried for my chances this year. I knew it would be a difficult battle, that if Hanna's strength held up, he might have the votes to toss me out of here. But still, I looked forward to it, the speeches, the travel, so many eager faces, the cheers, the applause. He and I have had some marvelous arguments."

"Sir, respectfully, the election is almost certain to go your way now. There is no one strong enough to defeat you, certainly no Democrat."

"Never depend on that. William Jennings Bryan is still lurking out there, and anything can happen with the electorate." He tried to smile. "Someone could come along with more of a silver tongue than I have."

"Sir, you have earned the right to another term, and right now the nomination is yours. The majority of our delegates will vote for *you* because of *you*, not because Senator Hanna's name is not on the ballot. I still don't believe he could have beaten you."

Roosevelt folded his hands, shook his head.

"Well, George, I don't know if that's true. But now we will never know."

CHAPTER 47

Since the first of the year, Roosevelt had known that the aging Elihu Root had an increasing desire to step down from his position as secretary of war. Root had been one of Roosevelt's closest advisors and confidants, but had seemed to drift away from Roosevelt's inner circle, though neither man found fault for that in the other. But with Root finally resigning that position, Roosevelt had an opportunity to bring in a man very unlike the overly critical Root, a man very much like Roosevelt himself. Since the Spanish-American War had ended, William Howard Taft had served as governor-general of the Philippines, a job that most Americans could ignore but that was often rife with conflict and scandal, especially with rogue American army officers abusing what remained of hostile Philippine guerillas. More recently, the Philippines had calmed considerably, in large part because of Taft's management. For Taft, it was time for a change, and as the new secretary of war, Taft could only be seen as an asset to Roosevelt's cabinet and to Roosevelt himself.

Roosevelt was known to nearly all as a man larger than life, but Taft, at three hundred twenty pounds, was quite literally the larger man. Roosevelt accepted that his own back-straining, knee-scraping jaunts through Rock Creek Park would not be for Taft.

Roosevelt enjoyed the spring in Washington, trees coming alive with their blossoms, so much of the landscape around the White House rising into lush green. Though he absorbed the energy of the change of seasons, he already felt drained by the upcoming Republican convention, hoping it might be a less controversial affair than he had experienced before. He would be, of course, the center of attention, which he never objected to. There was one thorn. Roosevelt knew never to disregard the powerful influence of men with money. The media mogul William Randolph Hearst, never Roosevelt's fan, had announced that he would launch his own campaign for president. Hearst would naturally be endorsed by the hundreds of newspapers in his control, and with a powerful message against a number of Roosevelt's policies, he might sway voters all across the country away from the president.

On the Democratic side, several names emerged as possible contenders, including the former president, Grover Cleveland, and the perennial candidate, William Jennings Bryan. So far, neither of those men was seen as a serious threat to receive the nomination, but the Democratic convention was yet months away. Anything could happen.

"WHY ARE YOU not concerned?"

Edith sipped her tea, said, "I'm enjoying my breakfast. The view here is as picturesque as any in Washington, even with the carriages and motorcars passing by. I am so pleased you have agreed to do this. We should have breakfast out here under the portico every day it isn't pouring rain."

He stared at her, saw telltale playfulness. "You really aren't concerned?"

She pretended to ignore him. "I must ask Louisa where the cook procured this sausage. It is especially good. Much better than that bacon yesterday. Too fatty." She sipped her tea again. "Now, why are you so agitated?"

"I was wondering if I should stand up and dance a Virginia reel in front of you to gain your attention. I am concerned, even if you're not. The convention is not far away, and there is all sorts of talk. As hard as this may be for you to believe, some people do not like me."

She crossed her arms, stared at him. Beyond, well out across the lawn, she glanced at her two youngest boys, playing around a sandbox, what seemed to be their favorite activity.

"Look out there, your sons. I assure you, Quentin and Archie love you. I love you. Ethel and the two older boys love you, even from afar as they pursue their studies. Even Alice, who can sulk and preen about like a homeless peacock, loves you. Every man who works for you, every cabinet secretary, your entire regiment of Rough Riders, your friends in the Dakotas, and nearly all of the people who gather in rapt attention to your speeches—they all love you. Not to mention our menagerie of pets and other creatures around this place who gallop to your side when given the chance. If, tomorrow, we were forced to leave the White House and return to Sagamore Hill, that very place feels loving to you and the rest of us too. You enjoy our lawn parties and receptions up there far more than you seem to enjoy them here. Your life there would be more than happy—it would be ideal. And there would very likely be far fewer newspapermen around to record everything we do. And in case I need to say this more than once, Teddy, *I* love you most of all. Now, what exactly are you concerned about?"

He knew he was defeated.

"You are correct on all counts, Edie. But . . . I *do* like being president. My hand is squarely in the middle of so much of what goes on in this world. That's an extraordinary feeling. My words, my utterances carry weight in countries everywhere. The Germans, the Russians, the Venezuelans, the Chinese . . . they may not agree with me, but they pay attention. Yes, Sagamore Hill is ideal, a place I treasure. But I do love it right here. And I am concerned about those who hope to toss me out. There is a chance they will succeed. Even my friends are concerned. You know that I love to talk, but I might talk too much about things that cost me an election."

Taft filled the chair, sat across from him like Roosevelt's personal bison.

Roosevelt said, "I am told that it is unseemly for a candidate for president to campaign on his own behalf. That seems utterly ridiculous to me. What better way for a man to put himself before the people than go before the people?"

Taft seemed to take him seriously, but still smiled.

"I'm familiar with that principle. I know that McKinley stayed at home while his team did his work. I'm sure that has been true throughout our history. The stump is, after all, a stump. Too undignified for a man seeking the highest office."

Roosevelt didn't agree, but couldn't argue with Taft's smiling face. He missed Root's critiques, often edging into sarcasm, but Taft's advice always seemed to build up Roosevelt's mood rather than poke holes in his behavior.

"Bill, since the people leading this campaign are doing their work without me, I'm going to rely on you a great deal. I suppose I will just keep working here until Congress goes home. Then I'll go to Sagamore Hill and spend the summer boating and hiking and wondering what people are saying about me."

Taft smiled again.

"That sounds right. Unless you make some horrendous mistake, you should have no difficulty being reelected."

"I don't like hearing that word, 'reelected.' No one has voted for me on a presidential ballot yet. This is my first time. It's no wonder I have concerns."

"Stop having them. You're in good hands."

Roosevelt shuffled papers, held up a small letter.

"Are you aware that the Republican Party has decided that the most suitable vice president for me should be Senator Charles Fairbanks, of Indiana?" He let out a breath. "All I know of him, other than minor skirmishes in the Senate, is that he never smiles, is conservative and boring."

Taft laughed.

"That is certainly better than the alternative. You don't need a vice president who outshines you. Besides, he is adored by Wall Street. Are you? And, tell me, what great challenges were placed in front of you when you were the vice president? Rest assured, he's unlikely ever to be in your way."

"No, you're right. He won't be a liability, and it doesn't really matter if he's an asset."

"Exactly. So, enjoy the tasks before you, let the convention run its course, then focus on what wax figure the Democrats choose to face you. It might even be fun." Taft paused. "By the way, I have received a rather strident request that you refrain from some of your more outrageous public activities."

Roosevelt was more curious than offended.

"Such as?"

"Swimming nude in the Potomac, for one. It's bad enough that you drive your Secret Service men to nervous fits and provide weeks of storytelling for the tourists. It's not seemly for the president of the United States to carry on that way. Imagine if it were me."

Roosevelt didn't respond, though those images forced themselves through his brain.

"And your constant gallivanting through Rock Creek Park, putting every hiker in peril, your rolling around in the mud with whatever child accompanies you, well, you certainly understand. It's the season for best feet forward. Your enemies are looking for reasons to humiliate you."

Roosevelt absorbed the criticism, said, "No. I understand deportment. But they're asking me to forego those things I enjoy about being here. I suspect the average voter prefers that I am a human being who enjoys getting a little mud on me and not some statue staring down on them from a lofty pedestal. Perhaps I should take to campaigning myself and toss the professionals to one side."

"Patience, Mr. President. It's perhaps your weakest quality, but I trust those people to get you elected. You should too."

He felt a heavy sulk coming on, the office suddenly stuffy.

"Fine. Let them do what they must. For me ... I'm going out to play with my dogs. Or rabbits. Or maybe even the zebra."

June 24, 1904
The White House

Gentlemen, I nominate for President of the United States ... Theodore Roosevelt of New York!

—*Frank S. Black, Former Governor of New York*

THE LUNCH HAD just been served, the family once more taking advantage of the pleasant atmosphere of the house's portico. As the plates were laid, Edith said, "Thank you, Louisa. This looks marvelous."

Roosevelt sat quietly, watched as Edith and Alice dipped out spoonfuls of something brown, lumps of meat and potatoes. They seemed to know what he was thinking, had the courtesy not to bother his thoughts. After a silent moment, he said, "We should hear something anytime now."

"Certainly, my dear. Please, eat some of this stew. It is most delicious. A gift from the Greek ambassador. A most charming fellow. His aides brought the dessert as well, something sinfully sticky."

Alice seemed especially cheerful, always a surprise. She poked at the stew in her bowl, said, "I'm here for the dessert, though if I must eat this, I will. Actually, it is rather good. The bread helps."

He craned his neck back into the house, imaginary sounds, tried now to focus on the food. "Just dip me a small amount, Edie, if you don't mind."

She seemed concerned now.

"Normally you'd eat the entire tureen. Please don't worry, Teddy. When word is received, you'll know."

Alice said, through dainty slurps from her spoon, "They're not going to keep secrets from you. Don't get yourself into such a fuss."

He ignored them, ignored the food, looked again into the house. He saw the servant now, at the door, pointing the way, Loeb hurrying out, the blessed paper in his hands. Roosevelt stood, felt annoyingly nervous, Loeb there quickly, handing him the telegram. Roosevelt read, reread, said, "They have agreed with me that Cortelyou should be chairman of the party. Good choice, excellent successor to Mark Hanna." He saw Edith now, her look bordering on the annoyed. "Oh, yes, there's more. It says here that I have been nominated by the convention for the office of president, by unanimous vote of the nine hundred ninety-four delegates."

He couldn't contain the wide smile, both hands rising high in the air, even Loeb responding with a hearty backslap. "Outstanding, sir. Outstanding."

Edith stood, Alice as well, both flanking him now, planting a heavy kiss on both cheeks. Alice said, "I'm proud of you, Papa. This will be wonderful. I love it in Washington."

Edith hugged him now, firm and soft. "My dear man. My dear Mr. President. I am so proud of my husband."

Loeb said, "Sir, there are newspapermen waiting. They're here for a statement."

"Even some of Hearst's boys?" He caught himself. "No, this is no time for sarcasm. This is a spectacular day. Let's share that with the reporters, and they can share that with the world."

HE WAS UNIMPRESSED by his running mate.

Senator Charles Fairbanks was a tall, gangly man, several years older than Roosevelt, who carried himself as though he was uncomfortable in his own clothes. Roosevelt watched him carefully as he sat, measured his physical appearance, one of those factors reporters always notice, the most superficial way Fairbanks would be judged. After settling onto the chair, Fairbanks said, "You know, Mr. President, I look forward to standing beside you in this endeavor. I have campaigned in many elections, probably when you were still too young for such activities. We shall make an effective team, especially since the Democrats have chosen Judge Parker. I know Alton Parker well and believe him to be unfit for the office. And frankly, sir, he is possibly the most boring man they could have chosen as their candidate. Shall we go over his alleged programs, his proposals that we must counter on the campaign trail?"

Roosevelt couldn't remove his eyes from the man's bald pate, the strands of hair in a carefully arranged comb-over.

"As you know, Senator, I won't be on the campaign trail at all. The powers that be of our party strongly suggest that I remain home, tending to the business of president while the professionals manage things. I assume you consider yourself one of the professionals."

He expected a chuckle, but instead Fairbanks seemed to ponder the words, nodding, as though paid a great compliment.

"By all means, Mr. President. Work is already underway, several of us planning to find ways to blunt some of your more radical policies, especially when it comes to courting the progressive wing of the party. We must not anger Wall Street by unwise programs that would only benefit the working man. As well, your tendency to wax violently poetic, to display outright passion in your speeches. Sometimes that could come back to haunt you, sir. I have here the transcript of your recent talk in Gettysburg, Memorial Day. Let's see, um, yes, 'attacked and defended, where finally the great charge surged up the slope, only to break on the summit in the bloody spray of gallant failure.' Yes, that particular reference is troublesome. In one stroke, by emphasizing the great failure of the Confederates, what I believe is called Pickett's charge, you could offend every southern voter."

Roosevelt was beginning to feel a fair amount of offense himself.

"I assure you, Senator, that speech was one of my finer moments. It was capped off by a marvelous ceremony by schoolchildren laying flowers on the gravestones. I stood where Lincoln stood, and that alone might have offended some Southerners, but I will not try to erase those moments. The southern voters may judge as they please. I expect the Democrats will carry the South in any event."

Fairbanks seemed completely unruffled.

"But your graphic use of the term 'bloody spray' . . . well, I assume you merely became carried away by a little too much energy in your rhetoric. This example is why the people managing your campaign suggest you keep a somewhat lower profile. As you often note, 'walk softly and carry a big stick.' We merely suggest you walk softly and leave it at that. Those of us with experience in these things will manage quite well. I am confident that we shall engineer a successful election come November."

Roosevelt crunched the word in his mind. *Engineer.*

"Well, if someone requires an apology for my Memorial Day offering, so be it. I don't agree. In fact, the crowd in Gettysburg reacted as though it was a bully speech. So, Senator, I hope you don't *blunt* me too much. And I hope my record thus far as president and my own ability to inspire people will add at least something to your engineering."

Fairbanks seemed oblivious to the jab, lost in thought in some other direction.

Roosevelt had endured all he could, knew there was the danger he might yet have another unfortunate outburst. He stood, the obvious signal that the conversation had concluded.

Fairbanks kept to his chair, looked at him with a blank stare, and Roosevelt said, "If you will excuse me, Senator, I must tend to my duties. Good day to you, sir."

Fairbanks stood now, seemed to unfold himself, much taller than Roosevelt.

"Well, then, I shall tend to my duties as well."

Roosevelt watched the man jangle his way out the office door, thought, *Duties*. Thankfully, the vice president usually has little to do. I just hope he doesn't get in my way.

THE DEMOCRATIC CANDIDATE, Judge Alton Parker of New York, proved to be even more colorless than Roosevelt's running mate. Parker was a man visibly uncomfortable in rallying anyone to his cause, if he was even able to spell out exactly what that cause might be. The primary tactic of the Democrats was to attack Roosevelt any way they could, yet they offered almost no plans or specific policies of their own. As the attacks against Roosevelt became more strident, he found it increasingly difficult to sit quietly perched in the White House while numerous insults were hurled his way.

Throughout the campaign, the issue of money couldn't be ignored. Roosevelt's campaign was well funded, contributions coming in from some of the largest financiers in the country, including, of course, Wall Street. The Democrats had little choice but to attack those contributions as the worst type of corruption, as though Roosevelt was simply being bought. The responses to those charges were quick and direct, including one statement issued by Roosevelt himself, a lengthy address to each of Parker's charges, labeling them "atrociously false." If the public had any qualms about Roosevelt's integrity or his fitness to continue as president, on November 8 it didn't show at the polls.

By nine in the evening on Election Day, Roosevelt received a note of concession from Judge Parker. The American people had given Roosevelt an overwhelming victory.

PART V

THE OLD LION

You only have to live with me,
while I have to live with you.

—Edith Carow Roosevelt to her husband

We must either wear out or rust out.
My choice is to wear out.

—Theodore Roosevelt

CHAPTER 48

It had been a bad night, waves of nausea he couldn't fend off, the fever returning. By morning, he was better, felt as close to normal as he had for several days, a full breakfast of pancakes and fruit, despite Edith's plea that he make some attempt at moderation, a request that had never worked before.

"Honestly, Teddy, just take some time, relax, read something. You are no longer in the business of pleasing the great crowds."

He rubbed his round belly, could smell the luscious bacon served to the others in the house, denied of course to him.

"Just one piece. Our little secret."

She couldn't help smiling at him.

"You have always been a four-year-old."

"Six. Most of the world thinks of me as six. I'll accept that. How about that bacon?"

"No. Not good for your stomach, and, besides, Mr. Longworth has devoured what remained." She lowered her voice. "His appetite competes favorably with yours."

"Baby Lee has trained him quite nicely. She required a husband who could be shaped to whatever she wished, whenever she wished. Longworth seems to fit that description."

Edith sighed, folded her arms. "It isn't polite to discuss your daughter's personal affairs."

"So what? Are they getting along any better?"

Edith looked down, didn't answer, and he said, "Well, Longworth won't tame her. I couldn't. We've had to accept her as she is, and Longworth had better do the same thing. Should they divorce, it will destroy his political career. He makes good stock of calling himself my son-in-law."

Edith kept her silence, but after a long moment her face brightened with a new thought. "Oh, yes, we have brought your former valet, Mr. Amos, to help take care of you. He should be here later this afternoon."

He wanted to protest the need for any more help, but he had always liked the man, had relied on him for every kind of assistance. He tried to hide his graciousness.

"That's good, I suppose. He can carry me on long walks."

She shook her head, pointed a finger at him, her silent scold, turned and left the room. He called after her, "Edie, what of that writer, Hagedorn? I expected him this morning."

She stopped, her back still to him, turned slowly, back into the room.

"We served him breakfast. He is outside, sitting in his overcoat on the piazza. I cautioned him that you had little stamina for yet another session. Honestly, Teddy, why must you open up our lives to him so completely? And, you are ill, even if you don't admit that. You should be left alone."

He knew how badly she despised intrusions into their personal lives, had proved to be the most private person he knew.

"It was *you* who agreed to this, Edie, who insisted I go along with the young man. Mr. Hagedorn has no evil agenda. He's recording my words and deeds for a new, younger generation, and generations yet to come. That's what *you* said. Those people would otherwise know of me because they might read a presidential history book. I want them all to know more. And besides, he was the first one to ask, and he's young and ambitious. That was me, once. That's worth something."

She looked down, nodded. "Then I shall fetch him."

She bent low now, kissed him on the forehead, and he took her hand.

"You're checking me to see if the fever's back. You can't fool me."

She backed away, couldn't hide the smile. "You seem fine, for now."

"Don't worry. I'm not planning to go anywhere. You may send in Mr. Hagedorn."

"WAS THE TREATY to end the Russo-Japanese War the high point of your presidency?"

"Oh, good Lord, no. Dealing with those ministers and diplomats, like so many intransigent children, was a nightmare. The czar, Nicholas the Second, couldn't admit his military had lost the war, even as his army was in shambles and his navy completely destroyed. They insisted that the treaty call for Sakhalin Island to remain in their control, even after the Japanese had completely occupied it. The Japanese weren't much better. Their entire culture seems based on the need to save face, to never admit mistakes or wrongdoing. There were times in our various meetings when I had to contain my temper, lest I toss their ministers into the sea. But"—he smiled now—"it worked. War over. Neither side was happy, which is how it's supposed to be."

"And you were awarded the Nobel Peace Prize for your efforts."

He thought a moment.

"That was bully. But I knew it wasn't just me. I actually used my daughter, Baby Lee . . . Alice, and my secretary of war at the time, Mr. Taft, to go over there and meet with those diplomats and such, to meet with several top people in a number of Asian countries. Alice, in particular, turned a good many heads, including the man who eventually became her husband, Mr. Longworth, whom I assume you met outside. I wanted to show those people that we were human, and frankly pretty nice folks. It was needed at the time. That was a nasty, overly bloody war, and *anyone* who stopped it would have been lauded. With the Nobel Prize came an award of thirty-seven thousand dollars. A president can't keep that kind of gift, so I donated it, established the Industrial Peace Commission. For all the good it will do. They weren't able to do much to stop the Great War. Trust me on this one, Mr. Hagedorn. The Germans aren't through yet. They lost the kaiser, but someone in that country always seems to rise to the top, and generally those kinds of people aren't very nice."

"Sir, your good work against the corporate monopolies, against the raw power of the trade unions, walking that fine line, that has to be particularly gratifying to you."

Roosevelt cocked his head, frowned.

"You want to talk about all of that business? Yes, yes, I shoved hard against Congress, and occasionally they shoved back, and we passed all manner of good bills, good laws. The railroad-rate bill, that was a good one. There will always be a war of sorts between the haves and the have-nots. It's up to the government to keep the peace, to maintain justice. That's what I tried to do. But important as all of that was, I'd much rather recall the good things we did for the natural world—the Forest Service, the parks, federal game preserves. Labor laws will change depending on who is in power. But the parks have been preserved for all time, more than two hundred thirty million acres of land. I'm confident no one will change that. It would be a crime against man."

"Sir, are you aware that you're the first president to travel outside of the United States?"

"Of course I'm aware. Panama. Took my wife down to see the big damn hole in the ground. Dee-lighted. That canal changed the world, Mr. Hagedorn, for all time. Now, you asked what I'm particularly proud of? The Panama Canal. I started that project, no one else. Had I just handed the project off to Congress to work out the particulars, I assure you, they'd be debating to this day, and for another five decades to come. But today ships move through that great ditch because we made it happen."

Hagedorn scribbled notes, seemed to be stalling, and Roosevelt said, "Tough question? I've had my share. What is it?"

Hagedorn let out a breath, said, "I was wondering if you would talk about the incident with the Colored soldiers, in Texas."

"I can't talk about the incident, because I wasn't there. All I know is what the investigators could tell me, that a number of soldiers went wild, shot up the town of Brownsville, assaulted people. I made those men pay the price, removed them from the army with a dishonorable discharge. That's all."

"Excuse me, sir, but I've read quite a bit of the criticism leveled against you . . ."

"I've had a good deal of time to think about that. I acted the way I did because I thought it was the correct and appropriate thing to do. Since then, I've seen various news stories, mostly out of the South, where some decent, upstanding, pure young white woman is set upon by a burly, vicious Black man. It's amazing how often the story remains the same, as though every virtuous white woman is a target for the uncontrollable urges of the devious Negro. To me, that seems like a ridiculous cliché, but consider, Mr. Hagedorn, that even now, the viciousness of white reaction to that horror has been the unwritten law of the land, mostly in the South. Lynchings have been staged for public entertainment, fed by the need to villainize any Black man who was convenient. I've read those news reports as well, the condemnation I received. I had made enormous gains with the Colored vote, and even in the South, those Lily-Whites I was so dismissive of, they began to mellow a bit as well, and in 1904 a good number of them actually supported my candidacy. In the end, I sacrificed the one to gain the latter. I'm not proud of how the whole Brownsville affair turned out. It might be the most purely political thing I've done." He paused. "I can't say I would have treated those soldiers any differently . . . but I can't say I would have exonerated them. I don't like your question, Mr. Hagedorn. Go on to something else."

Hagedorn seemed to know Roosevelt's mood had darkened, and Roosevelt saw a worried look on the younger man's face.

"Sir, I'm sorry . . ."

"No! Do not apologize. There is ugly in every man's life, and it can be an unpleasant thing to dig up old mistakes. I would rather embrace the good I've done. I cannot escape hindsight, and hindsight is not for recalling the good—it's for examining mistakes. It inspires guilt and causes anger. I've angered enough people as it is. Move on."

"Right. Yes, may we talk about your safari to Africa?

Roosevelt dropped his head for a brief moment, the fatigue returning.

"With the election in 1908, I knew it was wise for me to get out of town, so to speak. Either Taft or that moo-cow William Jennings Bryan would win, and in either case I didn't want to be confined to the audience, just a spectator, watching what might be a political disaster for this country. I'm ashamed to say that I had little faith that Bill Taft would make a good president for another four years. That's just the way I felt. Bryan, well, the country might as well sink into the ocean."

"What happened to sour your relationship with President Taft?"

Roosevelt thought a moment.

"He was a good friend, a good man. Everybody loved him, the big smile, nearly as big as mine. One of the most congenial fellows you'd ever meet, and so it was easy to vote for him. The problems came after, once he was in the White House. He backtracked on a number of issues that we had worked on together. It was as though he became timid, then . . . lazy. He seemed to be happier playing golf than he ever was in the White House. One by one, the alliances I had made with important senators dropped away. My friend Henry Cabot Lodge was explicit in his criticism of Taft. I was still in Africa when his wire came, that Taft was inept. What a word! But I had vowed to stay away, settle peacefully into my retired life, and focus on my writing."

He was scowling now, his heart racing, saw a look of concern on the young man's face.

"Then came 1912. I was approached—no, make that begged, assaulted—by well-wishers and a flock of Republican governors, pushing and pulling me to run for president again, to toss Taft out of office, to bring back the days when the country was running so much more smoothly. By then Taft was hardly in office at all, not even a good figurehead. He just seemed to lose the fight, to become an absentee president. I admit, I let my anger toward him take over, my frustration over what had happened to the Republican Party, so much of the good work we had done slipping away. So, I agreed to fight him, to run as a Progressive, a break with the Republican Party completely. The newspapers started calling the movement the Bull Moose Party. That name was foisted on me, but I admit I rather liked it. Most people thought it came from me, that I insisted on being called the Bull Moose. Well, maybe it *was* my idea. It was a chaotic time."

"Chaotic, meaning the attempt on your life?"

"Oh, you've heard about that, have you?"

"Sir, everyone knows about that. I'm just wondering how you saw it."

"I saw a lunatic with a pistol, shot me in the chest"—he put his left hand to his right breast, pointed—"right here. Didn't hurt too bad.

Scared the hell out of a whole lot of people, including, for a while, me. It was Milwaukee, thousands of people filling the streets, hoping to hear me speak. I couldn't . . . let them down. So, I ordered my people to drive me to the auditorium, and after a bit of a rest and a clean hand-kerchief applied to the wound, I gave my speech. Word had spread, of course, and most of the people didn't believe it, thought we were playing for sympathy, I guess. So, I raised up my shirt and showed them the wound. By now, it was pretty bloody. It had the desired effect on the crowd. I asked them to keep quiet so I could get through the speech. They did, and I did."

"How long did you talk?"

"About an hour, a little more. My speech, the papers had a damn bullet hole through them, and I'm told that the bullet hit the only place on my chest that wouldn't have killed me in minutes. The bullet is still inside me. Too tough to remove. Anyway, as the speech went on, I felt about as bad as I feel now. No, don't write that down. That whole mess was worse for Edith. She was in a panic that I was dead, or would be. She finally got through to me, and I calmed her down. That was the hardest part of the whole thing, listening to her crying."

"I read you looked at your would-be assassin, to see if you knew the man."

"I guess I did. Looked him in the eye. He wasn't there, if you know what I mean. Sad fellow, disheveled. They said he heard voices. He didn't really have a sane reason for trying to kill me. Thankfully, he didn't have a bigger gun. This country doesn't need any more public officials being killed."

"I followed that story in the newspapers. Everyone was pretty shook up about it."

"They should be. We're a country of laws, not people hearing voices."

"Oh, I did want to say, in that election my father voted for you."

"Don't toss grease my way, Mr. Hagedorn. I appreciate him, but it hardly matters now. A great many Republicans made big talk about how they wanted me back in office, but when the time came, they opted to stick with their party. There weren't enough of them to put Taft back in office, though. And so we have Woodrow Wilson. A Democrat and a peacemonger. He's supposed to be even more progressive than I am." He sniffed, shook his head. "Let me offer you a quote from Mr. Wilson. I've committed it, more or less, to memory. Someone, a reporter, asked Wilson why that year's groundhog was afraid to return to its burrow. According to him, the groundhog was afraid that I had put a *coon* in there. That was right when I was struggling to push through several policies liberalizing issues of race, appointing Negroes to government positions, and so forth. So here's the president of Princeton offering up a statement that could have been uttered by any Lily-White in Alabama." He paused. "You might not want to write that. No one will believe it. Some people actually like Wilson." He wiped his brow, felt a light sweat. "Not sure how much longer we can do this today, Mr. Hagedorn. Edith will no doubt intervene shortly."

"It sounds as though you can't really escape politics or the applause of the people. Is it that difficult for you to remain uninvolved?"

"I tried. That's why I took my son Kermit to Africa, a lengthy hunting trip, as soon as I vacated the office in 1909. It was a good trip, a long trip. We killed a great deal of big game, some of it on display right here in this house."

"You don't sound enthusiastic about that, sir."

"I used to love to hunt. We've had this conversation already. When you kill to survive, to eat, there's a nobility to that. But there have been a great many times that I have killed just to enjoy the feeling, to claim another trophy. There is a thrill to it, Mr. Hagedorn, something most people who have not picked up a rifle will never understand. The anticipation, the thrill of the chase, that heart-stopping moment when you see your quarry, the good shot, standing over the beast, inflated with pride as someone takes your photograph. It was good watching Kermit go through that experience. But these days, knowing I'm not likely to pick up a rifle again, my feelings have changed a bit. Unless it's for biological discovery or the need for meat, for survival, for me the days of gathering trophies are past. I felt that way at the end of that safari."

"But you went to the Amazon. And Kermit was with you again."

Roosevelt paused, fought against a slight chill, a nagging symptom of his long fight with a subtle case of malarial fever, originating in Cuba.

He looked hard at the younger man.

"I was too old, not healthy enough, but I went anyway. People had to accommodate me, take care of me, even Kermit. I am forever grateful to all those people. It was selfish of me, embarking on that journey for my own need to see it, explore it, discover it. I could have wrecked the entire expedition."

"But you didn't."

He leaned back in the bed, stared at the ceiling, a wide smile.

"No, I didn't. And I would do it all again."

CHAPTER 49

February 21, 1914
Near Buriti, Brazil

It was raining again. He couldn't quite get used to that, the relentless downpours that wormed their way into every part of his clothing, and every part of him. With the rain came the mud, drawing the horses' hooves deeper, the beasts struggling mightily to carry Roosevelt and the rest of the party closer to the headwaters of the river.

He was more concerned for Kermit than for himself. The young man had never seemed able to shake a bout of malaria, contracted years ago, returning now, combined with other strange symptoms of this place, diseases and parasites no one had ever studied, attacking Kermit now with a vicious spread of sores along his legs.

Roosevelt eased the horse out of line, looked back, saw the train of oxen and their carts, laden heavily with great mounds of supplies. Other men were looking at him, dark eyes beneath the brims of dripping hats. George Cherrie, the American naturalist, a thorough professional, was barely hiding his concern that Roosevelt was not physically prepared for what they might yet experience. The doctor, Jose Cajazeira, a different concern, watching Kermit as well, knowing that neither Roosevelt nor his son had ever tested the kinds of hardships or the various diseases that might confront them.

Roosevelt eased the horse alongside Kermit's, leaned closer, said in a low voice, "How are you feeling?"

"I am getting better, Papa. My legs aren't hurting as much. I'll be fine. I'm eager to reach the river."

"So are we all, my boy."

He knew Kermit was embarrassed for his condition, wanted no special favors, no one to treat him like the son of the *great man*. Roosevelt pulled his horse away, moved again to the front of the caravan, thought, He will be reckless, proving he is strong to me and to them. He will show me that he does not need me. In Africa, I had to teach him, but here there is nothing to teach but survive, pay attention, don't take foolish chances. He doesn't require his father to teach him that.

He reached the front of the line, the horse slurping its way through the drifting ooze beneath him. Roosevelt sneezed, wet and unpleasant, knew eyes were on him, and he raised his hat, flapped it high overhead, a loud cheer, then planted it back on his head. It was a gesture of defiance, that the weather was no obstacle, that rain was merely rain. He tried to chuckle, arrogant dismissal of the misery he felt inside. He wanted to believe it had the desired effect, the others drawing some kind of energy from his little show. Or, he thought, do they think I'm just a fool?

He glanced to the side, more eyes on him, the tight, wiry man, always concerned, yet with little time for coddling anyone. The man was now his partner, and the expedition's true leader, Colonel Cândido Rondon. Though the Brazilian government had labeled this as Roosevelt's expedition, mostly for the publicity that would garner, no one disregarded the authority that Rondon carried, the expertise and experience that made this entire operation possible. Rondon had been here before, his soldiers once working alongside native tribesmen to construct a lengthy telegraph line that would reach villages that never before had any means of contacting the world outside. Now, the telegraph poles, with their singing wires, provided the pathway, the poles spread so precisely apart that the men could measure their distance traveled by the number of poles they had passed.

Rondon was a short, tightly built man, the appearance of the spit-and-polish officer, but he was no martinet, had a warmth that Roosevelt found delightful. It didn't hurt either man that they had felt a mutual respect and friendship almost immediately after their first meeting. Rondon had arranged the means and the necessary crew to transport the amazing amount of supplies they would require. No one, not even Rondon, was quite sure just how long this journey would be or just what they would find along the way. As well, Rondon had hired the hands, the *camaradas,* the men responsible for every task the Americans and Brazilians could not easily do for themselves, including hauling supplies, paddling and steering the great canoes, preparing camps in places where no one had camped before, and keeping wary eyes on the jungle, both for potential game they could consume and for the native tribesmen, who might not welcome this intrusion into their territory.

The expedition had two primary purposes, spelled out for Roosevelt in an invitation he could not resist. It had come from a Brazilian minister, Doctor Lauro Müller, who laid out plans for a scientific expedition into the heart of the Brazilian wilderness to gather biological specimens that would benefit many of the world's most curious naturalists and the museums and universities that employed them. But there was a geographic purpose that intrigued Roosevelt the most. Accumulating game animals was nothing new, and he had often studied the habitat and the carcasses of all manner of creature, great and small. But Müller proposed that Roosevelt take part in a journey of discovery, a doorway into a completely new world. Roosevelt would have the opportunity to explore a part of Brazil no white man had ever seen, floating along a river that no white man had ever traveled. It appeared on no maps, had no official Brazilian name. And though Rondon knew of the headwaters, no one was quite certain just where the river flowed, how treacherous it might be, or if it was passable at all. It was Rondon who suggested that, by launching their boats at the headwaters, the river would eventually carry them to its terminus into a larger tributary of the Amazon or, possibly, into the Amazon itself. The river might wind through an area more than five hundred miles long. With so much uncertainty, it was Rondon who had given it a name. It was simply the River of Doubt.

ROOSEVELT HAD COME to South America with Edith, an official trip that for more than two months had carried him to several capital cities in a handful of countries, speaking engagements so reminiscent of those he had mastered back home. The people he met were no less enthusiastic than any crowd in any city in the United States, vast audiences full of good cheer and broad smiles, lavish gifts, state dinners with presidents of their countries. Through it all, he kept up the energy and the smiles, felt a genuine and somewhat surprised appreciation at the royal receptions they received. But then the time had come to begin Müller's planned operation. Edith departed for home with the usual tender tears, worry always that her husband and her son were venturing off into something outrageously dangerous. Even if Roosevelt agreed with her, he would never admit it. Comforting words came instead, combined with Kermit's bouncing enthusiasm that seemed to blunt her fears.

The trip had begun as a massive undertaking, volunteers from the community of biologists and naturalists, some just enjoying the association with Roosevelt. But very soon it became evident that the capacity for hauling supplies could not keep up with the number of men who would have to be cared for, either with food or their own baggage. The great train of oxen traveling overland could accommodate far more than the canoes built for the journey, which were waiting for them at the headwaters of the river. It was a painful yet necessary process, Rondon, with Roosevelt's input, choosing which men would not make the trip. Some would take a different journey down a river already mapped, the naturalists at least being given the opportunity to take specimens virtually unknown outside Brazil.

THE RAINS HAD stopped, at least for now, the sun dropping behind heavy overcast, dull darkness settling upon them. The *camaradas* had pitched the tents, campfires burning from dry wood carried on the oxcarts. Roosevelt sat heavily on his small camp chair, his boots in the mud, watched Kermit scrambling through the supplies to find a chair of his own. Along the train of carts, Rondon moved through the men, issuing instructions in Portuguese, words utterly foreign to Roosevelt.

The two men had found the only common ground for their mutual communication. Both spoke ragged French.

Rondon stood now with hands on hips, seemed to survey the activity, a sharp eye for detail that Roosevelt appreciated. He knows things about this entire operation, he thought, that I would not even dream of. Rondon made a tight pivot, moved toward him, a grim expression. He stopped outside the tent, seemed to shift his attitude, bent low, stepped inside with a tight smile.

"Ah, Colonel Roosevelt, we are closer still. Even in the rain, we made twenty kilometers today. I am, however, concerned for the condition of the oxen. We are working them too hard, and they are not fit. Like some men, they do not have stamina or the muscles for so much work, and, worse, many are not agreeable animals. They were raised to supply meat for the villagers or to plow small plots. There is simply too much for them to haul, and I know very well that when we reach the river, much of what we are now carrying must be left behind."

Roosevelt absorbed what seemed to be a double dose of bad news.

"Whatever you decide, Colonel. You are the authority here."

Rondon seemed relieved that Roosevelt had made clear the pecking order of authority. Roosevelt appreciated that Rondon did not refer to him as Mr. President, but chose instead his rank.

"I admit, Colonel Roosevelt, I was concerned there might be a bit too much ceremony with you and the other Americans."

"You mean we would come here and insist that America come with us."

Rondon looked down. "There is a bit of that even now, sir. Thus, the oxcarts, laden with so many items no one needs on such an expedition. I was hoping to make those decisions without controversy."

Roosevelt looked out at Kermit, digging through bundles of extra clothing, small pieces of furniture. Roosevelt smiled. "There will be no controversy. You make the decisions; we shall gladly accept."

Rondon followed his look. "How is your boy?"

Roosevelt knew that if Kermit continued to be sick, or got much worse, he would have to stay behind, which meant, of course, that

Roosevelt might have to remain with him. But he could not lie to Rondon or paint a false picture.

"The doctor says his fever is about one hundred two. The sores are scabbing over, but I know he is hurting. But he is improving, and I believe he will be fine. He needs a day or two to grow accustomed to conditions here. Perhaps both of us do."

Rondon didn't seem convinced. "When I built the telegraph line, we lost soldiers, natives too. Conditions were not so different than they are now. This is not a friendly place, Colonel. Even if the weather is agreeable, some of the tribes I have encountered seem angry at any intrusion. Others, surely, I have never encountered, but I know they exist, and they might regard our presence as a disease that must be cleansed. I only say this because once we reach the river and begin that part of our journey, we cannot simply stop or backtrack. On the land here, the high ridges, the telegraph line runs both ways, sir, and should anyone of this party, including you and your son, should anyone wish to turn around, they should do it before we move onto the river. For now, the wire offers a pathway back to the town, and the way to go home."

Roosevelt looked at Rondon, studied the man, wondered if there was some unspoken message, that Rondon was using too many words to say . . . *go home*.

Roosevelt said, "The naturalists on this trip are depending on both of us, Colonel. Your skills in the wilderness are invaluable. My name adds a legitimacy that will garner us a great deal of attention, which means financing for you to do this again, perhaps outside of Brazil. We are partners, sir. I will give you as much as I can, and Kermit will as well."

Rondon nodded slowly, seemed satisfied.

"We will be close tomorrow. I will begin to appraise the supplies. I will consult with you on any decision I make."

Rondon left the tent, and Kermit moved closer now, limping, had seemed to wait for Rondon to clear the way. He came inside, kept to his feet, the pain of the sores making it too difficult for him to bend his legs, a greater challenge when riding his horse.

"I'm not sure I like that man, Papa."

Roosevelt didn't need to hear this, not now.

"Why on earth not?"

"He's very . . . strict."

Roosevelt was annoyed, tried not to show it.

"Damn right he's strict. Our lives are in his hands. No one in this part of the world understands what we face here as much as he does. I for one have complete confidence in him, and you will too. Unless, of course, you're feeling as though you're too sick to continue. The telegraph wires will lead you back to town, if you wish."

He knew that tactic would work. Kermit's eyes widened, and he pulled up one pant leg.

"See? Better today than yesterday. By tomorrow I should be back to full normal. I will not turn around, not now. If you can do this, so can I."

"Then stop with any complaints. Do what you're told. In Africa, I watched you take unnecessary risks. There, you had a rifle to shoot a predator before he ate you. Here, the predator is everywhere, unseen or right beneath you." He stopped, could see something else in Kermit's eyes, knew that the young man had become engaged just as the journey was scheduled to begin, the starry-eyed stare of a man in love. "You cannot speed things up here just so you can return home all the more quickly. Your young lady will be far worse off if you never return at all. You and I have opposite goals here. Yours is to return to your true love and all of that. Mine is to stay as far away from Washington and the Democrats as I can. Woodrow Wilson is determined to unwind every program I put into effect. I don't need to stand by and watch that. Once we left Rio, we were free of newspapers, and I intend not to pay any mind to what may pass above our heads over that telegraph line. I promise you, do what Colonel Rondon tells you to do, and we'll all get home when the time is right. This river we're about to reach could kill us all, or it could be a gentle ride through a scenic paradise. If I die here, I am very happy to leave my remains in this jungle. I have lived and enjoyed a life as much as any *nine men* I know. I hope one day you will be able to say that, and mean it. So, no matter which way this goes, you will remember this for all time. Both of us will. I, for one, am dee-lighted by the prospect."

THE DAY HAD been unlike the past few, no rain, the sun rising high with a torch-like heat he had not felt since Cuba. They had passed a small river, the oxen forced to ford, a difficult feat with their heavy loads. Roosevelt felt the oily grime in his clothes, looked at the dark water, heard chatter behind him, saw Rondon trotting up toward him, then past, Kermit close behind. He was surprised to see they were naked. Now, the others were following, the first of the group reaching the water, a heavy splash, Kermit calling back to him, "Come on, Papa. It feels great! You need a bath!"

He turned, looked at the *camaradas,* nearly all of them laughing at the spectacle of so many white fleshy bodies. Roosevelt watched the commotion in the water now, the men floating about, and he could stand it no longer, peeled off the misery of his sweat-filled clothing, stepped gingerly to the water's edge, then, with a great shout, launched himself airborne.

He expected a chill, the water instead like well-heated soup. He looked at Rondon, the man smiling at him, and Rondon said, "Try not to make overly much commotion in the water. It could draw piranhas."

Roosevelt raised his head abruptly. "There are piranhas here?"

"Oh, most assuredly, Colonel." Rondon lay on his back now, held one foot in the air, missing a toe. "One did me no favor. They can attack you in a half meter of water, or even less."

The naturalist, Cherrie, said, "There are anacondas here as well, sir. Strangle a man in minutes. Saw an ox get pulled down once."

Roosevelt glanced about, tried to keep his feet motionless, felt a soft muddy bottom, stood quietly, water up to his chest. He had a sudden thought, glanced downward, nothing to see in the dark water, slid one hand down to his groin, a shield to protect himself as best he could. But he saw the others splashing about, enjoying the water, the one opportunity to wash away the sweat and grime of the journey so far. He removed his protecting hand, pushed himself up to lie on his back, his white belly skyward. Well, he thought, this isn't such a difficult trip after all.

The river was black and moved slowly into the jungle like spilled molasses. It was near twenty meters across, the steady current leading northward, disappearing quickly past a sharp bend.

He stood staring at the water, while behind him the *camaradas* did their work, Rondon already sorting out the necessary from the waste of weight and space. Rondon was beside him now, said, "So much is unknown about this place, this part of Brazil. Maps show nothing, or they show the river in the wrong place. They show mountains where there are none. This is important, Colonel. We shall draw the correct map."

If we survive. No, Roosevelt thought, none of that. This is a bully adventure. It's just a river, seems peaceful enough. He saw his gear being loaded into one of the supply canoes, his rifle protruding. Several rifles went aboard, a sense of security he couldn't ignore. If we need meat . . . or if somebody threatens us along the way. I don't want to kill anyone, not men. But if there's no choice . . .

"Colonel, right here."

He saw the doctor settling into the largest canoe, with Cherrie following. He moved that way, three *camaradas*, the canoe's crew, making way. He stepped in, the heavy wood unmoving, the canoe stout and solid. He looked across the rest of the group, Rondon and the Brazilian engineer Lyra in another, smaller craft. Kermit and two of the *camaradas* settled into the smallest canoe, pushing off quickly, Kermit looking back at him. Roosevelt did a quick count, had to know, to write down all of the experiences so all would know. Twenty-two of us, he thought. There were twice that many when we started. But it could not have been. It would have been a carnival on the river. Can't have that. This is too important.

He couldn't avoid the butterflies in his stomach, watched as each of the canoes slid farther out into the water. The canoe rocked slightly, the man in the bow paddling, the craft aiming downstream, the others moving out to either side. He felt the familiar blend, excitement and emotion, another look at Kermit, all business now, the young man insisting he help with the paddling. As if he felt his father's eyes, Kermit suddenly looked back, held the paddle in the air, shook it, a wide smile, and Roosevelt nodded, a smile of his own, thought, Yes, now we shall change the maps.

CHAPTER 50

March 1914

The River

He swiped at the air, a futile gesture, said to Rondon,

"What in blazes are these things? They're not like the mosquitoes from yesterday."

"Bees, Colonel. One of many varieties. These won't sting, unless you torment them."

"Not much chance of that. They're doing a fine job of tormenting me."

"I'm surprised the wasps haven't come. They will, likely tomorrow, at sunrise."

"Wasps? The stinging kind?"

Rondon laughed, swatted the air in front of him.

"Yes and no. Many varieties too. If you observe, the whine of the mosquitoes is really a pleasant singing voice. Each variety a different note. Much like a chorus."

Roosevelt smacked some kind of creature on his forearm.

"The insects didn't come until we came ashore. I guess there's not much we can do about that."

He could feel Rondon losing patience, no one else in the camp seeming to notice the great clouds of flying insects or Roosevelt's annoyance.

"That's how it is, Colonel. Stay out in the river, keep moving, you're mostly immune. The creatures, most all of them in this place, they stay on the land. It's as though they sit and wait for their prey. Right now, you are their prey. You can believe that one of them, a scout, has flown off into the jungle to bring all of his friends. We are, after all, a rare treat."

There was no comfort in that thought, Roosevelt moving to the makeshift shelter, his bedroom for the night. Around him, the *camaradas* worked to clear a camping area, small lean-tos pitched, camp chairs put in place. He watched a pair of men, deep copper skin, one man with a heavy axe. They moved to a small dead tree, chopped ferociously, the tree coming down quickly, firewood for the night.

The camp would do for at least the next two days, forced upon them by the first real rapids they had seen. With the crafts so heavily laden, they could not take a chance that their precious supplies could be lost to an overturned canoe. The *camaradas* teamed up to beach the canoes, empty the cargo, and after constructing a corduroy roadway, they would haul everything, including the heaviest canoe, downriver, below the rapids. At first, no one knew just how far they would have to go, since no one had any idea just how long the rapids were or when they might confront the next one. Rondon himself scouted the situation downriver, and then, with a crisp order, the labor had begun.

The other nagging problem for Roosevelt was the slow pace of their advance. Rondon had more than one duty to fulfill on this voyage, and an important task was carefully mapping the river's course. In the lead canoe, Kermit pushed forward to each curve in the river, disembarked onto the river's edge, and held up a marker, which Rondon would glass from upriver. The measurement of distance would be made, one small piece of the river's course now documented. The science behind the surveying made perfect sense, but for Roosevelt the task itself was enormously time-consuming and severely limited their progress.

To ONE SIDE of him, Kermit sat, rubbed his hands carefully down both legs, obviously hurting.

"I thought you were better."

"I am, Papa. The boils have mostly drained, and I'm not as tired. I've gone through this before. It will pass."

"You haven't gone through it in a roadless jungle. Just be honest with me, let me know if anything gets worse."

"Of course. I want to do my part, even if I'm not well."

Roosevelt tried to keep quiet, never his strong suit. "You enjoy the surveying?"

Kermit looked at him, knew the hidden meaning. "I know it slows us down, but Colonel Rondon told me it is good work, important. I enjoy being a part of that."

Roosevelt grunted. "I'll tolerate it for a while, but I have no patience for dragging our feet. We might be out here for a very long time, and I pay close attention to our supplies, especially the canned food. That's all we have before we have to live off the jungle."

Roosevelt sat back, blinked at an enormous horsefly, hovering, swirling, dive-bombing his face. He waved at it, another futile gesture, and Kermit laughed.

"Mother would not do well out here."

Roosevelt tried to see the humor, applied the stinking ointment, a fly dope, designed to fend off the hungriest of insects. Thus far it had barely worked and proved utterly useless in the rain.

"Your mother can be an excellent pioneer when she wishes to. I would be more concerned about Baby Lee."

Kermit looked at him with a smile.

"Alice would command Mr. Longworth to kill the insects for her."

They shared a good laugh, others turning to watch, no one else with much good humor.

And then it began to rain.

He slid beneath the canvas cover, Kermit into one of his own. But the rains had come daily, and often now they seemed to come every hour, with blasts of hot sunshine in between, drying only the surface of whatever had been soaked. There was a carpet of rotting leaves beneath his feet, water beneath that, the mud reaching up to him, the canvas above him dripping a sheet of rain.

The naturalist Cherrie was there now, rain flowing off the brim of his hat. George Cherrie was a few years younger than Roosevelt, a thin, fit man with a wide, drooping moustache. He had been sponsored to accompany the expedition by the American Museum of Natural

History in New York. Their hope, of course, was that Cherrie would discover one or more species of birds or even small mammals that the museum did not have in its collection.

"How are we doing, Colonel? Enjoying the tropical weather?"

"I am dee-lighted, George. This was exactly what I anticipated. Not so sure about the extraordinary number of insect species. You'll likely have your hands full finding the birds you're hunting. Most everything I've seen is high up, tops of the largest trees."

Cherrie glanced skyward.

"You have an observant eye. The mammals seem scarce too. That's a bit of a surprise. I expected them to linger near water, but with this much rain, every mud puddle is a watering hole. This shower should end pretty quickly. Usually does. Then, of course, the steam comes. I was wondering, since we're probably not going anywhere for a couple of days, if you would accompany me, with your rifle, of course, into the jungle. There are some bird specimens hereabout I would like to retrieve if possible. And since we have no actual meat to eat, I thought we might have the good fortune to bag a monkey, perhaps even a tapir."

Roosevelt retrieved his rifle from his gear.

"Let's go."

He crawled out into a steaming mist, the rain already lightening, saw Rondon, who said, "Good hunting, gentlemen. Be careful."

They stepped farther from the river, a makeshift trail provided by the machetes of the *camaradas*. Once they were well away, the trail ended, Cherrie picking his way through vines and wet, leafy brush. After a dozen more yards, Cherrie turned to him. "Thank you for the company. It isn't wise for any one of us to wander away from the river alone. And never leave your rifle behind. This is not a friendly place, Colonel."

Roosevelt pushed aside an enormous wet leaf, a swarm of bees suddenly finding him, darting about his head, seeming to aim for his ears, then his eyes.

"Ahh, they're relentless."

Cherrie moved closer to him, said, "They'll leave you alone after a time. They're looking for a source of honey, I suppose. You're not it, so when they figure that out, they'll leave. Probably come to me next. Excuse me if I don't stand too close."

Cherrie moved away, Roosevelt still working his hands to ward off the new torment. They pushed farther away from the river, Roosevelt looking up as much as ahead, the canopy of tall trees shielding the jungle from the sun. He realized now that the ground beneath his feet was mostly bare. Few things can grow down here, he thought. Very little sun gets through.

Cherrie stopped, focused on something, and Roosevelt did as well, tried to hear . . . anything. He realized now there were almost no sounds, no singing birds, no chirping of insects. It was so very different from the nighttime, when the jungle seemed to come awake, every creature competing with the rest to be heard. Cherrie glanced back at him, shook his head, moved away, stopped again, made a small yelp. Roosevelt moved closer, and Cherrie held up a finger, blood in a small stream.

"Damn. Thorn got me. Be careful. Some of these thorny things can be deadly. Some are just annoying. I hope this one is the latter."

The sound came suddenly, ripping through them, a piercing scream, the horror of a child being tortured, the awful image erupting into Roosevelt's mind. The sound stopped now, and Cherrie was laughing.

"Howler monkey. Scares hell out of me every time I hear it. He's a good bit away from us, but we need to watch above. A monkey is a prize feast around here."

Roosevelt strained to hear, nothing but silence.

"It doesn't seem that there is much game here."

Cherrie nursed his punctured finger. "There isn't much, not in the jungle. We get to some grasslands, higher ground, there could be. You have to take what the jungle will offer, and if it's a monkey, or a bush deer, some kind of pig, that has to do."

"Nobody's mentioned much about fishing."

Cherrie thought a moment.

"The river is our nemesis, the challenge, the obstacle. The *camaradas* know it isn't a kind place, and they don't care much for talking to it, coaxing out a fish. If we get hungry enough, we'll go to the river, asking for some help. It can happen. Piranhas are good eating, and there are several other species here that would make a good feast. For now let's keep our sights above ground. Um, Colonel, you might wish to raise your foot."

Roosevelt looked down, saw the bright colors of the coral snake sliding alongside his boot. He did as Cherrie suggested, stood on one shaking foot, set his boot down far past the snake, which slid silently into the leaves.

"They're not particularly aggressive, unless you step on one. Their poison is especially deadly, but they have to chew on you with their short teeth to make it work. Not like a viper. They have fangs. Just watch your step."

Roosevelt scanned the ground around him, kicked at a rotten log, saw a swarm of white termites, an enormous black beetle with a horn-like appendage. Cherrie said, "Rhinoceros beetle. Fascinating creature. I must say, I'm already enjoying this trip, Colonel."

Roosevelt stepped past the log, careful this time.

"I knew there were plenty of strange creatures out here. It's just how it is, much like Africa, much like the Badlands. But I didn't expect to run into so many of them the first week."

And, once more, it began to rain.

HE HAD SLEPT in fits, engulfed by the steam of the ground around him. The rains had stopped for now, a starless sky thick with clouds. He had slept on the ground often, especially in the Dakotas, but this seemed very different, and much more dangerous. The thought of coral snakes never left his mind, along with insects and other creatures he could only imagine. But his concerns spread past himself, worry about Kermit, about the *camaradas* doing so much work in increasingly hostile conditions. He tried to recall their names, even one, had heard Rondon speaking to them so many times. I should know their names. They are too important for us to just take them for granted.

He woke again, stirred, his back stiff, his injured leg aching. He realized suddenly that the jungle had come alive, cries and squawks, buzzing and chirps of every kind, every tone, every volume. He stared into the darkness, fully awake now, tried to sort the sounds, identify anything at all. What kinds of noises does a jaguar make? Is it just monkeys? How many are there, how many types? Frogs, what types? Night birds of all kinds, certainly. He began to energize, absorbed by the sounds, thousands of voices seeming to blend into a high-pitched roar. He raised his head, a glimpse in the dark, saw Cherrie sitting up, staring at the sounds made by specimens he might never have seen, might never have imagined. How does he go into the jungle at night to do his job? Simple answer to that: he doesn't.

THEY HAD PASSED by the first rapids, the canoes back in smooth water, aided along by the current. But the distant roars were frequent, the river's clear message that more lay in their path, perhaps many more, perhaps the entire river. Rondon and Kermit continued their work surveying the river, but Roosevelt continued to be annoyed by the slow progress. As days passed and more of the tumbling rapids were skirted by the rugged hands and strong backs of the *camaradas,* Roosevelt had to intervene, his own fears, mirrored by some of the others, that they were simply taking too long to make progress. Rondon's plodding had finally resulted in a brief, if not sharp, conversation, Rondon accepting Roosevelt's argument that his crew, including of course Roosevelt, was the priority. The longer they remained on the river, the greater the risk of catastrophe. If not that, simply running out of food might be the greater problem for all of them.

HE HAD HEARD the shots, stared out that way, all the *camaradas* doing the same. He heard whooping now, knew Kermit's voice, saw the engineer, Lyra, pushing toward them through the brush, Kermit just behind. Kermit yelped again, the sound Roosevelt had heard often in Africa, saw now Kermit dragging a pair of monkeys.

"We've got meat!"

Roosevelt was surprised at the enthusiasm of the *camaradas,* the men stopping their work, calling to the others downstream, a spontaneous celebration.

IT WASN'T YET fully dark, the campfire still high, Roosevelt staring that way, his tongue tasting the monkey meat still, a greasy film inside his teeth. Quite tasty, he thought. It wasn't his first time eating monkey, but this was a variety he had never seen and quite likely would never see again. Cherrie had already gone to work, retrieving the skin of one, the good work of the expert taxidermist, something Roosevelt had not done since he was a teen. There had been a large bird killed as well, which was made into a rich, dark soup, even tastier than the monkeys.

He looked at Cherrie now, nearer the fire. "What was that bird again?"

"*Jacu.* Looks much like a pheasant."

"Tasted like pheasant, grouse maybe. Very good."

Cherrie seemed lost in a haze of weariness, kept his eyes on the fire.

Rondon was there now, as though on patrol, the man seeming rarely to sleep.

"You must learn more of my language, Colonel. We have observed that your lessons are progressing slowly. The only two words you seem to remember are *mais canja.* Rondon smiled. "In time, you will do better than only to ask for *more soup.*"

March 15, 1914

He had taken his ritual morning bath, others had as well, discretely slipping into the river, paying heed to Rondon's warning about stirring up a school of piranhas. The *camaradas* had been hard at work repairing and replacing canoes, the damage coming from unavoidable collisions, rushes of high water, or simply the wear and tear the river and its banks inflicted on boats of solid wood, especially ones that rode so low in the water, weighed down with their human and other cargo.

The day seemed to offer them good progress, smooth water for several kilometers. He sat in the rearmost canoe, could see a sharp bend ahead, heard it now, the thunderous roar of yet another span of white water. His pilot, a *camarada* named Luiz, eased the canoe to the bank, slid it solidly ashore, leapt out, anchoring the bow, Roosevelt, Cherrie, and the doctor stepping out. He saw Rondon now, hurrying back, and Rondon said, "There is an island. The river is split into two, both very rough. I shall go with Lyra to see if the left branch is passable. I have ordered Kermit to halt his boat where he is. I shall tell you as soon as I know what we are to do next."

Rondon moved off quickly, and Roosevelt followed, Cherrie with him. The jungle seemed to clear slightly, no great obstacles, and Roosevelt could see the bend in the river, saw Rondon and Lyra on the left side, Kermit and two of the *camaradas* on the right branch, anchored at the bank. There was a rock outcropping to Roosevelt's front now, halting progress, and Cherrie said, "Nothing for us to do but prepare another camp. I'll go back and see if we can find a suitable spot." He paused. "Don't worry, Colonel. Your boy will be fine. Rondon will see to it."

He watched Kermit, the other two men, a hard discussion, all three standing at their canoe. Kermit bent low, shoved the canoe into the water, gesturing frantically, the other two men seeming to obey, stepping in, taking their positions at the bow and stern. They shoved off, slid into the white water, the two *camaradas* paddling manically, a desperate attempt to keep the craft straight downriver. Roosevelt felt a deep cold, thought, What the hell are you doing? Rondon said to stop. So, stop!

The canoe disappeared in the rocks and white foam, Roosevelt staring helplessly. He wanted to follow, to keep up, but there was no hope, nothing for him to do but back away, one last pleading thought: What are you doing?

HE SAW RONDON first, the engineer Lyra with him. Kermit came behind, and even from a distance, Roosevelt could see he was completely soaked. Rondon was moving quickly, a hard look, said to Roosevelt, "We must search. Joao and Simplicio are missing. Colonel, you and the doctor remain here. Mr. Cherrie, if you will join us."

The other *camaradas* had gathered, fell in with Rondon as they moved back down the river.

Roosevelt looked at his son, saw pain and sadness, blended with guilt.

"Why aren't you helping them? What did you do?"

Kermit shook his arms, wiped at the water still dripping from his clothes.

"I thought there would be a clearer passage to the right, so I insisted that my men go that way." He paused, and Roosevelt saw tears, a rarity. "We hit the rapids pretty hard. I thought we would make it, but they didn't end. We must have gone half a mile. The water finally capsized us, threw everybody out. The canoe is gone."

"Blast the canoe! What happened to your men?"

"I don't know. I thought they would swim to the bank. I caught a tree limb. Saved me."

"Rondon will want more than that. Did you try to help the others?"

"Papa, I could barely help myself. I nearly drowned. I think I'm falling ill. At least I was able to salvage my rifle."

Roosevelt cringed, added up the "*I*'s he had just heard. It had been much the same in Africa, Kermit taking risks, no matter the danger to anyone else. But no one had died in Africa.

THEY NEVER FOUND the canoe. Kermit had continued a search on his own, found a single paddle, the only piece remaining of a craft they desperately needed, along with the small crates of food and supplies the canoe held.

Rondon's search had been more productive. One of the *camaradas*, Joao, was found clinging to the riverbank, wet and coughing, but alive. But the tragedy had a name, Simplicio, most certainly a victim of the rapids, his body never found, assumed by now to have been swept well downriver.

Per custom, Rondon created a sign, dug it into the edge of the river. Whether anyone would ever read it made no difference to Rondon or his men. It said simply, IN THESE RAPIDS DIED POOR SIMPLICIO.

The mood of the entire expedition had changed, and Roosevelt did as he was told by Rondon, remain to one side while the *camaradas* cleared yet another camp. He saw a change in them as well, none of the smiling, backslapping teasing that had so often eased their labor.

The rain had begun again, a hard, soaking storm, and Roosevelt watched the men working, couldn't escape the guilt he hoped that Kermit was feeling. Kermit was in his shelter off to one side, and Roosevelt looked that way, saw the young man staring out as he was, pensive, expressionless. He saw Rondon coming up from the river, another fruitless search. The colonel was trailed by his dog, a preciously obedient hound named Lobo. Roosevelt heard the sound now, a hard howl coming from far into the trees. To his surprise, Lobo suddenly darted into the jungle, chasing the sound. Rondon shouted, the dog too caught up in the chase to listen. Rondon disappeared, and Roosevelt crawled out from the canvas, the rain too intense for his spectacles. He could only listen, saw Cherrie and the others doing the same. The chase belonged to Rondon, the rest helpless, another yelp, then more. The gunshot came now, adding to the agonizing mystery, Roosevelt recognizing the sound of a rifle, certainly Rondon's. The tension in all of them was unbearable, all the men, Kermit included, standing now in the rain, staring at the thickets where Rondon had gone. Roosevelt slipped back, a hand on his own rifle, thought, We don't know what it is.

Kermit said, "You can't go, Papa. Too dangerous."

Roosevelt wanted to protest, but he saw motion in the brush, Rondon emerging, rifle on his shoulder, carrying the dog. Roosevelt saw now, two long arrows passed through the dog's body. He stepped closer, Rondon laying the dog down at his feet. He looked up at Roosevelt, a glance to the others. "Indians. I didn't see them. But they saw Lobo. This is their sign. *Leave.*"

Roosevelt moved closer still, looked down at the dog, motionless, small rivers of blood blending in with the rain. He wanted to offer the man something, comforting words, Rondon now with his face in his hands. But there was only silence, the grief spreading through them all, and Roosevelt backed away, moved instead to his canvas shelter, sat, ignored what might lay beneath him. The arrogance, he thought. We come here to spread our civilization, to open up this land to the eyes of the world, as though we are doing a good thing. But already the jungle, the river have given us a lesson, that we do not own this place, that we will not win. I have dared to believe that I could come here and stand tall, Roosevelt, the famous man, so powerful in Washington. But here there is no authority but nature. None of us is in command. And unless we understand that more men will die.

He stared out at Rondon, the man's grief, knew he had to give something, even a gesture. He tried to stand, one hand pushing on the soft ground, but sat again, a cough coming, a hard, raspy sound, a dull pain in his chest, the chill of a fever.

CHAPTER 51

The rains had let up, the ground around him a pool of brown mud. On the river, the *camaradas,* aided by Kermit and the engineer, Lyra, were roping the canoes, dragging them up onto the makeshift pathway, hoping to transport them overland yet again, a full kilometer to the next smooth water. The supplies had been hauled ashore on the backs of all the men, Roosevelt included, but the heaviest work was almost always left to the *camaradas,* taut ropes and taut muscles working to protect each craft from destruction. It wasn't a perfect system, hidden rocks grabbing and tearing at the bottoms of the waterlogged wood, some of the canoes splitting apart simply from wear and tear, others capsizing, forcing the men to halt their progress while they worked to pull the canoe out of the water.

The night before, as the *camaradas* had labored to chop out yet another replacement canoe, Rondon had called the rest of them together, his own version of a council of war. They had sat together with a smoking fire, nearly extinguished by a drizzling rain, which only added to the gloom of Rondon's message. So far the expedition had traveled approximately seventy miles, with an unknown distance still to come. Food was becoming a serious concern, the original rations reduced by a third. What had not been consumed by the men had simply been lost in the rapids. The wild game they had hoped to hunt had been far more scarce than even Rondon had predicted. It was the occasional monkey and larger bird that had been responsible for supplying the necessary protein the men needed to keep up the labor required to maneuver and build the canoes. Of the original seven canoes that had begun the trip, five were gone—sunk, smashed, or simply useless from waterlogging. Already, the *camaradas* had been busy at nearly every camp, seeking out and cutting larger trees, digging them out with their tools, a hollowed-out tree eventually coming into service as one more canoe. But that work was laborious and time-consuming, and of course required a daily amount of substantial rations for men who never asked for any favors.

Roosevelt sat alongside the one remaining tent, which, despite his protests, had been set aside as his shelter. He watched Kermit working alongside one of the larger men, pulling a canoe up away from the water, the necessity of patching yet one more leak. It was curious to him how different the *camaradas* were from each other, their skin a variety of colors from almost white to dark brown. They don't seem to pay the slightest bit of attention to that, he thought. A lesson there. They're just men working together for a common purpose.

He studied Kermit now, the young man's shoes nearly gone, rotted away by the constant soaking. He can use my spare pair, he thought. Spare *anything* will be a luxury we cannot afford soon. I think I have one more pair of underdrawers. Unless the termites get them.

It had been two nights earlier, termites invading Cherrie's gear, devouring every piece of soft material, including a hat, canvas leggings, and the duffel bag itself. One more kind of torment in this place, he thought. But somehow Cherrie keeps up the good cheer, wants us all to appreciate the astounding variety of creatures, as he does. But he certainly didn't expect to have his gear consumed by ravenous insects.

Rondon appeared now, emerging silently from the dense thickets nearby.

"Colonel, you should see this. Come. Bring your rifle."

There was no smile in Rondon's orders, but Roosevelt obeyed, the familiar nagging stir in his chest, the potential for some new kind of disaster.

He followed Rondon, Cherrie coming as well, and Rondon motioned with his hand, *quiet.*

They pushed slowly through dense, uncut vines, Roosevelt curious why Rondon wasn't using his machete. But he knew better than to ask questions, could see a break up ahead, Rondon suddenly squatting down as though surveying what lay ahead. He pushed forward again, now stood, the jungle giving way to a wide swath of open ground more than a hundred yards across and, scattered in uneven rows, large grass huts. Rondon stood frozen for a long moment, and Roosevelt stepped up close to him, wondered at the man's thoughts—revenge, hatred, or just natural curiosity.

Rondon said, "They left a short while ago, and maybe not because of us. There are some utensils, clay pots, some with spoiled food, mostly a kind of soup. And ants."

Cherrie reached down, slapped at his bare ankles.

"Ants. They're everywhere. That's why these people left. The ants came. I've heard of this. Swarms just arrive out of nowhere, call it a bloom, like flies. You can't survive them crawling over everything."

Roosevelt felt the itch, mostly in his own mind, but now he saw them on his boots, circling their way up to his calves. He brushed them away, mostly, felt the first sting now. Rondon did the same, said, "We should withdraw."

They made their way back through the dense thickets, and Roosevelt realized just how close they were to the water. Well, of course, he thought. The Indians would be discreet if they could, stay back, hidden. But they still need the water, probably worshipped the river. They certainly wouldn't worship us.

March 27, 1914

"I can't say I've ever eaten a toucan. Always thought they were a beautiful bird. They're certainly tasty."

Cherrie was beside him, said without smiling, "Nature provides. If you ask nicely."

No one responded, faces down, focusing on whatever remained in their bowls. It was becoming harder every day, the weakness from the astounding amount of labor each man had to contribute, whether they were white or *camarada*. There was no longer a division of labor, every man now adding what he could to the survival of the group.

The insects had become routine, the kinds of torment changing with the time of day or night. Fortunately, Roosevelt's ointment repellent had proved partially effective, keeping the worst of the blood-sucking flies and other varmints away from his exposed skin. He had learned quickly that if a man didn't sweat and if the rains stayed away, the gooey stuff usually worked. At least, there could be a few hours' sleep.

Rondon stood, a signal they all recognized. The meal was over.

"Please move with me, Colonel, Kermit. All of you. I have something very special to say."

They followed him to the edge of the water, the rapids above, calm water below, a tributary flowing into the river from the east.

"I have given this much thought. Brazil is honored that the former president of the United States has chosen to lead this expedition, with so little known about our trials and so much peril to face. On behalf of the Brazilian government, I hereby name this river Rio Roosevelt. This tributary shall now be called the Rio Kermit. Salutes to these men and to the United States."

The cheering was long and loud, Roosevelt responding with cheers of his own, offering a toast to the government of Brazil, to every member of the party. Rondon had made a wooden sign, as official as it was crude, planted now on a pole a few yards away from the water's edge. Roosevelt stepped forward, stared for a long moment, said, "I did not come here for this, for my name to emblazon this place. Your graciousness has been overwhelming. But I feel we go about our duties now, to make this journey a profitable one, and that we may all return to our families. I am quite certain our families would prefer that as well."

"We must transport the lighter canoes downstream again. The rapids should allow them to float without damage, but we must man the ropes to maintain control. You all know what to do. I'm not certain how many more canoes we can make, not as weak as we are becoming." Rondon looked over at the group of *camaradas,* mostly seated, some squatting, focused on one.

"Paishon, how many are sick?"

The man rose, enormous, deep-brown skin.

"Seven dysentery. Three fever. They'll work. No one will say they cannot help."

The men nodded, brief words of agreement. Rondon looked back at Roosevelt, Kermit and the others scattered behind him.

"Half the men are in poor shape. I must ask you all to assist with the ropes, even more perhaps than you have done before."

Roosevelt studied one of the *camaradas,* the man they called Julio. He was a large man, black skin, a hint of rebellion in the man's face. There had been arguments among the *camaradas,* words Roosevelt didn't understand, but the tone had been clear. The senior men, Paishon for one, had confronted Julio more than once for slacking, failing to pull his weight at a time when every man's effort was critical. The white men had stayed completely out of any conflicts the *camaradas* might have had among themselves, only Rondon launching an angry tirade when it was appropriate. But Roosevelt had been paying more attention lately, knowing now how important each man's work could be for everyone's survival.

The fever he had felt days before had never really gone away, the shivering sweat that rolled over him each night something he kept to himself. He had caught the glimpses from Doctor Cajazeira, the man watching over him, mostly by staying away, something Roosevelt appreciated. He wanted no special attention, nothing special at all, including rations. It was not helpful that, for the past few days, their remaining tins of canned meats had seemed to empty on their own, as though some of the supplies were being stolen.

He saw the usual smirk on Julio's face, wondered what the man was thinking.

The group dispersed, several of the *camaradas* making the trek upstream, Kermit joining them. Roosevelt moved toward his shelter, began to gather his gear, rolling and folding, stuffing most of what he now carried into his duffel. He glanced over to Cherrie, the man already packed up, gathering a different kind of gear: the specimens he had brought to camp, taken down with his small-gauge shotgun, birds mostly, every type and color. They had been skinned carefully, salted from the inside, eliminating any problem with the smell. Roosevelt stood straight, stretched his back, said, "Well done, sir."

Cherrie looked up, smiled. "Perhaps. I dare say, some of these are unknown to science. Nearly all are unknown to the museum. All I require now for a successful expedition is to survive."

Roosevelt heard shouting upriver, turned, saw a pair of the smaller canoes, lashed together, upended, the two men guiding them launched into the water. The men scrambled to the safety of the shore, but the canoes were dragged low into deep water by the swirling current, pressed hard against a submerged ledge. Roosevelt moved quickly, jumped into the river, others following, all hands trying to save the precious canoes. He was buffeted by the violence of the current, the canoes too deep, and he felt a hand on his shoulder, pulling him up.

On the surface again, he heard splashing, loud shouts, saw Kermit and others standing out on large rocks, ropes tossed, several of the *camaradas* diving deep, securing the ropes to the canoes. They worked together, the crafts finally brought up, now clear of the swirling water, eased to the shore.

Their relief was obvious, none of the *camaradas* wanting to delay their journey for days while constructing more craft, no one seeking any more futile struggles against the swarms of insects that met them at every portage. Roosevelt sat on a fat rock, wiped at his face, his spectacles gone. He rose, moved toward his duffel, many more pairs of the precious glasses inside. And now he saw the blood. He tried to ignore it, moved to his gear, heard Cherrie.

"Colonel. You are injured."

The doctor was there quickly, squatted low.

"Please sit, sir."

Roosevelt obeyed, tried to ignore the stinging pain, his shin scraped, a deep wound. The doctor slid his pants leg up, the gash flowing blood. Cherrie stood over him, said,

"We must patch this, Doctor."

Cajazeira said, "I am aware, Mr. Cherrie. First is to stop the bleeding. I have very little in the way of antibiotics, and I'm afraid that's what is most required here. We don't know what kind of organisms are swimming around inside this wound."

Roosevelt appreciated the doctor's touch, the man swabbing at the open wound, trying to stop the bleeding.

"By Godfrey, Doctor, but that is tender. It's my other leg that always needed care. I don't wish to be a no-leg cripple."

"I can only try to keep the wound clean and attempt to keep you off your feet."

Cherrie said, "Good luck with that, Doctor."

THE WOUND GREW rapidly worse with the infection that Doctor Cajazeira was helpless to prevent. Roosevelt stayed flat on his back now, aided by a vicious rainstorm that prevented anyone from doing their work effectively. They had placed him inside the sole remaining tent, his protests useless against the resolve of the men who seemed to have more concern for his agony than he did.

They watched over him in shifts, Kermit, Cherrie, the doctor, and as the rain began to lessen, the work began, sounds Roosevelt knew well, the boats lashed together, the larger canoes stocked with supplies. But there was despair as well, voices reaching him, more rapids just downriver, the scouting parties, usually Rondon himself, returning with the news that put a heavy drag on the moods of the men. For now the rapids seemed unending, higher hills on both sides of the river funneling the water into a tighter chute, increasing the speed and roughness, creating far more danger than they had faced before.

For Roosevelt, that kind of news brought even more misery than the sharp pain in his leg. He was helpless to offer any kind of assistance, and of course the men who cared for him were taking themselves away from other duties.

He had tried to walk with the rest of the camp, doing as they had done before, hauling the canoes overland, the supplies. Roosevelt did his best to put on the good show, but the weakness was increasing rapidly, the infection all through him, and, no matter the smooth ground, he limped clumsily, stumbled.

They pitched the tent again, Roosevelt too weak to protest. They laid him down on the camp's only cot, the thin mattress long since devoured by termites or any number of other creatures. As he lay, shaking with anger, shaking as much with the chills from the return of his fever, he swore at himself, stared out at daylight, had to believe they had stopped here only because of him. There is more time, he thought. They should go on. This is madness.

The doctor was there now, sitting on the lone camp chair.

"Your fever is no better. Perhaps worse. Kermit says you have had heart pains before. That can't be helping you now. You need as much strength as you can muster. There is only so much we can do to help you."

Roosevelt fought against the anger inside him, the feeling of uselessness.

"Doctor, in my knapsack, a side pocket, there is a small bottle. It is morphine. I have always carried it on journeys such as this. I always knew there was a chance of being seriously injured or of becoming, as I am now, a serious burden, risking the lives of others. I cannot do that, Doctor. I wish for you to observe me carefully, and if I become delirious, unable to continue, you will administer the morphine."

"No, sir. I will not."

Roosevelt was surprised by the man's abruptness.

"Then you must leave me here. Just . . . go. I would rather die here, in this jungle, than have the world know that I forced the entire expedition to wait on me, like some mewling child. Where is Kermit? I must tell him."

Roosevelt was surprised to see Rondon at the entrance to the tent.

"Colonel, forgive me for hearing your conversation. If the doctor were to abide by your wishes, it would be murder. I will not have that any more than he would. You are not our burden, sir. You are the reason for this expedition, you are why the world cares about us, waits for us, hopes for our success. You are as important to us as any boats or laborers or rations. I will tell you that we have scouted downriver several kilometers. There are rapids and falls like none we have yet seen.

We cannot go by boat, and I have instructed the men to create a portage road, to transport everything until we are past the rough water. I assure you, Colonel, it is no great burden to transport you as well." He looked at the doctor. "What is his temperature?"

"One hundred four. I will administer quinine, which should combat the malarial fever. I do not know how much of his suffering comes from the infection in his leg."

"Do what you must, Doctor." Rondon looked outside the tent, skyward. "There is another storm coming. The clouds are green. That means violence. There could be hail. I must help secure the supplies."

Roosevelt was even angrier now.

"This is foolishness. I cannot be an invalid."

The doctor pushed firmly on his shoulders, held him on the cot.

"Colonel, right now, you are my patient. You can be the president another day. For now, you will do as I say. Lie here quietly, allow the fever to work through you, allow your body to fight the infection."

Roosevelt tried to focus his eyes, realized they had removed his spectacles.

"I am not afraid of death, Doctor. But I do not take well to weakness. I will not admit to anyone that I am too fragile, too frail to attack life."

"Colonel, right now, life is attacking *you*. Rest up. There will be other fights."

"THE DOCTOR TOLD me what you asked of him."

Roosevelt knew Kermit's voice, was too bleary-eyed to see his face.

"He should not have . . ."

"Papa, I am not leaving you here, whether or not you are a corpse. We began this together, and we shall end it that way. This expedition is in a bad way right now, and you cannot assume you are the cause. The river has become evil, steep gorges we must traverse, every man doing what his strength will allow. Food continues to disappear, and there is suspicion about that among the *camaradas*. The weather has been brutal, the hardest rains I have ever seen. Our best hope is that we can pass by the worst of the terrain and find calm water. The larger hills appear to flatten out several kilometers ahead, which might allow the river to widen." Kermit leaned closer to him. "I will not abandon you, no matter how much you want to leave your bones in this jungle."

He glimpsed a smile on Kermit's sunburned face, then closed his eyes.

"You have grown up, my boy. I would have it no other way."

April 3, 1914

They were preparing to move again, another day struggling against rapids, bordered by sheer cliffs. Kermit had worked alongside several of the *camaradas,* hauling canoes by ropes, lowering them into smoother water by climbing foot over foot along the ragged rock faces. But the toll on the men was near a breaking point, food supplies seriously diminished, Rondon and the others aware that with hunger and desperation comes the chance of mutiny, that should any one or more of the *camaradas* become desperate enough to steal the entire food supply, no one would ever know what became of the half dozen white men.

Roosevelt's fever had pulled him downward for several days, Kermit and the others standing watch, wondering if today would be the time when Roosevelt's heart would simply give up. Finally, with the doctor's quinine, the fever seemed to break. But the infection in his leg continued to fester, keeping him off his feet. The men had rigged up a canvas tent draped over a pole in the larger canoe. But there was nothing resembling a mattress, Roosevelt forced to make a bed out of old ration boxes.

He could hear the clatter of movement, slid out from under the makeshift shelter, but there was no sign of the larger canoe. He saw Cherrie, gathering up his specimens again, a few added the day before. "What's happening?"

"Nothing for you to be concerned about, my friend. They're still carrying the dugouts downriver, even the larger ones. Brutal ground, rock faces forty feet high. Kermit is doing an outstanding job of it. Several of us had our doubts, but he's proven us wrong. He's first class. I hope you know that."

Roosevelt sat up, probed the sharp burn in his leg. Cajazeira was there now, the doctor shaking his head. "Rondon wanted to shelve the whole operation, have us take to the woods, every man for himself. Damned fool. That's a death warrant for every one of us. We've talked him out of it. Even the *camaradas* wouldn't hear that kind of nonsense. I think Rondon is pretty discouraged."

Cherrie said, "We all are. But he's responsible to his government for all our lives. That has to be an enormous weight. Game has been nonexistent, and we need meat. The *camaradas* are in rough shape. Almost every one of them is suffering from dysentery. They don't wear shoes. Have you seen their feet? Busted up, bleeding, swollen. Not sure how they do it."

The doctor said, "There is one problem with those fellows, though. Julio is obviously a bit of a slacker, not pulling his weight. The head man, Paishon, gives him hell fairly often. It's a bad feeling watching them go at each other."

Cherrie looked out toward the river, said, "That's him, there. What the hell's he doing?

Roosevelt could see a stack of rifles against a stout tree, Julio picking one out, moving quickly into the jungle.

The doctor said, "Maybe he's going hunting. Can't fault him for that. He might have better luck than we do."

After a long minute, the shot reached them, then silence, and Roosevelt slid himself out into full open, said, "I hope he got something. Wonder what?"

The shouts came out of the jungle now, three of the *camaradas* running headlong toward them, stumbling, out of breath, hard, panicked voices.

"Julio has killed Paishon!"

Roosevelt struggled to his feet, grabbed one of the rifles, followed by the others. He stared for a long second into the brush, expected to see the

muzzle of Julio's rifle, the man deranged, desperate, looking to kill anyone who stood between him and rations. But the jungle was silent, the
other *camaradas* gathering, Rondon there now, the men moving quickly
into the jungle. Roosevelt wanted to follow, cursed the agony in his leg.
But the search was brief, the men returning, Rondon glum, emotional.

"Julio has killed Paishon. We found the body. We also found Julio's rifle. That is one good thing, the only good thing. He cannot
shoot any more of us. I don't know where Julio has gone, but we must
maintain careful watch. The jungle will not feed him, so he will come
for food."

Roosevelt felt a boiling inside, far worse than the infection. "He
must be tracked, arrested, and executed!"

Rondon seemed surprised at Roosevelt's fury, said, "In Brazil, that
is not possible. If he is caught, he will stand trial. He will not be murdered."

"That's not how it is in my country. If you murder, you will die."

"Respectfully, Colonel Roosevelt, you are not in your country.
What is the greater concern now is that we have lost Paishon, one of
our strongest men. Colonel, please return to your shelter. We have
much to do to move past the obstructions in our path."

"What is Rondon doing about Julio?"

Cherrie lowered his voice, as though offering a secret.

"Rondon wants to search for him, send a couple of the *camaradas*
back and see what they can find."

"My God, why? We are barely alive now, and food is scarce. Stopping to make way for a search party is foolishness."

"Colonel, you are the only one among us who can state such a
thing. Rondon and Lyra have always insisted, quietly, that mapping
this river, doing their surveys, is our most important task. They might
send a search party back for Julio, but halting our progress is their
priority. It's all about maps, Colonel. Kermit and I have tried to medi-
ate this, keeping you out of the discussion. You are in no condition to
argue with anyone. But Rondon will not budge, and he controls more

here than you do. One more thing. According to the *camaradas,* when Paishon was killed, he fell forward. That means he will pursue his killer for all time. It's not a bad tale."

"It's fine with me."

RONDON WAS AS stubborn as Roosevelt was adamant, and though Rondon insisted that the momentary halt was to launch a search party, the colonel and his engineer lost no time mapping another tributary that flowed into the river from the east. Roosevelt was too sick to argue the point, and despite a few harsh words between the two colonels, Rondon got his way. Julio had approached the river, calling out to the passing crafts a mile or more back, the canoes in no position to turn about, and, as Roosevelt noted to them all, the party had no way to imprison or secure Julio until they reached civilization. As they continued downriver, there had been no further calls from Julio, no sign of him at all. Roosevelt assumed, as they all did, that if he was not simply swallowed by the jungle, the local Indians would find him, likely treating him as more of an intruder than they had Rondon's gentle dog.

HE TRIED TO keep up, the steps agonizing, a few at a time, then a pause, desperate breathing. Kermit was there, a shoulder bent low supporting Roosevelt's arm. He stepped again, a short way, the doctor with a finger on Roosevelt's neck.

"Your heart is racing. You must sit."

"I cannot, Doctor."

The words came as Kermit lowered him to a wide rock, Cherrie there as well. Roosevelt fought to breathe, said, "I do wish you would all just go on. This is madness, looking after me like mother hens."

Kermit said, "Let's try again. Come on, Papa. Stand up. I've got you."

"No. Too weak. This is a good place to sit. Just go. I've had enough coddling."

Cherrie sat beside him, said, "I had a friend, very good friend. One day, he asked me for a pistol, and I thought he had a good need for it, so I gave it to him. He killed himself that same day. I will not allow another of my good friends to die by his own hand. Get up. We have to walk."

April 6, 1914

Despite the quinine, his fever had returned, the doctor hovering over him anxiously. Kermit and Cherrie stood close, none of them expecting Roosevelt to survive another night. Through it all, Roosevelt mumbled and chattered, delirious, keeping the others awake, adding to their fears. But survive he did, facing a new day with clear eyes and an unusual burst of energy.

They launched the canoes, the river calming, at least for the next mile. At the next portage, the men insisted on carrying him with a makeshift sling, but Roosevelt would have none of it. He walked, staggered, sat often in his folding camp chair, but by the end of the day, he had reached their new campsite. And there was the first stroke of good luck they had seen in days. Three monkeys were shot, fish were caught, and the men finally had meat.

To Roosevelt's dismay, his momentary clarity of mind revealed that nearly every one of the *camaradas* was ill, mostly dysentery. But worse for him, Kermit had been suffering a fever for days, the same fever he had seemed unable to avoid from the first days of the expedition. And now the fever belonged to Cherrie as well, the man nearly as debilitated as Roosevelt, barely able to walk for the past several days. What energy Cherrie had been able to muster, he had devoted to caring for Roosevelt.

For Cherrie, there was one glorious sign that none of the others recognized. Large vultures had been seen, wide, arcing circles over the tops of the great trees. It took the naturalist, the bird expert, to reveal what that could mean. He knew that the preferred habitat for vultures was flatter ground. The flatter the ground, the calmer the river that ran through it.

For the next week, the river was indeed kinder, the canoes making greater distances between portages, the river widening, calmer still. And then, on April 12, Easter Sunday, one of the *camaradas* returned excitedly to camp with a piece of news no one expected to receive. Protruding from one bank of the river was a vine, cut with a sharp knife or axe blade. The Indians had never been known to traverse the river, so the cut had to have been made by a man in a boat or canoe. That could only mean that someone had come upriver from the other direction.

CHAPTER 52

April 15, 1914
The River

Rondon stood with his hands on his hips, enormously satisfied with himself.

"Rubber trees. Great clusters of them. That will draw workers, maybe even their families. We must be close to the tributaries of the Amazon. Perhaps very close."

Roosevelt managed to stand, Kermit helping him to his camp chair. He saw what they all saw, the strangely crude sign on each side of the river, carved by fire with the initials JA.

Roosevelt had questions, his mind fogging over, frustrating, raising his temper. "Who is that? Do we know?"

The faces turned toward him, concern again, as there had been for the past several days. Kermit moved close to him. "No, Papa. But it's a sign. This is rubber tree land. Colonel Rondon said that. A rubber farmer, maybe a ranch owner, had to leave these signs, sort of like staking his claim to this land. It is a very good thing."

Roosevelt slumped in the chair, his brain swirling with heat. "Don't speak to me as though I am an idiot. I don't know any JA."

Kermit seemed to give up, and Rondon moved closer, bent low, examining. "Put him back in the canoe, lie him flat. Use the canvas to make him comfortable. It is all we have. Shelter his face with his helmet. He doesn't need any more sunshine."

Kermit and Cherrie moved to the dugout, spread the canvas, as two of the stronger *camaradas* came forward, following Rondon's motioning hand. They lifted Roosevelt slowly, each one with an arm under his, carried him to the dugout, Kermit and Cherrie helping him in.

He was flat now, the crushed food boxes beneath him, covered in a futile attempt at comfort by a single side of canvas. Above him, a blinding sun blocked only partially by his pith helmet, his one feeble hand holding it in place. He felt the dugout rock slightly, wanted to see, to help, but the fatigue held him down, sweat running down his neck, soaking through his shirt. He began to feel angry, growing now into raw fury, anger at his own weakness, at the curse he was putting on the others, forcing them to care for this weakling, the handicap that could jeopardize the entire expedition. He wanted to call out, summon them all, give the order that, by God, he was *Roosevelt,* he was in command, and if he demanded to be left behind, they must obey. He saw movement, realized it was Kermit and the doctor, and he removed the helmet, the two men leaning over him now, one hand on his forehead, and still the rocking of the crowded dugout.

"What do you want? What is happening?"

"Please, Papa. Just lie still. We are moving again. The river seems to be smooth for a good ways yet."

Cajazeira said, "You are still very feverish, sir. I must put a drain in your leg. It is festering, perhaps more dangerous than before. We shall find shade after a bit, and I shall do the operation. There is no anesthetic, as you know."

"Is there never any anesthetic? Fine, I will endure. My leg hurts, Doctor, terribly. Any relief is welcome. But it would be so much better for all . . . leave me here. I would rather die in a place where the footprints of civilization don't trample my bones."

Kermit moved away, more rocking, low splashes as the *camaradas* worked the paddles.

How much more of this? he thought. Is this what happens to old men who trespass where only the strong will survive? And who the hell is JA?

He heard low calls, familiar voices, Cherrie and, farther away, Rondon. He tried to sit up, no energy for it, lay there in his own steaming sweat, the boat rocking yet again, infernal movement.

"What is it? What is happening?"

He felt a hand on his shoulder, Kermit's voice.

"Quiet, Papa. It's a house."

"Indians?"

"No, Papa. It's a *house*. A real house. Someone lives here. My God, Papa, we've reached civilization!"

"Is anyone home?"

"Please, stay here, stay flat. Colonel Rondon is going ashore. He is being very careful. There are at least two house dogs, and they do not seem wild."

"Damn it all, I can be careful. I want to see."

Kermit helped him to sit, and he saw them now, Rondon and a pair of *camaradas* probing around the house, not much more than a grass thatched hut with a smaller one beside it. He saw something unusual now, a rarity, as rare as a lonely hut in the midst of the jungle. Rondon was smiling.

THE MAN'S NAME was Joachim Antonio, JA, and, as Rondon had guessed, he was one of hundreds of rubber gatherers pushing their efforts deeper into the Amazonian jungle. Though the first house they reached was recently abandoned, Rondon led them on, more huts downriver. After reassuring the first locals they reached that they were, in fact, not hostile, and certainly not the feared Indians, they continued downriver. As Rondon predicted, they began to encounter more signs of the rubber tree workers, more huts, and then they came upon one old Black man, smiling and generous with whatever food he could offer, a man who lived only for fishing on the great river.

Below there were gentler rapids, then more huts, larger houses, smoking chimneys, children and their mothers, none resembling the naked Indians from well upriver. They spoke Rondon's native Portuguese, though they were dumbstruck by Rondon's explanation of how they arrived to this place, how many rapids, men and boats lost, and just why they bore this ailing man, older, larger, who Rondon told them was very special.

With the sun and rain showers still relentless, Roosevelt's pain and delirium and pure misery were even worse. He ordered them to prop him up, had to see the sources of so much cheerful talk. He could see it all now, the river wide and mostly flat, the *camaradas* maneuvering the four remaining craft with perfect skill, a relief for them as much as it was for the others. And now, a single shot from a rifle, far distant, downriver. Rondon stood, precariously in the other dugout, waved both arms, Roosevelt burning with curiosity. Trouble? Again? Indians? No, they don't have rifles. Do they?

He tried to shut down the voices in his brain, focused on Rondon, more waving, holding his rifle now, aimed skyward, firing. Rondon began to shout, a celebration, the words joyful, boisterous voice, louder now.

"We were right! *We are here!*"

Roosevelt lay back, too weak, could feel the energy in the rest of them, hard cheers, Kermit beside him, fast words, too fast. He felt sleep coming, no, fought it, had to know. And now, a heavy bump, the dugout colliding with the shore. The cheers and loud talk continued, and the hat was lifted away, faces looking down, Rondon cheerful, energetic.

"Colonel Roosevelt, may I present to you Lieutenant Antonio de Sousa. He is my man, sent to this place to rendezvous with us, in the event this was the mouth of our river, the Rio Roosevelt." He stood upright now, said, "Lieutenant, we have been in a bad way, but we have survived. It can only be better now. Our mission has been a success. And this, Lieutenant, is Colonel Roosevelt, my partner, the president of the United States."

April 27, 1914
Near São João, Brazil

He was still desperately ill, open sores and boils now spread across his body, gaunt features worsening from the unstoppable dysentery. He tried to absorb their energy, Kermit standing close, eyeing him, Cherrie and the others never far away. The ceremony was uniquely Brazilian, Rondon surrounded by various officials, some in uniform, some in the garb of businessmen, farmers, fishermen. Rondon read aloud from his carefully prepared document, a perfectly accurate account of what they had experienced, what Rondon could claim to his government as their glorious accomplishment. Through it all, most of the men who listened attentively kept their eyes only on the larger man standing with great, painful effort. No matter the formal introductions, to those men assembled around him, Roosevelt's illness and agony could not sway their beliefs that here, before them, stood a king.

CHAPTER 53

"I close my eyes and I can still see the stars of the Big Dipper. It's right out here, of course, but in Brazil, it's so different, almost touching the horizon. You couldn't see the North Star. Below the horizon. But there was something in that one constellation that pointed *home*. It inspired considerable emotion then. And it does now. We had started in some unknown and treacherous place, where nothing was familiar, and we had finally arrived back to our world. It was so satisfying, so fulfilling. And I never forget that there was, of course, a terrible cost."

Hagedorn looked up from his writing.

"I've read your accounts of the expedition. Was it worth that cost?"

Roosevelt stared at the man for a long moment, wasn't sure how to respond.

"I think . . . yes. Not because I'm more famous for it, or because I accomplished something monumental that will change mankind. But if there is no cost, if nothing is at risk, the thing is not worth doing. In Brazil, some of our men died. A tragedy. But they risked their lives because it was worthwhile to them. Their wish was to accomplish something that, in their world, meant something profound. I'll tell you something, Mr. Hagedorn. Many people believe I went down there to enhance my fame, my reputation. Hogwash. I wish Colonel Rondon had never made such a ceremony of naming that river for me. It's on maps now, forevermore. I didn't earn that. Rondon could have made that journey on his own, could have made those discoveries, seen those extraordinary sights, and, yes, he might have lost men in the process. The discovery, the route of that river, the kinds of Indians, the birds and snakes and other creatures never seen by science, those were *his* to discover, and men like George Cherrie. They did the real work. I brought my name. I got him attention, both from his government and the world. For me, there was very little risk in that."

"But, sir, you almost died."

"That's not a badge of honor, Mr. Hagedorn. I jeopardized the entire party. And I wasn't the only one to be sick. Kermit, Cherrie, nearly all of the *camaradas* . . . There is no celebrity in being a weak link in the chain. I fear I was that link."

"Sir, I must ask, since you have allowed me such access to your thoughts . . . why have you not undertaken this memoir yourself? You have written on so many chapters of history, as well as some of your own adventures. You dismiss what you accomplished in Brazil, but still, you have written of it. There must be some pride in that."

"Mr. Hagedorn, that expedition . . . *was my last chance to be a boy.*"

Roosevelt wiped his forehead with his bare hand, angry at the sweat. He adjusted himself on the couch, leaned back slightly, relaxing his back, finding some comfort against one of Edith's pillows. He tried to focus on Hagedorn now, ignoring the small jab in his lungs, the constant itch of pain in his legs. His mind was still drifting, hard to focus, and he forced his voice to push through.

"We sailed home on the USS *Aidan,* I think. New York Harbor was a celebration all its own, welcoming me back. It is gratifying to see that, to feel the affection of the people. Pride. Yes, you said pride. I am respected by the people, and for that I am proud. But too many, politicians especially, depend on the respect they've earned to be forever, as though by one great deed they will be revered all their lives. Some, perhaps. But consider Ulysses Grant. Great man, great general. He could have rested on the respect he had earned in the war. But he knew it wouldn't last, and so he had to do more. So, there was President Grant. Then, Grant the memoirist. And George Washington . . . Do you know why I have such respect for Washington? Not for being the general, the president. He could have been *king,* the United States emerging as a monarchy. It was there, handed to him, and he said *no.* There's an act that deserves respect for all time. I have done nothing to equal that. I will say only that I have a clear conscience. There is pride in that."

Hagedorn laughed. "For a politician, that makes you a rarity."

"Maybe not. Not everyone is a thief. Just most of them."

"I know you are not fond of President Wilson. Has anyone ever explained to you the reasons why he would not allow you to raise a volunteer infantry division? Surely you could have attracted thousands of good soldiers to the cause."

The question made him angry all over again, a pot he had stirred for nearly four years. He looked down, put his hands on his knees, tried to sort out his words. Be careful, he thought. You have enemies enough as it is.

"There are two thoughts about Woodrow Wilson. He is president; he has experienced personal tragedy, the loss of his first wife, as I have. He was a state governor, as I was. He has taken on the massive task of serving as our president, as I have. Draw a line right there." He stopped, wiped again at his brow, glanced at the open doorway, surprised that Edith wasn't watching over him. "Throughout my entire public career, I have acted. He talks. I inspire emotional responses, anger perhaps, envy, happiness. There are people who want to slap my back, shake my hand. Or they try to kill me. Do you know that the last time I was on a speaking tour, a fellow threw a knife at me? He missed. But that act requires passion. Woodrow Wilson inspires yawns and platitudes. He thinks too much. He *fondles* ideas. He stood by and kept his hands clean through three years of the Great War, while an entire generation of young men died. Englishmen, Frenchmen, yes, even Germans, Russians, the rest destroyed by the most bloody and costly fighting in the history of mankind. And his response? 'I am too proud to fight.' All he did was demonstrate to the world that we were too weak to help our allies. He Kept Us Out of War—his great campaign slogan. No, he allowed the war to creep up onto our doorsteps, American merchant ships sunk off our own coastlines. So, finally, backed into a corner, he decides it's time for us to do our part, and we enter the war. Even then, he has no policy to propose, no advice to give, nothing to tell the world of our great resolve. Instead of leadership, he inspires dread and platitudes. His secretary of state, William Jennings Bryan, that great bass drum of a man . . . he resigns in protest at any hint of our entering the war. Protest! I imagine him telling Wilson that the best strategy is to *walk softly* . . . and just keep on walking. So, Bryan did. He quit rather than accept that we have responsibilities to the rest of the civilized world. Yes, I offered to raise a division of volunteers, to join with the American Expeditionary Force. I would have led it myself if they wanted me to. They rejected my offer for no more reason than that the offer had come from *me*. General Pershing was desperate for trained troops, and when I offered my own, many of them former Rough Riders, I was dismissed. Worse. I was ignored."

"And yet after turning you down, they made William Howard Taft a major general."

"Yes, how about that? The Mighty Balloon gets a commission, not that he ever commanded troops anywhere outside of his own front yard. How the kaiser must have trembled when he heard the news." He stopped. "No, I won't speak so poorly of Taft. He was a lousy president, but he's a profoundly decent human being. All he ever wanted, really, was to be chief justice of the Supreme Court. He knew he wasn't the man for the White House. The job made him weak-kneed, afraid to take an unpopular stand. It cost him a second term and, for a good while, my friendship."

"What about your second term? By the Constitution, you have technically only served one term of your own. You could certainly run again."

He didn't want to respond, but the words wouldn't stop.

"Wilson is terrified that I will run for president in 1920. Idiot. I proved my word when I chose not to run in 1916. I'm older and weaker now."

"But will you run? It has been said that you can't stay away, that the Republican Party can still reel you in with high praise."

He looked at Hagedorn without smiling, slowly shook his head. "They've already tried. And it would be a lie to say it's not a flicker somewhere in the back of my head. A newspaper in Brooklyn said it well: 'There is no other man in this country who can draw so large a crowd as Theodore Roosevelt.' Since they're not throwing rocks at me, I have to assume a good many of them would vote for me." He smiled, a small laugh. "They insist that I am such a talker, such a crowd pleaser, that if I'm not running for a single office this fall, it's because I'm running for *all* of them."

He drifted away for a moment, a sudden rush of unpleasant thoughts. "You'll ask me sooner or later, so no point in waiting. Earlier this year . . . I was deathly ill. The first time in my life I was truly afraid it was the end. I will spare you the extreme details, but I had surgeries that no man should endure. My ears, my . . . lower areas. More agonies from the malarial fever, the injuries to my legs."

"I am aware, sir. I wrote on some of those details in my first book."

"Yes, you did, didn't you? Well, I suppose there are no secrets anymore. My point, Mr. Hagedorn, is that my days of campaigning, or bellowing at the top of my lungs all those things that matter to me, shouting my voice through great auditoriums and lecture halls . . . it isn't there anymore. Change the subject. I'm not talking about that anymore."

"I have to ask, sir, and you may shut me up, certainly. How did you feel about all four of your boys volunteering to fight in the war?"

"Nothing in this country is ours for free. I have friends who did everything in their power to keep their boys out of the war. Their sons have turned out to be nothing more than pretty boys who know all the steps of the tango, how to make small talk at parties, all the proper kinds of socks and neckties—all of them useless and mollycoddled. My boys all volunteered willingly, and they all served this country well. Archie nearly died, Ted was injured frightfully by gas . . ." He paused. "You know the rest."

Hagedorn stood up, unexpectedly, said, "Sir, I believe that will be enough for today. I have an appointment in the city, to visit with your sister Anna. She has graciously allowed me to ask a number of relevant questions."

"Bamie will not lie to you, Mr. Hagedorn. Be assured of that. I'm not sure, however, that I would approve of what she has to say."

"Don't be concerned, sir. There will be nothing scandalous, I promise. I shall return here on Tuesday, the seventh, if that is all right with you."

"Check with Edie. She has command around here these days. She and the doctor."

Roosevelt looked toward the door, Edith standing with arms crossed and, behind her, his old valet, James Amos. Hagedorn slipped away, a brief bow to Edith, soft words he couldn't hear. Yes, he thought, be kind to her. She has all the power here.

Edith moved closer to him. "I really wish you would put Mr. Hagedorn off for a time. You expend too much of yourself."

"Does it show?"

Amos moved up beside her, seemed to examine him closely, a hard stare into Roosevelt's face. He was a tall man, wiry, exuding strength and a firm voice, not likely to allow Roosevelt to intimidate him. He had once served as Roosevelt's bodyguard after the loss of Big Bill Craig, but with the constant attendance of the Secret Service agents, Roosevelt was discouraged from having his own private guards. Amos had gone on to a career in law enforcement and criminal investigation, an astonishing accomplishment for a Black man in a mostly white profession. Roosevelt could see from the man's frown that Roosevelt's appearance must have matched just how poorly he felt.

"I wish I could say I'm happy to see you, James. If they called you here, it's only because I might require lifting. You're the only man I know strong enough to do so."

Edith said, "Teddy, he's here because you require assistance, someone to watch over you."

"That sounds like I need an angel."

Amos made a slight bow. "I been called worse, sir."

Edith said, "Teddy, you need a bath. Do you feel capable of bathing yourself?"

He tried to sit upright on the couch, a sharp pain in his chest, his legs seeming to fail him completely.

"I suppose maybe later. Not quite up to it right now."

"And that, Teddy, is one reason why Mr. Amos is here. He shall bathe you. Lord knows, you need it."

HE WAS BACK in the bed now, helped by Amos's strong hands.

"I swear you to secrecy, James. I don't need the women in this house hovering over me every time I cough."

"Can't do that, sir. I'm in their charge. If you're ailing, tell me. I'll do what I can until the doctor gets here. He's nearby, so they tell me."

"Dr. Faller. Hovers over me as much as Edie does. Difference is, she smiles occasionally. He just grumps."

"Sir, I know of a whole herd of doctors who'd be here in a quick, if you called 'em."

Roosevelt slipped farther into the bed, Amos pulling the blanket closer to his chest.

"One's plenty, James. Thank you for the help."

"I'll be honest with you, sir. You need more help than you're letting on."

Roosevelt felt a pinch in his chest, tried to breathe it away.

"Whatever problems I have, and not even Dr. Faller seems to know them all . . . I feel awful. I tried to dictate some letters to my secretary, Miss Stricker. It was useless. No point in writing a letter when my brain doesn't have the strength to make words. My legs hurt worse than I can tell you, despite so many damn surgeries. My wrist . . . never mind. You can't possibly care about all of these ridiculous details."

"You're wrong, sir. Right now, I care about nothing else."

Amos moved over to one of the tall windows.

"This ought to do just fine. I'll set my chair right here, gives me a good view of the water. I'll ask Mrs. Roosevelt if that's all right."

"What do you mean? You're staying in here?"

Amos stood facing him, blocking the sun.

"That's why Mrs. Roosevelt has brought me here. I'll sleep in the chair, there. I don't need much of that. You wake up at all, uncomfortable, painful, you say something. I'll fix it or get the doctor."

Roosevelt crossed his arms, realized Edith was at the door again.

"This is madness. I'm treated like a child." He tried to squirm, the pain in his chest growing. "I need to sit up. Odd feeling, like my lungs are getting smaller. Harder to breathe."

She motioned to Amos, who was moving already, strong arms under his, sliding him upright in the bed. "Better, sir?"

He took several deep breaths. "Maybe. Thank you. I guess I'm a child after all."

He watched her face, saw concern, a forced smile.

"You always were a child, Teddy. I'll see what Clara is preparing for dinner. You rest and do what Mr. Amos tells you."

Amos stood tall, hands on his hips.

"No worrying about that, ma'am. He will."

January 5, 1919

Amos had stoked the small fireplace, a flickering glow on the small paintings.

Roosevelt sat on the couch, Edith beside him, holding his hand, running soft fingers through his hair. He glanced around, said, "I know this used to be Ethel's room. Still is, I suppose. But then she was so very small. I played with her on the floor, silly games. I doubt she recalls."

"She remembers every detail. They all do. They were so very proud of everything you did."

"Edie, I was president. It's easy to be proud of that."

"That didn't matter to them as much as you think." She smiled. "Except Alice, I suppose." But to all of them, you were Papa, and you still are."

"Edie, I wish I knew what is happening to me. Since my surgeries, all the treatments, the drugs . . . I feel like a great locomotive that has shoved so much snow in front, it has been stifled to a halt. I'm not me; I'm not the Bull Moose. It isn't there anymore, the energy, the voice. I wish I saw myself as they still do, running for president yet again, shooing aside the meek and useless, men like Wilson, even Taft. It was grand and glorious and, my God, I miss it all."

She stopped touching his hair, released his hand.

"Teddy, you're ill—that's all. I . . . didn't want to tell you, but I convinced Dr. Faller to administer a bit of morphine so that you can sleep. I know you have been restless."

He had no strength to argue with her.

"I stare out the window, even in the dark. I can hear James stirring, his breathing, and I know he is watching me. Where is he now?"

"Clara prepared him some dinner."

"Good. A man his size . . . he should eat as much as I do . . . as much as I used to."

"You will again, against my good wishes. This illness will pass, and you will stuff yourself as you always have. You will require all new clothes."

He caught her glance, looking away, no humor in her eyes. He took a deep breath, felt tightness in his chest, said, "I must sit up."

"Your lungs again?"

"I don't know. Just . . . discomfort."

She moved away quickly, a sharp call, Amos moving in, the nurse behind him. Edith said, "Please lift him upright, James. Prop up his head. He is having trouble breathing again."

HE KNEW IT was late, his one good eye blurring the pages, no more energy for reading. The book was his own, and he examined the words with a critical eye and a scribbling pen, going through work he had written long ago.

"This is terrible, James. If they would allow me, I'd rewrite the whole volume."

"Yes, sir."

He knew Amos would be no help, other than agreeing with everything he said.

"You read any of my work, James?"

"Certainly, sir."

"You're an admirable liar. I appreciate that. Someday, when you are bored to tears, this might bore you further. Mr. Hagedorn was right. *He* should write about me. I should write more about birds."

The couch was becoming crushingly uncomfortable, and he tried to roll over, a nagging pain in his lungs. He stared out through the firelit room, the oil lamp over his shoulder, glanced through dark windows, a soft breeze blowing against the glass. He saw her shadow, looked up at the doorway, Edith and the nurse. And now with them, the doctor.

Faller said, "Mrs. Roosevelt, we can administer the morphine now. It's very late and he should be sleeping."

"Certainly, Doctor."

"Miss Harvey, you may give him the injection."

"Yes, Doctor."

The nurse bent low, Roosevelt too weak to protest, desperate for sleep. She completed the brief task, backed away, Roosevelt feeling the first effects almost immediately.

The nurse moved away, the doctor hovering now, "You feeling all right, Colonel?"

"Fair."

"Good. Perhaps you should return to bed. The shot will affect you very soon."

"Already is, Doctor."

Amos was there now, lifted him slowly off the couch, the doctor assisting, Roosevelt surprised his legs held him at all. He sat on the edge of the bed, Amos raising his legs beneath the sheets, both men backing away. Edith came to him now, bent low, a kiss on his forehead.

Roosevelt said, "She's checking for fever, no doubt. She's doing that constantly, Doctor."

Faller laughed. "Good."

"And, I admit, I was wrong about your nurse, Miss Harvey. She's not bad."

The doctor made a short bow, and Edith smiled, said, "Yes, Teddy. And you're not bad, for a cantankerous old mule of a husband."

"Moose."

"Yes, fine. Moose."

She moved away, the shadows moving with her, the doctor leading her out of the room. He still tried to fight the morphine, felt a brief panic at being alone, saw James now, settling into his chair.

"James, might you get the blanket?"

"Certainly, sir."

The big man came close, pulled the sheet up higher, then the blanket. Roosevelt glanced at the fire, nearly out, red ashes, the room still bathed in the soft gold of the lamp.

"You relaxed now, sir?"

"Yes, thank God. But do you suppose you could extinguish the light?"

"Of course, sir. Very sorry."

The room went dark now, and Roosevelt stared at the ceiling, nothing to see, his mind swimming with the morphine, eyes closing now. He fought it again, as he always did, tried to speak, the voice only in his mind, a plea, begging, desperately. Where was it? *The New-York Tribune:* "You must be up and well again. We cannot have it otherwise. We could not run this world without you."

He wanted to sit again, to speak to Amos, any of them. His breathing was painful, worse now, the morphine keeping him flat in the bed. No. It cannot be time. I have not done enough. *I would do so much more.*

EDITH VISITED HIM one more time, checking his sleep, a kind word for the friendship and vigilance of James Amos.

As she returned to her room, she stopped at the doorway, focused on his breathing, soft and steady, and already she was planning for the new day, the meals, cleaning his bedsheets. She crawled into her own bed well after midnight, fell asleep comfortably, was suddenly jarred by a shaking hand, the voice of the nurse. She responded immediately, quick steps into his room, Amos standing over him, moving aside now, soft tears, Edith calling out to her husband.

It was 4:15 in the morning.

AFTERWORD

There was no organ music; there was no singing. There was only a quiet unemotional reading of the funeral service as the coffin was borne in under the flag and borne out again. Over the snow of the steep slope to the grave the bearers carried their flag-draped burden. The level rays of the sun blazed through the files of the wood across the hill.

And so it was that the scarred body of a hero was laid to rest. But the spirit of Theodore Roosevelt did not sleep. It stalked mightily through the hearts of his countrymen, raising dead souls to life.

—Hermann Hagedorn

Valiant-for-Truth has passed over, and all the trumpets sounded for him on the other side.

—Senator Henry Cabot Lodge, to a joint session of Congress

EDITH CAROW ROOSEVELT

Always the most devoted wife, she insists on absolute privacy for their homelife, even when it is not especially practical. After her husband's death, her passion to ward off prying eyes causes her to burn her husband's letters. Fortunately for history, many of her letters to him and their children survive. Staying mostly away from politics, she involves herself briefly in the 1932 presidential campaign, supporting Herbert Hoover over Franklin D. Roosevelt, and only then to educate the public in the most emphatic way that Franklin is not, in fact, Edith's son, as many assume. (Theodore's brother Elliott is Eleanor's father.)

Edith lives out her long life as a caring mother to her surviving children and the caretaker of so many of her husband's mementos. She dies at Sagamore Hill in 1948, at age eighty-seven.

HENRY (HARRY) MINOT

Roosevelt's great friend and fellow Harvard student pursues his love of ornithology and publishes several works on birding. He relocates to the Midwest and has a successful career in the railroad business. Ironically, he dies in a rail accident at age thirty-one. The city of Minot, North Dakota, is named for him.

HENRY CABOT LODGE

Considered one of the leading statesmen of his day, Lodge firmly opposes Woodrow Wilson's efforts at joining the United States to the League of Nations, thus carrying on the battle against Wilson's policies that Roosevelt would have waged himself. Lodge authors some two dozen political and biographical books, including a few with Roosevelt. Roosevelt's loyal friend serves in the U.S. Senate until his death in 1924, at age seventy-four.

LEONARD WOOD

After his enormously successful term as governor-general of Cuba, Wood is considered a leading candidate to command the American Expeditionary Force into the Great War, the position ultimately presented to John J. Pershing. Highly respected, Wood is a strongly supported candidate for president in 1920, though the candidacy goes instead to eventual victor Warren G. Harding. Wood serves then a brief term as governor-general of the Philippines. He dies in 1927, at age sixty-six, and is buried at Arlington National Cemetery. In 1940, Wood is honored by the naming of the army's installation Fort Leonard Wood, in Missouri, active to this day.

"FIGHTING JOE" WHEELER

In 1900, for his service in the Spanish-American War, Wheeler is promoted to the status of brigadier general in the regular army, four decades after he had resigned that same army to fight for the Confederacy. He dies in 1906 at age sixty-nine and is one of only a small handful of former Confederates buried in Arlington National Cemetery.

WILLIAM R. SHAFTER

The commanding general during the army's assault on the Spanish in Cuba, Shafter is assigned to command of the Department of California after the war's conclusion. His obesity contributes to failing health. He dies in 1906, at age seventy-one, and is buried in San Francisco.

GEORGE CORTELYOU

Secretary to both Presidents McKinley and Roosevelt, Cortelyou resumes his impressive climb up the ladder of the federal government and ultimately serves as postmaster general and, in 1907, secretary of the Treasury. He dies in 1940, at age seventy-eight. His funeral is attended by Edith Roosevelt.

JOHN LONG

With Roosevelt's ascension to the presidency, Long resigns as secretary of the navy, suspecting that his tenure will become a contentious one with his former subordinate. He continues to dabble in party politics. He dies at his home in Massachusetts in 1915, at age seventy-six.

WILLIAM HOWARD TAFT

A one-term president, Taft finally achieves his ultimate goal and, in 1921, becomes chief justice of the Supreme Court, the only man to hold both offices. He dies in 1930, at age seventy-two.

COLONEL CÂNDIDO RONDON

He becomes a national hero in his native Brazil and is nominated by Albert Einstein for the Nobel Peace Prize. He holds the distinction of mapping and navigating more of the Brazilian backcountry than any other explorer. He dies in Rio de Janeiro in 1958, at age ninety-two.

GEORGE K. CHERRIE

One of the world's most respected naturalists, he continues to work long after the Amazon expedition and is a major contributor to the knowledge and understanding of tens of thousands of species of birds and mammals. He dies at his home in Vermont in 1948, at age eighty-three.

THE LEGACY OF TEDDY ROOSEVELT

Entire books can be written (and many have) about the extraordinary trail that Teddy Roosevelt leaves behind him. In the area of the nation's natural world, his gifts to the American people are immeasurable: five national parks, one hundred and fifty national forests, fifty-one federal bird sanctuaries, eighteen national monuments. His efforts go far beyond acreage, although he is responsible for preserving nearly 230 million acres of natural land for all time. With the coming of the twentieth century, the American public's eyes are focused outward, on the value and the scope of the natural beauty that surrounds every citizen. As the Industrial Revolution consumes natural resources and begins to pollute American cities, Roosevelt inspires his countrymen to pay attention to the natural world before it simply disappears. In that area alone, he should be regarded as one of our most effective and valuable presidents.

Roosevelt is a prolific writer, author of countless books, short stories, articles, and essays on an amazing variety of subjects. He is best known for those works that focus on himself and his adventures, such as his extraordinary trek through Brazil, his safari to Africa, his time spent ranching in the Dakotas, and his experiences, of course, in the Spanish-American War. But his work covers a wide range of American history, including biographies on such characters as Gouverneur

Morris and Thomas Hart Benton, as well as the definitive reference work on naval tactics and strategies of the War of 1812. His autobiographies are many, some brief and episodic, most of that work edited for the modern reader into various collections (including children's books).

Roosevelt founds what is known formally as the Progressive Party, although that party never holds any major stake in Congress or state legislatures. The description reveals his devotion to trust-busting, splitting up the monopolies that arise during the Industrial Revolution, great corporations that benefit the great financiers and magnates at the expense of their powerless workers. During his presidency, Roosevelt sponsors forty-five separate bills designed to ease conditions for the American worker and bring down the all-powerful men at the top. Yet he is careful to tread into that political landscape not as a pure populist, understanding that you need both sides of that battle to win the war. His legislation and enormous influence at nearly all levels of government and industry result in a robust U.S. economy, throughout his presidency and after, and the unprecedented improvement of workers' rights and labor conditions.

Perhaps it is difficult for us today to understand just how visceral, how emotional, is the hold that Teddy Roosevelt has on his public. It isn't merely politics, great claims of deeds, real or imagined, or of programs to be enacted that are more fanciful than realistic. By his style, his substance, his passion, and his accomplishments, he captures the emotional loyalty of an enormous percentage of the public. It is widely believed that had he run for another term in 1908, he would have won that election by a wide margin. That he chooses not to, instead handing the reins over to William Howard Taft, shows a measure of the man's dedication to the quality of his life, to an active life, and to his disinterest in merely boosting his own ego. While Taft flounders through his one-term presidency, Roosevelt visits Africa with his son Kermit, travels through Europe, and accepts the Nobel Peace Prize, to name but a sliver of his experiences in that four-year span. Though he is beseeched by the Republicans to run again in 1912, he is disappointed when the party machinery chooses Taft instead. Roosevelt's attempt to sidestep the Republicans with a third-party effort fails (the Bull Moose Party), as Roosevelt himself begins to weaken. By splitting the Republican vote, it is quite likely that Roosevelt is responsible for the election of the Democrat, Woodrow Wilson, a historical footnote that Roosevelt would despise.

In 1914, with the outbreak of the Great War, Roosevelt clearly grasps that the United States cannot remain neutral, which causes a complete break with President Wilson. As the United States falls inevitably into the fray, Roosevelt offers to form and then lead his own division of troops into that war. Washington receives the offer as a fanciful, quixotic leap from a man who is only seeking to keep his name before the public. But Roosevelt is not delusional. He knows that he can successfully rally thousands of men to join his cause and accept his leadership. But there is a personal goal as well that he does not reveal to the officials who dismiss him. He firmly believes that the most fulfilling way a man can end his life is by dying in battle. Thus does he always salute his youngest son, Quentin, though he will not speak of his son's sacrifice while Edith is present.

In 1941 the famed sculptor Gutzon Borglum completes work on his fourteen-year project near Keystone, South Dakota, what we know today as Mount Rushmore. Carved into the massive rock are the images of four American presidents: George Washington, Thomas Jefferson, Abraham Lincoln, and Theodore Roosevelt. It is a magnificent park and should be visited by every American, not merely to marvel at the enormous rock faces, Borglum's great work, or to jump into debates about just what other presidents might be included down the road. Consider that what Borglum gave us is his image of four men, chosen among many, who are most responsible for passing down to us our culture, our laws, our history, and our nation so that we might, in turn, hand these down for all time. Looking back at the image of Teddy Roosevelt, this author expressly hopes that we are up to the task.

> I have always thought it strange . . . how any man could be brought in close personal contact with Colonel Roosevelt without loving the man.
>
> —*George K. Cherrie, naturalist*

Among many others, I would mention the following, whose work on the life of Theodore Roosevelt has been extremely helpful in the creation of this book. Listed in alphabetical order, they include original works by George K. Cherrie, Hermann Hagedorn, Corinne Roosevelt Robinson, and the Reverend J. A. Zahm, all contemporaries of the man. Several outstanding historians are worth mentioning for source material and episodic experiences of Roosevelt's life, including Mark Lee Gardner, Doris Kearns Goodwin, H. Paul Jeffers, David McCullough, Candice Millard, Edmund Morris, and Daniel Ruddy, among many others.

The greatest credit I can offer goes to Theodore Roosevelt himself. His own writings opened doors for me that are a gift I can never adequately repay. This book is my offering.

> Never before in my life has it been so hard for me to accept the death of any man as it has been for me to accept the death of Theodore Roosevelt. . . . The world is bleaker and colder for his absence from it. We shall not look upon his life again.
>
> —*John Burroughs, naturalist*